BROKEN

Anna. M. L. Koski

ISBN-13: 978-1-7751857-1-0

BROKEN

Also available in eBook and paperback with Amazon.

Cover Image by NASA

Cover Design by The Round Table

To Ericka.

For your unfailing support and dedication
in making this book the best it could possibly be.

Hero of Old

Here lies the Hero of Old
A sword in his hand, he once stood bold
Blood on his face, ash in his eyes.
He fell to his knees, unable to rise.

Flesh with wounds that had cut deep
Our brave hero must lie down to sleep.
Though many above him wept with cries
Without a sound, he closed his eyes

For the many, it is not known
Our hero must reap what has been sown
Blood for blood, a price to pay
We all know the hero cannot stay

Our brave hero knew it was his time to die.
He did so bravely, without a weep or a sigh
It was now here, what was once foretold
The end of days for our brave hero of old.

1

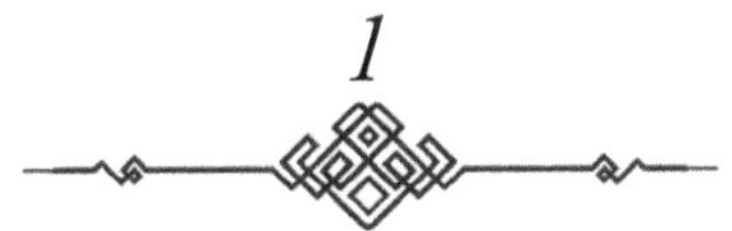

I sat down at the table, my hands knotted in my lap. Today was the last time they would try for me. My twenty-fifth birthday marked a day that would lead me to forever or the day I would be recycled. I felt sweat bead on my forehead at the thoughts. I wiped it away. The room was so warm.

Why did they keep it so warm?

I had been in this room so many times before but nothing had stuck, it seemed that there was nothing that would work for me. I had spent countless hours praying to nothing that it would work each time I tried. I prayed endlessly that something in my brain, my body or even my soul, would shift to allow the pairing to stick.

I once again rubbed at the sweat on my forehead before swallowing against the dryness in my throat. They never kept any water on the table and no one was around to ask for any. Ami'la, my case worker had sat me down and left. I hung my head, fighting back tears.

Why did it have to happen to me?

I had gotten wonderful grades. I hadn't been in any trouble. My father was a genetic researcher for the Orrians and my mother had been a specialist for interstellar plant growth. Everything should have been perfect, ***I*** *should have been perfect.*

I looked at my hands, wondering how they looked fine when I was so broken on the inside. Something they couldn't fix with medicine or surgery because when the soul was broken and unable to bond, there was nothing anyone could do. I lifted my head as Ami'la opened the door. Her ever-present high heels clicking on the tile floor as she brought another man in.

One last try.

"Liv, this is Tony." Her tone was soft and I closed my eyes tightly, sending up a silent prayer that this one would work. That he was the one that would make my soul sing and my world stop, the one that would be my forever. I opened my eyes slowly and looked at the man.

My heart sunk in my chest, there was nothing, just like the times before. My mother used to say the heart never lied and it wasn't lying now. I stood up looking at Ami'la before shaking my head.

Ami'la let out a large sigh. "Then there is nothing more we can do, Liv." The door burst open and my heart pounded harshly in my chest, as if trying to escape its bone cage. The fear was all-consuming but I couldn't move as hands and arms wrapped around me, forcing the air from my lungs. I couldn't breathe and black spots danced in my vision as I gasped for air that I could never take in.

I sat up in bed with a gasp, my lungs greedily taking in air as my limbs shook with the panic that surged through me. I pushed off the remnants of the nightmare and pressed my hand to my chest, feeling how hard my heart pounded. The fear lingered but the powerful pounding was calming. I was still alive, as long as my heart beat in my chest I was okay. The urge to cry because of the nightmare was nearly overpowering but I fought it off.

I should have been used to the nightmares by now. They had started when I had turned eighteen, right after the happiest day of my life had turned into the worst. It was when everything had fallen apart, when they had told me I might be broken. It was always the same nightmare, the same car, the same room, the same faceless person Ami'la presented as my soulmate. It always ended the same as well.

I died.

I looked at the clock and sighed heavily, rubbing at my face. At six in the morning there wasn't much sleeping I could do with my meeting in two hours. The very last meeting I would have with her. I wondered if I could lie, could tell them that we had bonded but I pushed the thought away. I couldn't do that to myself or Ami'la. She had been on my case since the beginning. She had taken it when no one else would because they were all certain I would just end up being recycled in the end anyway. Turned out no one really wanted to deal with dead ends and heartbreak. I couldn't blame them for that.

I had forty-three different men and forty- three identical failures. I had turned twenty-five and now it was time to pay the price for being broken. Ami'la had promised me one last chance and I had taken it. It was a fool's hope but one I knew I should have wanted anyway.

Humans needed to pair off, it was part of the way things had always been. Orrians had come to Earth over seven hundred years before to help us. We had followed the same paths of destruction over and over again and they wanted us to stop, to evolve. So they stepped in, they took over.

Not everyone agreed with the decision and the most vocal seemed to be a portion of the Orrians themselves. They wished to destroy humanity and build on our corpses but thankfully the more civil Orrians won out in the end.

The Orrians had instituted customs and laws, a lot of silly and unnecessary laws in my opinion, but it worked and nothing fell out of place. Humans were paired off in a soulmate system that the Orrians themselves used. I should have known how it worked considering how many times the system had failed me but I never understood how it functioned. I didn't much care to.

I closed my eyes and took a deep breath in before letting it out, my heart slowing to a more normal rhythm as I continued the deep breathing. I had been continually instructed about the relaxation technique due to my sometimes reoccurring panic attacks. I shook the thought away as quickly as it appeared. There was no need to think about it, not today.

My fingers absently played with the medallion around my neck, turning it around and around, twisting the chain it hung on. The medallions were an integral part of the pairing system. Ami'la told me that they were the physical representation of a person's soul. They were what the Soul Makers had created to house that soul. There were many different types of medallions, some had pictures, some had just colours, some were gemstones or rocks. No two were alike but in special cases your soulmate's could be similar or somehow complete yours.

I reversed the direction of my twisting, my fingertips taking in the familiar smooth edges of my medallion. It was like an oval coin but smoother and more plain with a set of engraved symbols that Ami'la told me were Orrian. The simple translation was that they were symbols for '*Love is*'. She also told me that in all her years of being a case worker, she had never seen a medallion like mine. The Orrian writing was uncommon with the Orrians and nearly impossible with humans but there I was.

I was her little oddity, her little freak show. I knew she never felt like that but sometimes, as I had people inspecting what was essentially my soul with such scrutiny, it felt like she was running a circus with me as the main attraction. I rubbed the metal with my thumb, a habit I had developed after I learned of what an oddity it was. Essentially I had been trying to rub the symbols out, to make it seem more normal. It never worked but the action comforted me regardless.

If the meeting today didn't work, I would be recycled. It is what happened to all the broken things and it happened to the people who had been born with life threatening disabilities that couldn't be cured. To be fair, an act of recycling wasn't a go to decision and the last person to be recycled had requested it and that was fifty years ago.

However, it was how it was, the law was the law. Broken things got recycled, even defective humans.

The Orrians had been helping humans remove all sorts of genetic flaws to negate the recycling by sharing their DNA with us. It was what my father did with his time and it gave me an inside look at how it worked. The Orrians shared their DNA with us to stop our genetic flaws and in turn humans would help the Orrians fix their infertility.

As a clause of the ancient contract, no human could be born with more than fifty percent of Orrian DNA. As far as I knew, there were no such cases. The Orrians were *very* adamant about it. Every human was tested in-utero for the DNA boundaries. If a fetus tested over the allotted amount, it would be aborted and another, more acceptable fetus, would be placed in the mother instead.

Some people found the system to be reprehensible but after seven hundred years it was now the norm. No one blinked an eye at it anymore, I certainly didn't. Even the thought of genetically engineering soldiers wasn't something immoral. It just was. Although, when I was younger I had sometimes wondered that they paired humans up at eighteen because the engineered soldiers would be put out in the intergalactic front at the age of nineteen. Almost as if they wanted them to have something to fight for back home.

It had made sense to me but Ami'la had told me that while it was a romantic thought, they picked the age of eighteen because it was when Orrians came into their adulthood. They then carried that age over to humans because it saved them from trying to adjust the system. Well that and the overwhelming majority of soldiers waited until *after* their time on the front before they were paired up. To my younger self, that thought was almost more romantic. They were protecting their soulmates even before meeting them.

I shook my head of the thoughts. I wasn't that young or naive anymore. I gave another heavy sigh as I pulled off the covers and shifted so I sat on the edge of my bed. The clock blinked quarter after six and I forced myself to stand up. It could be the very last time I ever got out of bed and the thought nearly made me crawl back into it. Human civilians needed to pair up by the age of twenty five. I didn't know why but we had to. The law was the law, even if it didn't make any sense.

I sighed before I pushed everything out of my mind. It was just another day, just an ordinary day that would end like every other day. I reached for a pair of jeans from my basket and pulled them on. I wasn't going to dress up for the occasion like I had when I was eighteen.

It had only mattered back then. I had picked my favourite sundress and had been allowed to wear my mother's heirloom ruby necklace. I thought I had looked pretty but if that mattered then I wouldn't have been in the position I was in now. I would have fallen in love with Mark, we would have had two children, and would have been living in a new house in a good neighbourhood with a pet dog. I had been so excited back then. Ready to take on the world but that sickening feeling of realizing I didn't love the man they presented to me was overwhelming.

I had rejected many men since then but that feeling was the worst I had ever experienced. The only feeling I had about the subject now was the inevitable disappointment. I tugged on a button up shirt and looked at myself in my mirror. Tired eyes gazed at me with a slight hollowness to them. I blinked and looked away. I didn't like looking at myself in the mirror anymore, the reflection always seemed to mock me. Like it was tormenting me over the fact that I couldn't see what was broken, no matter how hard I tried.

I undid my braid and carefully brushed my hair before redoing it. My hair was longer than normal. Women usually kept it shoulder length or a little longer but I kept mine even longer than that. It rested mid-back when loose and it drove Ami'la crazy. I couldn't remember how many times she had threatened to cut it all off if I didn't get it cut to the appropriate length. Long hair was reserved for the more important Orrians and despite being two separate species, humans adopted the custom but didn't enforce it like the Orrians did. I was looked upon very strangely for having longer hair but no one said anything to me about it, except for Ami'la of course.

I left my room and quietly made my way to the backyard where the sun was starting to rise over the horizon. I watched it until the light burned my eyes and I was forced to close them, letting my face warm up with the beams of a new day.

"You're up early. Another nightmare?" My dad's voice was low and I nodded, unwilling to open my eyes and spoil the moment. Everything was almost perfect, the sun on my face and a faint breeze that brought in the scent of the night. The faint scent holding out until the sun would warm it as well, chasing all the shadows from the night away.

"This could be my last sunrise, did you know that?" It was a morbid thought but I knew my dad would understand. He was the only one who would discuss such things with me, my mum seemed to be hell bent on ignoring any possibility it wouldn't work. I could understand but her refusal to actually think about the possibilities was almost as bad as the possibilities coming to pass. It was if she believed if we ignored it, it would all go away.

"I'm aware, Liv. I hope it isn't. I'm praying to the Source it isn't but we must be prepared if it is." His voice brought memories of my childhood. They flooded my mind until I felt like I wanted to cry. He said nothing else as he wrapped his arm around my shoulder and kissed my temple. "You're my little girl and you will always be my little girl. Never forget that, Liv." He let me go and I opened my eyes, the moment lost as the sun pushed further into the sky. I heard him go back inside but I stood still, not wanting to move. I knew that if I did, I couldn't go back.

It was now or never and even if I wanted never, I knew it wouldn't work. I let out a small sigh as I slowly turned my back to the rising sun and stepped back inside the house. I could hear my dad in the kitchen moving pans around and I knew he was going to make breakfast but the thought of food made me slightly nauseous.

I fought it back before stepping into the kitchen. "Do you need any help, dad?" I glanced towards him. His back was turned to me and he gave a small nod.

Nothing else was said as I grabbed a pack of eggs from the fridge and turned on the stove top. It was a simple thing to make breakfast, it was almost cathartic as I listened to the sounds of the food cooking and the shuffling of my dad as we moved around each other. A part of me was breaking inside but I ignored it. I had known for seven years that my life might end earlier than most and I had decided that if it came to it, I would meet my end like the heroes of old. To hold my head high and shed not a single tear because I was braver than that.

"Oh, you two are already up." My mum's voice sounded surprised and I looked over my shoulder with a tired smile.

"I couldn't sleep." I pushed my head to the side as she walked over to kiss my cheek. I tried to imprint the soft feel of the motherly kiss into my memory. I didn't know if I would ever feel it again. I watched as she grabbed a cup for some coffee and shuffled over to the coffee pot.

"Careful, your eggs will burn." At my dad's reminder, I flipped the eggs before turning off the stove. I dished up two plates and handed one to my dad as he walked by then set the other one on the table for my mum. She gave me a concerned look and I gave her another smile.

"I'm not hungry. Nervousness and all that." I watched as she went from concerned to sympathetic.

"Don't worry so much. This time it will stick, I just know it. Last time you were so close." At her sweet smile I looked down at my hands. I couldn't discuss it with my mum. She never listened. I couldn't hug her and tell her that she was the best person I knew or even hug her and cry because she truly believed I was fixable. "You were with him for nearly two months. This time will be the perfect one. Just believe in yourself, Liv."

I winced at the memory. One month, three weeks, and four days I had played at being a mate. I had tried for everyone involved but myself and in the end I couldn't pretend to love someone who was practically a stranger. Everyone had been so disappointed but I felt like an actor in a movie. I was saying the lines but not meaning them. It made me resent the people who pressured me to try, my mother included. She was under a false hope that somehow I could get better and it broke my heart.

"Eliza, let Liv be. She has a big day and doesn't need that pressure right now." Dad's voice was low as he scolded mum slightly but I just shook my head before looking up.

I gave him a tight smile. "It's okay, dad. Mum is right, maybe this time it will work. Or maybe it won't and I'll be shoved into a garbage disposal." I ignored her harsh intake of breath and pressed my lips tightly together. The words were meant to wound because I was angry that I couldn't discuss it with her, that I was stuck screaming about it in my head without a release because she couldn't handle what very well could be reality for me.

"*Liviya!* Don't you ever say something like that again! It will work! It has to. You have to *try*." The outrage in her voice suddenly brought tears to my eyes, tears I had been holding back for years. After the fourth try I had given up tears like I had given up hope of ever finding my soulmate.

"I've been trying for seven *years*. I'm tired of trying, mum. How many more do you think I have left? I turned twenty-five three days ago, this is the last one. There is no one else." I shook my head, wiping at my eyes, hating the wetness that made my vision blur. "Not for me." I stared at her and she pressed her hand to her mouth. I could see tears welling in her eyes and I felt my heart twist in my chest. I didn't want to hurt her but I couldn't pretend anymore. I was tired of going through the motions in a futile effort to bond with someone my heart didn't want.

"I'm sorry, Liv." She walked over before she wrapped her arms around me and I took in her scent. She smelled like dirt and lemons. A scent that permeated my childhood memories and reminded me of a time before everything had become so difficult. "I'm sorry." I knew what she was saying. She was sorry that I was born broken, that I had drawn the short end of the genetic lottery.

I wrapped my arms around her and realized she felt small and fragile almost like a baby bird. I felt for her, I really did but reality was what it was. "I'm sorry too, mum." The words were slightly choked but I cleared my throat. Someone needed to be strong and I had prepared for seven years to be that person. I pushed her away and lifted my chin, trying to show my strength but the action felt weak.

She grasped my face in her hands. "You were the prettiest baby. I loved you from the moment I knew we were going to have you." She let me go and returned to her spot at the table. I stood for a few more moments, trying to imprint the feeling of being in their presence into my mind before looking at the time. It was a quarter to eight, time to leave it all behind.

"I should go. I don't want to be late." It was a flimsy excuse but I held on to it as I turned away and walked to the front door. I pulled on my shoes and took a deep, shuddering breath in, trying to calm my nerves as I quickly opened the door and stepped outside. I looked at the government provided car. It had been programmed to take me to the Ministry of Soulmate Affairs and arrived last night. I quickly walked across the yard and got inside. As it drove away, I refused to look back, not wanting to shatter my strength with memories that would make me want to stay.

2

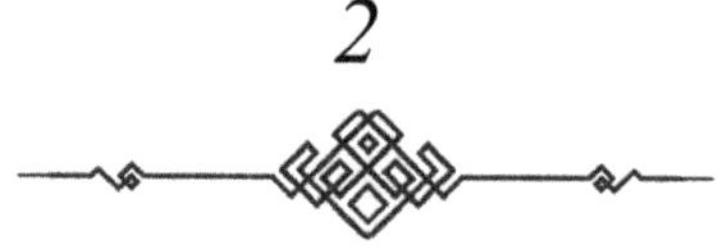

Ami'la looked at me with large, vibrantly blue eyes. They were the same colour as the electricity in plasma balls. They even shared the same pink colour around her pupils. I glanced down, her suit was pressed perfectly and her black hair pulled back from her face. Her mocha coloured skin, as always, was flawless even with the tiny lines that branched out from the corners of her eyes and mouth. She didn't have any seven years ago but dealing with my case I understood why she had gained them. I was quite a difficult and stressful person to work with.

"Liviya Burch." She let out a sigh and there was a soft look to her face. "Your hair's too long, I should cut it off." Silence fell after the slightly teasing words and I felt a small smile cross my face as I watched as a small smile crossed hers as well. A crack in the professional exterior she wore.

I felt accomplished, relishing the small smile. Not because I believed it would help me at all. No, I relished it because it was nice to see someone smile. I had been getting sympathetic looks or outright stares since my birthday. Watching that small smile as it crossed her face made it feel like any other day.

"Did you know that, that could be that last time you ever say those words to me?" I tilted my head at her and she raised an eyebrow at me. There were two things I *knew* Ami'la didn't like about me. The length of my hair and my morbid, sarcastic sense of humour I had cultivated carefully and lovingly since my eighteenth birthday.

Her eyes narrowed a fraction. "You get more morbid every time I see you, Liviya. It's not healthy." She let out a heavy sigh, suddenly the air felt oppressive. I shifted in my chair slightly, uncomfortable at the sudden heaviness. "You are the most difficult case I have ever had. I have never experienced such issues with a human before. It is as if your soul is rejecting any form of attachment. We have tried bonding, intimacy therapy, behaviour therapy, and every other therapy we thought could help you. We are out of options, Liv." I frowned at the use of my nickname. Ami'la never used my nickname and I felt a familiar tiredness enter my bones.

"You are aware that if this bonding doesn't work, that if you cannot form an attachment, you will be slated for recycling immediately, are you not?" Her words were soft and I gave a short nod. There was no need to drag the process out. "Liv, you could pretend." Her words surprised me and I looked at her, my eyes narrowing in confusion but her expression was sincere. "No one can tell if a human is mated properly or not because a child will result no matter the circumstances. Humans are incredibly fertile." Her gaze wavered slightly as she pressed her lips together.

"They don't test for anything else. No one would know." She said the last words softly, swallowing hard. I knew this was hard on her, we had spent quite a bit of time together in the past seven years. I was her only repeat customer, as she affectionately called me many times before. We were friends and I wanted to hug her as I told her it would be alright but I knew it would be pointless.

"I would know, Ami'la. It's okay. If this doesn't work, I've made peace with what will happen." I gave her a small smile and she appeared to try her best to force her expression to be professional but the sadness still lingered at the edges.

"I wish there was another way, Liv. I truly do." Regret and despondency mixed together in her voice and her eyes showed the sincerity of the words.

I tilted my head as I looked at her. "Oh, so there is no option of living under a bridge like a troll, scaring children with my horridly ugly face?" It was a familiar attempt at humour that wasn't lost on her and I watched the corner of her mouth twitch upwards. The familiarity seemed to lighten the atmosphere in the room and I felt like I could breathe again.

"Sadly, you don't qualify for that program." Her eyes were kind as she stood up.

I made a slight face. "Damn it all! I practised scary faces all night for nothing." I gave a small chuckle as I stood up, waiting for her to lead the way to my fifty-fourth chance at life. It was time to go. Time for my last chance.

Her back straightened as she nodded at me. "Please, Liviya, come with me." Her tone was back to being all business and I followed her out the door. I kept several steps behind her, listening to her heels clicking on the floor. I tried my hardest to commit the sound to my memory. I wanted to remember every single moment of the walk.

I remembered a similar feeling seven years ago. I had counted my footsteps, I wanted to know how many steps it would take to lead me to forever. I could still remember the number, ninety-four. It was funny to think that I was still counting those steps because my forever would never come.

"His name is James. He has spent the last four years on the front. He's younger than you but it shouldn't matter too much. You appear to be compatible on all counts." Ami'la's voice was chattering. She got like that when she was nervous and I felt the corner of my mouth twitch upwards.

"But that's on paper." It was a familiar statement I had made many times before and I could hear her sigh.

"Yes, that is on paper." She sounded tired and I didn't blame her as I kept my eyes on the backs of her high heels. She had worn her favourite black pair. My eyes glanced down to my sneakers, they were scuffed and worn. I gave a small smile. At least one of us had dressed for the occasion.

"Like the other forty-three." I let out a small sigh as we stopped in front of a door. She hesitated before grabbing the door handle.

"Maybe forty-four will be different." Her eyes had a glimmer of hope and I shook my head.

"I wouldn't count on it if I were you." I lifted my head and looked at her. She had been a great confidant the past seven years. I wondered if she ever took time off. I couldn't remember a time when she had. "I'm a bad bet." Wasn’t that true? No one could have ever thought I would be the losing bet in life but I had to deal with it.

"A broken clock is still right twice a day, Liviya. Is that not what you humans say?" The hope in her eyes had infected her voice and I shook my head. Why was it everyone wished for the best when they should have been preparing for the worst? I had forty-three strikes against me. The odds were stacked against me yet everyone wanted to hope.

"Then do I get to suffer through two of these? Don't I feel lucky." I give her a saccharine smile to hide the over bearing tiredness I felt. I just wanted it to be over. I was tired of trying all the time to make something out of nothing.

"You are impossible, you know that?" The words should have been biting but there were notes of affection in her tone that took all the sharpness from them. She opened the door and led me inside.

I looked at the familiar layout, taking in the plain grey walls and the equally grey tile. I had always thought it was an odd colour choice for a room where people fell in love for the first and last time. It seemed sombre in a way and seemed to fit my current situation better than the many excited faces who met their one and onlys.

"James Levi, this is Liviya Burch." Ami'la's voice pulled me from the thoughts and I finally looked at the man sitting at the other side of the grey table in the centre of the room. He stood up and held out a hand. Ami'la gestured me forward and I walked over before taking his hand. His palm and fingers were calloused, warm, and slightly damp, from nerves no doubt, but the gesture felt like the forty-three before it. Absolutely empty.

"Hello, Liviya. I'm very pleased to meet you." He let my hand go and I sat down in the chair. The click of the door closing behind Ami'la seemed to reverberate through my head. A still and almost awkward silence followed it.

I looked James over, he was handsome enough, sandy blonde hair, strong jaw. He looked like a person who spent time on the beach but his eyes held the same guarded, almost far-away look that all the soldiers had coming home from the front.

"Where were you stationed?" The question seemed to take him by surprise and he gave me an almost narrowed eyed look as if suddenly wary of me. It took him a moment or two before he relaxed.

"Third section, Delta quadrant. I was in the sixty-second Omega unit." His voice was controlled much like every other military man I had ever come across. Delta quadrant meant he was in the hot zone. The war between Orrians and Zengans. From what I had heard it wasn't a good quadrant to be in. Humans and Orrians were basically cannon fodder.

"Bad quadrant. From what I hear, you're lucky to be home." I glanced over his shoulder to the clock. It was strange but only a few minutes had gone by since I had sat down.

"Do you, see many of us? Soldiers, I mean." He looked genuinely curious and the look in his eyes was something I recognized. Something in his gaze wanted to connect to me but I knew he wouldn't find it. Not with me. It was if I was born unable to search for that connection or was just born without it. Everyone seemed to have it, that same something in their eyes that desperately searched my own in the futile hope that we would connect.

"I have known a few. Want to hear something interesting?" I watched as he leaned forward, as if curious to what I was going to tell him. "I have sat in rooms similar to this for forty-three times. You are number forty-four." His eyes went wide with shock then disbelief. It was the usual response when I brought it up. Disbelief because *everyone* had a soulmate and *no one* was *ever* broken. It made me want to scoff.

"No way." He said it firmly as he shook his head and I tilted mine, watching him with idle curiosity. He would find someone to connect to, they always did but not with me. I was intrinsically broken. My soul was flawed and nothing could change that. I was an impossibility, an oddity. I was born with a broken soul.

"Yup. I have been trying to find my soulmate since I turned eighteen. I'm twenty-five now." I crossed my arms and leaned against my elbows on the table top. "Do you know what happens when you turn twenty five without a mate? Not if you are in the army of course. You get a pass for that. Do you know what happens to *civilians* when they turn twenty-five without finding a soulmate?" I felt amused yet slightly morbid as he looked both uncomfortable and concerned but he shook his head anyway. Curiosity would always win out in the end. It had for the last sixteen men I had been introduced to.

"They get recycled, like trash" I watched as he flinched at the word. "Fertilizer mainly but sometimes, if you're lucky, you get atomized. Meaning your entire body is taken down to the atoms and then rebuilt into things. Mainly military equipment like bullets, clothing, helmets, or gun cases. If you're really lucky you could become part of a tank ship." I had learned that information after I had grown curious about what would happen to me if I never found my soulmate.

It was comforting in a way, knowing what would happen to me when I was gone.

James looked horrified and I smiled. It was always the military men who grew uncomfortable when people talked about recycling things. He didn't know that the last person had happened fifty years before but I didn't want to tell him. It would ruin my fun.

The tiredness I had escaped for a brief moment once again enveloped me and I let out a heavy sigh. My emotions had been all over the place the past week and I couldn't blame myself. Getting ready to die would do that to anyone. "James, you look at me but you didn't feel any spark, any *connection*. You didn't look at me and feel your world stop. You must be wondering if there is something wrong with you. It isn't you, James." I gave him a small smile of reassurance.

"*I'm* the broken one. The next woman you meet in a room just like this, you will fall in love with. You will have a wonderful life with her and I wish you both the best." I stood up slowly, resisting the urge to close my eyes. "I'm going to leave this room and I'm going to be taken away. I'm going to be recycled because that is what happens to the broken things in this world." I watched as a slightly sombre, uncomfortable look emerged on his face.

"It was nice to meet you, James, but there has been a mistake, you are not my soulmate." I held my hands behind my back, as I had been told to do, and waited. The door opened behind me and I watched as James's eyes went wide. Rough hands grabbed my arms and I was cuffed with forearm braces. The cold metal constricted my skin and made my shoulders ache as I was jerked backwards and pushed towards the door.

I didn't fight them, the Orrians were far stronger than I was and I had promised myself I would meet my death with my head held high.

"Liviya!" Ami'la rushed towards me and to my heart sunk as I saw tears in her eyes before her long arms wrapped around me tightly. "You were my favourite. You will always be my favourite." The words were a hushed whisper in my ear and I swallowed against the sudden lump in my throat. I didn't want to say goodbye to my friend, not like this.

She pushed away and looked at the two Orrians behind me. Her gaze was narrowed and slightly pinched looking as she spoke something sharply in Orrian and I blinked at her. Ami'la never spoke Orrian around me before. She repeated the words again and there was a sound of agreement from one of the Orrians holding me before I was pushed forward. I passed her and then the two Orrians stepped on either side of me. Each one held one of my arms, as if they were afraid I would try and escape.

I stood straighter, keeping my pace even with theirs as I held my head high. I wasn't going to give them a reason to laugh at me, to laugh at the poor broken human who couldn't fall in love. There was no love lost between the humans and Orrians and it had become clear to me that the Orrians who hated humans most always took the jobs where they could either hurt humans or lord above them. There was no middle ground for them. They were either for or against humans and it seemed as though I had gotten two who were against. It wasn't a comforting thought but it didn't stop it from being any less true.

We moved through the hallways, taking so many corners that I almost felt dizzy and I felt positive that if I did escape I would never be able to find my way out. They finally slowed their pace when they turned me down a long tunnel that ended at a black door. It drew closer and I realized it was a door to one of their ships. I guessed a shuttle ship that would take me from Earth to one of the recycle ships. I wondered if they were an actual thing or if they had a garbage disposal area on their other ships.

I let the thought drift away as the door opened and I was shoved forward into it. I stumbled and could hear the two Orrians laughing as they talked in between themselves. Their guttural language flowed through my ears almost harshly, a strange and angry language coming from them. I had learned something about Orrians, who they were greatly affected how they spoke their language. When Ami'la had spoken it, it was still guttural but there were softer edges, when the Orrian council spoke it during press conferences it was clipped and almost formal, and when these two spoke it, it was harsh and angry. It was an interesting concept to think on, to distract myself with.

I felt the ship lurch under my feet and I closed my eyes tightly. I could feel nausea swirling in my stomach and I fought to breathe. I hated flying. Even as a small child it terrified me. I hated flying and I hated ships. There had to be something solid and connected to the ground under my feet to make me comfortable. I felt the ship rise faster and the small room grew brighter. I cracked open my eyes and wished I hadn't. The Earth was quickly growing farther away and the sky seemed to become endless as we entered the stratosphere. I could almost taste vomit in the back of my throat and I swallowed compulsively trying to keep it there.

17

I was going to face my death with dignity but I couldn't do that if I threw up while flying. That was supposed to be the easy part, standing in front of an open recycler was supposed to be the hard part but in that moment if someone had given me a choice I would have taken the recycler instead of the flight. To my relief the ship started slowing down and I blinked at how dark it had become before realizing we were docking to another ship.

The two Orrian men laughed once again and I was reminded of gruff barking from two old dogs. I watched as one pressed a button on the instrument panel and the ship came to a jarring and shuddering stop. The force nearly sent me sprawling and as I caught myself once more the Orrians started laughing again. I felt my face heat up with embarrassment but I gritted my teeth and stood up straight. My dad's favourite poem ringing through my head, a mantra I forced myself to listen to it. Gathering strength from the words.

Our brave hero knows it is his time to die.
He does so bravely, without a weep or a sigh.
It was now here, what was once foretold.
The end of days for our brave hero of old.

I could hear the door open and I was jerked roughly forward, towards the gaping darkness of the new ship. The hands were needlessly cruel as they bit into the skin of my arm but I kept silent. I stumbled as the Orrian pushed me out of the ship and into the darkness. The door closed behind me and the lights slowly flickered on. The area looked empty and I could hear a hissing sound as the door sealed and mist flooded the room. I closed my eyes tightly repeating the stanza of the poem over and over again. I was terrified but I refused to let it show. I *would* be strong.

The hissing sound returned and I cautiously opened my eyes as the door in front of me slid open. I glanced over my shoulder, realizing I must have been placed in a sanitizer station. I turned my gaze back towards the open doorway and slowly walked towards it. I didn't know what lay ahead but I knew I couldn't go back.

I held my head high as I walked through the doorway, it closed behind me with a faint hiss. Orrians bustled around and I gave a slight wince at the pull on my shoulders. They were pulled too far back. As I was unable to stop the pulling, the joints ached. I watched with wide eyes as nearly everyone stopped to look at me. I stood straight and I waited. The door behind me opened and I was once again grasped roughly, fingers digging into my already tender flesh. I gave an involuntary hiss of pain as I was yanked forwards, the movement jarring my aching shoulders. The room was oddly quiet and it was unnerving having all those eyes on me in near complete silence.

I looked straight ahead. I knew I was going to die but there was no way in hell I was going to look at the people whose rules were the cause of it. I had accepted my fate but it didn't stop the slight resentment I felt for it.

The Orrian practically dragging me seemed to be muttering something under his breath when someone called something in the quiet. We came to a stop and I stared down the tunnel he had lead me to. It looked like an old electrical tunnel that was in the old ruins on Earth. I became aware of another Orrian walking towards us and the two seemed to start a conversation.

Even though I couldn't understand it, I could gather that it involved me as my escort tightened his grip on my arm, sending a new throbbing pain over my nerves. I stumbled as he jerked me closer towards him and away from the newcomer. His voice sounded like it was bordering on violent and I glanced up at his face.

His dark eyes narrowed with suspicion but the other Orrian said something and his face relaxed as he let go of my arm. It felt like it had a heartbeat. I turned to look at the newcomer when I was shoved roughly, I stumbled and fell but this time into a hard chest. Large hands grabbed my shoulders a bit too tightly as my escort said something and laughed loudly. I looked at him and his eyes were cold.

"*Slegrnd.*" The word sounded nasty and I knew it was directed at me as the Orrian spat at my feet before walking away. My gaze slowly turned back to the Orrian holding my shoulders and as my eyes locked with his, I felt my entire world grind to a halt.

3

The world had stopped, or it slowed down, as if seconds had turned into minutes as I looked at him. Slowly everything had fallen away until all that mattered was him. His hair was dark, I thought it looked black at first but it appeared more dark brown under the dull lights. It was in a standard military cut and my gaze fell to a scar on the right side of his face. It slashed across his cheekbone and then down, pulling the corner of his mouth down into a frown. It matched the stern set of the other half of his mouth. His nose had a slight bump in the bridge, as if he had broken it some time ago. Dark stubble shadowed his strong jaw and the edges of his face were hard.

I swallowed looking back up into his eyes, I couldn't see the strange thing in his gaze searching for a connection in my own. I *felt* it. I felt it pull something from the very core of my being, tying me to the man I had just been given to. It was if he had taken something from me, something important but I didn't know what. I had somehow been intrinsically changed by him and his gaze but I wasn't sure if it was for good or for bad.

20

It was like watching the world in slow motion as he dropped his hands from my shoulders and grabbed my arm. He turned his face away from mine and I pulled a ragged gasp into my lungs as the world jumped back into focus. Everything was different. I didn't know how but somehow this Orrian had done something that had tied us together. My knees felt weak but I offered no resistance as he pulled me down the tunnel.

His grip was a touch softer than that of the previous Orrian but he walked much faster. I had to practically jog to keep up with his long strides. I could hear him muttering under his breath but the words were a jumbled mess of Orrian. We turned several corners as I tried my best to keep up. Without warning he pulled me to a stop and pushed me none too gently against the wall. A large hand pinned me there, his palm scorching heat into my skin through my clothes.

Everything confused me, I didn't understand what I was feeling or what was happening. It was as if I had been thrown into the ocean and the large waves were sending me tumbling through the darkness, never letting me get my bearings as it tumbled me over and over again. I felt lost but at the same time it was as if everything I had ever been looking for had been revealed to me all at once. It was enough to make my head hurt. All of my emotions were jumbled and almost chaotic.

I watched as he pulled out a small device and jumped slightly as he pressed to my neck. I winced as it poked what felt like a needle underneath my skin right before he pulled it away. His entire focus on the small screen. Not once did his hand relax on my shoulder. I could feel the tension radiating off of him and I felt the same feeling build in me, as if my body was picking up on his cues. He started spitting out Orrian as he turned the device and pushed it close to my face. His gaze was livid and I could feel violence trembling in his hand and arm.

I looked at the small display but couldn't understand any of the symbols except a simple sixty-three percent that flashed red on the display. His voice sounded accusing and I shook my head. "Please, I don't know. I don't understand." I felt tears well up in my eyes. I didn't want them there but I was scared. It felt like he had taken something important from me and I wasn't sure if I could ever get it back. He seemed to let out a curse as he pushed away from me quickly and ran his hands through his hair. He looked almost as confused as I felt. He started pacing, long even strides that I realized came from his obvious military training.

I watched his form as he moved, the natural muscling that came to all Orrians didn't seem to have forgotten him. Muscles rippled across his broad shoulders and down his back as he paced. Watching him pace was like watching a tiger in a zoo only without the glass to protect me. He stopped and turned to me abruptly. He looked as though he had fought in many battles and had always emerged the victor. The thought made my mouth go dry.

He would defeat all who opposed him and all who got between him and what he wanted. His face looked carved from granite and I could see his fists tightening before he threw the device to the ground, shattering it. Bits of metal and plastic skittered across the floor and I jumped at the action but didn't have any time to react as he started pulling me down the tunnel once more. I stumbled slightly and he jerked me upright. I inhaled sharply at the pain the action brought.

My shoulders felt like they were on fire and I wiggled them, trying to ease the burning ache I felt deep in the joints. The pain seemed to bring everything into sharp focus and I tried to roll my shoulders forward but it almost seemed to increase the ache. An unwanted whimper escaped me and he stopped sharply. I froze, my eyes wide as he let my arm go and grabbed my shoulders, turning me so I faced him.

The expression on his face was hard to read and for a moment I thought he had squeezed my shoulders in an attempt to rid me of the ache but his hands were still as he looked at me with that strange, unreadable expression on his face. It was as if I were a puzzle that confused and intrigued him, as if I scared him but at the same time as if I made him feel something else entirely.

His right hand reached down and pulled my medallion from my shirt. I gave a slight noise of protest. My skin felt cold without it. I had never let anyone touch it before and the thought of him taking it from me made me want to back away from him and huddle in a corner. Without a medallion one could not form a bond and would feel empty for the rest of their lives. It was a harsh thing to lose a medallion, to lose your soul.

I watched with wide eyes as he pulled out his own medallion. It looked similar to mine but the symbols were different. He muttered something, as if he had read what was inscribed on the metal. I looked up at his scarred face and it looked as though the harsh edges had softened. He held both the medallions in one hand and pointed to them, repeating what he had just muttered. He looked at me intently.

"*Mehba illeehd sirbaht onshe halh.*" He said the words slowly and I realized he wanted me to say it.

"*Mehba illeehd sirbaht onshe halh.*" The repetition was slow and I stuttered over a few of the foreign words with a clumsy tongue but he gave a quick nod before removing my medallion completely. I started to give a noise of protest but the look he gave me silenced it in my throat.

I watched as he removed his and replaced it with mine. He muttered something I couldn't understand before he gently pulled his medallion over my head, letting it fall into place. My skin warmed at the contact, as if the small piece of metal had suddenly covered me in a warm blanket and I looked at him in confusion.

His gaze was as confused as mine but it appeared he had made a decision sometime during our trip down the tunnel. Slowly, as if he was afraid I would run off, he reached behind me and released the cuffs. My shoulders ached with relief and I went to rub my arms when he grabbed them instead. His rough fingers rubbed at the red marks on my forearms gently, his voice was low as he spoke.

As he looked at me his eyes were apologetic, letting my arms go before his hands moved to my shoulders, gently rubbing the stiffness from the muscles. I leaned into the contact and the relief it brought. I looked up at him and I finally noticed in the dark lighting of the tunnel that his eyes were a pale green, a colour no one had on Earth. Ami'la's eyes were wonderful but his eyes... his eyes... they were *beautiful.*

I lifted my hand slowly wanting to touch him. For some reason I wanted to brush my fingertips across his skin, to let his heat sink into me. I searched his eyes, trying to discern what it was that he had done to me, what he had taken from me. His gaze was almost tender and I recognized the look almost immediately. My breath left me in a whoosh as I realized what had happened.

He was my soulmate.

The Orrian with the beautiful green eyes and scar was to be my forever. The urge to laugh was almost overpowering but it was evenly matched with my urge to cry. I felt tears prickle at the corners of my eyes and I blinked them away not wanting to break down in hysterics. I let my hand move closer and I touched my fingertips to the line of his jaw. The stubble scratched against my skin and sent shivers down my spine.

A noise came from back in the tunnel and we both jumped. I dropped my hand and his head jerked towards the sound. His gaze was suddenly wary and I took a step closer to him without thinking. He said nothing as he grabbed my hand, pulling me away from the sounds. As we moved quickly through the tunnels he seemed to almost be debating something before he tugged me towards a door.

He said something and I shrugged, not understanding his words. He let out what seemed to be a frustrated sigh before he grabbed me around the waist and threw me over his shoulder. I gave a small cry of surprise that he shushed. It was a sound that was universal no matter the language and I kept my mouth closed as he carried me through the doorway. He barked out what sounded like a command before the doors closed.

Everything vibrated almost violently and I felt my very bones rattle inside of me, my head felt like it was in a squeeze press before it stopped abruptly and door once again opened. He carried me out, his strides seemed to have a purpose and I relaxed slightly, the after effects of the weird vibrating room slowly leaving me.

His arm shifted over my back to grasp my side and his other hand grasped my hip as if to balance me. I was a little disconcerted that I wasn't as upset as I should have been at the thought of someone carrying me around like a sack of flour. I fought back a laugh at the thought. I was slightly scared I was going to get emotional whiplash from my ever shifting emotions and I wasn't sure when the ups and downs of my emotional roller coaster would actually stop.

I looked around and everything looked white. The floor was white, the railing running around the edge of a large drop was white and the walls were white, the doors however, were a nice shade of light blue. I let my gaze linger on the symbols above the doors as we moved past them. Each one was different and I frowned, wishing I knew some Orrian.

He stopped walking and let my hip go to pound on a door. I felt my muscles jump at the sound and his long fingers twitched on my waist, tightening slightly. He banged on the door again and I glanced backwards just as it opened. An elderly man opened the door with a scowl. He took one look at my position and seemed to heave out a sigh before gesturing for us to come inside.

The large Orrian man carried me over the threshold and the old man said something and I was put down. Warm hands lingered on my waist and I took an involuntary step closer to him as I looked around. His hands dropped and I felt slightly cold at the missing contact.

"You look confused." The voice was slightly raspy and I jerked my head towards the old man in surprise. He waved me off as if not bothered by my surprise. "Yes, I can speak English. Don't look so surprised. If half of us put the effort into learning it we wouldn't be in this confusing situation." He held out his hand and I took it intending to shake it when he turned my arm, holding the inside of my wrist upwards.

He let out a cackle of laughter as he patted my wrist before letting my hand go. I took another step towards the man who brought me here and he took a step away. The old man scowled before saying something in a rather sharp voice. I looked at him and blinked. I had no clue what either of them were saying.

The old man let out a sigh. "Do you even know his name?" He pointed at the Orrian man who brought me and I opened my mouth then closed it with a frown as I shook my head. "Well go on, introduce yourself." I turned to face the man and he looked at me as the room flared brightly with a sudden light.

I swallowed and pointed at my chest. "My name is Liv." I searched his face for any recognition but got none. I let out a sigh of frustration that echoed the one he had given me a few minutes before.

"He won't understand full sentences. Keep it simple." The old man's raspy voice was slightly muffled and I let out another sigh.

I jabbed my finger at my chest. "Liviya Mary Burch. Liv, Liv." I frowned slightly as he remained silent before he stepped closer and grasped my chin in his fingers. Heat radiated from him and I looked up at him with some urging from his fingertips. The feeling of them felt scorched into my skin as if he had branded me.

"Liv." His rough voice saying my name sent chills up and down my spine but I smiled brightly. He had *understood!*

I nodded quickly and pressed my palm to my chest. "Liv, I'm Liv." I had no idea why but hearing him say my name and him actually understanding me made me feel like nothing I had ever felt before. It was freeing and so joyful I wanted to spin around and laugh like I used to as a child.

His face softened as he dropped his hand from my chin to touch his own chest. My eyes followed the movement before flicking up to his face. "Rhex. Rhex." His voice seemed to rumble through him and I smiled again. I felt like my face would crack.

I pointed at him, "Rhex. Your name is Rhex." I watched as he gave a small nod and I resisted the urge to cheer.

"Liviya. Liv." He pointed at me and had a slightly satisfied look on his face. I turned to look for the old man, who was bending over a large stack of books as if looking for something.

"My name is Ghilesh." The old man's voice was still muffled and I glanced over to him. "I am a Soul Maker. I am one of those that would have made Rhex's medallion when he was just a young boy or your own." He stood up, holding his back with a wince but he held two fancy cups in his hand. He said something in Orrian to Rhex and I watched as Rhex replied while stepping backwards from me. I crossed my arms over my chest and tried to focus on what they were saying.

"He wants to bind you two together." Ghilesh gave a small smile before turning to Rhex and asked something. A brief flash of confusion crossed Rhex's face at what he had just been asked. I kind of tuned out what Ghilesh had said as I moved around the room, feeling slightly bold as I let my fingers trail over the dusty stacks of books.

Rhex gave a reply to the question that had me glancing over to them both. Ghilesh nodded as if agreeing with whatever he had said. "He says that he is doing it to protect you. I can't say I blame him, you two are in for a rough time once the news breaks." He moved around the room, gathering a variety of different items and it was fascinating to watch.

"Why?" I walked over to see what he was doing and he shook his head, his face suddenly grave.

"You are human. If we don't bind you together some of the Orrians will see you as a target and kill you but even the law respects a binding. Once bound they cannot hurt you." Ghilesh shrugged and I looked at Rhex who stood perfectly still in the middle of all the clutter. I swallowed hard and wanted to wrap my arms around him and forget the world.

I rubbed the back of my neck before wincing at the pull on my shoulder. At the motion Rhex was suddenly at my side, his fingers gently manipulating my joint as if trying to figure out what was wrong with it. He muttered something angrily beneath his breath as he turned his head to look at Ghilesh and seemed to ask him for something. Ghilesh muttered something unintelligible and waved towards a cupboard. I watched as Rhex moved over to it with surprising grace considering his large size.

"What is he doing?" I rubbed at my right shoulder before moving to my left. I glanced over at the old Soul Maker, who seemed to be muttering nonsense as he pulled out what looked to be a cauldron.

He waved my question off, "Getting some healing salve. Leave me be, I need to focus." He went back to his muttering and Rhex walked back over to my side. He turned around as if searching for something and then moved a stack of books off of a stool before pointing at it while looking at me. It took a moment before I realized he wanted me to sit down. I did as he gestured and looked up at him right before he handed me a round jar.

I looked at it with apprehension before taking it. "What do you want me to do with this?" I fought back a smile at his blank look of confusion, he shook it off and pinned me with a look as he touched my shoulder again. He moved it around as if checking my range of motion.

With how stiff they were it didn't take much movement to make me wince at the sharp pain inside my joint. His hands moved to my other shoulder, repeating the tests to my movement. Despite the pain it felt strange having him touch me, delightful shivers plagued me as the warmth of his hand seeped into my skin.

He stopped suddenly, his hands dropping to his sides as he looked torn. He grasped my chin in his hand and lifted it, making eye contact with me. His eyes seemed to almost spell out an apology before he let my chin go. Warm fingertips brushed my collar bone before deftly undoing the top button of my shirt.

My heart jumped into my throat before beating quickly in my chest and I grabbed his wrist quickly with my eyes wide. The apologetic look was still in his gaze and he looked suddenly pained before saying something in Orrian. The rough tones of the language seemed almost smooth when he spoke it.

Ghilesh gave a bark of laughter at whatever Rhex had said. "He wants to put the healing salve on your shoulders to take away the pain and potential for injury. He needs bare skin." He let out another chuckle and I frowned at him before looking back up at Rhex. His gaze was expectant and with my heart pounding in my chest, I let his wrist go.

His hands slowly started to unbutton my shirt again. I felt heat rise up in my face as I looked off to the side, trying to look everywhere but at my soulmate. Heat curled through me as his calloused fingertips brushed against the skin between my breasts. He gently pulled my shirt down over one shoulder, part of his hand dragging across my skin the entire motion. It felt like my skin broke out in goosebumps following the motion but I didn't turn to see if it actually did.

Rhex took the jar from me and twisted off the lid. My eyes followed his hand as he swiped a finger through the pale, sweet smelling paste. I glanced up at his face, trying to keep from blushing as he gently smoothed the salve over my shoulder. I jumped at the unexpected iciness of the salve. He jerked his hand back, his eyes on my face. I couldn't help it and I gave a short and choked laugh at the absurdity of it all.

"It's cold. I'm sorry, I didn't expect it." I felt a small strained smile on my face as another blank look crossed his. I carefully pointed to the jar of salve and mock shivered while rubbing my arms. "Cold." The gestures seemed to do the trick and I watched as his lips twitched slightly in amusement as if he understood what I was trying to tell him.

He handed me the jar again before gently massaging the icy salve into my shoulders. It didn't take long before the heat of his hands warmed it up as he spread it over my skin. The ache faded and I looked at the jar, trying to ignore the pleasurable searing of my nerves as his hands and fingers moved across my skin, massaging the paste into the aching areas. I brought the jar up to my face and took a tentative smell. It was sweet smelling but I couldn't place the odour and the colour seemed to be a swirl of very pale green and pink.

Rhex gently pulled my shirt back over my shoulder and tugged it down my other one. I looked over and the tip of a bruise peeked out from under my shirt. It was almost a deep blue and small but I could see would grow into a decently sized bruise. The Orrian guard hadn't been nice when he was dragging me around. Rhex's hands froze as he looked at the tip of the bruise. His gaze went hard and he said nothing as he quickly undid several more buttons on my shirt, nearly tearing the fabric in the process.

I stiffened at the sudden and harsh movement before I glanced down. My head snapped back up with my eyes wide, I tried to focus on breathing as I looked down once again. Rhex had undone all the buttons down to my belly button. I swallowed hard as the shirt did nothing to cover my chest, my light blue bra seemed to feel inadequate and I wanted to cover my chest with my arms.

Rhex didn't seem to notice as he gently pulled my shirt down over my arm so he could look at the dark and aching smudges. I felt the curlings of warmth start to rise up my neck and head for my cheeks. I tried to fight it down as Rhex took some more salve and started rubbing it into my shoulder and arm. The bruised flesh was slightly tender and I gave a small wince, the small jolts of pain distracting me. I glanced looked over at him and his entire focus was on spreading the salve as if it could erase the bruises on my arm. I felt my heart lurch in my chest at the display of almost protective tenderness.

Without thinking I reached over with my other hand and brushed my fingertips down his cheek. His eyes snapped to mine, his expression unreadable. I bit the inside of my bottom lip slightly, afraid I had done something wrong. I took a deep breath in and I watched as his eyes flicked down from my face and immediately right back up. His eyes were slightly wide and he swallowed. I watched his Adam's apple bob in his throat before a small embarrassed smile forced its way onto my face as I tried to adjust my shirt with my free hand to cover myself.

"It's just skin, nothing to be embarrassed about, right?" I nearly croaked the words as he pointedly looked away from me and continued smoothing the salve over the dark marks. He said nothing as he pulled my shirt back into place and slowly did it back up.

Once the last button on my shirt was looped through the hole, one of his hands reached up and palmed the side of my neck. The warmth from it seemed to flow through my body and pool in my stomach. I look up at him and his eyes held a sincerity I didn't expect as he said something in Orrian. My gaze went from his eyes to his moving lips before back up again. I didn't understand what it was he had said but I almost didn't care.

I stood up slowly, feeling small next to him. I went only up to his shoulders and he was nearly twice as wide but it didn't scare me. His hand moved from my neck to my jaw, tilting my face up. A peculiar look crossed his face and he leaned forward.

For a heart stopping moment I wanted to go up on my tip toes and close the distance between us and press my lips to his. I felt my feet bunch in preparation of doing just that as he moved closer, his gaze on my mouth. I could feel my pulse pounding wildly and I felt suddenly alive for the first time in my life. I started to rise, my breath coming in small short bursts. I could feel his breath on my lips and I started to pushed with my toes.

"Just kiss him already." Ghilesh's voice snapped through the haze in my mind and suddenly Rhex was further away, his hands bunched into fists behind his back. Ghilesh laughed at his posture, shaking his head in stark amusement. He waved a finger at me as I felt that familiar heat of embarrassment flash across my face. "You are going to give him a stroke if you keep raising his blood pressure like that." He winked one of his amber eyes at me with a knowing smile and I looked at my feet in embarrassment. I wanted nothing to do with what the old Soul Maker was implying.

Nothing at all.

4

"Alright, I need your medallion." Ghilesh held out a wrinkled hand and I swallowed as I grasped it tightly in my hand. He narrowed his eyes at me slightly. "Girly, I need the pendant to do the bonding. I'll be taking Rhex's too." His voice was gruff but not angry and I quickly slipped the pendant over my head before I could think about it too much. I felt cold without it and I resisted the urge to shiver.

He took it carefully and turned to Rhex, who had already taken his own off. It was strange, we had exchanged medallions maybe fifteen minutes before but it felt like his medallion needed to be around my neck. It was if it belonged there and had always belonged there. I gave in and shivered at the chill I felt from the absence of the pendant. I rubbed at my arms trying to get rid of the goose bumps that had popped up. My shoulders and arm still ached slightly but the salve was doing its job in making them feel better.

I felt a large hand touch my lower back gently before it pressed more firmly. I looked at Rhex and he pressed his hand a little harder as if urging me to walk forward. I took several steps and he seemed to walk in tandem with me to stop in front of the table.

Ghilesh hastily wiped down the dusty surface. "I apologize for the mess. I do not get any bindings anymore." His voice seemed almost forlorn at the thought and I felt suddenly curious as to why. He looked at me with a rather amused expression on his face, his amber eyes twinkling. "That is a long story and I am far too old to tell it right now. I need to focus." His words trailed off into Orrian and I watched as he started pouring a shimmering almost opalescent liquid from the small cauldron into the two cups he had set on the table.

It didn't appear to have a scent or any colour but it shimmered with something I couldn't identify. Steam curled up and over the edges of the glasses and I watched it with rapt fascination. It was though the steam tendrils were alive as they moved, touching the sides of the glass before retreating back into it.

My focus went back to Ghilesh when the steam was no longer visible. He dangled the pendants, one over each glass before muttering some words in Orrian. I watched, awestruck, as the steam once again moved from the cups but instead of climbing over the rim, it twirled around itself reaching upwards to the pendants.

The display was beautiful and almost intimate in a way as the steam curled around each pendant with a bright glow. I stared at it, almost seeing pictures in the glow and wanting to see more. However it was too late to see anything as the glow subsided and the steam seemed to drop into the cup as if it had turned liquid. I glanced up at Rhex and his face was blank, there was nothing there to discern what he was feeling or thinking about the display.

"That was interesting." Ghilesh held out our pendants. I reached over and he handed me my old one. I took it with a small frown and Ghilesh's face broke out into an amused smile.

"You have to exchange your medallions in order to show your acceptance of the bond." He gestured to Rhex. "Your soulmate decided to forgo with tradition and switched them before coming to me. I don't blame him, it is natural to want to carry your mate close to your heart. Now you need to face Rhex and exchange your pendants." I turned to face Rhex and he reached over taking his pendant before turning towards me.

"Alright, Liviya. I now need you to repeat whatever I say in English. Okay?" At his words I nodded and he said something in Orrian which I believed to be a repetition of the words for Rhex. I watched as Rhex nodded as well before turning his gaze back to mine. "I accept you as my soulmate. I put my soul into your keeping."

"I accept you as my soulmate. I put my soul into your keeping." I held up the medallion and Rhex bent down slightly so I could slip the chain over his head. I followed the chain with my fingers, making sure it sat straight on his wide chest. I glanced up at him and realized the harsh edges of his face had once again softened. It almost made it hard to breathe with how he was looking at me.

"I entrust you with my body, my future, and my love. In this moment we are one until death takes us." Ghilesh's words snapped me back into focus and I took a deep breath.

"I entrust you with my body, my future, and my love. In this moment we are one until death take us." I wasn't sure if this was a more Orrian form of a binding because it was slightly different than the ones they did on Earth.

Ghilesh said something formal in Orrian and Rhex repeated the words as he slowly placed his medallion over my head, following the chain like I did so it would lay straight. Ghilesh said something else and Rhex repeated it, his words doing something to me. It was reaching a place deep inside and warming it. His voice seemed to smooth out the rough and harsh edges of the language and I could practically feel the words dancing on my skin. His green eyes held me captive and the urge to kiss him was overwhelming but Ghilesh clapped his hands, startling me slightly.

"Okay, here is the fun part." Ghilesh almost seemed excited and I quickly looked at him as he motioned us forward with a big smile. It seemed like he was anticipating something was going to happen but Rhex's hand was once again on my back, urging me forward and I felt the worry drift away as we moved closer to the table. Ghilesh coughed before sliding the cups towards us. "Go on, drink. Now you have to drink all of it or the binding won't work." I hesitated at the look on his face but Rhex carefully grabbed his cup and said something that had Ghilesh glaring at him coldly. The answering retort sounded scathing and I took my cup to avoid the confrontation, needing something to do if they started yelling at each other in Orrian.

I looked at the contents of the cup and it was clear like water and I cautiously sniffed it but there was no scent. Without overthinking it I brought it up to my lips and took a drink. The cool liquid seemed to burn a trail of fire right down to the core of my being but as it did I felt relaxed and rather tranquil. I finished it and I set my empty cup down. I truly liked the warm feeling the drink had given me.

I gasped at a sudden wrenching inside of my body. It didn't hurt but it felt strange and it happened again as I placed my hand on my stomach. I turned to look at Rhex as he set his cup down and I could feel the millions of little threads that bound us together. Tiny threads weaving around and around from his soul to my own that brought us closer and closer.

The final wrenching seemed to echo through me as I stared up at the man I had just bound myself to. I could feel his soul resting close to my own and I felt my breathing increase because of it. It was such an odd and intimate thing, feeling our souls connect, feeling how they bound together. My hands trembled and I looked at Ghilesh with wide eyes.

He looked positively overjoyed and clapped once. "To be honest, I thought you were going to throw up like the last couple did but that was something else." His amber eyes glowed with happiness and I glanced up at Rhex and I could see the shaking in his hands as well and felt relieved I wasn't the only one who had felt the wrenching. "It is sad that I had to wait seventy-eight years to get to see a true bonding of souls." I felt slightly wobbly as I tried to breathe and I placed my hands on the table, taking deep breaths in and out, trying to fix the disruption the bonding had done to the natural order of my body.

Rhex placed his hand on my back, rubbing up and down my spine, I appreciated the contact. I bent over the table, placing my forearms down with my head touching them.

"How do you feel, Liviya?" Ghilesh sounded curious and I looked up at him, my vision swimming slightly, trying to figure out how to focus. Two of the amber eyed Soul Maker danced in my vision and I felt a little nauseous.

"Like I'll never be the same again so a little freaked out but I don't feel... *alone* anymore. My body feels disjointed, like something has been pulled out of place and everything my body normally does needs to find a new rhythm. Other than that, I'm good." I pressed my face to my arms again, closing my eyes, focusing on my breathing.

In, out, in, out.

Rhex seemed to rub my back in time with my breathing and the motion relaxed me. After a few more moments I felt a bit better, the trembling had stopped and my breathing had returned to normal for the most part. I felt Rhex's hand slip off my back as I straightened. I blinked my eyes into focus and looked at Ghilesh who was furiously writing in what looked to be a leather bound journal.

"If you are feeling better. I suggest you go with Rhex, he will take you to his apartment. I need to document this." He didn't look up from his hasty writing and I looked over to Rhex who gestured to the door in almost a questioning way and I nodded quickly. I needed to lie down for a while, get a good night's sleep then re-group in the morning.

Rhex stepped towards the door and I fell in behind him. Everything felt slightly heavy and I was curious as to why I felt like that when Rhex seemed fine. I had to walk fast to keep up with his long strides and I gave a sound of annoyance. He glanced backwards then frowned before slowing down until he was walking beside me but slightly behind. I could almost feel the heat from his body as he moved closer.

There was an almost still wariness to him as we walked and I suddenly became aware of eyes staring at me. I looked around and the few Orrians that were around had stopped what they were doing and were staring at Rhex and I. I felt exposed under their disgusted and disgruntled looks. I had never been more aware that I was human before that point. There were a few gazes that were curious but most of them made me acutely aware that I was not wanted on their ship.

Rhex murmured something and moved closer to me, his frame almost leaning over mine protectively as we walked. I hugged my stomach, hunching under their stares. I felt each one almost like a heavyweight trying to pin me down. Rhex said something in a low voice, I couldn't understand it but I could feel as if he were trying to comfort me, telling me to ignore them.

I looked around as we walked. The white railing circled a large drop off where I could see ships flying in and out of, as if it were a centralized port for the different stations the ships could dock to. The height of it almost made me dizzy and I leaned away from it and towards Rhex. He moved away from me slightly at the movement, as if wanting the distance of space he had chosen rather than the one I had created. The thought hurt almost and I looked down at my feet, letting him walk me towards our destination.

We stopped and I looked up to see a familiar door. I shook my head quickly planting my feet. I had no want or desire to go back into the small room that had had attempted to vibrate my bones right out of my skin.

"I'm not getting into that thing. Once was enough. I thought my teeth would rattle right out of my skull." I shook my head the entire time I spoke, wanting Rhex to understand I didn't want to get back into the weird vibrating room. I looked up at him as he gestured to the room, his face even. "No, I'm not going in there." I clenched my hands tightly and shook my head again.

There was a slight look of irritation and his hand found a place on my lower back and he put pressure on it as he pointed at the open door. I ignored the hand trying to push me forward and I shook my head again. The room had been highly unpleasant the first time and I didn't want to repeat the process feeling as off as I did. The pressure increased and he looked decidedly annoyed as I pushed against his hand and planting my feet.

I could feel that stubborn look appearing on my face as I pushed backwards. My dad said there were two immovable objects in this world, mountains and me when I decided to set my mind to something. I gritted my teeth, prepared to fight against Rhex when he simply dropped his hand from my back and shifted so he stood in front of me.

I felt a bit surprised at the action but wasn't given time to react when he grasped me around my waist and lifted me up. I gave a sound of outrage as he carried me into the room and set me down. His hands never left my waist and his muscular chest was nearly pressed up against the front of mine. Any anger I felt at being man-handled drifted away as I became acutely aware of the sexual intensity he emitted in the small confines of the strange room. His hands on my waist seemed to burn through my clothes and into my skin as if marking me. I felt my breath come in short bursts as the heat pooled lower in my stomach.

My mouth went dry as I trailed my gaze from his chest up to his face. He muttered something in Orrian as his pale green eyes connected with mine. The vibration started and I felt my brain rattle in my skull as the room seemed hell bent on tearing me apart. It had been uncomfortable before but now it was borderline painful. My muscles seized as the vibrations continued and my heart seemed to pound irregularly in my chest, as if unable to beat with the vibration moving through it. It stopped as quickly as it started and I gave a pained gasp as my weak legs crumbled under my weight. They felt numb and if Rhex hadn't been holding me I would have hit the floor hard. My muscles didn't want to co-operate as they trembled from the aftershocks of the vibration.

"You're an asshole." I was surprised I managed to croak it out as he held me standing. I reached backwards and found a railing that I leaned against gratefully. His hands slipped off my waist and he started to walk out of the small room. I took a step to follow him but my leg buckled and I hit the ground. I was pretty sure if my extremities hadn't been numb it would have hurt. "Rhex." At his name he looked backwards and sighed at my position on the floor. I watched as the annoyance on his face slipped into the soft look he gave me that made my breath hitch in my chest. With two strides he was at my side and carefully picked me up.

I felt small as he cradled me to his chest, my head pounded and everything felt far too heavy to move. There was no way I was going to get into that god awful room again. The vibrations were terrible and painful. I wrapped my heavy arms around him and rested my forehead against his neck, closing my eyes. I could feel his pulse on my skin and could feel every step he took as they seemed to jolt my sore muscles. Everything seemed to pull me down to sleep and I didn't care to resist the urge my body was giving me. I settled my head closer to him and slipped backwards into the beckoning darkness.

5

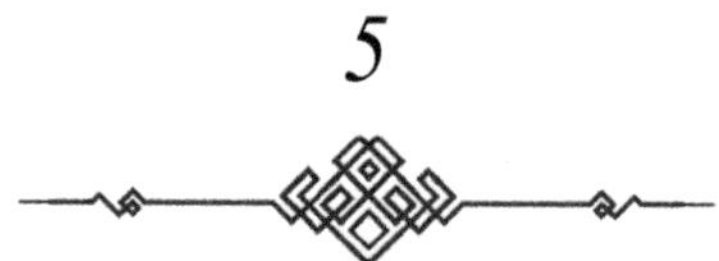

I was pulled out of unconsciousness by Rhex as he lowered me onto a rather comfortable bed. I went to roll over to go back to sleep when he gave me a small but firm shake. I let out a groan at the bright light that came on above me. It was like shards of glass digging into my eyes and my muscles ached with a pain I was pretty sure I had never felt before. I closed my eyes again and Rhex gave me another small shake to keep me awake.

I turned my head to look at him, trying my best to keep the exhaustion from taking over. It was obvious he didn't want me to sleep and I wanted to know why. He shook his head and held up a single finger as he said something in Orrian. I looked at the finger and blinked slowly, it was a similar gesture that my dad had given me growing up. If he was busy with work he wouldn't say anything and just hold up a single finger as if to say *'One moment, Liv.'* I wondered if that was what he was trying to tell me.

I blinked slowly, my eyelids feeling like heavy weights. When I managed to pry my eyes open again, Rhex was gone. I attempted to lift up my head to see where he went and failed miserably. I let out a breath and let my body sink further into the comfortable mattress.

The room was slightly cool and I wished I could wrap myself up in a blanket. I could hear someone moving around and the urge to try lifting my head again was rather strong but my neck felt like a wet noodle. Rhex appeared in my peripheral vision holding a cup in one hand and a small vial in the other.

He sat down beside me, the mattress tilting me towards his larger frame. He slid one arm under my back and practically lifted me to sitting. I felt my head loll backwards and his arm slid up my back, his elbow turning slightly holding my head steady. He murmured something softly as the lip of the vial was placed on my bottom lip. As if by instinct I felt my mouth open slightly before he poured the liquid into my mouth. It was incredibly bitter and I made a face but swallowed it, hating the strange aftertaste it left in my mouth.

I scrunched up my nose and a strange rumbling came from Rhex and I smiled when I realized he was chuckling. Cool glass replaced the vial on my lips and I glanced up at Rhex with suspicion. He gave me an amused smile and my eyes were drawn to his scar, it bunched slightly as if not used to the shape his mouth was making. I felt sympathy for him, hating that the scar was there but understanding why it was. Not everyone left the front untouched.

He pressed the rim of the cup to my lips again and I opened my mouth, the cool water seemed to wash away the bitter taste of whatever was in the vial. I drank for a few moments before he took the cup away and set it somewhere I couldn't see.

He gently laid me back down, his arm sliding back out from under my back. I missed the contact as soon as it was gone, he stood up and I jolted slightly as he picked up one of my legs slightly to pull my sneaker off. I watched as he untied the laces and I blinked sleepily as he pulled it off along with my sock before moving to my other leg.

Once my shoes were off he moved back to my side before picking me up off the bed. I wrapped my arms around his neck without thinking as he held me tightly with one arm and flipped back the blanket with the other. He lowered me back onto the bed and I let his neck go as he set me down, tucking me under the blanket.

I winced as a muscle group in my arm seized suddenly. I reached over to grab it but his hands were there first, massaging the cramp away. I let my hand fall on top of his, too tired to move it back. He stopped massaging my arm and gently moved my hand off of his before I closed my eyes, unable to keep them open anymore. The lights shut off and I could barely hear the door close as I fell asleep once more.

38

"Liv." The sound of my name pulled out from my sleep and I cracked an eye open, my brain feeling fuzzy. The pain in my muscles was gone and I stretched under the warm blanket, relieved that they moved as they should. "Liv." A strong hand brushed my cheek and I found my gaze latching onto Rhex's form as he grasped my shoulder and helped me to sit up. I ran a hand through my hair and blinked sleepily before rubbing my eyes, trying to rid myself of the fogginess.

"Rhex?" I looked up at his face and he gave a short nod before handing me a bowl. I took it with a confused frown, the food inside looked strange but it smelled alright. A fork appeared in my vision and I smiled before taking it. I crossed my legs, shifting on the bed.

The mattress tilted and I looked over as Rhex sat on the bed beside me, a bowl in his hands as well. I looked at my bowl and took a forkful of the strange slightly brown mush. I sniffed it experimentally and shrugged before taking a bite. It had a slightly spicy taste and was slightly chewy but I found it didn't mind it. It filled my stomach so I wasn't going to complain.

I finished what was in my bowl and straightened my legs before carefully standing up. The cold tiles underneath my feet seemed to jolt my entire body. I became aware Rhex had stood up as well. He took my bowl and walked out of the room without a word. I followed him, curious as to where I was. The door opened to a hallway and I could see Rhex as he turned a corner into what looked to be a bright room. I walked after him, looking around the doorway into a room that looked like a kitchen. Rhex placed the dishes into what looked to be a rack inside of a cloudy bubble.

"Rhex?" At my voice he looked over his shoulder, the look in his eyes questioning. "Is this the kitchen?" He raised an eyebrow and walked over pulling a small device out of his pocket. He held it up in front of my face before grasping my chin in his other hand and turning my face to the side. He slipped it around my ear and placed part of it in my ear. I shuddered at the strange feeling it gave me right before he seemed to turn it on. A piercing squeal filled my ear and I flinched, wincing at the painful noise. It stopped and Rhex turned my face back so I was facing him. I watched as he took out an identical device and put it in his own ear.

"Can you hear me?" A rough voice with smooth edges filled my ears and sent a shiver down my spine. I pressed my hand to my mouth, eyes wide. "Liv, can you understand what I am saying?" His mouth didn't match the words but it was *his* voice.

I nodded quickly, a sudden smile on my face. "I can hear you." I watched as the corner of his mouth moved upwards slightly. "What is this?" I pointed at my ear and he shrugged.

"A military grade translator. I took two of them from the military bay after I brought you here." He moved to the back of the space and moved around a corner, I followed him. The room I walked into seemed to be a living room, there were several chairs and a sofa. The glass table in front of the sofa was cluttered with some books and what looked to be some parts of a gun.

"You stole them?" I watched as he picked up the parts and started assembling them rather quickly. It looked like he had done it a thousand times before.

"Borrowed is a more appropriate term. They were meant for integrated Human-Orrian combat units. We don't use them because we don't integrate with humans anymore so no one will miss them." His words made me feel slightly cold and I wrapped my arms around my stomach, attempting to quell the faint tremors I felt growing inside of my muscles.

"Why not?" The words felt smaller than I had intended and Rhex didn't look at me as he slid the last part into place on what looked to be a rifle with a scope. He looked it over, as if double checking his work.

"The Council has declared it to be so. We must listen to the Council on matters such as that." His voice seemed stiff and I felt slightly hurt, it was like a rejection. He was my soulmate and I wondered if he hated the fact he was now tied to a human. I felt myself hunch forward like I had against the stares as he had walked me to the vibrating room.

"Then what about us?" The words made him freeze and he looked up, his face blank.

"We never should have been mated." The words made me wince, a phantom pain seemed to slice through me at his bluntness. I looked down at the floor, not wanting to see the blank look on his face. "A Human-Orrian pairing has never happened and it goes against all of our traditions and laws because *you* go against all of our laws." I forced myself to look at him and his expression softened as he set the weapon down on the glass table before standing up.

His large frame walked closer to me and I stepped back slightly, not trusting him for a brief moment. He ignored my retreat, his hand reaching out and touching the side of my neck. His thumb brushed my skin repeatedly and I tried to ignore the goose bumps that erupted over my skin at the gesture. It felt like my skin was charged with electricity as he moved closer.

"I tested your blood in the tunnel. I wanted to know the reason why I looked at you and saw no one else. I wanted to know why I felt you take something from me with your eyes. Your DNA is sixty-three percent Orrian." His thumb stroked the spot again. I realized it was where he had held the device to my neck earlier. The flashing red numbers danced through my head and I looked up at him. "You never should have been born. If they knew what you were, they would kill you. I broke the tester before it could upload to the main database and then took you to Ghilesh." His hand dropped and I watched as he placed them behind his back.

"Ghilesh said we would have a hard time when everyone found out. Does that mean they would still try and kill me if they find out about my DNA?" The words felt strange to me. Fear was rising as I understood what had happened, I had been born broken because I wasn't supposed to be born at all. Human embryos with more Orrian DNA than human DNA needed to be aborted but somehow I had slipped through the cracks. I could feel my heart pound against my ribs at the thought I would be killed for a mistake I had nothing to do with. I would be killed for the crime of simply being born.

"I chose you as my soulmate. It is protection enough. You cannot be denied your mate, no matter who they may be." He took a step backwards and I looked at the floor trying to process what I had been told. I wasn't exactly human but at the same time I wasn't Orrian. I was a half-breed, an abomination in most eyes. I bit the inside of my lip, my eyes wide. I was a mouse among vipers and I had a feeling Rhex knew it as well. "Liv, you must breathe. I can see you are panicking. Your emotions are new to me, I am unsure how to deal with them. I haven't dealt with another person's emotions before." I looked up at him, my hand trembling as I ran it through my hair.

My braid had loosened since this morning and the motion I made with my hand nearly unravelled it completely. Rhex reached out with his hand and I jerked my head back slightly as he touched a loose strand. There was a peculiar look in his eyes as he looked at it and I felt slightly uncomfortable.

"Your hair is beautiful." The words were a faint murmur as he rubbed the strands between his fingers. I felt my stomach flip pleasantly at the compliment but I felt a tad self-conscious. I had been given compliments before but I have never been given a compliment while being looked at with such stark truth.

"It's too long." I shivered as his hand ran through my hair, completely unravelling the braid. His eyes flashed with a sudden heat before he looked away, the look gone from his face entirely.

"I never liked short hair." He dropped his hand as I reached up and pulled my hair over my shoulder, tugging it slightly. He placed his hands behind his back once more and I felt his sudden tenseness, a withdrawal from the situation. It was confusing, his moments of tenderness were immediately followed by an icy withdrawal. "Come, I'll show you around. It is a smaller apartment but it functions well enough." He turned on his heel and walked by me. I let out a small sigh before following him down the hallway and past the door to the kitchen. He pointed at the far door.

"That is my bedroom. You have seen the kitchen and the sitting area." He pushed open another door. "This is the bathroom. I am sure you want to get cleaned up. It has been a long day." Rhex stepped inside of the small room before opening a cupboard and pulling out a towel. He handed it to me before stepped outside of the room and gesturing at me to go inside. I took a tentative step inside when he grasped my arm, halting my progress. I looked at him and he moved my head to the side and removed the translator.

"Is it because I'll get electrocuted if it gets wet?" I looked up at him and he nodded before letting me go and walking back down the hallway. I looked at his retreating back before I stepped back and closed the door.

The room was an off white and everything had a slightly metallic feel to it. I looked around, slightly lost as to what to do. Everything was similar to on Earth but looked far more complicated. There was a glass door across from the door to the hallway and I pulled it open.

Water started dropping down from the ceiling and I gave a gasp of surprise at how sudden it was but the surprise wore off as I stuck my hand into the falling water. The warmth made a smile cross my face and

I stripped quickly, uncaring of where my clothes ended up as I stepped inside the small piece of heaven I had discovered.

I let out a groan as the hot water pounded down onto my skin, I felt layers of tension slide off of my body. My muscles slowly loosened, letting all my emotions slide off my body like the water did. I was left feeling peaceful standing under the hot water. I closed my eyes, enjoying the feeling of everything washing away and disappearing down the drain.

I ran my hands through my hair and tilted my head back, letting the water hit my face. I straightened my head and pulled my hair over my shoulder. I opened my eyes, looking around the square room for shampoo but finding none.

I frowned when the water stopped and looked up. A warm tingling wrapped around my foot and I jerked my gaze downwards. The bottom of the shower was filled with a blue mist. I jerked away from it but it wrapped around my legs leaving goosebumps in its wake. I fought the urge to kick it off. It felt like tingling hands moving up my body. The thought made me move around, trying to avoid the mist. I shuddered as it slipped up my back and over my chest. Another portion of it ran up my belly and I held my breath holding my arms up. I closed my eyes tightly, wanting the weirdness to stop.

The tingling seemed to run through my hair right to the ends before it slowly stopped and started retreating. I let out a shuddering breath as it completely left. Without a second thought I jumped out of the shower with wide eyes, my hands searching blindly for a towel. I grabbed it and wrapped myself up in it tightly as I shuddered. That had been a highly unpleasant experience. I looked around for my clothes and blinked. They were gone. I spun around, my eyes on the floor. I hadn't missed them, my clothes were no longer in the bathroom. I felt my heart sink, I had practically been molested by a shower and now my clothes were missing.

I held my towel tightly to my chest and walked out of the bathroom. I made cautious steps towards the sitting area and stepped around the corner. Rhex was sitting on the sofa cleaning his rifle.

I shifted my weight nervously from foot to foot. "Rhex?" He turned to look at me as I said his name and I swallowed thickly. "I'm pretty sure your shower just molested me and your bathroom ate my clothes."

6

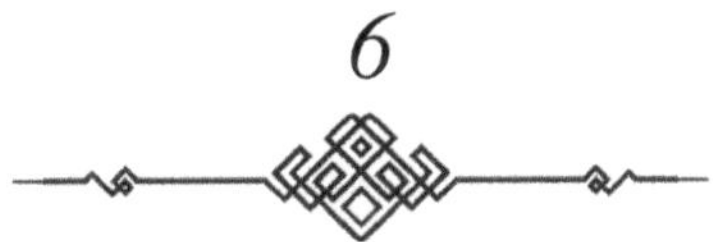

I could practically feel his gaze as it moved up my body and it left a trail of heat in its wake. I gave a small shiver as his eyes found mine. The desire in his gaze wasn't disguised for a brief moment and I watched as he shook himself, his eyes narrowing as he stood up. I rocked back and forth on my feet, becoming acutely aware of the water I was dripping everywhere.

I tugged my towel closer to my body as he walked over. He said something in Orrian that I believed was directed at me and I gave him a blank look. He handed me the translator, grasped the edge of the towel and then pointed to his ear.

I frowned wondering if I interpreted it right. "Dry my ear out then put the translator in?" I watched as he nodded before he walked down the hallway and into his bedroom. I shifted my towel so one half covered my chest before carefully tilting my head and using the other corner to dry my ear. I quickly adjusted the towel and put the translator in like I had felt Rhex do. I looked down at the floor and felt a shudder run down my back.

"They have rooms that try to kill me and showers that touch me inappropriately. This is going to be *so* awesome." I couldn't help the sarcasm that entered my tone as I held the towel tightly, terrified it would fall off. I was highly attracted to Rhex, it was a given with a soulmate, but at the same time he was always hot and cold. That wasn't entire conducive to a bond and I didn't want to end up in an uncomfortable sexual situation with him due to it.

"I had forgotten how sensitive humans are in regards to many of our devices. I apologize for not warning you." He was standing beside me and I jumped in surprise. He held out a few clothes that I took and clutched to my chest, staring at him with wide eyes as he ran a hand through his hair. "I shall have to shut off the cleaner in the shower. I don't wish for my shower to 'touch you inappropriately' again. I do not wish for you to be uncomfortable here." There was sincerity in his eyes and I felt myself relax slightly.

"It's okay, it was just really strange and unsettling. I'm not used to that method of cleaning one's self." I felt amused suddenly and I chuckled. "I'm sorry, this is ridiculous. Sexually deviant mist. That's a first... Well behind murderous vibrating rooms and bathrooms that eat clothing." I laughed at the look on his face and pressed a hand to my face, shaking my head.

"The vibrating room, as you call it, is actually a teleporter. They function similar to your elevators but they are much faster." He shrugged, his hands behind his back again. The gesture seemed to be happening a lot and I wondered why, it didn't seem like it was natural to his habits. "As for the bathroom taking your clothes. It did take them. They are going to be cleaned and then put in the closet. A lot of spaces on the ship are automated as such." I had to admit that it did make a lot of sense.

I felt a cool breeze blow across my shoulders and I swallowed. "I should probably get dressed." I shuffled to the side, letting Rhex pass me.

"They are built for an Orrian so they will be large on your frame." He walked back to the sofa and sat down. I let my gaze linger for a moment before I turned and headed into the bathroom. I set the clothes on the counter and lifted the first piece. It was a well-worn t-shirt that looked to be two sizes too large but I said nothing as I dropped the towel and pulled it over my head. It fell halfway down my thighs and I picked up the second item. I raised my eyebrows at the small pair of shorts. They looked to be too small for Rhex and I shrugged before pulling them on. They fit a little big on me but they covered what needed to be covered. I picked up the towel and hung it on the rack before leaving the room.

"I take it the shorts aren't yours." I stepped into the sitting room and watched as Rhex shook his head, his back to me.

"They were my sister's. I was surprised I still had them. Your clothes should been done in about twenty minutes but you can keep those if you like." He was taking apart the rifle again as I moved towards one of the chairs and sat down. I watched him work, he looked almost relaxed as he inspected each piece of his gun.

"I'm going to need more than two outfits." I stated it absentmindedly and then sat up with wide eyes. My parents. I had to tell my parents what had happened. "Is there any way I can call my parents?" I needed to let them know I was okay.

He frowned but didn't look up. "I can get you new clothes." The words had an edge of something I didn't understand, as if he was trying to tell me something without actually saying it.

"It's not about clothes, it's about letting them know I am alright. I left the house thinking I was going to be recycled and so did they. They need to know that I am okay." I could hear the bite in my voice and I took a deep breath, trying to keep my annoyance in check.

"You can't call them. This ship doesn't have any contact with humans unless it is through the Council." His tone was back to being emotionless and I sighed.

"Of course it doesn't." I let out another sigh, pressing my face into my hands. "Can I ever contact them?" The thought made my throat close with sudden emotion and lifted my head to look at Rhex.

His movements slowed as he took off another piece of his rifle, he let out a small sigh. "I will do my best to get word to your parents that you are alright." His words were comforting and I fiddled with my fingers in my lap, feeling an awkward silence creeping up as he went back to taking apart his gun. His movements were precise and slightly graceful as he placed each part on the glass coffee table.

"Can you teach me how to put it together?" I looked from the parts and back up to his face. He looked stiff but then suddenly relaxed, I saw his mouth twitch upwards slightly.

"I can." He shifted over slightly on the couch and I smiled before jumping up. I moved around the table and sat down beside him, looking at him with a touch of excitement. I had never really been allowed near guns before and it was almost exciting. He deftly took apart the rest of it then handed me the stock of the rifle. "Alright, I need you to grab that part right there." He pointed at a part on the table and I picked it up. I smiled at him and he gave me a crooked one in return.

"Okay, so this one goes here?" I snapped the piece into place and Rhex nodded. I had put it together and taken it apart several times and even though I couldn't name half of the parts, I had a general idea of where they were supposed to go. The rifle had been heavier than I thought and the metal was cool on my skin as I carefully set it on the table.

Rhex reached over and picked it up, looking it over. "It looks good. A few more times and you can do it with your eyes closed." There was a slight hint of teasing in his tone and I smiled, my face heating up slightly. I felt a yawn rise up and I covered my mouth. Rhex looked at me before looking at the clock on the wall. "It is late, we should probably get some sleep." I gave a nod, stretching my arms over my head with a yawn. The stretching felt good and my back popped in several spots.

"You can have the bedroom, I'll sleep of the sofa." He gestured to the hallway and I raised an eyebrow. There was no way he could fit onto the couch, his frame was too large.

"No, I'll sleep on the sofa. I had the bed all day." I stood up and gave him a small smile. "You are a little big to be sleeping on the sofa. It would be uncomfortable for you, besides it's your house and I'm the guest." He tilted his head at me, his eyes narrowing slightly as if he were trying to puzzle me out. I moved away, heading into the kitchen looking for a glass of water.

"I'll grab you a blanket and your clothes." His voice echoed slightly in the hallway as I pulled open cupboards in search of a glass. I found them and then looked for the tap but there was only the strange bubble on the counter I had seen Rhex place the dirty dishes in. "Here." I jumped at how close he was and he held out a blanket and my clothes. We switched as I handed him the glass and took the blanket and clothes. I walked towards the couch, placing the items on top of it. I could hear him walking over and I looked up as he held out the glass, now full of water. I took it with a small smile that wasn't returned.

"Don't forget to take your translator out. I'll be in the bedroom if you need anything." His face was even and I watched as he turned around and disappeared into the hallway. I listened as the door clicked shut and I moved my clothes to the side, spreading the blanket over the couch before crawling under it. I carefully took the translator, despite how much I had already slept I felt rather exhausted so when the lights shut off I closed my eyes.

I sat up in a panic, giving a small cry of fear. I did not know where I was and the remnants of a nightmare I couldn't remember hung off me. I clutched at my medallion, stroking it between my fingers. I let reality seep back into my mind, chasing away the heavy feeling of the nightmare, reminding me of where I was and what had happened. I took several trembling breaths in and out. The nightmare was so vivid but I couldn't remember anything, just the fear but it had been all consuming like it was eating away at me.

I paused before looking around, I was sitting on a bed, not the sofa. I pulled back the covers and stood up. I ignored the chill the tiles gave me as I slowly made my way down the hallway and into the sitting room. The lights turned on but just enough to take the edge off of the darkness.

I looked over the edge of the sofa and Rhex was sprawled on it. He was too tall to lay on it properly and one leg rested on the floor and the other hung over the edge of the arm rest. One of his arms covered his eyes and his mouth hung open slightly. His breath coming in soft puffs.

My eyes felt gritty and I rubbed at them, noticing the blanket had fallen on the floor. I moved around the sofa and picked it up before gently covering him with it again. I went to walk away when a hand grabbed my wrist tightly and I was pulled down onto a hard chest, my face close to his. I let out a small noise of surprise, my heart beating hard in my chest as his arms wrapped around me tightly, practically forcing the air from my lungs. He barked something in Orrian, his voice laced with sleep.

"Rhex!" It was practically a squeak and the arms immediately loosened. His voice rumbled up his chest and through to mine. The lights brightened and I looked at him with wide eyes. He rubbed at his eyes with one of his hands, he looked at me in sleepy confusion. "I'm sorry, I had a bad dream and I came out here because I was in the bedroom and then I put the blanket back on you. I didn't mean to wake you up." I felt his arm tighten slightly around me as his eyes finally focused on mine. I was so close to him I could feel his warm breath on my face, I swallowed hard as heat curled through me once more.

Everything about him seemed to hit a chord deep within me that no one had ever struck before. When he was around me the air seemed to be charged with electricity. When he touched me, my skin fairly burned as if each touch was a brand into my skin. His scent drew me in turning my brain into a hazy and foggy mess where I didn't know up from down. I had never truly experienced such a potent desire before and it almost scared me.

It wasn't an urge to touch him or to be near him, it was a bone deep *need.* As if he was just as important to my survival as breathing. His arm around my waist and his warm breath in my face made me light headed and almost dizzy. Everything seemed almost too warm but at the same time not warm enough.

I felt my breathing grow shallow as I looked into his eyes, everything in me wanted to close the few inches and press my lips to his own. To see if they were as hard as they appeared or it they would soften as he kissed me. I couldn't help myself and I dropped my head down, brushing my lips against his in the barest hint of a kiss but the heat of it surged through me like an inferno.

I felt the groan Rhex let out more than I heard it. My heart was pounding in my ears as his arm tightened around me and his other hand cupped the back of my head, pulling me back down. His lips captured mine in a searing kiss that threatened to burn me to ash but I greedily wanted more.

I reached up, freeing my pinned arm and pressed my hand to the side of his neck, feeling his pulse pound harshly against my palm. The heat from his skin sent little shocks through my nerves. He moved his mouth on mine and his lips were both soft yet firm. My mind felt like it had turned to mush and everything faded away except for the raw need that suddenly surged through my body.

He pulled back with a gasp as if he was taking in air that had been denied him before he sat up quickly, pushing me away and putting a significant amount of space between us as he did so. The rejection was a sharp pain that sliced through me. I pressed my hand to my chest as if trying to stop the pain from consuming me. I watched as he paced, his hand in his hair. I looked down at my hands before I brought one up to touch my lips, they tingled pleasantly. The only evidence that the kiss had happened, that he may have enjoyed it as well.

He started speaking in rapid Orrian and I glanced up at him. He looked frustrated as he paced and I blinked, watching his even pacing. His voice was enough to send shivers up and down my spine even if I couldn't understand a word of what he was saying.

"You do realize I don't understand, right?" I blinked as he froze into place. He turned to look at me and I felt suddenly pinned under the intensity of his gaze. He moved towards me slowly and I shifted back, feeling somewhat like a mouse being watched by a hawk. He picked something up off the coffee table and moved closer. My heart slammed into the front of my chest as he gripped my chin and pulled my head to the side. I felt him place the translator into my ear before he turned my face towards him. He wasn't looking at me and it felt like something was wrong.

"I cannot touch you. It makes things complicated." His words were even and controlled. I looked up at his face and winced at the blank look he had on. "I have training to do so I will be gone in just over a week. I must serve my people and you are just a distraction."

7

There was silence, an unbearable silence, that fell as I tried to let the words sink in. They had been needlessly harsh to say the least. The hurt bloomed in my chest and I tried my best to ignore it. I understood duty, I understood the need to do what a person had been assigned in life but it didn't mean I shouldn't have a chance.

I had spent seven years thinking the worst of myself and by some strange twist of the cosmos I had found the one piece that I had been missing my entire life. Now it was like everything was laughing at me. I was a distraction from duty, I was once again second. I threaded my fingers together and squeezed until my knuckles turned white.

The dull, aching pain gave me room to think, gave me the ability to see things clearly. "How long will you be gone?" The tone felt empty and I inwardly winced. I didn't want to sound so hollow because I wanted to be strong. I wanted to show Rhex that I would be okay, that his rejection didn't hurt me and that I understood his need to do his job.

"Four months." At his words I winced slightly. Four months was a long time. The thought of being away from him was crushing but for some reason I knew four months would be excruciating. We were bound tightly and I was scared of how it would affect me when he was gone.

Even my parents had never been separated long, I doubted any bound couples had. It wasn't done.

"Where will I be staying once you are gone?" I felt one of my joints pull painfully and I loosened my grip slightly, not wanting to cause further damage.

"Here, most likely." It was such a civil and polite tone. It was if we were discussing politics or the weather, making small comments about the decorations. It made my stomach churn slightly. I wanted him to express *some* emotion over the situation.

"What will I be doing?" I bit the inside of my lip, worrying the flesh with my teeth but not actually biting down. It would be a long four months if I was to stay locked up without anything to do.

"I have to speak to the Council." His words, for some strange reason, made me angry. He referred to everything he did not know or did not wish to discuss to the Council. I already disliked the Council for their rules and regulations and I was terrified of them for what they would do if they ever found out about what I was. Now my soulmate was emotionlessly parroting everything they said as if he was pre-programmed. *Great.*

"Of course." I gathered up enough courage to actually look at him. "How long will it take, after you are gone, before they try to kill me?" A muscle in his jaw ticked, as if he had clenched his teeth together but his face remained expressionless.

"They won't. Our binding will provide adequate protection for you." It was that same polite tone that made me want to rip my hair out. I felt a mask slip over my face, the same one that had always fallen when my mum had discussed pairing options with me. It was like a withdrawal from a situation I no longer wanted to be in.

"Are you sure?" I knew it was a combative question but at the same time I was scared. If he left and I was left on the ship alone they could do anything to me and he wouldn't know for weeks. I could be dead and gone before his first report back because he would not be able to return in time to stop them. A thick silence fell and I dropped my gaze back to my hands. I started to pick at my nails, trying to ignore the fact he was staring at me.

"You should get some more sleep." His words pushed into my head but I pushed them out again just as quickly. I hated how I was feeling, this sad almost scared feeling made me feel weak. I hadn't even felt like that on my way to being recycled. I had been scared, yes but I had been firm in convincing myself that it was partially my decision. I was broken and broken things needed to be recycled. The feeling I had now was just wrong, I wasn't sure I ever wanted to feel it again. "Liv, get to the bedroom." There was annoyance in his voice and I shook my head, pulling myself out of my thoughts.

"Sorry, I forgot where I was for a second." I stood up, looking up at Rhex at the same time. I gave him a half-hearted smile. "Probably just tired." It wasn't a lie. I felt tired-no *exhausted.* It would be difficult to be bonded to someone who seemed to unknowingly jerk your emotions back and forth rapidly but I knew I would have to deal with it.

He lifted his hand slightly before letting it drop back to his side. I watched as he stiffened before pulling his hands behind his back. "Get some sleep." There was a slight bark in his tone that made me bristle slightly but I was too tired to really care. I moved passed him and down the hallway.

Everything was so confusing, I didn't know where my emotions were half the time and I had no clue what to expect with a bonding. Everyone I had talked to about it said it was easy, that everything fell into place but then again they weren't bonded to an Orrian. The very idea of it wasn't easy let alone trying it out in real life.

The bedroom was quiet and I pulled the translator from my ear, placing it on the bedside table as I flipped back the rumpled covers. I sat on the edge of the bed rubbing my forehead, trying to understand what was going on. I gave up, I knew I would have to figure everything out but at that moment I was too tired to think straight without wanting to cry. I lay down and pulled the covers up to my chin before curling up and trying my hardest to fall asleep.

8

I stood beside Rhex in front of the Council. I could feel their stern gazes on me and I looked at the floor, tracing the patterned tiles with my eyes. I had known they would find out eventually but I thought they would have been quicker. It had taken them three days of me being on the ship before they realized I was there.

"Have you lost your mind, Rhex DharSon?" The man's voice was cold and I lifted my head slightly, trying to see who it was. He stood off to the left, his face was twisted into a sneer and his eyes were a cold grey.

"I am perfectly aware of where my mental faculties are, Councilman Khos." Rhex's words were even and bland but I could hear the slight gritting of his teeth. I lowered my eyes back to the floor, continuing to trace the patterns with my eyes.

"You have just broken every law, tradition and code we have. You have paired with a *half-breed!"* There was venom in his words and I flinched at the last one. *Slegrnd.* I learned that it was a favourite word for Orrians to use in regards to me and other humans. I hated the word. I had been called it more times than I could possibly count in the past few days. It seemed more and more Orrians hated humans, at least on this ship.

"Watch your tone, Khos. We must discuss this rationally." It was a soft feminine tone and I glanced up once more. Her hair was so blond it was nearly white and her eyes were a vibrant lilac colour. Her gaze locked onto mine and she gave a small smile. "Now, Liviya Burch, I'm going to state some things. I need you to let me know if they are true or not." Her words matched her mouth and I realized she was speaking English.

She tilted her head and I gave a small nod. I could feel Councilman Khos's eyes on me and the gaze was so cold it felt like the air around me had lowered several degrees.

"Your name is Liviya Mary Burch. You grew up in the Northwest Settlement near the Old Ruins. At the age of eighteen you found you could not pair with your chosen soulmate." Her tone was soft and I nodded. I looked at her, trying my best to ignore the stares of everyone else. "You spent seven years with your caseworker, Ami'la, trying to resolve the issue of being unable to bond." I gave another nod and she gave me another small smile before turning back to her notes.

"That is enough, Nadila! She needs to be recycled. Enough with your sympathies! She has broken our law and needs to be taught what that means." The councilman's voice sent a shudder down my spine and I could feel Rhex stiffen at the words.

Councilwoman Nadila turned to look at the cold man and gave him a serene smile before turning back to her papers. "You have been introduced to forty-four possible mates but found no bond with any of them despite the many forms of therapy you had to try." She looked up at me and I gave another nod. She set the papers down and clasped her hands together, resting her chin on them. "You were aware that on your twenty-fifth birthday, if you didn't find a bond you would be recycled. Am I correct?" I lifted my head a bit more, feeling a touch braver at her soft kindness. Not every Orrian hated humans and I was glad there were a few on the Council.

"Yes, I was aware." It came out strangled and I gave a small cough, trying to clear the tightness from my throat.

A strange smile crossed her face. "So, after you last meeting with Ami'la, where you failed to bond with one James Levi, you were taken up to this ship. Correct?" There was something about her smile, something secretive that made me almost uneasy. I didn't trust what I didn't know or people who knew things that I didn't. I wanted to trust her, she was one of the only Orrians who had shown me kindness, even if it was a smile. To be fair I hadn't really looked at the others either but having someone want to kill you would keep your curiosity tamped down.

"That's correct, yes." I swallowed hard feeling the tension growing in the air. Something was happening in the energy in the Council. I felt the hair on the back of my neck stand up, the energy they were putting off was intense.

"You made it onto the ship and your handler was taking you to the recycling bay. Did you fight him? Attempt to escape?" Nadila seemed to lean forward her smile tugging at the corners of her mouth. Her gaze, unflinching on me, seemed almost predatory.

"No. I had accepted my fate and why would I try to escape? I'm human and more than aware that any Orrian could kill me without thinking. It would be tantamount to suicide." The words tumbled out with my confusion before I could stop them. I swallowed again, goosebumps erupting on my skin and I looked at her with wide eyes.

"Did Rhex tell you what he was doing when he brought you to the Soul Maker, Ghilesh? Did he ask you for your permission before he took you to another part of the ship?" Her gaze looked expectant and I shook my head.

"No, I didn't understand what was going on. All I knew is that I looked at him everything felt right, in place." I felt almost panicked, the very air was oppressive and I felt my breathing start to constrict in my chest. Her eyes lit up and the smile finally emerged. The predatory smile of a snake catching a mouse.

"So, Khos." Her words had a bite to them but the smile never left her face. "A human without a mate reaches her twenty-fifth birthday. Is prepared to meet her fate, as corroborated by her caseworker of seven years. Reaches our ship where by some twist of fate finds her soulmate among us and he essentially kidnaps her, binds her to him without her full knowledge or consent. Which is the very thing *any* one of us would do when faced with our soulmate. Yet, *she* has broken our laws? Our customs? Our codes?" There was a harsh edge to her voice that hadn't been there when she had spoken to me.

"Enough, Nadila! We need to show humans that this type of bonding is an abomination! I will not stand by while you defend this Source forsaken half-breed!" As he words erupted the very air seemed to lose the expectant oppressive edge and gained a heated one from his anger.

"Tell me, what laws has she broken?" Nadila's voice is calm and she turned to look at Khos with that same smile on her face. I suddenly realized what was going on, there was a serious power play going on between the two of them. The hatred was evident.

"She has bonded to an Orrian!" The words were spit out and I looked at Khos, his face was twisted with rage and his grey eyes looked deadly. I felt my breath hitch in my throat and I took a small step towards Rhex. To my surprise he didn't move away and actually seemed to lean partially in front of me as if trying to subconsciously hide me from Khos's angry gaze.

"That isn't a law, Khos. You are baying for innocent blood." Nadila spat the words out before pointing at me and standing up, her gaze completely on Khos. I could see her chest heaving and her eyes were narrow slits. "She went through forty-four meetings with men she couldn't bind to. Followed every law written and when the time came to be recycled she accepted it." She shifted her pages around again before she clasped her hands together.

"Her entire life she has followed the law and you are getting pissy because she followed the very one you want to punish her for." She gave a heavy scoff at him and Khos' face turned red.

"He is Orrian and she is nothing but a fucking half-breed! It isn't done!" Khos stood up as well and Rhex was suddenly in front of me, his hand behind his back as if telling me to stay there. I peeked around him to look at Nadila, she looked ready to become violent at any moment. The other people on the Council watched them with slight frustration or amusement.

"You cannot control who someone bonds to, Khos!" She pointed at him in a jerky movement as the muscles in her jaw clenched. "You have *no* say in what the Source does when it comes to souls. The Source has brought them together, Khos, and the worst crime would be you taking them apart. Now that is a law you can actually pay attention to." I watched as she picked up a book and hurled it at the other man. I felt my mouth drop open in shock. This was how they did politics on the Council? What the actual fuck?

"Two souls brought together by fate, one must never separate. After they discover what is found, by ceremony they are forever bound. Tear apart what the Source has wrought, to death you will be brought." She straightened suddenly, smoothing her hair and her suit with a sudden smile. "If you touch them, Khos, you sentence yourself to death." I watched as Khos's face went eerily blank before he moved away from his position and left the room.

"Now, do I hear any opposition?" She looked around expectantly and I watched as a stern looking man with dark eyes stood up. "Yes, Bilsh?" The serene smile is once more on her face as if the screaming match had never happened.

"Khos is right, this isn't something we should celebrate. This is a cause for concern." He gestured to me and Rhex shifted so he blocked the man's view. I swallowed hard, when one enemy disappeared another popped up.

A frail old man shifted in his seat, drawing my attention. "How is it a concern, Bilsh? For years we have been trying to figure out a way to unite our peoples. To finally get rid of the separation between our races. This pairing, it goes against everything we have ever known but maybe it is for the best." His voice was thin and wavered slightly. "I have lived over a hundred years and I have never seen a pairing such as this. The winds of change are upon us and we must decide if we will stand firm, unbending and break against its force or if we will bend and move with it." I narrowed my eyes slightly in confusion before I realized his eyes were cloudy.

He was blind.

The male who spoke before gave a low scoff. "Oh please, old man-"

"*Do not* disrespect me, Bilsh." His voice was booming all of a sudden and I watched as the people on the council bowed their heads in obvious respect. "Where is this remarkable woman?" Rhex stepped to the side and gently placed his hand on my back, leading me forward. I looked around with wide eyes, my breathing growing harsh in my sudden nervousness.

"Do not be afraid." His voice was soft and I was reminded of my grandfather. Rhex and I stopped in front of the table separating us from the old man and he motioned me to come closer. I leaned over the table and his hands reached for my face. I closed my eyes at the strange feeling of his papery skin brushing over mine. His fingers moved over my features as if trying to create a picture of me in his mind. He gave a thin chuckle. "Send her to the Learning Centre while he is away. Teach her our ways, our language, our laws. Let her learn what it means to be one of us. She will make friends." His hands dropped and I leaned back.

"She is a pretty one." He chuckled, it was a wheezing sound that was almost alarming, as if he were having troubles breathing. "Rhex, my boy, kiss her every once in awhile or someone else will." He started to chuckle again and I felt my face slowly heat up.

"I shall keep that in mind, grandfather." There was a mixture of fondness and embarrassment in Rhex's voice and I looked between the two, trying to see the family resemblance but I couldn't see much of Rhex in the old man's wrinkled face.

"Well, Rhess has suggested sending her to the learning centre. I have no objections to it. Does anyone else object to it?" Nadila's voice was calm and I turned my head to look at her. She is almost lazy in her confidence and I smiled suddenly, she was a good ally to have. She looked around and I followed her gaze, many of those on the Council shook their heads. Her gaze met mine. "Alright, Liviya Burch, I hereby official declare you an Orrian citizen." Her smile was sweet and kind and I couldn't help but smile back.

9

Rhex knocked on the door in front of him and I smiled as Ghilesh opened it. He raised an eyebrow as he took us both in. The look he gave was questioning and I tilted my head, my smile widening. "You're supposed to babysit me." I wanted to laugh at the look on his face but I refrained.

"Liviya, you are twenty-five years old, you do not need a babysitter." His tone was sharp and I shrugged, giving a flippant gesture towards Rhex.

"Tell that to Rhex. We were at the Council today where I was given an Orrian citizenship but Rhex needs to go report to his commanding officer." I ignored how Rhex stiffened at my words. "And as I refused to be stuck inside of that apartment by myself any longer and there is the ever present threat of someone throwing me over a balcony if I'm alone. It was decided I needed a babysitter." I could feel my smile turn brittle as I clenched my teeth.

I watched as a flash of amusement crossed Ghilesh's face. "I could use some amusement for the day. Besides, I am in need of someone with your expertise." He held up the door for me to come in and I gave him a smile, ignoring Rhex as I moved past the older man into his cluttered apartment.

"Liv, I will be in the military bay if you need me." Rhex's voice made me turned around so I could give him a tight smile but didn't reply. I was a little testy from being thrown into the teleporter after being told Ghilesh would be 'watching' me for a bit.

"Go do what you need to do, Rhex. She will be fine. Not much trouble we can get into I'm afraid." Ghilesh waved him off but Rhex continued to look at me intently.

I gritted my teeth. "Ghilesh and I are going to be *fine*. Just go." I turned away from his gaze to look around Ghilesh's sitting room. Dusty books littered the area and there were odd trinkets hanging from the ceiling. I reached up, letting my hand run through the polished glass that hung from the ceiling above my head. I could hear the door close and Ghilesh's mutterings as I continued to reach up and touch the odds and ends hanging from the ceiling.

"Those are important, make sure not to misplace any of them." At his words I pulled my hand back and turned to look at him. He had grabbed a leather bound book and picked up a pen. "Okay, Liviya, I have a few questions for you." He took a stack of books off of a chair before sitting down.

I gave him a small smile as I cleared off the chair across from him to sit on. I settled into the high backed chair, pulling my feet onto it. "Alright, go ahead." I wrapped my arms around my knees, waiting for him to begin.

He paused, muttering under his breath as if trying to gather his thoughts as he shuffled through the pages in the leather book he was holding. "Okay, where is it? Oh, here we are." He pulled out a folded piece of paper and opened it. He scanned it for a few moments and then looked up at me. I gave him a smile. "Alright, Liviya. When you saw Rhex for the first time, when you realized he was your soulmate, what happened? What did you feel?"

I frowned slightly. "That's a really odd question. When I first saw him I had no clue he was my soulmate." I chuckled at the puzzled look on Ghilesh's face. "I had spent seven years believing I had no soulmate and wasn't capable of having one and then suddenly I was confronted with someone who seemed to be the impossible." I shrugged with a small amused smile. "It was impossible. *He* was impossible."

I shifted in my seat. "I was broken. I had felt that way for seven years. So being given what I had believed was an impossibility made it not click in my head right away." I let my knees go before putting my elbow on the arm of the chair and leaning my chin against my palm. "I was seriously flawed and he was Orrian. It was impossible but he made my world stop anyway. I remember looking at him and for a moment as I looked at him, as I took him in, we were the only two people in this world." I felt the smile grow on my face as I remembered that moment. It was a moment of pure *connection* to another person, of being suddenly completed for the first time in your life.

"It was if my world had finally made sense. I felt completed, *whole,* but I was confused. I had no clue what was going on or who he was." I watched as Ghilesh wrote in his journal and I thought back again. "His gaze took something from me and tied me to him." I gave a lazy gesture with my hand as I spoke. “Keep in mind I had been prepared to be recycled so this had completely thrown me for a loop."

Ghilesh looked up at me suddenly, his eyebrows pulling together slightly in a frown. "What does that mean?" His amber eyes were confused and I was reminded his native language wasn't English. It was easy to forget, he spoke it so well.

"Thrown for a loop?" I watched as he nodded and I bit the inside of my lip trying to find the words to explain the odd idiom. "It confused me. I think that's close enough to what it means." He nodded and turned back to his journal. "Where was I?" I frowned and thought for a second before finding my train of thought. "He scared me to be honest. I wasn't scared *of* him, I was scared of what he was doing to me. He had changed something in me that I hadn't even known existed." I scratched the inside of my wrist lightly.

"When did you become aware he was your soulmate?" He glanced up at me, his amber eyes searching my face as if he could read my very thoughts. It was almost unnerving to have that vibrant intensity directed at me.

I gave a small frown, directing my thoughts towards the moment he was referring to. "There was a moment when we were in the tunnels.. He had removed my cuffs and was trying to rub away the soreness they caused but he did it for me.. He gave me this look, it was almost tender but I recognized it. It was the same look my parents give each other in the little moments." I shrugged slowly. It had been a moment of instant recognition because that is what I had wanted for so long and there it was. "As soon as I figured out the look then everything made sense." I shifted, putting my feet back onto the floor. I was getting a bit restless.

"Are you attracted to him?" His question made me laugh and I nodded my head with a smile.

"Highly. It goes without saying." I felt a slight flush crawl up my neck but I forced it down. I was twenty-five, there was no need to be prudish about my sexual identity or preferences. I was supposed to find my mate attractive and want to be with him. It was normal and okay. There was nothing about it that should have brought me embarrassment but I still had that faint heat to my cheeks as I looked away from Ghilesh.

"Have you ever felt attraction with anyone else?" His question made me inhale sharply at the painful reminder of the Intimacy Therapy I had been essentially forced into.

"I have." I felt an angry sharpness in my chest at the memory. It was a mixture of pain and anger. Pain because it hurt to remember I had been pressured into it and anger that they had thought it was okay to do so. "There was one man, his name was Theodore. When I told that there was that tiny spark of attraction, I was told I needed to try intimacy therapy. Basically to try and fuck my problem away." I rubbed at my sternum, trying to rub away the emotional ache the memory left me.

"I don't want to continue with that." I closed my eyes tightly, rubbing at my forehead. I still felt dirty and used, even after three years. There had been no emotional connection and I discovered sex needed to be more than just two bodies making motions. There had to be a connection for me to feel fulfilled or satisfied with the intimacy.

"I'm sorry. I wasn't aware Intimacy Therapy was an actual form of therapy beyond theories in books." His voice was soft and I looked up at the ceiling. I didn't wish to continue the conversation.

"It isn't traditional. They were grasping at straws, Ghilesh, they were doing their best to try and save my life." I blinked back tears. I needed to be done with the conversation. It only served to make me feel shitty and hurt. "It's best if we just drop the topic. Please." I took a deep breath in, forcing my body to hold back the emotion. It was best not to think about, to dwell on.

"Okay, Liviya." His voice was soft with understanding and I felt a great sincerity from him. I appreciated it greatly. "Would you like something to drink?" He set his journal and pen down and I glanced at him before I shook my head.

"No thank you." I slowly turned my head upwards to look at the various things hanging from the ceiling before confusion had me turning to the old Soul Maker once more. “Why are you asking me about all this?" I watched him carefully as he pressed his hands together.

He paused for a moment, his eyes narrowing, as if debating on whether or not to tell me. "You and Rhex are one of the few couples who I have seen who appear to be actual soulmates." He seemed almost sad and I sat up straighter, my interest piqued.

"What does that mean?" I watched as he shifted, his fingers interlocking before he leaned back in his chair.

"Over nine hundred years ago, Orrians started to go against the Source and started pairing off based on money, power, and connections rather than what the Source had decreed. They started to reject the option of finding their soulmates and went with what would further themselves in life." He sighed, it was a heavy sound, as if the world rested on his shoulders. "Two hundred years after, it started to become difficult to find a soulmate. Three hundred years after that, it was nearly impossible. Now, we are lucky if there is one pairing born at all." He steepled his fingers and he frowned, his white eyebrows pulled low over his eyes. There was anger in his gaze that surprised me.

"The last pairing I saw was my niece's. Vila was a sweet, *sweet* girl and she thought she had found her soulmate in a man named, Khos. You probably met him today, crying for your blood like some sort of savage." His words were bitter and I felt my eyes grow wide. His amber eyes fairly burned with an angry fire. He had a far-away look on his face, his gaze focusing on something that wasn't there. "He rejected her for a more 'suitable' pairing. She wasn't from a good family, wasn't from money, didn't have political leanings or connections. She didn't 'fit in' with his life so he cut her out of it." I held my breath, not wanting to interrupt the story he was telling.

Heavy emotions painted his face, sorrow and anger mixed in his eyes. "She could barely eat, she slept all the time, she lost all motivation to do the barest necessities of life. Vila wasted away before our very eyes." He gave a slow shake of his head. “There was nothing we could do, that *I* could do, because we could not fix her soul." I watched as his hands clenched in his lap.

"I went to Khos and I *begged* him to stop his nonsense. To do what was right but he cast me away, his eyes colder than ice." Fire burned in his eyes as he told me, making the colour glitter and nearly spark. “I realized then what he had done. He had bonded to a more suitable woman. He had given away his soul to a different woman and he no longer cared about Vila." The fire died out and he gave another sad shake of his head.

"She died a few months later." He let out a pained sigh and I bit my lip, sympathy beating at me for his loss. "We all tried to move on but her twin sister, Nadila, refused to leave it be. They were identical twins and when Vila died, Nadila made it her goal to made Khos' life as miserable as possible." A small smile tugged up the corner of his mouth. "She fought her way up the political ladder until she held political sway and a chance at a seat on the Council." His words suddenly made what I had seen in the Council more clear. "He fought against it, of course, but she held more sway than him and was given a seat."

"That would explain what she meant." I blinked at the sudden clarity I had. His gaze met mine and I gave him a small smile. "Nadila was talking about how Rhex had basically kidnapped me and brought me to you to bind us together. She said it was what anyone would have done if they discovered their soulmate. It was a dig at Khos' rejection of Vila, wasn't it?" The anger made sense now. She was angry at Khos for essentially killing her twin and he was angry at her for reminding him daily of what he had done and lost.

There was a vengeful gleam of amusement in Ghilesh's eyes and he smirked. "Nadila always was a bit spiteful. I also heard she threw the Book of Law at him, spouting off the number one Orrian law of never separating chosen mates." He let out a small chuckle. "You two would get along. She has a big heart, it is closely guarded but I think you could break through to it." He rubbed his hands together, the sadness still lingering in the as he stood up.

"She was kind to me. I knew she reminded me of someone, I'm not surprised it was you." I watched as he waved me off as he moved to his kitchen area.

He came back with a glass of water. "You need to drink. The atmosphere is highly recycled and it dehydrates a person very quickly." I took the glass with a nod before taking a small sip.

A comfortable silence fell as I looked around. "So why aren't you mated?" The question came out unexpectedly and I felt heat rise up into my face. I wasn't normally so blunt. "I'm sorry, that was rude."

Ghilesh laughed loudly. It was a happy and jovial sound that floated in the air. "It isn't rude, Liviya, it's curiosity. You look around and see a mess and you noticed my habit of incessant muttering. It is only natural to wonder why I have not mated because it is obvious I haven't." He smiled widely, the corners of his eyes crinkled. "But the thing is, I *am* mated. I've been mated since the day I was conceived." I tilted my head, confused at his words.

"I am a Soul Maker, we are mated to the Source. We are her, or if you prefer, his, living conduits. We cannot mate because we already are. We are content in our life because she is always with us." He gestured to the air around him, a curious little smile on his face as his head tilted as if he were hearing something that didn't reach my ears. "My incessant mutterings may appear as though my age is getting to me but I am actually speaking to the Source. I am hearing her murmurs, her instructions. She is a good mate, I am content with her. Together we make a difference." He gave me another bright smile and I was helpless not to return it.

Humans had never really been given history lessons on the traditions and systems that had been placed in our hands by the Orrians so I was happy he was telling me.

"Every soul medallion I make, it is not just me making it. She is there, telling me how to put it together so that it can house that person's soul perfectly. It was her who told me about you when I looked at your wrist, it was her who told me of your blood, your future." His smiled softened. "She is the one who told me you and Rhex will help fix what we as a race have broken so badly. She told me you were part of the future." His words hung in the air and I wasn't sure what to think of it. It was a heavy thing to have that placed on my shoulders.

There was a loud knock on the door and Ghilesh patted my shoulder as he walked by. I looked over the back of the chair, taking another drink of the water from the glass. I looked around as he went to open it.

"What do you want?" His tone was gruff and I looked over my shoulder and grinned as Rhex gave him an unamused look in return. "I told you, Liviya and I would be fine. There is no need to check on us like a mother hen." Ghilesh looked over his shoulder and winked. I gave an amused chuckle as I sat the cup of water down on small empty space on the table.

I stood up and moved towards the door, my head tilted slightly as I kept my eyes on Rhex. "Yah, Rhex, what do you want?" I smirked as he raised an eyebrow as he crossed his arms over his broad chest. The action as a bit distracting and I had to fight to keep my eyes on his face.

"You." It was such a simple word but it practically knocked the air right out of me and forced myself to give him an even look, not wanting him to see how the small words affected me. "I want you to come with me." His eyes narrowed slightly as I tilted my head once more.

"I was having a nice conversation with Ghilesh, Rhex. What if I wished to continue it?" I fought against the smile that wanted cross my face. I still hadn't forgiven him from forcing me into the teleporter so I wanted to needle him for it.

"Don't argue with me, Liviya." His eyes narrowed slightly and I narrowed mine in return. We glowered at each other before Ghilesh gave a small snort.

"It's not arguing, she's merely asking a question." Ghilesh sounded amused and I gave Rhex a smug smile. At least Ghilesh was on my side for the time being.

"Yes, Rhex. It's just a question." I shifted my weight onto my other leg and Rhex said nothing as his jaw muscle ticked slightly under his skin. He dropped his arms to his side and moved past Ghilesh. I felt my muscles stiffen immediately. I had felt safer when he had been on the other side of the door. Now I felt like a prey in the sight of a large predator.

He moved closer and stopped only when his chest was nearly touching mine. I resisted the urge to take a step back. I clenched my teeth, trying to fight against my attraction to him. It was hard, everything about him was pulling me towards him.

He lifted up a hand and moved to touch my cheek and I gave him a cold look. "No touching, remember?" His eyes narrowed and I lifted my chin up.

"You didn't make that a rule did you?" Ghilesh sounded disbelieving and I tightened my arms over my chest.

"Yes, no touching because I'm a *distraction.*" Despite how brittle the words sounded Ghilesh started laughing. I looked around Rhex and he turned to look at the Soul Maker as well.

"You can't do that, Rhex. It isn't going to work, you will break." The smile on his face looked almost devilish and I gave him a wary look. "And you will break hard." I frowned in confusion, unsure of what the words exactly meant.

"Liviya, we are leaving." Rhex grabbed my wrist, the heat from his skin sending shivers down my spine.

I tugged against it, my jaw closed so tightly I could practically hear my teeth groan. "I'm not being shoved into the stupid teleporter again." I spat the words out and looked at him with narrowed eyes. "It feels like my bones are going to rattle out of my skin and my arms and legs get numb." The teleporter made me feel horrible and I was resentful for being ignored when I said that.

He met my gaze evenly, he was angry but I was too. "This isn't about what you-"

"Rhex, I think it is best if you listen to her." Ghilesh sounded slightly concerned. "There is a reason we did not let humans use the teleporters. It interrupts their physical systems, like the heartbeat. It could kill her." Rhex stiffened at his words then looked at me, he frowned almost in worry.

Vindication soared through me at Ghilesh's words. "I *told* you! I knew the stupid room wanted to kill me." I pointed at Rhex and he stepped closer to me, my eyes level with his collar bone. He reached up and ran the back of his hand down my cheek. I shivered at the contact and looked up at him, I felt sad for some strange reason. He was always so hot and cold with me and it caused a pang in my chest.

His skin brushed against mine softly as his gaze met mine. "I am sorry." His hand dropped back to his side and I tried to smile but it felt more like a grimace so I stopped.

"Take the service stairs if you are with her. There are no cameras there." Ghilesh smirked and I gave him an unimpressed look.

"Like that would ever happen. Distraction, remember." I pointed at myself and let out a sigh as I walked out the door. I could feel Rhex walking behind me. I froze mid-step and he leaned closer, his cheek close to mine and his chest nearly pressed against my back.

"You do not need to remind me of that, Liv." Despite the words I felt myself shiver as they rumbled through his chest, the vibrations of them dancing on my skin. "You *are* a distraction. I cannot think when you are around because all I can think about is running my hands over your soft skin and kissing you until we both can't breathe." My breath caught in my throat at his words and my heart started a harsh rhythm in my chest.

I fought the urge to lean back into him and I closed my eyes, taking in his scent. It was musky and almost seemed to have an edge of something wild, something that warned me off as if he were dangerous. At the same time it called to me on an almost primal level and I resisted the urge to whimper.

"Rhex, I was serious. This no touching rule will break you. Your grandfather is right, if you don't start kissing her. Someone else will." Ghilesh laughed and closed the door behind us. Rhex moved away from me, leaving me feeling chilled and frustrated and I glared at him.

"That is not fair, Rhex." I blinked back tears, "You know it isn't fair."

10

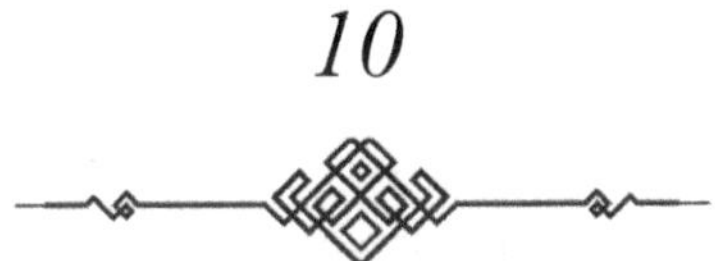

"Come on, Liviya." Rhex grabbed my wrist once again and pulled me towards a dark blue door.

I stumbled behind him before leaning against his hold with a scowl. "No, Rhex! It's Liv and you can't do things like that to me!" I jerked back hard and he let me go, turning around slowly. I wanted to stamp my foot on the ground like I used to do as a child to show him my frustration.

"I'm only human, Rhex. I can feel everything about you, you are *that* intense. Being around you is like being in an ocean that is swirling around me, pulling me down and then you go ahead and touch me." I gestured at him with my hand. He just needed to understand how I felt. "You don't even *have* to touch me to affect me. Just being around makes everything that much more intense. My skin feels like humming when you are near me and it feels like fire when you touch me. I desire you in a way I have never desired another person in my entire life and that's terrifying." I took a deep breath in, holding out my hands towards him, imploring him to understand.

"Then you make the rule no touching because I'm a distraction. Then you proceed to break that rule and *then* withdrawal from the situation right after. You don't feel it when you shut down but I can. It's like a bucket of icy water dumped over me that hurts. It's like a vicious slap to the face." I closed my eyes and rubbed my forehead, trying to rub the sudden ache away. "I don't want to be this sensitive to you, Rhex, but you put out a goddamned energy and I'm only human." The differences between us was right there in front of us but it was like he didn't see them like I did. He could shut everything down, withdrawal, I couldn't.

"Please, if you are going to play this weird game with me, take that into account." I felt drained but in a good way, as if all of that had been festering inside of me and having it out in the open was a good thing. I looked up at him and he had a look on his face that frustrated me, it was nearly undecipherable.

"Come on, Liv. We have things to do." His voice was even and I levelled him with a glare but kept my mouth shut. I had said what needed to be said and I wasn't about to say anything else. He opened the door and I walked into to the dim stairwell. I gritted my teeth as he closed the door and moved past me, starting down the stairs. I followed behind him slowly.

I envied the way he was able to push everything away as if it didn't bother him. I wanted to be able to do just that, to push everything away like I didn't have a care in the world. Instead I had half of a Council who wanted my head on a pike, more than half the population on this ship wanted me thrown down the recycler. Not to mention one person wanting to wage war on humans all because the Source had decided my soulmate had to be Orrian.

We walked down several flights of stairs before he opened another door and led me out. I blinked, the doors on this floor were red and there were far more Orrians than I was comfortable with. I resisted the urge to step closer to Rhex as we started walking towards a door sitting beside clear windows. It appeared to be a clothing store and I almost balked. I didn't like clothes shopping on Earth, let alone surrounded by Orrians who would probably smother me in the clothes while Rhex wasn't looking.

I paused at the doorway and as if sensing I had stopped Rhex looked over his shoulder with a frown. "Come on, Liv. Into the store, I said I would get you more clothes and it wasn't an empty promise." He levelled a look on me that demanded he be obeyed and I wanted to stand just outside of the door to spite him. I clenched my teeth tightly, my jaw aching at the pressure, as I stepped inside of the store. "Pick out what you wish to wear." I looked around, the styles were similar to Earth styles but I had no clue where to start.

I moved over to a rack and moved some of the shirts around, the fabric was nearly sheer. I frowned, most of the pieces would need to be layered and it irritated me. "Can I help you with anything?" The worker's voice sounded stiff and I looked at her with a small smile before shaking my head.

"No thank you, I'm just looking." I watched as the smile slid off her face and her eyes grew cold. I leaned away from her slightly, she suddenly felt overly hostile towards me.

"I'm sorry, we do not serve humans here." She pointed at the door and I felt my cheeks heat up.

"She just arrived." The voice was familiar but the tone was almost too polite. I looked over my shoulder and Nadila stood with a brittle smile on her face. "A human exchange student. She is going to learn about our culture, laws, and language. To better help us understand each other." Her lilac eyes were cold as she looked down at the worker.

"Councilwoman Nadila! I am sorry, I did not see you there." There was a slightly frightened look on the saleswoman's face and I glanced between the two women, wondering if the clothes hanging on the racks would be enough for me to hide in.

"Of course you didn't." Nadila let out a sniff as she walked over and placed a hand on my shoulder. It was a comforting feeling and I felt myself relax. "Now this is Liviya. She will be spending some time at our Learning Centre and as you can see she is in need of a wardrobe." Her tone was haughty and stiff as as she spoke to the other woman. "Please put it on my bill. My treat." She gave my shoulder a soft squeeze before giving me the same kind smile that had bolstered my courage in the Council Chambers.

"That is not necessary, Councilwoman Nadila. I am perfectly capable of paying for Liviya's clothing." Rhex's voice rumbled slightly with agitation and I glanced over to him right as the store worker managed to slip away. I felt a bit envious for her slippery escape. I didn't have it so easy, it was like I had a big billboard flashing over my head that spelled out *'Look at me!'*. If they weren't looking because I was human, the fact a Councilwoman was talking as if we were good friends was more than enough reason to stare.

"Oh hush, I need to speak with your lovely soulmate. Besides you don't really want to be in here, do you?" She waved him off like you would a stray dog and I fought back an amused smile. "Go on now. This is a situation that requires a feminine touch, not your masculine barking. Go find her a nice binding bracelet. I'm sure she would like that and her wrist is basically screaming that she is single." She gave him a kind smile before wrapping her arm completely around my shoulder.

"I would prefer not to leave her alone." Rhex's eyes narrowed and Nadila let out an unladylike snort of disgust.

"She is with me. In case you forgot I'm the one who granted her citizenship." She pressed her hand to her chest as if he had insulted her. "Do I look like Khos or Bilsh? No, I'm far too pretty. Now go." Without waiting for his reply she pulled me further into the store. "Silly boy, he is rather protective over you." She let her arm drop from my shoulder to grab my left wrist.

She lifted it up and turned it over. "This *is* looking rather bare." She gave me a crooked smile, her eyes crinkling at the corners slightly as she patted my face gently. "You are something special, you know that? My uncle is quite fond of you. Please sit." She let my wrist go before pointing at a comfortable looking chair and turning to a clothing rack. I sat down in it and watched her with slight curiosity, she seemed to be far more at ease than in the Council Chambers.

"They have much simpler clothing on Earth. Nothing too flashy. I almost prefer it. Your colour scheme is more professional, black, greys, blues, browns, purples. So many can be used to make a suit look fun but professional." Nadila smoothed her a-line skirt down almost fondly. "I only get my clothes from Earth stores. The people are much more accommodating and the fit is so much nicer." She pushed some clothes across the rack. "When you are built like us, Orrian clothing hangs strange."

She flicked through more clothes. "I don't have much hope in finding anything off the rack so we will probably have to get most of this tailored for you." As she spoke she pulled clothes off of the racks and shelves around her. I watched her with a strange fascination, her movements were reminiscent of Ghilesh while he had gotten ready for our bonding.

"Thank you, Nadila." The words surprised me but they were true.

She stopped and tilted her head at me. "Please don't thank me. I am using you to piss Khos off." Her words were blunt and I frowned in confusion. "Don't get me wrong, you are a good person but making him mad makes me happy. So if helping you out makes him mad. I will make sure you are the most well taken care of person on this ship." She gave me a smile and I raised an eyebrow.

"I thought looking at you every day would be enough to hurt him." For a moment I thought I had gone too far but she simply smirked.

"That had been my original intention and it still works. I see you have been speaking to my uncle on personal times." She brushed a stray lock of hair away from her face. "No matter, Liviya. Khos is a harsh and cruel man and I will do everything in my power to break him like he broke my sister." She straightened her blazer with a firm tug and shifted the growing armload of clothes.

Her pretty eyes softened as she moved over and touched my face gently. I became aware of the slight wrinkles around her eyes and mouth. She wasn't as young as I thought she had been when I first saw her. "I may be using you, Liviya, but you *are* special. You are here for a reason. Rhess was correct, we have been seeking for answers on how to unite our races for far too long and now here you are." She patted my face gently.

"You and Rhex have done what was once thought to be impossible. You have united, human and Orrian, as a cohesively perfect unit." Her hand slipped to my neck and pulled out my medallion. "Never easy. Love is never easy. Those are the words that were placed on your medallions. The Source knew this would happen before anyone could comprehend the magnitude of it. Your love will never be easy but facing change never is." She let the medallion drop and I watched as sorrow flickered across her face but as quickly as it was there it was gone. I knew it must have been hard for her after everything she had gone through.

"Come now, into the tailor." Her hand grabbed mine and she pulled me to my feet. Her small body hid a deceptive strength and I was once again reminded of just how fragile I was compared to Orrians.

I glanced at the stack of clothes she had draped over her arm. "Please tell me I don't have to try all that on." I gave the clothing a look of disgust that fell to a smile as she laughed. Her entire presence was calming and it was nice to be around something that wasn't sending me into a panic due to intensity.

"No worries, Liviya. The tailor will take your measurements then tailor everything to them. Perfect fit every time." There was a small booth in the back of the store that she gently pushed me into. "Hold your arms out and give the machine a few seconds. It will feel like someone is touching you but don't move." I gritted my teeth, my mind immediately thinking of the blue shower mist. I gave a small shudder right as it felt like hands were moving up my legs under my clothing. I took a deep breath and the feeling went over my stomach and up my chest and down my arms in a very linear pattern.

I cracked open an eye as it left and Nadila smirked. "You looked uncomfortable." Her amusement was apparent as she smirked at me.

I gave her a sarcastic smile. "I had a run-in with a shower. I still haven't gotten over it." To my surprise she laughed, it was a soft and delicate sound that made me want to join in. It was like listening to pure happiness.

"I had forgotten about those. Here." She handed me the stack of neatly folded clothes. "We are going to go pick you out some bathroom essentials. The cleaners are effective but they strip away all scents so you are left smelling kind of bland. Clean but bland. If you want to smell nice, you need to use toiletries." She said it almost offhandedly as she moved away.

I followed her up to a counter and she took the clothes from me, setting them down. "Place these on my bill then send them to Military Apartment eighty-six, Rhex DharSon." Her words were cool and clipped and she didn't wait for a reply as she moved towards the door, her steps even and quick. I blinked before rushing to catch up with her. She gestured to the red door. "The floors are colour coded. Red doors are shops, light blue are apartments, darker colours signal service stairs. Grey doors mark teleporters." She pointed out the colours while we walked, her heels clicking on the floor.

"Every floor has a balcony overlooking the shipping bay. There are hundreds of floors but you will be most likely staying in Sector B." At her words I gave a wary glance towards the balcony and the open space where ships pulled in and out of. "This is the section that Rhex's apartment is in. There are fifty Sections in this ship but you won't really see any of them but Sector B so I wouldn't worry too much about the rest." Her voice was professional as we turned into another store.

Nadila didn't look around as she moved straight to the counter. "We need some toiletries. Body wash, shampoo, conditioner, all of that." She glanced at me with a thoughtful expression. "Make the scents lightly fruity and feminine. and please place it on my bill and send all of the packages to Military Apartment eighty-six, Rhex DharSon." The clerk nodded quickly before moving away from the counter more than likely going to find what she had requested. I guessed being a Council-member had its perks.

Nadila tugged on my shirt to get my attention before she moved out of the store. "We are going to get a small snack. There is a nice little café around here somewhere." She looked around and I followed her, ignoring the stares I received as she finally grabbed my wrist pulling me into a small café close to the balcony.

We sat down and entered into a slightly awkward silence. I didn't know entirely what to say. "So what is a binding bracelet?" I looked at my left wrist and frowned slightly. She had mentioned it and had held my wrist so I was guessing it was an Orrian custom I wasn't familiar with.

"On Earth you exchange rings. On Oria, we exchanged bracelets. It's more symbolic than anything. You don't notice when medallions are exchanged but having a binding bracelet lets everyone know you are taken." She tapped on the table with perfectly manicured nails. A waiter came over and Nadila ordered a small sandwich and a tea.

She looked at me expectantly and I shook my head, giving her a small smile. "I'm not really hungry." I watched as her eyebrow rose slightly.

"Get her the same." She gave me a look and the waiter left. "You need to eat something. Rhex would probably throw me off the balcony if I didn't make sure you were appropriately taken care of." She sounded half amused at the thought.

I wrinkled my nose slightly. "He needs to stop sending out those signals. I'm twenty-five, I am perfectly capable of taking care of myself." I gave a small sigh and leaned on the table slightly. I didn't particularly like the idea of them buying me anything either but I knew my money was on Earth and I didn't have any of my cards with me. I was shit out of luck on that front.

"We all understand. I doubt there is one of us who doesn't but Rhex is very much aware of your limitations now. Orrians are much stronger than you and it isn't exactly hidden that many of them do not care for humans." She gave me a strange look, as if she were feeling a bit sympathetic over my plight. I honestly didn't appreciate the reminder that lots of people wanted me dead. She waved her hand slightly. "Rhex is military. He has lived, breathed, and fought in death. It must have saturated him a thousand times over."

She leaned against the table, her hands clasped. "He was engineered to be a solider and I bet that you are the single most important person in his world right now. So you are the one thing he would fight death itself to keep." Her words were sweet and I picked at my nails, a faint heat touching my cheeks.

I wanted the discussion to be over because currently all he saw me as was a distraction from his duties. I understood he was engineered to protect his people but I didn't appreciate being labelled as a distraction by the one person who was supposed to love me above all else.

"He's domineering and I don't appreciate it." I didn't like being told what to do like a child, ordered around like I didn't have my own mind.

"He's military and he's just trying to keep you safe." She moved her cutlery around, trying to make it sit straight on the table.

"I know." Everything he said I could or couldn't do was based on my safety first and foremost but it didn't mean I liked being ordered around.

Nadila let out a heavy sigh as her fingers stilled on the cutlery. "You don't know how lucky you are." Her words were quiet and I frowned, trying to figure out where that had come from. "Vila would have given anything to be where you are now. Khos broke her so badly that there were too many pieces to put back together." Sorrow twisted her face to a sharper degree than it had Ghilesh's

"She died without knowing what it felt like to be protected by the one person who had the ability to love her to the ends of the universe." She looked up and her eyes almost seemed hollow, as if there were something important missing in her gaze. The corners of her mouth were twisted down into a small, sad frown.

"I'm sorry, Nadila. I was going to be recycled. Rhex was the best thing that ever happened to me." I swallowed, feeling guilty about bringing the subject up. She had lost her twin because her soulmate had turned his back on her. I didn't want to sound petulant or spoiled when mine was ordering me around when he actually *wanted* me.

"Liviya, I wasn't giving you trouble. It's just hard seeing the bond you have with Rhex and knowing that was the bond she could have had with Khos. He was a cruel man, I know that now but at the time he was all she wanted and he should have wanted her too." She gave a small pause, her lips pressing together slightly. "Love is never easy." She let out a heavy sigh before looking out into the shipping bay.

Her mouth twitched upwards slightly. "For Vila and Khos it was impossible but for you and Rhex it just happened. It's funny. It should have been easy for them and it should have been impossible for you." She gave an empty smile. "I miss my sister. She died thirty years ago and there isn't a day that goes by that I do not miss her." She looked down at the table, lacing her fingers together.

"She was my twin, my other half, and Khos took that from me. What he did to Vila was like he punched a hole in my chest and took out my heart before crumbling it into dust." Her hands twisted together tighter. "I will never forgive him and I will do whatever it takes to bring our races together because it would kill him to see it happen." She said it with an edge of vengeful hatred. "I am a selfish woman, Liviya. I was a selfish woman before Vila died and it is even worse now. I don't hide who I am." I looked at her, taking in the sorrow that etched deep lines into her beautiful face.

"It is not wrong to be selfish about this." He had taken something very important from her. "He hurt you, he took something from you that couldn't be replaced. Do the same and take away his war." I wasn't foolish. I knew what Khos wanted and I was slightly fearful of the lengths he would go to achieve it. "He scares me, Nadila." The admission was hard to say and her eyes flared with a sudden fire.

"Do not worry about him, Liviya. He will not touch you." She smiled brightly as the waiter returned with the food. All traces of her grief and sadness gone from her face. "Thank you." I looked at the small sandwich and picked up a quarter, taking a bite. I wasn't overly hungry but Nadila had ordered it for me.

I glanced at her as we ate. There was a question that had been rolling around in my mind for awhile and I knew she would be the only one who would give me a straight answer. "Rhex told me the only communication between the humans and this ship is through the Council." I watched as she gave a quick nod.

"That is true." She picked up her cup of tea and took a sip, looking at me over the rim.

"Is there any way you can get word to my parents that I am alright?" I felt the harsh burn of tears at the thought of my parents and I did my best to blink them away.

Nadila said nothing as she looked at me from over her cup. She set it down on its saucer before pulling out a cellphone. "It's connected to the intergalactic communications link. Call any number and you will get through." She slid it across the table to me before she took a bite of her food with a happy smile. I reached over and picked it up, punching in the familiar numbers on the delicate feeling touch screen.

My hands shook as I brought it up to my ear. "Hello?" My mother's quiet voice brought tears to my eyes and I couldn't help but smile.

"Hi, mum." There was silence on the other end of the line before I could hear heavy breathing and sniffling.

"Liviya? Is that really you, baby?" Her voice cracked and I couldn't stop the tears from pooling in my eyes and rolling down my cheeks. It felt wonderful to hear her voice again. I hadn't thought I would ever hear it again.

"It's really me, mum." I gave a shaky laugh, covering my mouth with my hand. I could hear a faint scraping sound over the receiver.

"Louis! Liviya is on the phone. Our baby is on the phone." My mum's voice was muffled and the scraping sound returned before I could hear her breathing. "Are you okay? What happened, baby girl?" I swallowed against the lump in my throat.

"I-I found my soulmate. I bonded, mum." I smiled at her shocked inhale. "His name is Rhex, he's in the military." I looked over at Nadila who tilted her head, as if the conversation intrigued her. I wiped at my face with my sleeve, trying to clear the stickiness away from my cheeks.

"What is he like? What type of person is he?" The questions made more tears fill my eyes as I locked gazes with Nadila. I didn't know how to answer the question. I wasn't sure if I was even allowed to tell anyone on Earth that Rhex was my soulmate.

I tried to ask Nadila what to do with my eyes, my voice has fled me. She narrowed her own eyes before smiling and giving a nod. I rubbed at the new wetness on my cheeks, wiping it away. I opened my mouth but froze, the gravity of the situation slamming into me.

"Are you okay, Liv? Is everything alright?" My mum's voice was slightly frantic and I swallowed as I watched Nadila who nodded again, urging me forward.

"He's Orrian, mum." The words were slightly straggled and I gave a weak cough, feeling a touch light headed.

"Pardon?" Her tone was suddenly sharp and I closed my eyes.

"He's Orrian." I took a trembling breath in, trying to calm myself. I let my eyes focus on Nadila once more, her calm energy was soothing the nervous jitters in my stomach.

"Is this some kind of sick joke?" Her voice rose slightly and I could hear the phone exchange hands.

"Liviya, sweetheart. What did you say?" My father's rich voice filled my ear and I felt another fresh wave of tears flood my eyes.

"My soulmate is Orrian, dad." There was a frightening pause, for a moment I thought he wouldn't believe me. There was a heavy sigh on the other end of the line and I relaxed slightly.

"How did you meet him?" His voice was even and I took a drink of my tea, trying to find something to focus on other than the jitter of my nerves.

"They took me onto the Council ship for recycling. He saw me in the recycling bay." I twisted the cup on the saucer. This conversation would have gone easier in person but I was thankful for just the chance to talk to them.

"That's a pretty big coincidence, sweetheart." He sounded on the edge of disbelief and I felt a small flash of anger.

"You're telling me, I had no clue who the fuck he was when I first saw him. Let alone that he was my soulmate." I narrowed my eyes and took another sip of my tea. It was hard to believe, I knew it was. I had *lived* it.

"Language!" My mother's voice was sharp and I felt a bit of the anger leave as I smiled.

"Sorry, mum. I got onto the ship, went through sanitation and my handler was taking me to recycling when Rhex stopped him." I looked up at Nadila who was finishing her sandwich. "He took me to a Soul Maker so we could be bound. He was scared, dad." I ran my fingertip along the rim of the cup.

"Of what?" He sounded curious and I stared into to the murky liquid.

"Of them taking me away." I could hear another pause and then the phone shifting hands again.

"Can we meet him? Is there any way we could possibly see you two? I won't believe you are okay until I can hold you in my arms again." My mum's voice was back to being soft and soothing and I felt suddenly unsure. Nadila reached over, gesturing for the phone. I handed it over quickly.

She pressed it to her ear with a winning smile. "Hello, Mr. and Mrs. Burch. This is Councilwoman Nadila. I am sitting here with your daughter, we're having lunch. Well, *I* had lunch, she is staring at her food." She placed her hand on the bottom of the phone. "Your mother says to eat because you are too thin." There was amusement in her voice and I picked up the sandwich and started eating.

"Yes, I am very aware of the complications of the situation.... No, we aren't going to do anything like that." She paused and I took another bite. "Three, no, four days ago, I do believe.... No, he's nothing but charming..... Yes, I do believe he cares. He's very protective over her." I finished the sandwich and took another drink of the tea, the warm liquid was soothing.

"You can actually. Does tomorrow work for you? I know it's short notice but Rhex has to prepare for training. He leaves at the end of the week." Nadila shrugged and I watched the action with interest. "I understand but it was too late to pull out from the training. It's nothing dangerous and he should be back in no later than four months." There was another pause before she tilted her head. "Liviya is actually being enrolled in our Learning Centre. She has a wonderful opportunity to learn everything about our culture. She will learn our language and our laws. This is really a one of a kind opportunity." She gave me a bright smile at the words. I still wasn't sure about the whole Learning Centre idea.

"I wouldn't worry so much. She has made a few friends already." She gave a heavily amused laugh at whatever she got in reply. "Oh yes, even with that sense of humour." An amused grin crossed her face as she looked at me. "Well thank you again and I have to go. I need to drop her off with Rhex and continue on with my day. You will see her tomorrow and no need to thank me, it is my pleasure." She smiled brightly and I felt my mouth open in shock. "No worries, I'll let her know. Okay, bye now." She hung up the phone and shook her head.

"They sound like really wonderful people and close your mouth, it isn't very becoming." Her smile took the sting from the words and I closed my mouth with a slight snap. "Your parents say good bye and that they love you."

I gave a small nod of acknowledgement. "I get to see them?" It almost seemed too good to be true but the smile on her face wasn't hiding anything that I could see.

"Yes, tomorrow." She stood up from her chair and I followed suit. She had done so much for me. She had saved my life, bought me a fair amount of clothes and now had arranged for me to see my family again.

"I don't know how to thank you." I truly didn't. Nothing seemed right, no simple 'thank you' would ever repay what she had done for me.

She smoothed down her suit jacket with a Cheshire cat grin. "No need to thank me, sending you down to Earth with Rhex is going to piss

Khos off." She chuckled, a vindictive smile on her face. "Just remember you are here to make me look good. I'll be holding more sway if I have a human pet." I watched as she started walking away and smiled. She had a good poker face but she was a terrible liar.

11

I wandered around with Nadila as we looked for Rhex. The stares I was receiving were starting to make my skin crawl. I kept my head down to avoid looking at them, to avoid seeing their disgust. Each gaze was like a weight pressing down on me. Nadila was talking but I found I couldn't focus as the stares increased.

"There he is. Stupid boy." At her words I looked and felt a relieved smile cross my face at Rhex's familiar form. He seemed relaxed as he leaned against a wall next to a door but his gaze scanned the crowd in a way that made it perfectly clear he was far from relaxed. "Rhex! Get over here." Nadila's voice was sharp and I felt amusement rise up at it. She was definitely demanding.

Rhex's gaze zeroed in on us and he said nothing as he pushed off of the wall and moved through the crowd to reach us. He was silent as he gave Nadila a short nod and pressed a hand to the small of my back, leading me away.

I looked over my shoulder and waved at the blond haired councilwoman. "Thank you, Nadila." She gave me an amused smirk, saying nothing before she turned and walked away herself.

I let Rhex lead me away from the crowds, happy to be away from their probing gazes. We walked up the service stairs and back towards the apartment. The silence was almost stifling but I didn't want to speak unless he spoke first. The silence dragged on as we walked up the stairs and out the service door.

"Did you enjoy your time with Councilwoman Nadila?" His tone seemed actually curious, as if he actually wanted to know the answer.

I smiled, relieved that the almost tense silence had been broken, as well as feeling a bit smug that he had been the one to break it. "I did. She's an interesting woman." We made it to the apartment level and I looked at the doors, looking for the one that signalled Rhex's apartment. It was hard to point out because the light brown doors looked same and I couldn't understand the symbols on them.

"It is good you make some friends with those on the Council. It will make your stay here more pleasant." He stopped in front of a door and opened it. Nadila had told me the doors worked on DNA. Your DNA was inputted into a scanner in the door and when you touched the door handle it automatically unlocked at the presence of the DNA coded into them.

"She said we could go see my parents tomorrow." I felt excited and he didn't appear to have any reaction to the news. I paused, frowning at him as we moved into the apartment. "Is that alright?" He was always so reserved that I couldn't tell what he liked or not.

He dropped his hand from my back leaving me feeling bereft from the loss of contact before moving to sit on the sofa. "I am fine with such a meeting. Councilwoman Nadila was very kind in providing you with such an opportunity." His gaze was lazy and I slowly closed the door before stepping further into the small apartment. His behaviour was strange and it made me uneasy. I watched him intently as he leaned his head on the back of the couch with a sigh. It made him look vulnerable.

I faintly trembled from the urge to go over and curl up next to him, tucking myself against his side. "She was very kind. She bought me some clothes and some toiletries so I don't have to use the cleaner intheshower." I clasped my hands together and looked at him carefully.

His shirt stretched and bunched across his bulky chest as he reached up to run his hands over his face. "I'm going to have a nap. Stay out of trouble." His words were soft and I could hear the clear warning in them. I felt a little more at ease, that was the Rhex I was used to.

I noticed several packages by hallway and Rhex gave a slow gesture to them. "They must have arrived while you were with the Councilwoman." His voice sounded slightly rough and I said nothing as I kicked off my shoes and moved through the sitting room to pick them up.

I carried them into the bedroom and set them on the bed before opening some of the drawers. I started opening the boxes, I was impressed by the selection Nadila had picked for me. It was mainly pants and a large variety of shirts which was the style I had preferred. I wasn't a skirt or dresses type of girl. There was a dress in one of the boxes and I folded it and placed it in the bottom of one of the drawers before covering it with the other clothes. I wouldn't be wearing it any time soon.

There were also several shoes that I placed inside the closet before grabbing the last box and taking it to the bathroom. I opened the shower door and placed the shampoo, conditioner, and body wash inside. I grabbed the box and moved back to the bedroom to collect the others. I stacked them up and placed them by the kitchen before looking into the sitting room. Rhex hadn't moved, his eyes were closed and he looked peaceful.

I slowly gazed around the apartment before letting out a small sigh. There was nothing for me to do. I couldn't read because all of the books were in Orrian. He didn't seem to have his rifle so I couldn't practice taking it apart and putting it together.

I moved closer to Rhex, unsure of how to broach the subject. I sat down on the couch beside him. "Rhex?" I looked at his face and he gave no indication that he had heard me. "Rhex?" I leaned closer but he didn't move. His expression didn't even twitch and I reached out and gently touched his arm.

"Mmm?" The rumble startled me slightly and I swallowed, my mouth suddenly dry.

"Can I sit with you?" I watched as his mouth twitched upwards. His arm lifted before it wrapped around me, pulling me close to his chest.

"Mmhmm." The noise rumbled through me and I smiled, curling up to his side. I didn't want him to wake up fully and push me away again so I held still before letting myself sink into his side. It was closeness and even if I wasn't tired, it was good enough for me.

12

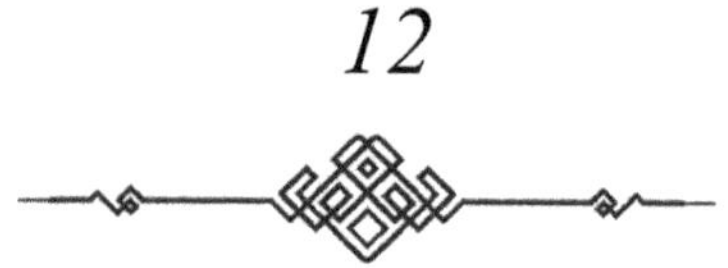

I felt arms shift around me and I jolted slightly, unaware I had actually fallen asleep on the couch. I became aware I was being carried somewhere. Panic filled me as I opened my eyes completely. *Someone was taking me.*

"Easy, Liv. You are okay." Rhex's voice rumbled through me and I felt myself slowly relax. I looked around carefully, we were going up some stairs and I felt slightly concerned. He was taking me somewhere I didn't know.

"Where are we?" The words showed my apprehension and Rhex said nothing as he pushed open another door, carrying me over the threshold. The room was lit but it was from the light of millions of stars. I let out a gasp of delight as Rhex set me down on my feet. I did my best to take it all in as I slowly turned around. The tiny pinpoints of light marking the stars surrounded us. It was beautiful and I walked forward a smile spreading across my face.

"I come here sometimes to think." Rhex was behind me again and he pulled me over to a blanket laid out on the floor. He sat down and I sat beside him, staring up at the night sky with awe.

"It's beautiful, Rhex." I smiled up at the stars and Rhex grasped my shoulder. I turned to look at him and he tugged me backwards slightly.

"Lay down." The words were soft and despite my confusion I did. He moved his hand from my shoulder and lay down beside me. "I brought you up here so we could talk." His words were even, as if he had planned each one carefully.

"Talk about what?" I swallowed hard and looked up at the stars, trying to figure out what he meant.

There was a faint pause that made my heart beat quicken. "Everything, Liv. I want to talk about... *everything.*" He paused once more and I wondered if I needed to say anything when he spoke again. "There is never any pressure while I am up here. I feel less closed in, more able to freely express myself. Orrians don't talk about such things and I'm trying to figure out how to deal with all this." I watched as a shooting star flew across the sky.

I could tell he was nervous and tense and I bit my lip, trying to think of a safe subject, something that would put him at ease. "I was born May twenty-fourth to Louis and Eliza Burch. I was two and a half months premature and weighed only three pounds and eight ounces. My dad used to tell me that I barely fit into both his hands cupped together." I gave a small chuckle and shook my head. "He used to call me his little potato. Not my most favourite nickname in the world but it was mine. Other little girls were called princess, dolly, or cupcake but I was the only little potato." I smiled at the memory before laughing at the absurdity of my dad's nickname.

"He doesn't call me it much anymore." I frowned slightly before returning my attention back to the cluster of stars that made up the arm of the Milky Way galaxy. It was like a bright ribbon of light across the sky. "He's a genetic researcher helping try and find the cause for Orrian infertility. My mum is a specialist for interstellar plant growth, her research is helping feed soldiers on the front and the Orrians in ships." I rested my hands on my stomach, drumming my fingers, listening to the slight patter they made.

"I had a good childhood. Actually my entire life up until my eighteenth birthday was perfect. I had doting parents, good grades." I let out a heavy sigh holding my hands still on my stomach. "After my, eighteenth birthday I spent the next seven years feeling like I was deformed. I couldn't bond. I was an oddity, a freak. I was referred to as 'the broken one' at Ami'la's office." That nickname haunted me for a *very* long time. "The only human unable to form a soulmate bond. I hated myself every day for not being normal like everyone else." I felt tears clog my throat and I swallowed, trying to force them away.

"I am glad you aren't like everyone else." His smooth, deep voice startled me. I had almost forgotten he was there. I watched as he reached over, grasping my hand in his, threading his fingers through mine. I shivered at the contact, his skin was warm and rough against my own.

I looked at our clasped hands with a small smile. "You scared me, you know. Well not that I was scared of you but of what you had done to me. I was so scared, confused, as to what had happened to me. Everything was changing when I looked at you and I didn't know how or why." My words were quiet and I turned my head to look at him.

His profile was strong and I traced the edges of it with my eyes. He was handsome and I became aware of a curious buzzing in my veins from being so close to him. There was a thick silence and I turned back to look up at the sky. It was a soothing view and I closed my eyes, enjoying the feeling of being under a blanket of stars.

"The day you came onto the ship I was only down in the recycling bay because I had been assigned recycling duty. It was passed off as a clerical error because soldiers do not get put on civilian jobs. I was upset but I did it anyway. I got to the recycling bay just as you arrived." He let out a small breath, his hand squeezing mine. "Everyone had been talking about the human slated for recycling but I didn't care. I had enough of dealing with death while out on the front, I didn't want to see it at home." He paused and I closed my eyes tighter, not wanting to ruin the moment.

"I saw you and I watched how he was treating you. You were in pain but he didn't care and it made me angry. I had never wished to hurt one of my own before but in that moment as your face twisted with the pain he caused you I wanted to make him stop breathing." He let out a deep breath, his hand tightening on mine slightly once again.

He brushed the back of it with his thumb, his hand made mine look small but I didn't care. "I stopped him, I don't remember why but I told him I could take you to the recycler. I told him it was better for me to waste my time than him. He let me take you." He gave a small smile at that. "Just like that. I felt like I had pulled off a crime to be honest. Like I had just completed the heist of the century." He chuckled and the sound surprised me. I hadn't really heard him show amusement before.

"No one had told me what to expect when I found my soulmate. People were always telling me to bond with someone who would raise my status, who would increase my political standing. The talk of soulmates never entered the conversations." That made me feel for Orrians, to never actually be given the choice to find their soulmates, to be told they would have someone out there that was perfect for them. "Then none of it mattered because there was only you." His words made my heart squeeze slightly. He brought my hand up and kissed the back of it gently. I felt my breath hitch in my chest and I turned my head to look at him again.

"There can be only you, Liviya Mary Burch, and that is a terrifying feeling for me." He shifted, moving closer to me a fraction. "I was engineered to be a soldier. My loyalty was designed to be for the protection of my people but now I find it shifting to you. I have spent my entire life protecting my people and now all I want to protect is you." He turned his head, locking his gaze with mine.

"I cannot allow my allegiances to shift, not now. My people need me to protect them but you are changing that. You are changing how I think, what I need to do." His words hurt but I nodded, turning my gaze back up to the dark sky. He removed his hand from mine and I pulled it back to my stomach.

As terrible as it was I wanted to cry because I ached for a soulmate who wanted me just as much as I wanted them. I sat up, my eyes on the stars above me. I pulled my knees up to my chest and wrapped my arms around them.

"It's good that you're honest with me. I appreciate it." The words were quiet and I gave a small cough, trying to clear my throat of the sudden lump that had formed.

"I was born on October twelfth, twenty-seven years ago. My mother is a woman named Ha'li. My father is a political soldier named Ber'reth. I have a sister named Kati. They live back on Oria." He said it said each word precisely as if he had practised them a hundred times before. "I haven't seen my parents in ten years and I haven't seen my sister in five. It takes months to reach Oria and I have always been too busy to visit them." I winced for him. I couldn't imagine being months away from my parents, not being able to see them or truly talk to them.

"Unlike on Earth, children often leave their parents shortly after they visit the Soul Makers. We are all assigned a job and we are expected to train for it as soon as we are able." His tone was slightly cold and I leaned my chin on my knees, looking out across the dark edge of the

Earth. It still looked like a blue and green marble but the pale haze of the stratosphere was still visible despite the darkness.

He made a noise of frustration before sitting up. "Liviya, I have been taught how to fight since I was ten years old. I am expected to die for my country and I have nearly done that a dozen times over. I was taught how to kill without remorse but this? I have never been taught how to handle *this*." I could see him gesture between us in my peripheral vision and I tilted my head to look at him.

Resting my cheek on my knee I noticed the frustration clearly on his face. "Do what comes naturally." I shrugged, turning back to the view, hoping the soothing feeling would come back.

"*None* of this feels natural." His tone was flat and I winced slightly at it. It pretty much summed up our entire relationship, emotion and then back to being emotionless. Hot and cold, never being consistent.

"Then I don't know what I can tell you, Rhex. I'm trying to understand your position. Trying to understand why you are pushing me away. I get that you need to protect your people, your planet. I get that I'm a danger to that but I can't understand why I can't have a small piece of you for myself." I felt agitated, feeding off his energy. I wanted to stand up and walk away. Why was it that whenever we started talking it devolved into an argument that would never be resolved?

"I was taught that Orrians do not show affection to their mates nor their children. It was how I was raised, it is how it is done. It is the natural order of things, Liviya." His tone was sharp and I gave into my urge and stood up.

I scowled at him, anger filling me along with the agitation. "Stop calling me that! It's Liv. *Liv.*" There was nothing worse than the feeling of him using my full name to keep distance between us. As if he were using it as shield. "There is *nothing* natural about us, Rhex. Our very *bond* is unnatural to your people." It was something that people continued to remind me.

"Affection is a natural reaction to being around someone you care about, someone you love. Withholding it is cruel and it hurt me when you do it." I was humane and humans weren't Orrians. "I crave your contact with me, Rhex. I need it like I need to breathe but you are so easy to push that away. I just want to understand why." The hurt poured out before I could stop it and I pressed my hand to my mouth, narrowing my eyes at him. "I can't stand it when you put this space between us that I feel like I'm not allowed to breach but it makes it so much worse when I don't know *why.*" I ran my hand through my hair and tugged on the strands in frustration before crossing my arms over my chest, hunching forwards slightly.

"Because you *terrify* me. You threaten *everything* about my life and it terrifies me more than anything I have ever known before. I have fought on the front seven times and I would rather be there than be standing here because at least there I knew where I stood. I knew what I had to do." The words were like a slap to the face and I nearly reared back away from him

"Then go fight on the front then, Rhex. Leave me here and go if things are simpler there." I felt tears in my eyes and I wiped at them furiously, hating the fact they were there. I had done enough crying. I turned my back to him and stared at the sky,. It didn't seem as beautiful anymore, it had lost its magic.

"I'm fucking this up." He let out a heavy sigh and I looked at the floor, tracing the tile pattern with my eyes. "What do you want, Liv? What do you need?" He sounded tired and I shrugged, not trusting myself to speak. "Liv, I need an answer." There was a thread of agitation in his voice and I turned to look at him holding my hands out in a gesture of defeat.

"I need contact, Rhex, and you have made it very clear you don't want that." I avoided his gaze, letting out a shuddering breath.

"Touch me." The words confused me for a second and I turned to look down at him.

"What?" My voice had an edge. I was getting tired of him jerking me back and forth like a dog with a rope.

"No rules, no judgment, no pushing away. *Touch* me." He grabbed my hand and pulled me down abruptly, practically forcing me to straddle his lap. His pale green eyes darkened slightly. "Touch me, Liv."

13

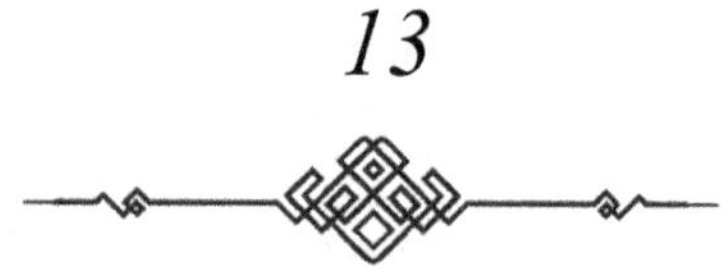

I felt a bolt of anger rush through me at his words and I narrowed my eyes. "*Excuse* me?" I couldn't believe what he had just said. "You can't just say all of that shit and then just demand I touch you. That isn't fair, Rhex. I can't handle doing this hot and cold thing anymore. You pushing me away then pulling me back only to push me away again. I'm done with it." I pushed against his chest and he said nothing as he reached around my back, spreading his large hands across it before pulling me close, ignoring my attempts at putting space between us.

"Touch me, Liv, then shut me out. I want to know what you go through when I do it to you." The words were harsh in my ears and I blinked, taking him in. He was serious, if his expression was anything to go by. He loosened his arms and I slowly reached up and traced the scar on his face. He winced. "Don't touch it." I was curious and I wasn't going to let this opportunity pass me by.

"Why?" I smoothed my hand over his cheek, scar included. I liked how his slight stubble scratched my palm. The jagged scar was smooth and I brushed my thumb over it lightly.

"It's disgusting and I know it's hard to look at." The words were filled with self-loathing and I leaned closer, kissing the corner of his mouth that the scar pulled down. I felt him stiffen at the contact but I pulled back to look at his eyes.

"How did you get it?" I shifted my hand so it cupped his cheek, my thumb brushing over the place I had just kissed. His skin was warm and it made my hands and palms zing as my nerves lit up at the contact.

"Explosion in the third section, Delta Quadrant. Zengan suicide bomber. Tore most of my squad to pieces and I was left with this pretty thing and a giant scar on my side." He practically spat the words out and I let my heart ache for him before I dipped my head and kissed down the entire length of it. His muscles didn't loosen and I wrapped my hand around the back of his neck before pulling him to me.

I hugged him tightly, glad that he survived to be with me. I slowly let him go. "War takes away many things, Rhex but it didn't take your life." I let my fingers trace his cheekbones and jaw-line. It was nice to be close to him, to actually touch him. It almost settled something deep inside of me, relaxing it.

"It took away people's ability to look me in the face. They are repulsed by it." There was so much anger emanating from him it was almost oppressive in its heaviness.

"They're foolish then." I cupped his face in my hands and gave him a sad half-smile. "If I could, I would take away this mark and all the negativity that goes with it. I would remove the memories it has because you should never feel like this, Rhex." I traced my finger down the pale line again, mesmerized by the jaggedness that made his face look so severe and unapproachable. He looked dangerous with it and I almost appreciated how harsh it made him.

"I can't take away your scars or your memories, Rhex, but you can let the negativity go." I brushed my fingers across that mark once more. "If they cannot look you in the eyes then they are not worth your time. You protected them and that should not be the thanks you get." I settled slightly in his lap, sitting eye to eye with him.

His gaze was angry and I dropped my hands to his shoulders, letting my fingers dig into his muscles. I massaged at the stiffness I found resting in them before reaching down slowly and grabbing the edge of his shirt.

A large hand snapped out and shackled my wrist in a tight grip. I looked at him tilting my head slightly. "Don't." The word was low and angry and I could feel him withdrawing from the situation and I narrowed my eyes.

"No rules, no judgment, no pushing away, remember?" I watched as he narrowed his eyes as well before he let my wrist go. I tugged up on the hem of his shirt and with a low sound of irritation he pulled it off for me.

"Happy?" He looked angry but I leaned back as I took in the muscles that roped across his chest and down his abdomen. I was *very* happy. I reached out and gently brushed my fingertips across the scar that rested on his rib cage. I could feel him stiffen at the contact and I pulled my hand back before returning to massaging his shoulders. His skin was warm under my hands and I smiled slightly before leaning closer.

I pressed my chest to his and laid my cheek on his shoulder before wrapping my arms around him loosely. I let my right hand smooth down his back, drawing nonsense patterns across his skin with my fingertips before trailing up to his neck. I gave a small sigh of contentment as I continued to trace patterns into his warm skin. His scent swirled around me, relaxing me but heating me up at the same time. It was a delicate balance that comforted me.

His arms moved to wrap around my back and I smirked. "You don't get to touch, Rhex. Hands to yourself." I chuckled at the sound of annoyance he made as his arms dropped back to his sides. I could feel the tension in his body and I smirked once more, continuing to draw lazy patterns in his skin before trailing my hand back up to his neck and scratching the back of it with my nails. My smirk turned to a smile as he gave a small shiver at the action.

"What are you doing?" His voice was sharp and I closed my eyes rubbing my cheek across his warm skin, relaxing into his body a bit more. I liked how my body moulded to his hard edges, I liked how I felt pressed against him.

"Enjoying the moment. Don't ruin it." I enjoyed the moment as desire curled through me slowly. It wasn't like the flash fire of when we kissed but it was just as enjoyable. Being around him was something I wanted and something my body needed. I didn't want to think of how it would be when he would be gone.

Four months without him would be painful. I pulled back from the embrace to look at his face. His jaw muscles twitched slightly and I bent down, kissing his shoulder gently. The heat from his skin practically burned my lips as I moved my head to kiss the crook of his neck. I could feel him stiffen a touch more, like a wind-up toy wound to the point of breaking. I trailed small kisses up his neck, wiggling slightly in his lap, feeling my need for him sharply.

"This isn't fair, Liv." His words were straggled and I smirked against his skin as I kissed below his ear.

"What was that?" I chuckled before kissing his jaw before trailing my lips up to his scar. "Hmmmm, that sounds awfully familiar." I pressed my lips to his scar, moving them slowly down the jagged line in soft kisses.

I stopped just before the corner of his mouth. "Now where have I heard those words before?" He made a noise in the back of his throat as I pressed my lips to the corner of his before moving so I hovered over his lips slightly. I could feel his short breaths on my mouth and I brushed my lips to his in a hint of a kiss before I pulled away. I stood up and moved away from him, forcing myself to try and block him out, despite every fibre of my being urging me to go back to him. I crossed my arms over my chest, trying to ignore the heat curling through my veins as I put more space between us.

I looked out to the starlit sky as a heavy silence fell. I forced myself to try and be unaffected by what had happened. I couldn't withdrawal from the situation like he could but I was trying my best. He had wanted me to show him what it was like but I wasn't sure if I even could. He didn't seem as sensitive to me as I was to him so I had no clue if it would even work.

"Liviya." His tone was almost sinuous and I tried to fight against the shivers it caused. I became aware that he was moving closer, my entire body attuned to his presence. Warm hands grabbed my waist and turned me around. I held my hands up, as if trying to keep space between us. His green eyes had darkened with the heat they held and I felt a flush crawl up my face. His hand touched my cheek before sliding around to cup the back of my head. He pulled me close and suddenly it was hard to breathe as his mouth nearly touched mine. He paused for a single heartbeat before he pressed his lips to mine and everything I had been thinking disappeared like smoke.

I spread my hands across his chest, letting the heat from his skin sink into my palms before I slid them up and wrapped my arms around his neck. I sunk into his embrace, enjoying the feeling of his lips on mine and the fire that was slowly consuming my body. The kiss grew more demanding and the hand on my waist, slid across my back before pulling me tighter against his frame. A low rumble moved through his chest and I gave in. He was everything, the taste in my mouth, the scent I breathed in, and the warmth that I touched. There was nothing but him in that moment. He was like a warrior claiming what was rightfully his.

Everything seemed overcharged and the heat was building up in my body as his lips moved on mine. His presence surrounded me and it pulled me into a vortex of heat and need. It was strange having someone who had that much power over me. I felt a whimper build in my throat as the kiss tapered off before he pulled back.

"Never think for a moment that I do not want you, Liv." His words were a husky whisper and I could feel his heart beating in his chest as it matched my heart's frantic rhythm. He peppered my face with soft kisses that sent shivers down my spine each time his hot lips touched my skin. "You are the only thing I want, that I crave." His lips brushed over mine and I inhaled sharply at the motion.

"You want contact, Liv. I will provide that for you but I cannot claim you as mine." His words were soft as he pressed a gentle kiss to my cheek before nuzzling his way to my ear. "I am afraid if I do I will never be able to let you go." His slight stubble scratched at my sensitive skin making me shiver.

He pressed a kiss to where my pulse danced under my skin. "Four months, Liv, I promise you. Nothing more than that. Four months and I will be all yours." He smiled, I could feel it on my skin. My breath hitched in my chest and I tightened my grip on him slightly, feeling his muscles bunch under my hands.

"All mine?" I hated how breathless the words sounded and a chuckle reverberated through his chest.

"Yes." The word seemed to skip across my skin indecently and I bit my lip with uncertainty. He pulled back but his grip on me didn't loosen as he ran his hand through my hair.

"What did it feel like when I left you sitting there?" I looked into his eyes and his expression went slightly hard.

"Rejection, an icy cold slap to the face. Frustration and agitation." His face softened slightly and the heated look returned to his eyes. "An overwhelming need to press you up against the nearest hard surface and teach you a lesson." My heart lurched in my chest and I felt my eyes grow wide at his words.

"What lesson would that be?" I tried not to shiver as his trailed his hand down my back, his fingers spreading wide.

"Not to tell me no touching." His voice rumbled through me. I tilted my head with a small smile before giving into impulse and nuzzling his neck. I took in his masculine scent, the headiness of it had a slight spice scent to it. I took a small breath in trying to identify it. Cloves, it had a slight clove scent mixed with musk.

I nuzzled his neck again. "Sounds like someone I know." I pulled back to look at him with a small smile. His gaze was almost tender and he brushed his nose against mine.

"We should get back to the apartment. We have a big day tomorrow." He let me go and I watched as he walked over to the blanket before picking up his shirt and pulling it on. I felt a slight pang of disappointment as his muscled form was covered. He picked up the blanket and looked at me before running a hand through his hair. "Come on, Liv." I turned from him for a second to look out at the stars one more time.

"Okay, let's go home." I ducked my head in embarrassment at the words but followed him out the door and down the stairs. The walk wasn't awkward like before, it was just silent. We kept a respectable distance between us and for once it didn't hurt me to see it. A mantra beat into my head. Four months, just four short months. I pressed my fingers to my lips, they still tingled slightly and I bit back a groan. Four *long* fucking months.

14

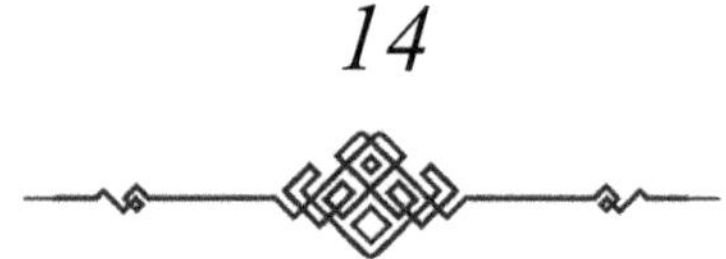

The trip to the apartment took longer than I expected and I was amazed that Rhex had carried me all the way up to the observatory. "You seriously didn't carry me all the way up there, did you?" My question seemed to startled him and he gave a small smile as he pushed open the door to the apartment.

"I did." He looked down at me, that smile dancing along his lips. "You aren't exactly what I would call large. Dainty is the word I would use. Humans are all so delicate but you are dainty." He raised an eyebrow and I felt a smile cross my face.

"Orrians look like roided out jocks." The words echoed ones I had heard my father say too many times to count.

"What does that even mean?" His face twisted with confusion and I laughed, shaking my head.

"I honestly can't tell you, my dad uses it sometimes. I think it means someone who is really muscular?" I frowned. "I think it's also an insult. I don't know it's an Old Earth term. As I said my dad uses it sometimes." I shrugged, biting the inside of my lip.

"Well we tend to be a larger race of people but genetically we aren't much different from humans." He walked inside and I followed him, closing the door behind me. He shrugged, lifting one muscular shoulder before letting it drop. I got the overwhelming urge to run my hands over the muscles, feeling them move under my palms. "I am a soldier, not a scientist so I do not really care."

"I found it more interesting after my eighteenth birthday. I had a morbid fascination with trying to find out what made me tick instead of tock. Never found out anything important. My DNA tests I gave my dad always came back corrupted for some strange rea-" I stopped mid-sentence thinking back on what Rhex had told me. I had sixty-three percent Orrian DNA and I had always given the samples to my dad. He had *known* and he had hidden it from me. The thought was almost crushing, I knew he had done it to protect me but it didn't make it hurt any less.

"Don't over think it, Liv." Rhex's voice pulled me back out of my thoughts and I gave him a weak smile, my stomach feeling suddenly nauseous. My entire life I had been lied to. It was a lot to take in. "Parents will do things to protect their children that may not seem right. Obviously he loved you enough to risk his own life in hiding it from people." His words made sense and I nodded, fighting down the hurt I felt.

"We should probably get some sleep. I'll take the sofa again." I watched as he levelled me with an even look.

"You take the sofa every night and as soon as you fall asleep I carry you to the bedroom. It is best if we avoid all of that hassle and you just go sleep in the bed." His tone was serious and flat and I sighed, shaking my head. Back to emotionless, it was never even keel with him, it had to be one or the other.

"If that is what you want." I moved past him and into the hallway where I became aware that Rhex was following me. I wanted to stop and give him a look of '*what the fuck are you doing?*' but I refrained and entered the bedroom with him walking a few steps behind me. I went to the closet and grabbed Rhex's t-shirt and the shorts and tossing them on the bed behind me. Rhex reached around me and took a pair of what looked to be flannel pyjama pants from the stack on the shelf before leaving the room. I paused, staring at the closet before changing into the sleep wear..

I stared at the immaculately made bed, a habit Rhex more than like had gotten from the military and I felt guilty. I was the one messing up Rhex's life. I had been forced into it without so much as a '*Hi, how are you?*'. I understood that was how soulmates worked but when a person wasn't looking for one it almost felt like an inconvenience. I didn't want to crawl into the bed and I certainly didn't want to go to sleep. There was too much going on in my head to make it seem even a remote possibility.

My father had *known* of the fuck up in my DNA. He had *known* I was born illegally. He had *known* that was the reason I had been broken. The worst part was when I had been rejected again and again, crying over the many failed attempts, asking why I was broken. He comforted me and said nothing. It was selfish to want him to tell me that when he knew it put our entire family in danger but it was something that would have been slightly comforting to know. I wasn't broken, I was different. My DNA was different than the other humans and that was okay. It made sense it was an explanation that I needed to understand who I was.

I sat on the edge of the bed, staring at my hands in my lap. I didn't want to be upset at him, he used to sing me silly nursery rhymes and drink pretend tea out of stupid plastic tea cups. He was my dad and I loved him but I was hurt because he hadn't trusted me enough to tell me what was actually wrong with me. I let out a sigh and stood up before moving to the bedroom door. I cracked it open, my heart beating hard in my chest.

"Rhex?" To my surprise my voice was clear and even. There was no shaking and I watched as he walked into the hallway with a frown. It was difficult to keep my eyes on his face without him having his shirt on. "We could share the bed." I watched as he stiffened at my suggestion before levelling me with a withering look that made me want to shrink to the size of a bug and hide in a corner. "I don't want to be alone right now. Please." I fought against the tears I knew wanted to fall and I watched as he ran his hand through his hair in a rather angry gesture.

"No touching. I promise. I just don't want to be alone." I pulled my hand behind my back as I said it. "You can bring your own blanket and pillow. No judgment." I watched as he gave me a narrowed eyed look before moving out of sight. I felt my heart sink slightly but he reappeared, a blanket draped over his arm as he walked towards me.

I opened the door wider before slowly moving to sit on the edge of the bed. He said nothing but I could feel the agitation swirling around him as he pulled the blanket on the bed back and threw it over to my side of the bed and covered his side with his own blanket. I stared down at my bare knees.

I didn't want him to be upset with me but the thought of sleeping alone wasn't a pleasant one. Nightmares tended to flock to me when I got into this state and it made me almost afraid to sleep. I didn't know what type of nightmares they would be now but I didn't want to find out. Something told me it would have something to do with cold eyes and hands pushing me into a recycler. I winced slightly as I brought my knees up to my chest, resting my heels on the edge of the bed. There was a lot of hurt that I was trying to ignore but it wasn't going to work.

Sleep was a bitch because it was when all of the feelings I had ignored while I was awake, came back to bite me in the ass. Nightmares plagued me for seven years because I refused to deal with my feelings by becoming a rather morbidly sarcastic bitch who enjoyed making people feel uncomfortable. It gave me a semblance of control in my out of control life. I paid for it when I was most vulnerable. All the fear and the hatred and the desperation I had bottled up leaked out into in my dreams, twisting my sleep into hopeless nightmares. It was if my body had punished me for trying to fight off what it was trying to make me feel.

"Liv, what are you doing?" Rhex sounded irritated as he sat on the bed, making the mattress tilt slightly towards his bulky frame.

"Letting myself be scared of the dark." I felt the truth in the words. I was terrified what horrible concoction of nightmares my brain would have cooked up from my hurt and my fear. I didn't want to linger on the thoughts but I knew for a fact it would happen.

"You are afraid of the dark?" He sounded incredulous but also curious and I shook my head with a sigh.

"I'm not fond of what it brings with it. Sleep and dreams that inevitably turn into nightmares." I let my knees go, letting my bare feet touch the tile on the floor. "I'm scared of nightmares, Rhex." At the admission I felt the agitation faded and I was left wondering what had replaced it when Rhex grasped my shoulder and turned me to face him.

"I will be right here, Liv. There is no need to be afraid." He sounded so earnest that I wanted to believe him but the niggling doubt in my head refused to yield but I gave him a small smile anyway.

"Okay. I trust you." I stood up, shaking his hand off as I reached down and pulled the blankets back. I carefully took the translator out of my ear and set it on the bedside table before crawling into the bed and curling up into a small ball under the covers. Rhex leaned over me and murmured something in Orrian before he kissed my temple. His lips lingered slightly before he turned away and lay down. The lights dimmed and I gave a small sigh. There wasn't much choice for me.

15

I cracked an eye open, fully aware that I had gotten very little sleep the night before. I had vague recollections of waking from nightmares and Rhex pulling me close, whispering sleepily to me in Orrian until I drifted back to sleep. I was thankful I couldn't remember the nightmares, it was worse when I did because then I could dwell on them. I closed my eyes and pulled the blanket over my head as the light came on.

"Liv." Rhex's voice made me groan. The blanket was pulled off of me and I curled up into a ball, trying to keep the light from hitting my eyes. "Liv." I waved my hand in the air, trying to keep him away as he grabbed it gently and placed the translator in my ear. I groaned again, rubbing my face in the pillow, trying to ignore the cold breeze on my legs.

"We need to get ready to go." At his words I cracked open my eyes and was greeted to the sight of his sculpted abdomen. I felt my body more than my brain wake up in the moment as I traced the well-defined ridges with my eyes. His scar covered a good portion of his ribs and I trailed my eyes up to his face. He raised an eyebrow at me and I covered my face with my arm.

"My mum and dad won't mind if I miss seeing them for more sleep. They will understand." I reached for the blanket with my other hand and Rhex crouched down beside the bed. I could feel his warm breath on my face and I tried to ignore it as I grasped the edge of the blanket triumphantly.

"Liviya." His voice seemed to caress each syllable of my name in such a way it sent shivers through me, as if his voice were a physical caress. "Get your ass out of bed." I tugged the blanket closer and a large hand grabbed my wrist, stalling my blanket recovery.

I let out a huff of air in irritation. "I didn't sleep well." I knew I was pouting but I always got irritated and petulant when I didn't get enough sleep. Ever since I was little, if I didn't get enough sleep I woke up with my bottom lip sticking out in a perpetual pout.

"I know. You had a few nightmares. Do they happen often?" His voice was soft and I lifted my arm to look at him. His eyes were concerned and I nodded slowly.

"More than they should. I need to learn not to bottle up my emotions in order for them to stop. At least that is what my doctors used to say." I let the arm fall back onto my face and Rhex moved it before brushing my hair from my face. The light was too bright and I resisted the urge to cover my eyes once more.

"Liv, you need to get out of bed." He let my wrist go before standing up, giving me another nice view of his muscled physique. I groaned before pushing myself to sitting, running a hand through my hair. I carefully untangled the soft strands with slightly blurry eyes.

I did my best to wipe away the blurriness and yawned. "You don't have to dress fancy if you don't want to. My parents won't care." I pulled my feet over the edge of the bed and blinked sleepily. I hadn't gotten nearly enough sleep. I ignored the cold chill of the tiles as I moved to the closet and pulled out a random shirt and a pair of jeans. I threw them on the bed and looked over at Rhex who was doing the buttons up on what looked to be a dress shirt. I gave a snort of amusement at his choice.

"You look stiff in that. My parents would prefer it- No, actually *I* would prefer it if you were dressed in something more comfortable." I pulled a shirt from his neat stack of clothes and threw it at him. He gave me an even look with slightly narrowed eyes and I blinked slowly. "What? You are going to act more stiff wearing something that looks like it belongs in a funeral. It's just my parents, Rhex. You don't have to impress them. You just have to show up to prove that you aren't a figment of my imagination." I moved back to the bed and sat down on it before for falling onto my back and closing my eyes.

"So, they wouldn't care no matter what I wore?" There was a strange tone in his voice and I gave an unladylike grunt as an answer. It was far too easy to fall into the vortex of sleepiness that was promising me sweet dreams. I was nearing the edge of oblivion when the bed dipped and I became aware that Rhex was hovering over me.

My eyes snapped open and Rhex smirked at me from his position above me. One hand was pressed into the mattress by my shoulder and he had one knee pressed against the mattress as if balancing him. A warm hand touched the bare skin of my side and I was instantly awake as I inhaled sharply at the contact.

"Even if I wore nothing at all?" His eyebrow quirked up and I felt a sudden flash of heat move up my neck and to my cheeks.

"What are you doing?" My voice was practically a squeak and he brought his head closer to mine before rubbing his nose along mine. His lips were too close to my own but at the same time too far away.

"Making sure you don't fall asleep." A rich chuckle erupted from him as he stood up.

I blinked at him, my heart pounding in my chest. I glared at him before grabbing the closest pillow and throwing it at his head. "You're an asshole." I watched as he caught the pillow with ease and it made me almost angry. I gave a sharp exhale, trying to stave off my irritation at him. I watched as he unbuttoned the shirt he was wearing and shrugged out of it. I had to tear my eyes away from him as I gathered my clothes and hurried to the bathroom.

I closed the bathroom door and sunk to the floor, my heart pounding and my body aching with desire. I had almost liked it when he was aloof, at least then I wasn't the subject of all of his sexual intensity. I gave a small groan. It was my own damn fault. I told him I needed contact and he was just giving me what I asked for.

16

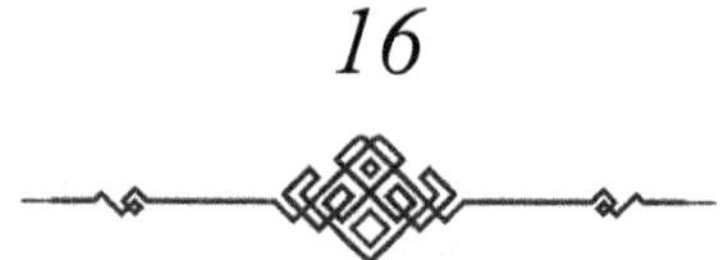

"Rhex, I hate flying." I looked at the black door to the shuttle. My heart pounded in my chest and I felt panic rising up sharply. I had been able to forget that I was on a ship orbiting Earth because of how solid and stable it felt but a small shuttle ship was a completely different story.

"You have spent the past six days on a spaceship that is orbiting your planet and you are telling me you are scared of flying?" He sounded amused and I resisted the urge to grab him tightly and never let go.

I clenched my teeth until my jaw ached. "Yah." My world felt wobbly as we moved towards the shuttle ship. I could feel the blood drain from my face. I hadn't had a choice the last time I had been placed in a shuttle ship and it helped that I was already scared but this was just me being a coward.

I froze slightly, ignoring Rhex's tugging on my arm as he tried to get me to move closer to the door. "I'm *really* scared of flying." My voice felt weak and I honestly felt like I was going to black out.

"Are you okay?" His voice was sharp with concern and I swallowed against the breakfast that wanted to make a return appearance.

"Nope." I looked at him and I couldn't stop the trembling that had taken a hold of my entire body. He said nothing but slowly wrapped his arms around me. There was a lot of comfort in the action and I found myself clutching at the back of his shirt. The fabric bunching in my hands.

"We are going to get on the shuttle and I promise I won't let you go until we reach Earth, okay?" The words rumbled through his chest and I closed my eyes tightly before nodding, not trusting myself to speak. He took a few steps backwards and I followed him, clutching him tightly.

I could hear the shuttle door close and the floor jolted under our feet. I squeaked, like a frightened little mouse, if I hadn't had been so terrified I would have been embarrassed. It would be hard to show Rhex how strong I was when the mere thought of flying made my knees go weak and my stomach lurch.

I felt the shuttle start descending and I felt my breathing increase. Flying was stupid, birds flew, humans did not. Space shuttles crashed all the time and killed everyone when they did. If the universe wanted humans to fly it would have had us evolve wings. Rhex didn't say anything but his arms tightened around me and I pressed my face tighter to his chest.

I gritted my teeth as I told myself that it would be over soon but the thought of the shuttle malfunctioning and crashing in a fiery explosion wouldn't leave my head. I focused on my breathing, trying to take deep breaths in before letting them out slowly. It was easy to forget you were flying through space when the ship was gigantic and it never had so much as a bump to let you know it wasn't on the ground.

A rumble moved through Rhex's chest and I was aware he was chuckling. I would have scowled if I hadn't have been so worried I was going to throw up the strange concoction of eggs Rhex had made for me for breakfast.

"It's not funny." I practically croaked the words out and squeezed my eyes tighter, praying the ship would settle down on the Earth quickly.

"You are right. It is really not." His words held amusement and I resisted the urge to push away from him. Getting away from him meant seeing the shuttle flying, meaning I would probably get a huge sense of vertigo and probably pass out. "I am sorry, it is just. You were not this scared when you were being taken to the recycler and you were not scared when Councilman Khos threatened to take your head but you are terrified of the one thing that has a lesser chance of killing you than either of those options." He shook slightly with his silent laughter and I hoped he would choke on his own spit.

"It's *not* funny." It was a repetition of what I had just said but it was the only thing that I could get out at the moment. He said nothing and after what seemed like an eternity the shuttle jolted to a stop and the door opened. I released Rhex and with weak and wobbly knees, I tried my best exit the small space quickly. I still felt nauseous and I wiped my forehead with the back of my hand before crouching slightly in the hallway.

Rhex reached down, pulling me to my feet and I leaned on him heavily. "Are you okay?" He sounded sincere and I breathed deeply, feeling the nausea and the dizziness fade away.

I gave a quick nod as I was able to stand up without leaning on him. "Yah, it's going to be brutal going back up." I avoided looking at the door and looked up at Rhex whose expression was even.

"I will be with you." He gave a small nod before gesturing to the hallway. I started down it, my heart pounding slightly. It was exciting to be able to see my parents again.

A familiar face appeared at the end of the hallway and I felt a watery smile break across my face. "Liv!" Ami'la's voice was a welcome sound as she hurried towards me as quickly as her high heels would allow before wrapping me in a tight hug. I hugged her back just as tightly. "I thought you were gone. I thought I would never see you again. When Councilwoman Nadila let me know that you had bonded I nearly threw a party." She released me before cupping my face in her hands.

"Look at you. I am so proud of you." She blinked rapidly before patting her face. "Look at me getting all teary eyed." She turned her gaze to Rhex and her eyes went wide in shock. "A military man." She smiled brightly before nudging my shoulder with a wink. "He doesn't speak any English does he?" I shook my head and pointed to the translator.

"No. Communication was an issue so he got us a pair of translators. So at least we understand each other." I put my hands in my pockets feeling almost shy. "Ami'la, this is Rhex. My soulmate." I looked at Rhex then back to Ami'la who smiled at him.

"I have been Liv's companion for seven years and you are definitely not the type of soulmate I pictured her having. No offence but you are terrifying. Like I thought Councilman Khos was terrifying but he looks like a kitten compared to you." She looked him up and down. "You need to be terrifying to keep everyone off of Liv. How is that anyway? Are you being treated alright?" The concern was evident on her face and I nodded, trying to ease her fears.

"Councilman Khos doesn't like me and I feel like people are trying to stab me with their eyes but other than that I'm good. Councilwoman Nadila and Councilman Rhess are on my side. Then there is the Soul Maker, Ghilesh who I know. He's really wonderful." I gave her a small smile and she gave me another hug.

"I missed you like you wouldn't believe. Things got really quiet down here after you left. It was strange and I didn't like it." She pulled back and looked at Rhex. "Do you not talk?" The tone in her voice made me chuckle and I bit the inside of my cheek slightly, trying not to smile.

"I speak just fine. I figured you would rather speak with Liv than her over-glorified body guard." There was a slight bite to Rhex's voice and I looked at him a frown on my face. The words would have hurt if I hadn't known he was uncomfortable with the situation.

"Don't sell yourself short, Rhex, I'm pretty sure Liv finds you to be the right amount of glorified." Ami'la gestured down the hallway as my face heated up at her implication. "Okay we have a car waiting for you to take you to your parents and it will take you back later today." She started walking and I followed her, aware that Rhex was close behind me. I rubbed at my wrist, aware that it was bare. I hadn't noticed it until Nadila had pointed it out and now it was hard to ignore.

"Stop." Rhex grasped my wrist. "It is a rather distracting gesture. It reminds me I have to get you a binding bracelet." His eyes were narrowed slightly and I shrugged.

"No need to worry about that right now." I smiled at him, trying to put him at ease. "No judgments here. It's just a habit I picked up, I'll try to stop." He let my wrist go and I resisted the urge to rub at it again.

We followed Ami'la to her office where she had a single file on her desk. "I have been waiting to do this for a long time, Liviya. You have no idea." She pulled out a stamp and pressed it against the top corner of the file before showing it to me. I smiled when I realized it was my file and a big black 'Mated' had been stamped on the corner. "There. I wash my hands of you. My job is done. I never want to see you in my office again." There was a teasing note in her voice and I laughed.

"You wish you could get rid of me that easy." I watched as she placed the file in her cabinet.

"Too late. It's going in the cabinet. It's done. No more of your morbid humour. James Levi actually asked me if what you said was true before he left and I couldn't lie to him." She wrinkled her nose in distaste. "Poor boy looked horrified. Luckily for him, the next meeting he had was his soulmate so that brightened his day considerably." I could imagine it did but it didn't stop the slight flush that coated my cheeks

"That was a bitchy move on my part, Ami'la. I apologize." I scratched the top of my head with an embarrassed smile and she rolled her eyes.

"Your hair is still too long and there is no need to apologize. Now come on. We need to get you two to the car." She pointed to the door and I gestured for her to go first.

"You want me out of the building so it only seems fair that you get to open the door and kick me in the ass on the way out." I couldn't help but smile as I looked at her. Ami'la was my friend and she had been there for me through seven years of hell. She had been the one to pull me out of my slumps, the one to offer me comfort or to make me laugh when I wanted to do nothing more than curl up into a sobbing ball.

She walked from the room with a nod and I felt the smile linger. Rhex moved to stand beside me. "You two are good friends." It wasn't a question but more a statement and I nodded with a small smile.

"She's seen me at my worst and I trusted her when I hit rock bottom. That type of relationship doesn't stay professional very long. Her entire profession is to make people happy and I was the only one who couldn't be." I started towards the door. "She got a little invested in making me happy." It was nice being on the surface with the people I cared about, where no one looked at me like they wanted to throw me over a balcony.

17

The drive to my parents was quiet. Ami'la had sent us off with a smile and a promise that she would see us later. I had to smile at the memory, she was truly one of a kind. I could feel Rhex's stiffness as he looked out the car's window. He was uncomfortable and I had no clue how to make it better. I was nervous that he would be meeting my parents but I had no clue how he felt other than I could feel he was uncomfortable.

I let out a sigh and reached over to place my hand on top of his. "Are you okay?" I watched as he swallowed before looking at me with small nod. I gave him a small smile. "It's okay to be nervous or uncomfortable." It was only natural. He hadn't expected to have a soulmate and now he was meeting said soulmate's parents. "I know it's weird. We've only known each other for less than a week and I'm taking you to see my parents. This is beyond weird for me." I pulled my hand back but Rhex reached out and took it in his.

"I am not used to these things. My parents did not show me very much affection as I grew up. My grandfather and my grandmother did but it was always sporadic. They were very busy people." His expression was serious and I felt my heart squeeze in my chest at the thought of

Rhex not having anyone to show him love growing up. "The way-" He paused, looking almost uncertain.

"Orrians-" He seemed to be at a loss for words and I squeezed his hand slightly. He seemed to collect himself and frowned slightly. "I am nervous because I was raised by Orrian customs and the way humans are is very difficult for me to process because I am not used to any form of affection." He lifted our hands and stared at them."This, right here. I like the feeling of your hand in mine but my brain is screaming at me that it is not proper. I am at odds with myself and now I am going to be stepping into an area I have never known before."

He gave a heavy swallow. "Orrians do not meet parents, we do not hold hands, we do not feel things like humans do." He gestured between us and I kept silent letting him finish. "My body and its reactions are the complete opposite of everything I have ever been taught." He tapped the side of his head. "My brain is not willing to let things go. Especially this meeting with your parents. I am uncomfortable because I do not know what to expect because this is not done." He looked so lost that I wanted to smile.

"Rhex, you are over thinking things." I brushed some hair from my eyes and chuckled. "My mum will probably give you a hug, my dad will most likely shake your hand. Then they will promptly sit us down and we will talk. That's it, there is nothing else involved." A realization slammed into me and a smile broke across my face. "Actually this is a good thing. My parents have been mated for over twenty-six years. They can help you understand what is going on. They can help *us* understand what is going on." I narrowed my eyes slightly, thinking it over for a moment.

"Ghilesh said that soulmates within the Orrian race are incredibly rare so everyone is raised to ignore it but Orrians gave humans the soulmate system. The humans understand it more than any Orrian right now because we still use it like we have for the past seven hundred years, while your system started to decline." I watched his expression but it remain unchanged. "My parents can *help* us understand what it is we are going through. Just treat it like a training session. It is data recovery, essentially." His face was even but he gave a slow nod. He pulled his hand from mine and I looked at his as he turned back towards his window.

I gave a small sigh and moved closer to him on the seat. "Rhex. Rhex, please look at me." I grasped his arm in my hands and after a moment's pause he turned his head to look at me.

His eyes were expressionless and I fought the urge to scowl. He was like a turtle, retreating into his shell when he became uncomfortable or scared.

I reached up and pressed my palm against his cheek. "It's okay. I'll be with you." I couldn't help myself as I repeated the words he had told me right after the terrifying flight towards Earth. I watched his mouth twitch upwards slightly before he fought to get it back under control. I didn't have his self-control and started laughing.

It took me several moments to stop and I looked at him before removing my hand from his cheek and wiping my eyes. "You are scared of meeting my parents. I don't understand it." I fought to get rid of the smile off my face but I was failing miserably.

"You are terrified of flying. I do not understand that." His voice was sharp, he was pushing me away and I narrowed my eyes at him.

"Hey, those flying cans can and *have* killed people. My parents cannot and have not. Thank you very much. My fear is perfectly justifiable." I crossed my arms over my chest and he tilted his head slightly, his eyes looking me up and down. I tried to ignore the heat that started crawling through my veins at it.

"So is mine. If you father so much caught a glance of what goes on in my head when I look at you. He would probably shoot me for even thinking of doing half the things I want to do to you." His voice was low and he turned in his seat so he was almost facing me.

I swallowed hard and tried my best to keep my breathing under control as I realized the car was far smaller than I had first thought. "Well that seems a bit specific." I cursed myself as my words seemed a bit uneven. He seemed to almost leaned towards me and the car seemed to get even smaller. I felt my breathing grow a little jagged.

"That is because it is a very specific scenario, Liv. Your father would kill me." He leaned closer before reaching up and brushing the back of his hand down my cheek with a soft smile. He leaned forward, his lips moving closer to mine. I resisted the urge to close my eyes. "It would be worth it though. Only if I managed to get to do at least one of the things that I want to do to you." He pulled back suddenly and chuckled as my cheeks flushed red. I glared at him darkly for his little trick.

He looked out the window. "We are here. It is best not to be caught in a compromising position by your parents." True to his words the front of my house came into view and I could see my mum waiting on the lawn. She looked worried, concerned, fearful, and happy all at the same time.

I clung to the car door my muscles tense as I waited for the vehicle to stop. I didn't wait for Rhex as I threw open the car door and threw myself at my mother. "Liviya!" Her arms wrapped around me tightly and I took in her familiar scent, dirt and lemons.

It was like being wrapped up in my memories of her. I felt tears build in my eyes. I had only been gone for six days but it felt like an eternity. "My baby girl. My sweet girl. I thought someone was playing a nasty trick on me. Ami'la told me you hadn't bonded to that last boy and I was devastated. I thought I had lost you." She gave me one last tight squeeze before letting me go to cup my face in her hands. She peppered my face in kisses, her brown eyes so much like my own were filled with tears. "I've been standing on this lawn for the past hour. Your father is probably having a fit right now. I've been ignoring him."

She had a soft smile on her face as she brushed my cheekbones with her thumbs. She dropped her hands and took in a deep breath. "Okay, where is this bo-" Her voice trailed off and her gaze was just over my shoulder and I glanced back. Rhex had finally stepped out of the car and pushed his long sleeves up to his elbows as he looked around.

"He's handsome and definitely *not* a boy." My mum blinked rapidly before nudging me with a sly smile. "Introduce us, Liviya. I want to meet the man who bonded with my little girl." I felt a slight embarrassment rise up at her words but I took a deep breath in and gestured at Rhex who slowly made his way over. I opened my mouth and he shook his head before handing me a translator.

I stared at it for a second before realizing what he had meant. "Okay, mum. This little device is a translator." I held up the small device before pointing at the one in my ear. "I have one too because Rhex doesn't speak English and I don't speak Orrian. It was actually quite thoughtful of him to remember to bring them. It completely escaped my mind." I shook myself out of the thoughts before reaching over and putting the translator in her ear and turning it on. I winced with her as the high pitched whine emitted. I knew what that sound felt like in my ear.

"My name is Rhex DharSon. I am your daughter's soulmate." He held out his hand and my mum blinked several times before smiling so wide I thought her face would crack before she waved his hand away.

"You are part of the family now. No need for such formality. Come here." She took one step towards him before wrapping him in a hug. I forced my face to stay neutral but the smile forced itself onto my mouth anyway. Rhex looked confused, not just confused but a little bit afraid of my small, human mother. She let him go and I tried not to laugh at the relief he had on his face. "My name is Eliza, you will meet my husband, Louis, shortly. Please come into our home." She gave him a brilliant smile and I couldn't help myself and I started laughing. Rhex looked like he was being lead to his death.

"Liv, are you okay?" My mum's voice was sharp with concern and I waved her off, stifling my giggles.

"It's just this funny thing I just remembered." I blinked innocently at Rhex who looked completely unamused with my giggles.

My mum walked by me and Rhex wrapped his hand around my wrist and tugged me to his side. "You will be with me. Every Source-forsaken step of the way." His words were whispered between gritted teeth and I fought back a chuckle.

"I *did* promise." I linked my arm through his, ignoring how he stiffened at the action as we walked inside of the house. He was so tense it almost made me feel guilty for laughing at him. He was scared to meet my parents. I didn't blame him. He was being introduced to a completely different culture and he didn't have a clue on what to do with it. "I'm sorry for laughing at you. Just relax. You are going to make my parents nervous if you look like that." I grimaced as I looked at him.

"I can literally *feel* how uncomfortable you are right now. Just relax, okay?" I met his gaze and watched as his face softened slightly, the feeling in the air shifted slightly but he was still tense. I watched as my mum disappeared into the kitchen.

"Liv." My father's voice was soft and I smiled at him before letting Rhex go. I walked over to my dad and kissed him on the cheek before hugging him tightly. "My little potato." The name made me fight between wanting to cry or laugh.

"Dad, you haven't called me that in years." I looked at him with a smile. I had missed them both *so* much.

"I was getting a little nostalgic. Sue me." He kissed my forehead and I held him tighter. I had no idea what he meant, another one of his strange phrases but it made me love him even more.

"I love you." I couldn't help it but say it and he kissed my forehead again.

"I love you more." He let me go and looked Rhex up and down. There was a tense moment and I watched as Rhex stiffened once more. "You Orrians really are like roided out jocks. I mean seriously." To my surprise my dad gave a bark of laughter before his face was once again serious.

"You need to be in order to protect my little girl. I know how half the Council is. I know what it is like up there. You protect her from them, you understand me?" His voice was low and he seemed almost pained as he looked at me. I glanced at Rhex in turn whose face was almost severe. He held out his hand towards me and I quickly took the translator from him before handing it to my dad.

He didn't look confused as he took it and put it in his ear. "I am perfectly aware that there are those among my people who wish to kill Liv. It is a fact I am reminded of daily." Rhex's gaze met mine and there was a coldness in it that surprised me and almost scared me a bit. "If I hear word of her being hurt in anyway while I am gone, I will return and find the person who did it before removing their head from their body and delivering it to the Council."

He grasped my hand, holding it tightly. "*Tear apart what the Source has wrought, to death you must be brought.*" Hearing Nadila say the words and then hearing Rhex say them were two completely different things. Nadila's version wasn't nearly as terrifying as Rhex's. I resisted the urge to shiver at the coldness in his voice. "I will not allow any harm to come to my mate. The thought is inconceivable." His voice had turned almost soft and I gave him a small smile before stepping closer to him.

"You are so sweet even if you were just talking about ripping someone's head off." I smirked at him and he raised an eyebrow, the tension slowly leaving his body. There was a moment of silence and I froze, remembering why I hadn't had a good sleep the night before. "Dad." I turned to look at him and he gave me a loving smile. "I *know,* dad. Does mum?" I watched as his smile turned almost brittle and his shoulders slumped.

"How?" The word sounded almost defeated and I sighed. I was upset and I was hurt. I had been lied to for my entire life.

"Rhex tested my blood." At my words my father's eyes snapped up in an angry panic.

"Why the fuck would you do that? Do you have any clue what they would do if they found out?" His words were a harsh whisper and Rhex shrugged almost lazily.

"I broke the tester before it could upload to the mainframe. I am a soldier. I am not stupid." He looked down at me with a curious smirk on his face. "They would have taken her away from me and I was not really in the mood to kill the people who would try." His hand tightened slightly on mine and I leaned against his arm.

"Does mum know?" I looked at my father and he shook his head quickly.

"No. I told her you were normal, that everything was fine. She loved you from the moment she heard we were going to have you. I couldn't do that to her." He looked genuinely sad at the thought and I shrugged.

"I don't blame you. You would assassinate a world leader if it made her happy." I couldn't hide the amusement from my voice but I winced again as the hurt shot through me. "Why didn't you tell me? I spent seven years worrying about being broken, dad. That is a lot of psychological damage." He looked guilty.

"It was too dangerous. I couldn't tell you in case it got out. It needed to be a secret from everyone." He sounded sincere but I knew he was hiding something from me but I couldn't place my finger on it. "I'm sorry, potato. I did it to protect you and your mum. By the time you were old enough to keep it a secret on your own it had gotten too big to just say." He rubbed his hand over his face and he actually looked stressed.

"I told her not to overthink it. She did not listen." Rhex's voice sounded almost amused and I looked up at him in confusion. "She rarely listens." I raised an eyebrow at the insult but Rhex ignored me and stared at my dad.

"She gets that from her mother." He gave a smile and I watched as my mum came around the corner with a scowl on her face.

"I *heard* that, Louis." Her voice was even and I nearly laughed at the look on my dad's face. He knew he was in trouble. "Liv, sweety, you and Rhex go ahead and sit down in the sitting room and your father and I will be right there." She gave me a happy smile and I nodded before leading Rhex towards the room.

"You are actually relaxing. That's good." I smiled at him and he gave me a strange look, as if he were confused but amused at the same time.

"I have common ground with your father. We both seem to have an overwhelming need to protect you." At his words I let out a groan and rolled my eyes.

I let his hand go before sitting on the comfortable sofa in front of my mother's antique coffee table. "Just what I need." I smiled as Rhex sat next to me. He was close enough to touch but far enough away to be proper. I wanted to comment on it but I thought better of it.

"Two men who are concerned for your well-being?" He sounded curious and I smirked.

"No, you two finding common ground." I tried to hide my smile as he chuckled before leaning over and kissing my temple. I leaned into the contact before reaching over and taking his hand in mine. I threaded my fingers through his and held it on my lap. "Before you know it, you two will be inventing ways to keep me and mum in a cage while you two go fishing or whatever Orrians and humans do to bond." His hand twitched in mine and I looked at the scarred knuckles and calloused fingertips. He had hard working hands. I tried to keep away from the thought of how the hands felt on my skin but it was becoming difficult.

"I do not know what fishing is but locking you in a cage sounds like a good idea." He was smirking I didn't need to look at him to see it. I could hear it in his voice.

I resisted the urge to roll my eyes at him. "You're a terrible person. Wanting to lock up your mate like she was some animal." I turned my face to look at him. I gave an amused huff of air and the corner of my mouth twitched slightly. His eyes went slightly dark before he leaned over and pressed his lips to mine suddenly. All the playfulness of the conversation went out with window along with my ability to think straight.

I leaned into the kiss, pressing my lips more firmly against his. The hand I wasn't holding onto cupped the back of my neck and pulled me close. I didn't know where the kiss had come from but in that moment I didn't care. I let his hand go before wrapping my arms around his neck and practically sprawling on his lap. It wasn't hurried or aggressive and I felt like he was enjoying the moment as much as I was. He moved his lips against mine and I gave a low groan at the action, my finger nails scratching lightly at the back of his neck in response. I felt him shiver and moved to properly sit on his lap.

"Well, this is awkward." At my mum's voice I pulled back like I had been electrocuted. My eyes went wide and I was pretty sure my face was the same shade as a tomato as I practically launched myself from Rhex's lap. I covered my face with my hands and prayed for the couch to swallow me whole to save me from the embarrassment of having my mother walk in on that.

18

I hid my face in my hands trying to ignore the searing heat that had settled on my face. That had been almost mortifying but to be fair I was glad it was my mum who had walked in and not my dad. As Rhex had said, he was protective over me and just because Rhex was my soulmate and an Orrian probably didn't matter if he would have witnessed that. I had to concede that maybe Rhex's fear wasn't exactly unwarranted.

"You know that feeling you get when you are close to each other? The feeling of wanting to touch each other, to have contact?" My mum's words were soft and I peeked at her from between my fingers and her expression was gentle. "That won't go away. Even after twenty-six years with your father, Liv, the feeling is still there. There isn't a day that goes by that I don't have that feeling." I removed my hands from my face, the blush receding. I glanced over at Rhex who looked actually interested in what she was saying. She sat down in a chair across from us.

"How do you cope with it?" His question as quiet and she looked almost confused for a second.

"Cope?" She laughed lightly. "You can't just *cope* with it. I understand that you're Orrian and all that's going on is different for you but there's no coping." She gestured slightly as my dad walked into the room. "Your bond runs deep. That's what a soulmate is. They're the other half to who you are. You can't cope with that, you accept it." My mum's eyes were on my dad and a small smile ghosted the corners of her mouth.

The love between them was evident as was their bond. It was impossible for me to imagine my mum without my dad and vice versa, they were a team and always had been. My dad picked up her hand and kissed the back of it with similar smile on his face before he sat down on a chair beside her.

"Orrian traditions are quite... strict. I haven't had the privilege of knowing all of them but the ones I have become aware of are difficult to process." My dad looked between us and I placed my hands in my lap. "For a race of people that is so technologically advanced, you're very, very stupid when it comes to dealing with what nature intended." He smiled in amusement. "You're a race that prides itself on status and power. You were different before but your race has been in a slow decline since humans have known you." There was a sad look on my father's face and I glanced at Rhex whose expression was guarded.

"I have been searching for a solution to Orrian infertility since I started my career and it's difficult to pinpoint the cause. Many think you have actually bred out the ability to have children because you have gone against what the Source has decreed. You give up your soulmates, you give up the ability to have children." My dad looked thoughtful for a moment and my mum rolled her eyes.

"He's so serious." She gave my father an affectionate smile before turning to Rhex. "So how were you raised? Did you have a good childhood?" It was clear that she was going to keep Rhex busy.

I stood up and looked at my father. "Do you mind coming with me for a moment?" I watched as he nodded and I headed for the kitchen and into the backyard. There were a few moments before he followed me.

"What is it, Liv?" He pulled out a patio chair and sat down in it. I followed suit and rested my hands on the table. I needed to have some closure with what had happened.

"I don't think we had enough of a conversation regarding what I am, dad." I looked at him, I needed to know what had happened, why he had lied and he gave a small grimace.

"I can't explain it, Liv. I didn't want to lose you. Your mother would have been devastated if she learned we would have to abort you. So I tailored the results and made sure your actual DNA never reached the main database." He let out a heavy sigh but he didn't elaborate.

I worried the inside of my lip slightly. "Why didn't you tell me after everything? It hurts that you couldn't trust me." I took a deep breath in and slowly let it out. I frowned slightly as his face closed off. I wanted to let out a sound of frustration. There was something he was hiding from me, I could feel it.

"I couldn't. I trusted you but you have to believe me when I say I couldn't tell you." It was another deflection and I scowled at him. I just wanted to know *why*.

"Dad, you are avoiding the issue." The words were slightly snappish and he gave me a slightly cold expression. I blinked in surprise, my father had never looked at me like that before and it was almost alarming.

"And you are pushing, Liviya. I cannot elaborate so I suggest you drop the subject." His words were icy and I leaned back in my chair, suddenly wary of the man sitting across from me. Silence fell and he ran his hand through his greying hair with a sound of frustration. "Liv, if I could tell you I would. Let's just leave it at that. I don't want to ruin this." He looked almost sad and I avoided his gaze. I looked across the yard and towards the old ruins that lay beyond the small forest behind our house. It was clear he wasn't going to give me any answers.

He looked around like I did before he scratched the back of his neck. "So four months." His tone was questioning and I gave a short nod before wincing.

"It's going to be painful, isn't it?" The thought of Rhex leaving was terrifying. We were bound together tightly and the thought of separation made me anxious and panicky.

"Yes." He looked at me before reaching over and placing his hand on mine in a comforting gesture. "I haven't spent a lot of time away from your mother but there was one time before you were born that she had to go up into one of the ships for a few weeks for work. It was difficult. The separation between us made me feel like I was being pulled too thin. I was tired constantly and I couldn't sleep. They were the worst three weeks of my life." He looked pained at the memory and I wrinkled my nose.

"You could have lied and said '*It's okay, Liv. The time will fly by and you won't even realize he is gone!*' instead of telling me the truth.

Now I have another thing to worry about." I clenched my jaw and he squeezed my hand.

"It might be different for you. You two haven't completed your bond." He gave me an even look and it took a second before I understood what he had just said. I felt mortified and my face flushed warmly and my eyes went wide.

"Well this is awkward." My choked words echoed my mother's and I pulled my hand from my dad's and avoided his gaze.

He laughed loudly before shaking his head. "Liv, don't be embarrassed." He was trying to be comforting but it just seemed to further my embarrassment at the situation.

"How can I *not* be embarrassed? You are talking about sex! I don't want to hear my father talking about sex." The thought made me feel a little nauseous and I looked at the glass top of the patio table.

"You're twenty-five years old and you never get flustered about anything. It's obvious." His words made me wince and I started at the evergreens that signalled the start of the forest. "Liviya, there's no need to be embarrassed. I remember you coming home after therapy with Theodore. You weren't embarrassed then, even though we both know what type of therapy it was." The words were like a jagged knife to the chest, it made it hard to breathe.

"That was different, dad. That was-" I fought to look for the right words to explain it when he reached out and took my hand in his again.

"Painful for you. I know." His tone was sincere and I met his gaze, trying not to tear up at the ache the memories brought. "I begged Ami'la not to try it because I knew it would hurt you but I understood her position in making you try." He looked sombre and I knew a similar expression lay on my face.

"Please don't bring it up. I just want to forget that it happened." My voice was practically a whisper and tears flooded my eyes. Even the memories made me feel slightly used and in need of a shower.

"You can't forget that it happened, Liv. It will always be there. That's why I didn't want you to go through with it because I knew you wouldn't be able to handle the emotions it would bring you." He let out a heavy sigh and I grimaced before giving him a sharp look.

"I don't want to talk about it, dad." The words were spoken between clenched teeth and he gave me an apologetic look.

"I'm sorry." The words lingered in the air before a heavy silence fell. I didn't wish to be reminded of Theodore or the Intimacy Therapy.

It had happened and it was done and over with and it didn't do well to bring it back up.

"How did you know Rhex and I haven't exactly- well you know." I felt my face redden at the question and I stared at the table top not wanting to look at my father in that moment.

"He looks at you like he wants to drag you off to the nearest bedroom and you have pretty much the same expression on your face when you look at him." There was amusement in his voice and I closed my eyes tightly, wrinkling my nose.

"Is it that obvious?" I glanced up at him and he looked amused before nodding.

"Only to humans. Orrians wouldn't know desire if it bit them on the ass. Us humans are physical creatures, more in-tune with our emotions. Orrians are like bricks." It was almost insulting and I gave a small chuckle, the embarrassment leaving my body. He was my dad and we could talk about pretty much everything.

"You do remember that my soulmate is Orrian, right?" I felt a smile twitch at the corners of my mouth and I saw a similar one forming on his face.

"I hadn't. Your soulmate is a brick, an emotionally deadened brick." His words made me laugh and I smiled at him unable to help myself. I had missed joking with him.

"I thought he was a roided out jock." I pointed at him while raising my eyebrow and he laughed. There was always an ease when I was around my dad, I had missed that, I had missed so much since I had been gone. I hadn't been gone for long but the fact I was living on a ship with a lot of people that wanted me dead, I figured time was dragging by me so slowly that it felt so much longer.

"All Orrians are roided out jocks, that goes without saying but your soulmate happens to be a brick *and* a roided out jock. Aren't *you* lucky?" There was a teasing note in his voice and I laughed again. It was easier to pretend that everything was okay when I was on Earth. At least no one down here wanted to kill me.

"I'm incredibly lucky, dad. He's a good guy, well when I can get him to open up." I shrugged before standing up. "We should probably head inside." The urge to be near Rhex was growing and I hated how it made my skin itch slightly. I felt like a drug addict.

"You are getting the itchies aren't you?" My dad's voice had a high note of amusement at my slight discomfort and I resisted the urge to scowl at him.

"I do *not* have the itchies." I narrowed my eyes at him and a smile crossed his lined face that made me narrow my eyes a touch more.

"Yes, you do my little Orrian addict." His smile was so wide that it was causing my face to twitch with its own smile. I fought it down, unwilling to let him see my humour at his words. It was true, I was a little bit addicted to my mate.

"No, I don't and don't call me that." I fought to keep my face even, I didn't want him to see how much he was amusing me.

"You're a little addict. Your skin is starting to get itchy and you want to go back inside so you can snuggle with your mate." He wrapped his arms around himself as he said snuggle and a laugh built in my throat but I fought it down.

"You're not helping." I lost the battle and the smile broke free as did the laughter as I looked at him. It was nice to have everything back to how it was. I was upset he wasn't telling me things but in that moment he was my dad. The man who wore a tiara and a feather boa to my pretend tea parties. He was the one who would let me put makeup on him and do his hair.

"It looks like you aren't the only one who has the itchies." He pointed towards the door where I watched as Rhex slid it open. "You're both little addicts. Itchy, itchy." The words were whispered as he stood up and nodded to Rhex who I could feel standing behind me. Large hands grasped my shoulders and almost immediately the uncomfortable feeling on my skin vanished.

My dad smirked and I glared at him playfully. Just because he had been right it didn't mean he had to get a big head about it. He gave me a knowing smile before waggling his eyebrows slightly at me and heading into the house.

"Your mother is an interesting woman but I am afraid I did not learn anything new." His fingers massaged my muscles and I let out a small groan as he rubbed away a knot in my right shoulder. I leaned into the touch, my eyes closing slightly as his hand moved to massage the back of my neck.

"That feels nice." I felt myself relax further as he seemed to rub all the stress away with his hands. "Did you guys talk about much?" His hand stilled slightly on my shoulders and he chuckled. The rich baritone of his voice slid across my skin and I resisted the urge to shiver as his hands started moving on my shoulder again.

"Not really but she showed me a picture album. I was surprised to see it actually, no one has them anymore. It had pictures of you when you were a baby." He chuckled again before leaning over and kissing my neck, it sent a sharp spike of pleasure through me. "You were an adorable child, Liv." His breath fanned across my neck and collarbone. That time I couldn't help the shiver that ran through me.

"I'm almost scared to ask what type of pictures were in there." I chuckled slightly before leaning my head to the side and inhaling sharply as his lips trailed across my skin.

"Just pictures she told me were to be brought out when you found your soulmate." His breath swept across my skin leaving goosebumps in its wake and I could feel his smile on my skin.

I let out another small groan as his fingers removed another knot from my shoulders. "So embarrassing ones." I opened my eyes as he leaned back, his hands moving down my arms in a caress. I fought the urge to turn around and kiss him at the action.

"Well there were a few when you were in the bathtub as a baby." He chuckled again and I made an embarrassed sound in the back of my throat. That was all I needed my mother to show him, pictures of me naked as a baby.

"She's terrible." I stood up and his hands dropped from my arms leaving me feeling almost chilled.

"She is a good mother." He sounded amused and I turned to look at him, he had a single eyebrow raised.

"I never said she wasn't. I just said she's terrible." I paused, he had the same look in his eyes that he had when we had been sitting on the couch. I narrowed my eyes slightly. "Don't look at me like that, Rhex." His gaze was on my mouth and I tried to keep my breathing under control. The intensity he put out sometimes was distracting.

"Like what, Liv?" His voice was low and I swallowed, my breathing was becoming slightly more laboured as he looked at me. I felt my body temperature increase as he leaned towards me. His presence was all around me and every breath I took in had his smell and it made me almost dizzy with desire. My mother's words ran through my head.

You know that feeling you get when you are close to each other? The feeling of wanting to touch each other, to have contact? That won't go away.

At the moment I honestly didn't want it to. I wanted Rhex more than I wanted anything in my life. I forced myself to breathe and I could barely hear anything over the harsh pounding of my heart as he took a step towards me, his chest brushing mine.

"Like you are going to kiss me." The words were breathless and I didn't want them to be. I wanted to be somewhat unaffected by the man who stood in front of me. I wanted to be able to function when he focused all of his intensity at me because at the moment I was practically a puddle of mush.

"I am." His words broke through to my mind and I felt my heart jump into my throat before settling back into my chest.

19

I didn't have time to think as Rhex wrapped his arms around me and captured my mouth with his. Heat flooded me and pooled low in my belly. I wrapped my arms around him, opening my mouth for him as I ran my hands through his hair before attempting to pull myself closer to his large frame.

Nothing mattered but his lips on mine as his hands pulled me closer. I wasn't quite sure where all the random kisses came from and I didn't exactly care. I felt him trail a hand up my back to cup the back of my neck. I relaxed into him, letting my body mould to his.

His fingers dug into the muscles on my lower back before his hand slid to my hip, gripping it tightly before moving me backwards so the backs of my legs were pressed against the patio table. I bunched my hand in his hair before wrapping my arm around his shoulder and pulling him down slightly, my fingers gripping his shoulder muscles tightly. It was like there was a raging inferno moving through me as his mouth claimed mine and he was the only thing keeping me from going up in flames.

He pulled back suddenly before burying his face into my neck. There was silence as I fought to get my bearings. I tried to sort through the chaos that was now my brain but it was difficult as my lips still burned and tingled.

My pulse raced and I tried to calm my breathing. "What was that about?" I felt my breath hitch as he nuzzled my neck. Silence fell again as he held me tight to his body, nuzzling my neck slowly.

After a few moments he pulled away before touching his forehead to mine. His eyes were closed and I traced the features of his face with my gaze. He had a strong face, it was severe and hard but I loved every edge of it. It was terrifying for me to love the man standing in front of me yet I knew little about him.

"Your mother told me that it would get worse." His tone was low and it seemed intimate in the small space between our bodies.

"That what would get worse?" I leaned forward and rubbed my nose along his, needing the contact. soulmates were a difficult thing to understand. I hadn't known how much I would need the contact with him, how much of my life was now tied to his.

"My need to touch you. She said it would get worse until I complete the bond." His words made me shiver slightly and I closed my eyes. "I am leaving in two days. I cannot back out of training." I had known that so the words didn't surprise me as the hand cupping the back of my neck moved to cradle my jaw.

"I know, Rhex. It's okay." I let myself enjoy the embrace, they didn't come often and I knew that in two days they would be gone for a very long time.

"This is very difficult for me." He sounded frustrated and I ran my fingers through his hair, trying to sooth the tension that bunched his muscles.

"You and me both, Rhex." I let out a sigh. "I'll miss you. I barely know who you are but I'll miss you when you are gone." He finally opened his eyes, a small smile turning up the one corner of his mouth.

"I don't really know you either." He pulled back and stepped away. I missed the contact almost immediately. He ran his hands through his hair as if trying to put it back into place. "Could we use the time apart to get to know each other?" He looked earnest and I nodded.

"That sounds like a great idea. That way we will have some idea as to who each of us are when we get back together." I crossed my arms over my chest and scuffed the toe of my sneaker on the ground feeling almost shy. I hated the feeling. I had never been shy before but with Rhex I couldn't help myself. I wasn't sure if I would ever be good enough for him and I felt like I was eighteen again and feeling shy before getting introduced to a soulmate I would ultimately reject.

This time there was no rejection but it didn't stop the shyness from being there. I looked up at him and he looked almost nervous as he ran his hand through his hair again. Another silence fell and the urge to touch him was starting again.

"We should head back inside. Your mother is making us lunch." He gestured to the back door and I gave a small nod of agreement before moving past him and into the house. I could smell grilled cheese and I smiled as I stepped into the kitchen.

"Grilled cheese?" I looked at my mum who was currently putting plates on the table.

"And chicken noodle soup." She nodded to the stove and I went over to a drawer and grabbed some spoons before placing them on the table as she grabbed some bowls. I turned back to the stove as my dad took the grilled cheese off the frying pan. I took the plate of them and set them on the middle of the table.

Before long the pot of soup was placed as well and I looked towards the door where Rhex stood, looking almost awkward at our flurry of activity. I waved him over and he looked almost hesitant before he slowly made his way over to me.

"It's nothing fancy. We prefer to do wholesome in this family." My mum's smile was bright and I gestured to a chair before sitting down beside it. Rhex hesitated before sitting down, I smiled slightly before reaching over and placing a sandwich on his plate as my mum ladled him some soup.

"I know Orrian food is a little different but this tastes just as good." My dad sat down as he grabbed a sandwich before taking a bite. I chuckled as I got myself some soup, letting the familiar scent wash over me. It reminded me of the days when I was little and stayed at home with my mum. It was a nice feeling and one that I knew I wouldn't feel again for a long time.

20

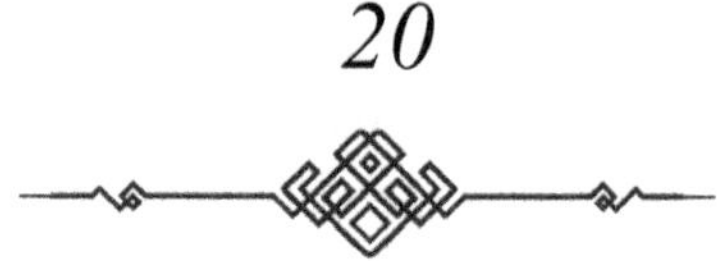

I looked around my room and let out a sigh. There wasn't much I could take with me back to the ship. I pulled out a suitcase from my closet and started to pull clothes from my drawers. I folded them tightly and placed them into the suitcase, trying to make sure there was enough room for all of it.

I paused at the knock on my door, my mum opened it with a sad smile. "Hey, sweetie. Do you mind if I help?" She hovered in the doorway her hand on the doorknob as if expecting me to tell her no.

I gave her a smile and nodded quickly. "I definitely could the help." I gestured to the mess I was making in my drawers. She moved into the room with a nod before starting to place things into my suitcase. Silence fell and I handed her another stack of clothes before I turned to my desk, looking at the books I had stacked on it.

"I know for the past few years we haven't exactly gotten along." Her words were quiet and I grabbed a few of the novels on my desk before placing them on the bed beside where she had sat down. She was twisting my shirt in her hands to tightly I was afraid the fabric would rip. "I was a terrible mother to you the past seven years. I was so scared of losing you that I did everything I could to keep you even though some of the things may not have been right." She looked up at me and I my chest ached at the sadness that etched her face.

"It's okay, mum. In the end you were right. I did find my soulmate. It just took a little longer than normal." I gave her a wavering smile and she let out a heavy sigh before slowly untwisting the poor shirt and folding it.

"I denied the possibility of you being recycled and I shut you down when you tried to discuss it. That's not right. I'm supposed to be the person you can talk to about those things and I let you down." She sniffled and I turned back to my desk to grab a few more books. "I never wanted to do that but all I could see was you as a little girl with sticky fingers and pudgy cheeks. I didn't want to lose you so I pretended I couldn't. I shut you out along with the possibilities of what could have happened to you." I turned to look at her, the books in hand before I moved back to the bed.

"Mum, I understand your position but that's behind us now. I'm still here and you were right. Now, how many books should I take?" I lifted the stack of books in my hands and she gave a watery chuckle before wiping her eyes.

"I would think most of them. Need to keep you distracted while your man is gone." She straightened her back and resumed packing my suitcase in an orderly fashion. She tucked a strand of her greying black hair behind her ear. From her position I could understand why my father said I looked more like her than I did him. "He's quite the catch. Very handsome." It was odd to see my mum look giddy but she almost did. "That man cares about you a lot. I can see it, Liv." She gave a wistful sigh and I had to smile as I helped her place the rest of my clothing into the suitcase.

"He's everything I could have dreamed for you, sweetie, but he's far more handsome than I thought." She winked at me and I ignored the flare of embarrassment it brought me.

"Don't say that too loud. Dad might get jealous." I chuckled as she threw a t-shirt at me with a laugh.

"Oh, what your father doesn't know won't hurt him." Her smile was wide. "Don't ruin my fun." Her eyes were bright with happiness. I smiled at her, remembering all the fun we used to have as I grew up. *This* was the mother I knew and loved. She was a strong woman but she didn't always remember it.

"I love you, mum." As I said the words I watched as her face softened, a gentle look appeared on her face and she held out her arms. I sunk into her embrace trying my best not to cry.

"I love you too, my baby girl. We'll see each other again." Her smile was sweet as she pulled away from the embrace to look through the books. I watched her movements as she placed the books into the suitcase, trying to make them lay flat.

"Do you remember that day I was sick and I stayed home with you? I was probably eight years old and you took me to see the Old Ruins." I watched as she tilted her head, her hands slowing in her task. "I sat tucked into a blanket as we sat on the edge of one of the blast zones. You told me about Old Earth." I watched as recognition filled her face and she nodded.

"I remember. I told you about the bombs and the vaults. You were oddly morbid for a child. You actually enjoyed the story when many children would have hide in their blanket. You didn't hide, you actually seemed to look out further across the Old Ruins." Her smile was nostalgic and I remembered that day clearly.

"And then I threw up." I gave a laugh as I remembered that particular day.

"Yes, then you threw up." She chuckled and I smiled at the memory. I hadn't been feeling well but for a moment as my mum had held me as we looked over the ruins of Old Earth I had felt peaceful and fine. That was until reality crashed through and I had thrown up everywhere.

"It was fun while it lasted." I gave a wistful sigh and glanced out my window to where I could see the skeletal frames of the Old Ruins. "I still love going out there." I hadn't been out there in weeks and I knew I didn't have the time to go before Rhex and I had to leave. It made me rather sombre at the thought. I liked the peace that the ruins brought me.

"You liked the history the place had. Your father used to tell you that every place you visit has a history and if you sit long enough it will tell you stories." She zipped up my suitcase and I turned to my jewellery box, my mother's heirloom ruby necklace sat on top and I lifted it up. "That always looked so beautiful on you, Liv." I could see her in the mirror behind me and I turned around, holding it out for her.

"You keep it, mum. Save it for your grandchildren." I handed it to her before pulling out my pendant from my shirt. "I don't need anything but this." She reached out and lifted it off my chest.

"Do you know what it says?" She set it back down and smiled at me, her eyes questioning.

"Never easy." I grasped the warm medallion in my hand with a smile.

"And yours was?" She tilted her head and I chuckled. She should have remembered it, Ami'la was the one who told her.

"Love is." I shook my head at the saying before meeting her gaze again.

"Love is never easy. The Source had a sense of humour when it helped create those medallions." She laughed softly at that and I had to agree with her statement. The power at be had one *hell* of a sense of humour. I joined in with her laughter.

"Are you two quite done? I thought a pack of hyenas had taken up residence in my daughter's room." My dad's voice was amused and I watched as my mum grabbed a pillow from the bed and throwing it at him. It seemed I had come by that habit naturally.

"Just finished packing her up." My mum's eyes went teary and I resisted the urge to do that same. I would see her again. My dad came into the room and grabbed the suitcase before kissing my mum on the cheek with a soft smile.

He pulled the suitcase off the bed and gave an exaggerated oof. "What did you pack in here? Bricks?" I gave him a blank look as I nodded.

"Emotionally deadened ones." I was surprised at how well I kept my voice deadpanned but I couldn't help but burst into laughter as my dad snorted loudly in amusement.

"I knew I raised you right." He winked at me before carrying my suitcase out the door. My mum left with him and I looked around my room, feeling sad that I wouldn't be coming back for a long time. Even after Rhex was done with his training I wasn't sure if we could go back and visit.

"Liviya! The car is going to leave if you don't hurry." My mum's voice entered my room from the front entrance way and I smiled.

"I'm coming!" I took another look at the room committing it to my memory before leaving. I made my way to the front door where my mum wrapped me in a tight hug.

"I'm going to miss you, baby girl. The second you can get a chance to come see us you do it, okay?" She let me go before cupping my face in her hands and kissing my forehead. "I love you and you stay safe." She let me go, her eyes watering. I fought against the tears but it was a losing battle.

"I love you more, mum." I was pulled into a strong hug and wrapped my arms around my dad, trying not to cry into his neck.

"Don't forget about me. I love you the most, my little potato." He let me go and handed me my suitcase. "Now go before we tie you up and lock you in the basement so you can never leave." He kissed my cheek and gave me a push towards the door.

I gave a teary smile that I didn't really mean as I left my childhood home once more. I watched as my dad wrapped my mum in his arms before I turned around. I moved towards the car and towards Rhex. He said nothing as he took my suitcase from me before putting it into the trunk of the car.

I got into the car and rubbed at my eyes, trying not to cry. I was only vaguely aware when Rhex got in beside me but I became fully aware when he wrapped his arms around me and kissed my cheek. "It will be okay, Liv. You are not going away forever." His lips lingered on my skin as he kissed my cheek again and I leaned into him.

"I'm sorry. Tears seem to be this function my body does." I threw up my hands in disgust while the tears continued to leak from my eyes.

He chuckled, the sound vibrating through his chest. "Do not apologize, Liv. It is a difficult time, letting go of family is hard." His words were comforting but I shook my head.

"I'm twenty-five years old and it's not like I'm never going to see them again. The tears are pointless." I made a frustrated sound in the back of my throat as I wiped at the tears again. I gave a frustrated chuckle at the futility of my actions as the car drove us back to the Ministry building. I grimaced as I remembered what lay ahead. "Rhex, can you knock me unconscious before we get on the shuttle again?" I looked up at him with hopeful eyes and he gave me a crooked smile while shaking his head. I let out a huff of irritation.

"Can't even trust my soulmate to knock me around when I need him to. What use is he?" I nearly regretted the words as soon as they left my mouth because the small space in the car seemed to heat up considerably.

"I can think of a few uses I would be good for." His voice was slightly husky and I I leaned away from him with wide eyes.

"No. I can't believe I am actually saying that but no." I wiped at my face. "I'm a mess right now and you do not get to use all that sexual intensity you have, on me right now." He laughed, it was a rich sound that I couldn't help but smile at. I had never heard him actually laugh before and it was almost like a treat for me.

"You are beautiful no matter what you look like, Liv." His words were sweet but I scowled at him, narrowing my eyes.

“You're only saying that because you have to." I bit my lip to prevent a smile from crossing my face at his expression.

He slowly raised an eyebrow at me. "A mate must do what a mate must do, Liv." His words made me chuckle and I sighed after my chuckles had subsided. I was going to miss this. We were just getting to know each other and he was going to leave.

"I'm going to miss you." I looked at him and he nodded before pulling me into his side. Two days and then I would be all alone on a ship where I wasn't exactly wanted. I allowed myself to relax in his embrace knowing it would be one of the last ones I ever got from him for four months.

21

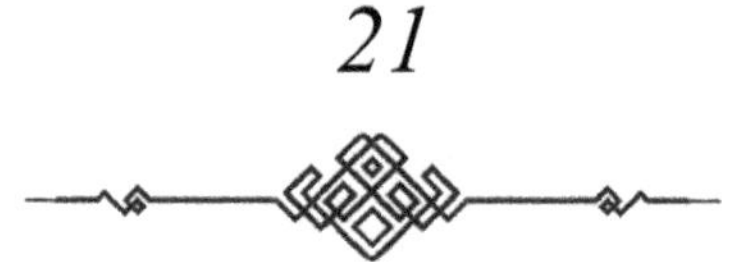

I swallowed against the lump in my throat and looked up at Rhex. His face was clean shaven and his expression was blank. I swallowed again, trying my hardest not to reach out to him. He was dressed in his army fatigues and I could see the barrel of the rifle sticking up from behind his back. This was the first time I had seen him since we had returned from Earth. He had been called to stay with the other trainees until they left. I had been alone for the past two days, it hadn't been fun.

"You look handsome." I pulled my hands behind my back and tried to keep my breathing even. A muscle in his jaw twitched and I felt my chin tremble. "I'll miss you." I watched his hand tighten on the strap of his pack before he swallowed.

I looked around us, there were only a few others saying their goodbyes and I blinked away the tears, trying to be strong. I was terrified of him leaving but I didn't want to show it. I wanted to be strong. I didn't want to fall apart but the longer the silence grew the more I felt like I was going to shatter. I turned my gaze back to Rhex and his eyes looked almost sad as he reached out into the space between us. I stared at his hand unsure of what it was he wanted.

He gave a small gesture with his fingers and I tentatively reached out with my left hand. He grasped it gently before sliding a plain gold wedding band on my ring finger. I blinked in surprise at the ring and he said nothing as he stepped closer. I was confused but he brought my hand up to his mouth and kissed my knuckles.

"I'll miss you too, Liv." His words were low and I felt tears blur my vision and I pressed my lips together tightly, trying to stop the trembling of my chin. I blinked away the tears and watched as he closed his eyes before rubbing my hand against his cheek. "More than you will ever know. Stay safe." He dropped my hand and backed up I clenched my hands into fists to keep from reaching for him. He turned his back to me and started walking away.

"You be careful, Rhex." I felt the tears again but I didn't fight them back. He gestured with his hand as if to acknowledge he had heard me and I took a shaky breath in as I watched him enter the shuttle.

"It's not him you should be worried for." Nadila's voice was sharp and I turned to look at her as I wiped at my eyes. Her lilac eyes were furious and I tried to ignore how my breathing started to increase with worry. I became aware of two large men with severe faces standing behind her.

"Is everything okay?" I knew my voice was too quiet and she inhaled quickly as if about to say something when the two men behind her pushed past her. I took an involuntary step backwards, suddenly scared as they grabbed my arms with unnecessarily tight grips. I was jerked forward and my heart jumped into my throat.

"Let her go!" Nadila's voice was vicious and the two men ignored her as they pulled me away from the docking bay.

"Nadila?" I hated how small I sounded and I looked over my shoulder at her. Her face was twisted with rage. The fear was nearly paralyzing and I tried to focus on getting my legs to work properly.

"I order you to let her go this instant! She is an Orrian citizen, not a criminal." I could hear Nadila following behind us and people were starting to stare. The man on my left grunted before squeezing my arm tightly. I gave a small yelp of pain as he pinched my skin slightly. "You are *hurting* her!" Nadila's voice was frantic and I tried to focus on breathing.

"We have orders-"

"Orders to take her to her new lodging. Not to drag her there like some animal." Her words were harsh and the man on my right let out what sounded like a scoff.

"She is a half-bre-"

"That does not make her an animal!" Her voice was practically a bellow and the two men froze in place. I fought back my panic as more people stared at us with curious gazes. "You are to treat her with respect and dignity. She is not some creature that is below your notice or feet. She is mated to an Orrian and that alone demands your respect." She pushed past the two men and stared at them, her face lined with anger and it practically vibrated the air around her. I felt nauseous at the tension and I focused on her face hoping the familiarity would make the nausea go away.

"That is an abomina-" It was the man to my right and Nadila's eyes flashed with fire as she cut him off.

"Don't you *dare* finish that statement." The words were dangerously cold and her face went into an icy mask that terrified me. It was easier to know what someone was doing when you could see what they were feeling but Nadila was beyond pissed off. I didn't know her well but I knew that the icy mask was not a good thing.

The man on my left shifted uneasily, as if sensing we were in dangerous territory. "Councilman Khos has stated-"

"Does it look like I care what Khos has stated?" The words were so cold I almost felt the air around the two men drop in temperature. "*Does it?*" The words were brittle and I felt them loosen their grips on my arms. "While I am on this ship she is under my protection. If I hear of a single instance that *any* Peace Officer has tried anything towards her I will take that as an act of aggression against her bond with her mate. I will deal with that aggressive action the only way the Council will allow me to." The threat hung in the air and even though she didn't state what the action was I was fairly positive that they knew what she meant. The hand dropped from my arms and I rubbed at the spots hoping they didn't leave bruises.

Nadila stared at me and I fought the urge to lower my gaze to the floor. The silence was nearly unbearable and I pushed at the panic that was growing in me. I looked into her eyes and at the mixture of emotions that were in them. The two men beside me shifted their weight and Nadila's gaze was on them immediately.

"Let me make something perfectly clear. Liviya, the *abomination*, the *half-breed,* as you have so labelled her, will be treated as though she is of my own blood. This means I want no Peace Officers touching her without her express permission. Do you understand me?" Her voice was low and the two Peace Officers murmured their agreement and she wrinkled her nose as if they disgusted her. "Get the fuck out of my sight." She waved them away before grasping my wrist and tugging me away from them. I felt my muscles loosen as soon as I was away from their sides. I was still scared but without their bulk on either side of me caging me in it was easier to relax slightly.

"Councilman Khos-"

"I said *leave.*" Nadila wasn't letting them talk and I watched as the two men turned before walking away. "Are you okay? They did not bruise you did they?" She grasped my arms and I felt my breathing hitch and within a few seconds I had started hyperventilating as I started crying.

She wrapped her arms around me tightly. "Breathe, Liv. It's okay, they won't touch you again. It is okay." The words were whispered as she tucked my head underneath her chin and embraced me much like my mother would. "Shhhhh. Breathe, remember to breathe." I fought to take in air but the fearful sobs wouldn't end. I didn't have Rhex to protect me anymore and I was terrified. I didn't want to know what would have happened if Nadila hadn't been there.

"I will kill that bastard. I will kill him for going behind the Council's back like this!" The words were hissed and I wiped at my tears, finally getting my breathing under control.

"What?" The word was more of a croak than anything and I winced at the sound but Nadila didn't comment as she wiped the tears from my cheeks.

"Khos went to the Oria Council with your living situation. He basically told them you were a student living in a military apartment. They reprimanded us for letting that happen and you are to be moved to the student apartments." Her face was tight with anger and I blinked in confusion.

"That's not that bad." I didn't like the thought of leaving Rhex's apartment where I was comfortable but moving apartments wasn't such a bad thing.

"It *is* bad, Liv. You were safer in the military apartments, the student apartments still rely on lock and key. They are very easy to break into not to mention Khos's son is living in your student section. I should have known he would pull this." She let me go and pinched the bridge of her nose in frustration. "I am sorry. I tried to get them to move you to my apartments but they refused. As soon as they did I came here to try and stop all of this." Her gaze was worried and she met my gaze and I swallowed hard at her expression.

"Do not trust the Peace Officers. Do not go near them. They are in Khos' pocket. If you need any help, look for the Peace Keepers." She pointed at a red and white robot that stood still by a railing. "They started out as medical bots and are now programmed to keep citizens safe. They cannot be corrupted and they will help you." I watched as she straightened her suit jacket with a sharp tug before making sure her hair was still in place.

"Let us get you to your new apartment. I had some strings pulled and you have a roommate that speaks English." She gestured to the service door that was further away. I followed her towards it wiping at my face, hating the slight stickiness the tears had left. "Your apartment is four levels above the military apartments and two levels below the Learning Centre. I want you to walk to and from the Learning Centre with your roommate." Her voice was sharp and I nodded quickly.

"This is important. If your roommate needs to stay at the Centre longer than you do, you will wait for them." She opened the door and I stepped inside and started climbing the stairs. "I know you cannot use the teleporters and I hate that you have to take the service stairs but it is unavoidable. Do not linger in those areas. There are no cameras in the stairwells." I knew Nadila was just giving me a heads up but everything she said made my heart sink lower in my chest. I was terrified but now I had to adjust everything so that no one could possibly get me cornered. I shuddered at the thought and we passed another level.

"Khos has a son?" I glanced at Nadila whose face twisted into a nasty scowl.

"Yes and he is just as nasty as his father." She stopped and grabbed my arm. "Stay away from Kher, Liviya. When I say stay away from him I mean if you see him you turn and go the other way. He's a vile man and I do not want him near you." Her words were harsh but her eyes were soft. "I *know* this is terrifying but I'm trying to make sure you will be okay. I would be more relaxed if you were in my apartments but it isn't allowed so I am trying to make sure you understand the danger you are in." She grasped my shoulders in her hands and I nodded. There was concern in her eyes and I appreciated it.

"I'm trying to understand, Nadila." The words sounded shaky and I hated how weak they were.

"I know you are, Liv. You do not have to keep trying to be strong. I know I would not be in your situation." She squeezed my shoulders comfortingly. "There is no shame in being scared. This is terrifying. *I* am scared for you, Liv." She let my shoulders go and gave me a small smile. My stomach felt too queasy to return the gesture.

"Let uss go." She pointed up the stairs and we continued our climb to the student apartments. If Nadila was scared for me then it did not bode well for my situation. The severity of what was happening was immense and terrifying. There was a big chance that someone would try to hurt me and without Rhex there to calm my fears it was somehow worse.

Nadila pushed open a door and we walked through. The area was mainly empty and she gave what appeared to be a sigh of relief. She walked quicker as she handed me a key without a word. I took the cool metal and gripped it tightly, trying not to panic or break down. We passed the purple doors and I tried to focus on the symbols but their meanings were nothing I could decipher.

"Your apartment number is one hundred and forty-two. Do not forget it, Liv. If you ever get lost make your way to the nearest Peace Keeper and stay by its side until someone you trust comes for you." She pointed at a door and pulled me towards it. "This symbol is your room number but I am getting someone to put some numbers you understand on here for you." Nadila looked tired suddenly and she let out a heavy breath. "Stay safe, Liviya Burch." She patted my cheek before she walked away. I turned to the door and unlocked it. It was dark and I tried to ignore how my heart beat faster as the light slowly turned on.

"Hello?" My voice echoed slightly in the empty apartment but there was no answer as I closed the door making sure to lock it behind me. I slumped against it, suddenly exhausted. I let myself lean against it for a moment before I pushed away from it, kicking off my shoes. The sitting room was small and was attached to the kitchen. I stopped, looking at the couch I got a sudden urge to cry. I sat down and pressed my face into my hands.

I didn't want to cry, I hated having the mopey feeling hanging over me but when a thin band of metal on my finger pressed into my forehead I couldn't help it. I looked at the ring Rhex had placed on my finger and I couldn't stop the tears from falling. It had been my great grandmother's wedding band. My father must have given it to him before we left. A sob crawled its way up my throat and I pressed my hand to my mouth, trying to muffle the sound. I lay down on the couch and curled inwards, letting the wracking sobs escape.

There wasn't much I could do but go through the motions. I missed Rhex, as pathetic as it was, but I hadn't seen him for two days and then only to say good bye. I remembered how he held me in the shuttle and my chest hurt as more sobs tore through me. It was the last time he had hugged me and I missed the contact. I pressed the heels of my hands to my eyes. My head hurt and my chest ached but the sobs didn't stop.

Everything in my world felt out of balance and off kilter. It was like my world was suddenly in chaos and the only thing keeping me grounded was gone. In a way it was. Rhex was a steady constant in my chaotic life. I had known him for eight days and he had somehow become the most important person in the world to me in that small amount of time.

The tears tapered off and the sobs lessened and a heaviness settled into my limbs. I was tired but I knew it wasn't just exhaustion, it was if I were being pulled in two directions. I was stuck in one spot but a part of me was flying further and further away.

22

I woke up as the door to the apartment closed. I sat up quickly, my eyes wide as I looked at the woman standing in front of me. My heart pounded in my chest and she had her own hand pressed to her chest as if I had startled her.

"I am so sorry! I did not realize you were sleeping." Her voice was quiet and I tried to calm my breathing down as I ran my hand through my hair. I hadn't meant to fall asleep but sometime during my inner reflection on just how shitty I felt, I had.

"That's okay, I probably shouldn't be sleeping right now anyway." I felt a fleeting smile cross my mouth before it disappeared. She gave me a bright smile in return and I rubbed at my eyes. "My name is Liviya but you can call me Liv." I stood up and extended my hand towards her.

She took it quickly and gave it a rather excited shake. I felt the jarring movement all the way to my shoulders. "Ani'tah but you can call me Ani." She let my hand go and tossed her satchel onto one of the chairs. "Councilwoman Nadila put us as roommates. I am so glad because I have never really spent time with a human before. You are so *fascinating!"* She looked excited and I smiled slightly, amused by her excitement. At least she was friendly.

"It's okay. I've spent more time with Orrians in the past few days than I have my entire life." I had only seen a spare few when I had been on Earth and now I was surrounded by them. My thoughts were distracted as she jumped up and down slightly. She reminded me of an excited puppy.

She shook her hands in front of her before smiling brightly. "Is it true you are bonded to an Orrian?" The words burst from her and I blinked in surprise as she clamped her hands over her mouth with wide eyes. "I am sorry. I do not have a filter." She gave an almost sheepish look and I chuckled, it sounded empty to my ears but if Ani noticed she didn't let on.

"It's okay. Yes, I've bonded to an Orrian. His name is Rhex." Just saying his name sent a sharp spear of pain through my chest. I absently rubbed at it, hoping the sting would go away.

She was watching me with wide-eyed curiosity and pointed at me. "Are you okay?" She tilted her head much like a curious puppy would and I nodded quickly.

"Yah, it's just the bond. We are separated for a few months. He had to go to training." I watched as her face went pale. It was a similar reaction to everyone else I had told, apparently it wasn't healthy to separate bonded soulmates for extended periods of time.

"They *still* sent him to training? That is, what is the human phtase? Oh yes, *bullshit*." She flopped down in one of the chairs and I sat back down on the couch. "Orrian politics are so weird sometimes. *Everyone* knows that separating bonded pair is going to be painful for both parts." Her eyes were wide as she gestured rather angrily with her hand.

I shrugged with a ghost of a smile on my mouth. "We expected it. We haven't completed the bonding so hopefully it's not too painful." I leaned against the back of the couch with a sigh. I felt drained but my dad had warned me about that.

"How did you manage not to complete it? The bonding that is." Her silver eyes seemed to sparkle with curiosity and I shrugged, a faint blush on my face.

"We have boundless self-control. Well he does anyway." My tone was dry but she laughed anyway. I smiled at her, at least she had a sense of humour. I was glad, not very many Orrians seemed to even know what humour. was, let alone have a sense of it.

"You are funny. I think I am going to like you." She giggled as she wiggled in her spot. "Everyone on this ship has a stick shoved up their asses. Everything is always so *serious*." She giggled again as she wiped her eyes and I couldn't help but give a small laugh at her words.

"You know, I thought the exact same thing but no one has ever corroborated it for me till now." I let out a sigh and looked around, trying to find a clock. I rolled my eyes when I remembered there wouldn't be one I could read. "What time is it?" I gave a small frown as I looked around. I wasn't entirely sure how long I had been out for.

She frowned slightly, matching my expression before she broke out into a smile. "It is about noon. Are you hungry?" She stood up and I shrugged. I didn't have much of an appetite since Rhex and I had left my parents and I was pretty sure it had everything to do with our separation.

"I'm okay." I watched as she pursed her lips with a slight frown.

"You should eat. Councilwoman Nadila said you might experience some appetite loss but you should still eat." She held out her hand and I tentatively took it. Without much warning she yanked me to my feet and pulled me towards the small kitchen. "To be honest, you should probably hold back on the apathy a bit. You need to keep your figure for your man." She bumped her hip into my mine playfully and I laughed suddenly at the unusual action. I had seen friends do it to each other when I had been in high school but I had never really had anyone do it to me before. It felt nice.

"Alright, I concede. What are we having?" I watched as she pulled a container out of one of the cupboards and pulled a tab on it.

"Something tasteless but filling." The sarcasm was evident and I chuckled. I was finding I liked Ani more the longer I was with her. "Human food is so much tastier. I've only had a few dishes but it is just so good." I gave a sound of agreement as she pulled open the container and a spiral of steam floated upward.

The scent was almost minty and I frowned slightly. "That smells like mint." I looked into the container and to my surprise it was a strange burnt orange colour.

"It probably does not taste like it." Her voice sounded disgusted and I looked at the container with apprehension as it wiggled like some type of burnt orange jello.

"If I had an appetite, I'm pretty sure I would have lost it." I glanced at her as she grabbed two plates and doled the questionable food out in even portions. Orrian food was so strange at times, I corrected myself, Orrian space rations were strange. It made me miss the grilled cheese and chicken noodle soup my mum had made Rhex and I.

"I understand that. At least it does not taste weird. That and this is the only food we have up here. Plants don't grow up here." She let out a sigh and handed me a plate and a fork before gesturing to the living room.

I followed her before sitting on the couch, setting the plate down in front of me. "My mum actually is a researcher for interstellar plant growth." I poked at the mush with the fork and was surprised that it didn't move away. I looked at Ani who had taken a bite of the food with a strange expression on her face as she swallowed.

"Hopefully she figures something out because the texture is off putting." She placed her plate on the table. "We need to get some groceries. This was all we have to eat." I looked down at my food and cautiously took a bite. It had that similar spicy taste like all the food had but the texture was off-putting just like Ani had said. I forced myself to swallow, ignoring the sudden nausea I was feeling. I wasn't sure if it was from the food or from actually eating something.

"You look pale." Her remark was casual as she picked up her plate. She looked like she wanted to eat it about as much as I did.

I gave a sigh but forced a small smile onto my face anyway. "I don't feel the greatest." I turned back to my food and forced myself to finish it. I didn’t want to but I knew I had to.

There was a slightly awkward silence that fell as we both ate. "Is your mate hot?" The question caught me off-guard and I stared at her for a moment. Her cheeks flushed slightly as she poked at the food on her plate. "I know it is a weird question but is he?" I felt a slow smile cross my face as I thought of Rhex. The strong angles of his face, his beautiful green eyes, the harshness of his scar. He was far too handsome.

"From the goofy look on your smile I would say, yes, he is." Ani's voice was teasing and I felt a flash of heat on my cheeks. "Oh do not be embarrassed. From what I hear having a soulmate is a wonderful experience." I watched as her expression slowly fell. "I am jealous, you know. The chance of me finding a soulmate is pretty much zero." Her silver eyes were downcast and I felt guilty, I hadn't realized that some Orrians would have wanted what Rhex and I had.

"Things are changing. Maybe there is someone for you. A human perhaps." I watched as her face brightened slightly at my suggestion. I didn't want her to feel down because I had what she wished to get.

"Hey, you could be right. I mean you found Rhex and he's Orrian." There was a tiny bit of hope in her tone and I couldn't help but smile at her. "I wouldn't care if he was human or Orrian. I would love him to the ends of the universe and back." There was a wistful tone in her voice and I set my now empty plate down, ignoring the sour feeling in my stomach.

"He would love you the same." I knew the words were true. It was what soulmates were. Rhex and I cared for each other and I knew it would eventually be love but I also understood that we needed to get to know each other first. Our bond had forced us together but we were choosing to get to know each other, to make use of the time we were apart to learn about one another.

"I know. It would be wonderful." Ani's voice snapped me back to reality and I smiled at her again. She was a sweet person and she deserved all the love a soulmate bond could give her.

"And don't worry, it probably won't be as difficult as my bonding." I gave her a teasing smile and her face looked concerned. "Don't worry about it so much. I promise you no one is going to want to make your life difficult." I kept my tone teasing but she glowered at me.

"I am not worried about my non-existent soulmate. Councilman Khos is probably going to want to kill you." At her words I gave a loud snort of laughter. It wasn't new to me. I knew that from the beginning.

"I already knew that. He's wanted to recycle me since I came on the ship." I waved my hand flippantly. It was difficult with Khos and everyone else that wanted me dead but I knew I could manage. Nadila and Rhess and Orrian law were on my side.

"Do not be so apathetic about it. Kher is going to be at the Centre as well. That is dangerous!" Her face was almost pale and I felt sorry for her. She was feeling everything all at once. I had time to almost get used to the fact most Orrians wanted to kill me.

"Nadila said I had to stick by you. To and from the Centre every day." I watched as she slowly shook her head. Her black hair swayed around her face, it was barely brushing her shoulders and I was reminded of the Orrian custom with hair. Nadila's hair was below the middle of her back, my hair was only a few inches shorter than hers. I felt a smile grow on my face as well as a chuckle building in my throat.

"I cannot stop Kher if he gets something in his head." Her voice sounded small and I couldn't help the chuckle that escaped. "It is not funny!" Her voice was harsh and I shook my head.

"I know. It's just I was looking at your hair. Humans have the same custom as you guys but we don't enforce it." I tugged on my hair, twirling a strand of it around my finger absentmindedly. "So how important am I?" I couldn't help the smile on my face as I wiggled my eyebrows.

She gave me an incredulous look before bursting into laughter. "I never noticed your hair. It is a really pretty colour." She reached out and I let her grab a small chunk. I was reminded of Rhex telling me I had beautiful hair. "It is kind of brown but too light. How do you get it so soft?" She rubbed it before letting it drop. Her face was bright and I smiled back at her, glad the conversation about Khos and Kher was over.

"I use actual shampoo and conditioner." I watched as a surprised look crossed her face as she touched her own hair.

"*Seriously*? I never thought about that. Would my hair be that soft if I used it?" She sounded almost self-conscious and I nodded. It seemed that Orrians were just as self-conscious about their appearance as humans, the thought made me want to smile. There was common ground after all.

"But you need to turn the cleaner off in the bathroom. Last time I used it, it practically molested me." I shuddered at the memory and she laughed loudly.

"Oh you probably enjoyed it. I know I do." She wiggled her eyebrows suggestively and it took me a moment to understand what she was saying.

"Oh that's *gross*. I didn't need to know that." I couldn't help but laugh at her expression. She was still wiggling her eyebrows and I reached over and pushed at her shoulder. "Stop that! I get it."

She laughed and smiled brightly. "I will turn it off and we need to seriously go shopping. I had to move yesterday so I did not get anything then." She stood up and I followed suit. Ani was a fun person. It was nice to be around someone who wasn't cold towards me or focusing all of their intensity on me. I never really had friends that I hung out with outside of high school, I never thought I needed them but I knew I needed friends more than anything at that moment. More than friends I needed allies. "Oria to Liv." Her voice pulled me back to reality and I shook my head, realizing I had missed what she had been saying.

"Sorry, got lost in my thoughts." I gave her an apologetic smile that she rolled her eyes at with a smile.

"Well I do not have a map for that so I cannot help you. However I can help you figure out how to get your ass out of the apartment so we can get groceries." There was a teasing note to her voice and I nodded quickly, trying to ignore how the thought of leaving the apartment makes me feel drained of energy. I wondered if it was starting, the feeling of being exhausted and tired that my dad had warned me about. I didn't get a chance to think about it as Ani grabbed my hand and pulled me towards the door.

"You're so demanding." I chuckled as I put my shoes on and she rolled her eyes once more.

"My mother tells me that all the time but she is more demanding than me so I come by it honestly." There is a smirk on her face and I shook my head with a smile.

"I'm stubborn just like my mum so we make a great pair." I ignored the tired feeling that was filling my muscles as she looped her arm in mine and pulled me from the apartment.

23

Ani and I walked towards the Centre, the service stairs were almost darker in this part of the ship and I repressed a shiver. Ani had her arm looped through mine and we walked in a comfortable silence. After we had gone shopping and had put everything away, we had sat down and talked about meaningless things for hours. It had felt good to talk to someone even if it was about nothing important. The endless flow of conversation helped take my mind off the ache that was slowly building in my chest.

"You are probably going to have to take your translator out." Ani's voice cut through the silence and I glanced at her. Her face looked pale in the poor lighting and I gave a small nod before pulling the translator out of my ear and sliding it into my pocket. "The teacher here is kind of an asshole."

I bumped her slightly with my hip. "I think it is easier for you to tell me who *isn't* an asshole on this ship." I smirked as she laughed loudly.

"Well, at the top of the list is me." She batted her eyelashes and winked at me.

I rolled my eyes and tightened my arm on hers. "Of course you are." I truly liked Ani, she was easy to talk to and it helped that she seemed to make it her mission to keep me from dwelling on the separation I had with Rhex.

"Hey, so you were saying last night that you and Rhex were going to use this time apart to get to know each other. You do not speak or read Orrian so does that mean I get to be privy to all of your relationship talk?" She wiggled her eyebrows and I smiled in amusement. I looked at her, thinking about what she had said. I hadn't thought about that aspect of our separation.

"You know, that would probably be a big help, Ani." I looked at her and her face brightened considerably as we pushed open the door to the Centre's floor.

She gave a small fist pump. "Yes! I get to practice on you two and that means I will be an expert by the time I find my own mate." She looked so excited that I couldn't help but laugh. Ani was a bubbly person, being around her was like a mood booster.

"Well, as long as I can help you out. So do we share the same types of classes?" I tried to ignore the strange stares we were getting and Ani nodded.

"Councilwoman Nadila put you in all of my classes. We will not be separated." Her tone was reassuring and I gave a small nod, trying not to let the nervousness fill me as the Orrian chatter filled my ears. I missed the translator and I had to resist the urge to put it back in my ear. I didn't like how I couldn't understand what they were saying. Ani took a step closer to me and leaned her head towards mine. "They are not talking about you. Actively avoiding you is a good term." She gave a bright smile to the Orrians around us and they all turned their backs or looked away. "See?" There was laughter in her voice and I smirked.

"I must say I prefer avoidance to attempted murder." I kept my tone light and she threw her head back and once again laughed loudly.

Her hand pressed to her stomach as she leaned forward, taking deep breath in. "Don't we all?" She wiped at her eyes and I chuckled.

"I didn't think it was *that* funny." I almost stumbled as she pulled me towards a door without warning.

"It is not *what* you said. It was *how* you said it. You have some serious deadpan humour." She pushed open the door and drug me inside. "This is our classroom. We will be here for pretty much the entire day. Our instructor is Mr. Dahgme, he is a total hard ass and does not particularly like humans." She pushed me towards a table and I sat down with a raised eyebrow.

"I told you it would be easier to tell me the people who liked humans." I watched as she set down her bag and sat beside me.

"Well it is hard. I am still trying to figure out who is on the list." She looked almost peevish at the thought and I chuckled. It wasn't a long list, I knew that much. The door opened again and more people poured in. They actively took the seats far away from us except for one man. His face was cold and his grey eyes were far too familiar. There was a sneer of disgust on his mouth and Ani tapped my shoulder as he took the table to the left of me.

"Switch seats with me." Her words were a hushed whisper and I quickly switched seats with her. After we had settled she looked over at me, her eyes wide. "That is Kher." There was a large amount of fear in her voice and I felt my shoulder instinctively roll forward. I could feel his pointed glare on me and Ani shifted so she was blocking his gaze.

"He is acting weird and scary." Her words were mumbled and I silently agreed with her assessment. "I have never noticed it before. He was always intimidating but this is a whole new level of crazy coming from him." I couldn't help the small snort of laughter that escaped at her words. I covered my mouth and stifled the rest of the laughter that wanted to escape. I wasn't sure if I was laughing because I was scared or if it was just plain ridiculous.

The door opened again and an older man with dark eyes stepped in. He looked like he was permanently angry with how low his eyebrows were over his eyes. I watched as he scanned the class, his eyes immediately zeroing on me. His eyes were cold and he barked something out in Orrian.

"He wants to know your name." Ani's voice was low as she nudged my arm to get my attention.

I swallowed thickly. "Liviya Burch." I stated it loud enough that he could hear and he gave a look of distaste.

"Liviya Burch, *agun slegrnd.*" The words were harsh and I felt Ani stiffen beside me. I knew the reason, she didn't have to tell me what he had said. It had been spit at me more than enough since I had been on the ship.

"I am not translating that." She sounded pained, her form tense.

I gave a small shrug. "I already know what he said. That's a favourite for Orrians." I tilted my head and stared at the teacher. I smiled suddenly remembering what Rhex had said to me in the tunnels my first day on the ship. *"Mehba illeehd sirbaht onshe halh."* Ani's head whipped toward me and her gaze was wide with shock.

"Where did you learn that?" Her voice was a hushed and straggled whisper as she grasped my wrist.

I frowned slightly. "From Rhex. I think it's what our medallions say. Love is never easy." I shrugged once more. It was one of the very few Orrians words that I knew.

She gave a small frown, shaking her head. "That is not really what it means. Well that is the easiest translation in English. The literal translation is '*The first of many loves will never be easy for the winds of change blow harshly.*' It's part of our history, from when the Source started to experience the universe." She shook her head slightly. "Can I see your medallion?" I took it out of my shirt and she picked it up with a raised eyebrow.

"I never knew the Source had a sense of humour." She let the medallion drop back onto my chest and I tucked it back into my shirt. It felt strange as she studied my face, like I was something under a microscope that she was inspecting. A slow smile crossed her face as she started to shake her head. "The first of many loves. Let's hope one of those 'many loves' finds its way towards me before I break down and turn on the cleaner again." She wiggled her eyebrows playfully and I pressed my hand to my mouth, not wanting the chuckles to escape.

"You have a filthy mind." I smiled to take the bite out of the words and she let out a huff of pretend irritation.

"Oh I forgot, you have a mate. Leave me to my steamy affair with the shower and enjoy your mate." She rolled her eyes and pulled out two notebooks and handed me one with a pencil.

"Steamy affair?" I bit my lip to keep from laughing out loud and drawing unwanted attention to ourselves.

"Pun intended." She chuckled as she flipped open both the notebooks. "Mr. Hardass won't be speaking English at all in any of the subjects so I'll take the notes and translate them for you later. You doodle and distract me and cause trouble. Maybe if you do you can get us both kicked out and we can do something fun." She winked at me and I bit my lip harder to keep the laughter from bubbling out. Ani was one of a kind.

24

"I swear on all that is holy that if he hadn't shut up I would have pushed him down a flight of stairs." Ani was practically vicious as she drug me from the classroom and towards the service stairs. I chuckled under my breath and smiled at her.

"I would have helped." The thought of Mr. Dahgme's lecture made me shudder. His voice had droned on and on in Orrian about subjects I had no clue about and couldn't understand. My boredom had been nearly unbearable.

"I knew I liked you." She bumped her shoulder into me playfully and I laughed at the action right before a sharp pain flashed through my chest. I winced and rubbed at my spot. It had been happening sporadically throughout the day and it was starting to get alarming. "I do not know much about bonds but that whole wincing thing is starting to worry me." Her silver eyes were slightly dark with concern and I let out a sigh.

"We could go see Ghilesh. He might know what is causing it." I looked at the service stairs door and frowned, unsure if his apartment was up or down.

"Who is Ghilesh?" Her tone was questioning and I blinked, forgetting she was there for a moment.

"He's a Soul Maker. He's the one who bonded Rhex and I." Once again I struggled to figure out which way to go when Ani grabbed my arm and pulled me down the stairs.

"If he can explain some of what is going on then I do not care." She said nothing else as we rushed down the stairs and towards a familiar looking dark blue door. She pushed it open and tugged me through it. I felt another pain run through my chest and I rubbed at the spot with a frown. It was starting to get irritating.

I caught sight of the back of Ghilesh's head and I waved frantically. "Ghilesh!" At my words he whirled around, his eyebrows pulled low over his amber eyes.

He caught sight of me and his face brightened. "Ahhh, Liviya. How are you?" Just being in his presence relaxed me and made it seem like everything would be explained. Ghilesh was someone I trusted completely and if anyone could help me find out what the whole flashes of pain were, it would be him.

"I've been better. Do you have a minute or twenty?" I gave him a small smile and his eyes flashed with concern before he opened his door and waved us in.

"Of course, of course. Please come in." He moved inside, holding the door for us and I tugged Ani forward. The dusty room didn't seem to have changed since the last time I had been in there but it seemed as though some of the book stacks had grown larger.

"This is pretty cool." Ani reached up, trailing her hands over the odd and ends hanging from the ceiling like I had before.

"Thank you but do not touch. Liviya, who is your friend?" Ghilesh looked between us and I jumped slightly. I had completely forgotten that Ghilesh didn't know Ani and my cheeks fairly burned.

"Oh, I'm sorry. This is Ani, she's my roommate." At my words he frowned darkly. He looked between us and I almost winced at his expression.

"Why aren't you staying in Rhex's apartment?" The question hung in the air for a few moments before Ani let out a loud sigh.

"Why do you think? Councilman Khos was being a prick, as per usual." She waved her hand flippantly and almost instantly the tension disappeared and Ghilesh gave a small smirk.

"I like you." He shook his head before turning his gaze to me. "What seems to be the issue?" He rubbed at his chin with a curious expression

I winced as another sharp pain flared through my chest. "I've been getting sharp pain in my chest. It doesn't happen regularly. It's actually pretty random but they are getting irritating." I watched as he tapped his forehead with a confused frown before he started muttering to himself and moved towards a stack of books, rifling through them.

"He is kind of strange isn't he?" Ani's voice was a whisper and I chuckled slightly. Ghilesh was slightly odd but it was what made him so interesting.

"You get used to him. He's very informative. He's actually Nadila's uncle." I watched as he moved to an overflowing bookcase and went through those books as well. Dust floated through the air and I waved my hand in front of my face.

"Really? That is kind of cool." Ani looked completely enamoured with the space, there was a look of wonderment on her face that I had to smile at. "This is so- just so *awesome*." She closed her eyes and breathed in deeply. I chuckled at her before shaking my head.

"Found it. I have found it. Misplaced it but I have got it." Ghilesh came back holding a thick book before he opened it up. "Where is it? Where could it be?" He drug his finger down what looked to be a table of contents. He tapped on a line of symbols I couldn't read before he flipped the book opened.

"Okay. Okay. Separation. Physical symptoms. Pain. Ahhhh here we are." He looked at me with a soft smile. "It says that when two bonded mates are separated they may experience some physical pain. Your bodies are supposed to be in-sync with one another but because you are separated that is far harder to do. It causes some discomfort, loss of sleep, loss of appetite, chest pains. There is a whole list of other symptoms here that I do not want to bore you with. Basically it boils down to you are going to feel sick and crappy for four months and the only cure is Rhex."

I gave him an unimpressed look while narrowing my eyes. "That's great. So I have to just deal with this?" I gestured to the book and he shrugged nonchalantly. If I didn't know any better it seemed like he was excited. "Wait are you using this for research?" I narrowed my eyes at him and he froze, his eyes wide.

Busted.

"Ghilesh! Come on! I thought we were friends." I let out an aggravated sigh and he chuckled.

"I apologize but you and Rhex are the first bonded soulmates I have ever met. Everything that you are going through fascinates me to no end." He tilted his head to look at me and I smiled at him, an unexpected chuckle escaping me.

"You're not sorry. Now, is there any way to lessen the symptoms?" I looked at him expectantly and he looked thoughtful for a few moments.

"Talk to him. Find a way to communicate with him. Maybe the sound of his voice will help ease some of the issues you are experiencing." The idea was actually half decent and I felt the corner of my mouth twitch slightly. "However he is probably in hyper sleep right now and will probably be for the next week or so. So you are probably going to have to wait but take that time to talk to Nadila about arranging the call." The words made me grimace but I had to concede.

"Soooooooo, is there any chance that I could find my soulmate?" Ani's voice was curious and hopeful and I rolled my eyes and Ghilesh frowned at her slightly.

"Well, I do not see why that could not be a possibility. Why are you asking?" He shifted on his feet and I turned to look at Ani who had a sad smile on her face.

"Because I, unlike all the others on this ship, want to find him." There was a soft cord in her voice and I turned to look at Ghilesh who has a curiously soft expression on his face.

"My niece, Vila, sounded just like you. The Source rewards those who stay with tradition. Out of everyone on this ship I do not doubt you will have a soulmate somewhere. You just need some patience. All things will come in good time." His voice was so soft I was almost shocked. "There are very few that are like you, Ani'tah. You are rare." He gave her a small smile and I looked at Ani's shocked expression and I had to agree with him.

25

"Well, Rhex is going to be in hypersleep for two more days, then he is going to need to be processed for training so I do not see why you could not talk to him in three days." Nadila took a graceful drink from her cup and I gave her a grateful smile. I wasn't the healthiest looking, the separation between Rhex and I was taking its toll. "I will worry about the details, Liviya. You should probably focus on sleeping." She gave me curious look and I gave a tired chuckle.

"I can't sleep. The separation is hard." I looked into her lilac eyes and she gave me a bright smile, waving me off slightly.

"No worries, Liviya. I am sure you will be fine. Ghilesh told me you visited him and I am sorry I could not come to see you sooner. Khos has been all over me constantly about protocols. I think he is just doing it so I cannot spend time with you." She took another drink and I sipped at my water. "Kher is not stepping out of line, is he?" I shook my head. He had been glaring at me constantly but he hadn't tried anything so far. Ani was very careful about staying by my side while I was at the Centre.

"And the schooling? How is that coming along?" Her gaze let me know the change of subject was deliberate. As if it was her way of getting me to focus on something that wasn't almost terrifying.

"It's alright. Mr. Dahgme is difficult but with Ani's help I'm actually learning about things. I feel kind of bad, she has to translate all of her notes into English for me." I set my glass down on the café table in front of me. Nadila had taken me to the same café she had taken me before.

"She is an intelligent girl. I bet she finds it oddly fun." There was a slight smirk on her face and I smiled at her. Ani had said it was good practice and that before long I would grasp the language well enough to read it.

"She *has* mentioned that." I took a bite of my sandwich and Nadila seemed to watch me carefully. The sandwich was good but my stomach always tried to rebel against food, no matter what it was.

"Are you sure you are alright, Liviya?" Her tone was soft and I took another drink of my water.

"I can't sleep, I'm tired all the time, I keep getting random chest pains, and I have no appetite but I am okay." I gave her a small smile as I set the glass back down on the table. "I know it will all be okay when Rhex gets back. It's only temporary." I watched as she gave a small nod.

"I wish I could get the phone call sooner for you, Liv. I really wish I could." She reached across the table and grasped my hand and I gave it a slight squeeze. It was nice that she cared. It was nice that Ani cared, having people care about me in a sea of others who didn't was nice to experience.

"It's alright, Nadila. You have done so much for me already." I let her hand go and picked up the sandwich once more, forcing myself to eat it.

"Liv!" Ani's voice made me turn around and she waved her arms wildly. It made me smile as she came over.

"This must be Ani'tah." Nadila smiled brightly and stood up before holding out her hand. "It is a pleasure to meet you." I watched as Ani shook it quickly before grabbing my shoulder.

"Do you mind if I steal her? I have today's lessons translated." She smiled and I watched as Nadila nodded.

"By all means, learning is important." Nadila stood up and I did as well and she surprised me by pulling me into a tight hug. "You will be okay." She let me go with a smile and I gave her a small wave as Ani grabbed my hand and pulled me away from the café.

"So, in the star year 85,437, the Kengans declared war on the Orrians?" I looked at Ani in confusion and she frowned slightly.

"No, in the star year 85,437, the Kengans attacked the Orrians without declaring war. Which caused the Orrians to retaliate. No one formally declared war until star year 85, 500. Which was sixty-three years after the attacks started." She tapped on a paragraph further down on my notebook.

I looked at the translated text with confusion before I read what she meant. "Ohhhhh." I read the passage and scratched my forehead. "That makes no sense." I looked up at her as she threw her hands out.

"I *know*. It's ridiculous. Who waits that long to declare war? They were fighting for sixty-three star years! It was just like someone stopped and was like. '*Oh yah, we should probably declare war.*' It was like an afterthought." She frowned and rolled her eyes slightly. "Nothing they did back then made any sense. The war is still going on and it's been like fourteen hundred star years." I smiled at her and couldn't help but laugh. She had a point, the declaration of war after fighting for so long seemed a bit trivial and out of place. I winced as a sharp pain speared my chest, I resisted the urge to rub at the pain. After a few seconds it faded as I knew it would.

"So how are you doing?" She set her notebook down and I smirked.

"I hope when Rhex wakes up that he gets this just as bad as me." At my words Ani started laughing. I watched as she fell backwards onto the couch, grabbing her stomach. I couldn't help but chuckle at the display.

"That will make his training so hard!" She managed to speak between her fits of laughter before wiping her eyes. "I can just imagine this large Orrian soldier sitting there because his chest hurts because he misses his mate. The image is just so oddly hilarious." I had to admit it was slightly funny but at the same time it made my chest ache. I didn't want him to experience the same things as I did especially considering I could take the pain away. It wasn't right that he would be hurting and I was the only thing that could take the pain away but I couldn't. I just hoped he felt that way about me.

I let out a sigh before looking down at my notebook. Ani had left some words in Orrian, she said it would help me grasp the language easier. I didn't disagree with her, I knew the Orrian words for Kengans and star years. The pronunciation was more difficult. Orrians spoke low in the back of their throat, a task I had yet to manage. Silence fell between us as I continued to read about the Kengan-Orrian war. I was lucky they didn't really do tests.

"I do not like this, Liv. You look so tired and sick all the time. I know it is because of the separation but looking at you, I feel terrible." Ani's voice was soft and I looked at her with a shrug.

"It's not your fault. Fate had us separated for a time." I watched as she scowled darkly. I liked Ani but she liked to take things personally. I didn't like how she felt bad for Rhex's deployment. It was if she was blaming herself for everything other Orrians did to me.

"No. Rhex should have been let out of training as soon as you two were bonded." She made a disgusted sound in the back of her throat. "It is a sad state of affairs when they would allow the separation between mates. It is stupid, Liv." Her silver eyes were almost down cast and I shrugged again.

"I can't argue with that, Ani, but it isn't your fault." I reached over the table and grabbed her hand. "You're my friend. I know you are feeling guilty for the entirety of the Orrian race but please don't. They are responsible for their own actions." I let her hand go before setting down the notebook. We had been at it for close to three hours and my brain hurt. I was tired but that was nothing new.

"I say we stop for the day. I do not think my brain can handle any more information." I rubbed at my face and she chuckled before nodding.

"I agree with you there. I would ask you if you wanted to do something but then I remembered this ship is boring and there is nothing to do." She smirked and I rolled my eyes at her statement. Ani made mention of how boring the ship was at least a hundred times per day. I was positive she was trying to tell me she wanted to go to Earth but wasn't sure how to approach the subject.

"You know, I could ask Nadila if we could go to the surface on one of our spare days. I could take you to the old ruins behind my house." I watched as her face brightened significantly. I had guessed right.

"That would be awesome. The surface looks so cool. I've never been down there and it would help with my studies to visit some of the old ruins." Her expression almost looked dreamy and I tried my best to make my expression even.

"It's going to be even more awesome when you realize that if we go to the surface, you get to meet my parents." I watched as her eyes went wide with a bright smile on her face.

"That sounds even better! I heard that your dad is a genetic scientist!" She looked so happy that I couldn't help but laugh. I didn't know what I would do if I didn't have Ani. Her emotions were always so positive that it made you feel better just by being near her. It actually helped with the separation.

Another sharp pain jolted my nerves and I winced. "Stupid separation." I muttered it before standing up and moving to the kitchen. Ani had showed me how most of the kitchen worked. The bubble on the counter was actually a dishwasher and because there was no sink, the cooler in one of the cupboards filled glasses with water. I wasn't sure how they did but you put the cup in and after a few moments it was filled with water. "Must be magic." I placed a cup into the cooler and closed the door, waiting a few brief moments before taking the cup out.

"Boo!" The sudden shout by my ear caused me to practically throw the cup away as I clutched as my chest. I scrambled away and Ani burst into laughter. She gripped the edge of the counter with her hand, as if she couldn't stand without it.

"Fucking Christ, Ani! Don't ever do that again!" I took several deep breaths in trying to calm the harsh pounding of my heart. She had nearly given me a heart attack. I watched as she was practically on the floor, tears streamed down her face and her other hand clutched her stomach.

"Your face! You should have seen your face." She sounded like she could barely breathe and I crossed my arms over my chest, trying not to smile

"You made me spill water everywhere. I was going to drink it but now it's all over the kitchen." I tapped my foot as I waited for her laughing fit to be done but every time she looked at me it just seemed to renew her laughter. "Ani, please stop." The longer she laughed the harder it was for me not to smile at her. It *was* funny. I didn't like being frightened but the more I thought about it the funnier it became.

I watched as she wiped her eyes, random bursts of giggles erupted from her and she clutched her stomach with both arms. "My tummy hurts. It hurts so bad right now." She winced but another bout of giggles erupted from her.

"That's God's way of punishing you." I fought hard against the smile that wanted to cross my face at yet another one of my dad's strange phrases.

Ani looked confused, her silver eyes narrowing slightly as she tilted her head. "Who is God?" She looked so confused I couldn't help but chuckle and soon the chuckles turned into full-blown laughter. After holding all of it in it just decided to escape.

"I don't know." I shook my head, trying to stop the laughter that escaped but I failed miserably. Another sharp pain lanced my chest and I felt tears in my eyes and to my horror the laughter turned to sobs. I pressed my hand to my mouth trying to stop the sobs from escaping but it didn't help.

I hadn't cried at all since the day Rhex had left and it had been as if Ani had been keeping the feelings at bay but now it was like a tidal wave of sorrow had slammed into me. I closed my eyes, the tears burning fiery trails down my cheeks as I gave into the bone wracking sobs. I slid down the counter and sat on the floor. I felt thin arms wrap around me and I leaned into Ani's embrace.

"It is okay. Let it out, Liv. Let it all out." Her words felt almost empty. Everything was empty without Rhex. My heart felt heavy in my chest like it was a burden to carry without him. Breathing without him was damn near impossible and all of the feelings I had, terrified me. I wasn't prepared for how much he would mean to me. How much I needed him to survive. I wasn't prepared for any of it and now that I was feeling the effects I realized just how terrified I was of all of it.

"I'm scared." I managed to get the words out between sobs and Ani shushed me before pressing my face into her neck.

"I know, Liv. This is scary." She stroked my hair gently as I clung onto her, the tears seemed endless and I let out the emotions I had been avoiding. The fear, the terror, the pain, the hurt, the anger. They all came out in a torrent of tears that I wasn't even sure I wanted to stop. It felt good to cry and I hated that it did at the same time. Tears were a weakness, they showed a vulnerability that I knew people would exploit but at the same time they seemed to be a release for the emotions I was unwilling to show the world.

"I miss him *so* much and it scares me." The sobs had lost their intensity but the shuddering breaths continued. I was scared because he meant so much to me and I had never been so connected to someone that intensely before.

"The first of many loves will never be easy for its intensity is that of a thousand fiery suns." Her voice was low and soothing and she smoothed her hand over my hair again. "Two beings caught in a raging inferno of the Source's creation. One cannot survive without the other and the other cannot survive without the one. Their love will be the spark that creates the beacons for those lost in the darkness. Their love will ignite the passions that have been faded for a millennia and it shall draw the lost ones from the darkness." Her voice trailed off before she sniffled slightly. I clutched her tightly, trying to bring her the comfort she was giving me.

"Without the first of many loves their souls are darkened, awaiting for the other half that will never come. Banished to the darkness as they had forsaken the light they wait without hope for the first of many to call them back home." She let out a sigh. "The first of many loves will never be easy for the winds of change blow harshly and the darkness will fight back against its fiery light." The words were almost chilling and I pulled back from her embrace, wiping at the tears.

"It is okay to be scared, Liv. Having a passion that burns like a thousand suns for a single person seems terrifying." She gave me a look and I pushed her shoulder gently. "But embrace the fear because Rhex would never let you burn." She pressed her forehead to mine, clasping the back of my neck gently.

"He would never let you burn." Ani's voice brought me so much comfort it was like I had been wrapped in a warm blanket. She was right, Rhex would never leave me to burn from the intensity of our bond. He would be standing right beside me holding my hand.

26

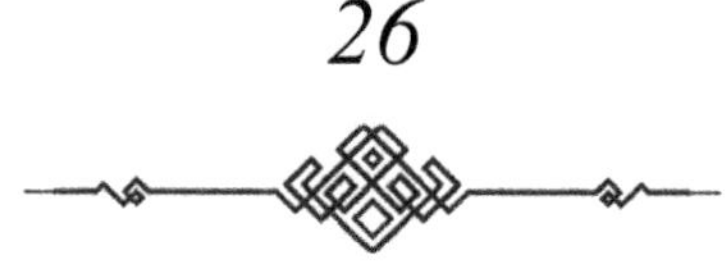

"Liv." Just hearing his voice was enough to make me feel better. I let out a shuddering breath, holding the phone to my ear tightly. The roughness of his tone still sent goosebumps across my flesh, as if the hundreds of light years that separated us were nothing more than a foot of space. I missed him and just being allowed to hear his voice was enough to ease that ache slightly. It had been a week and I missed him more than I had ever thought was possible.

"Rhex." My voice was a faint croak. It had been a long week without him. The Learning Centre had only done so much and while Ani was great for keeping some of the feelings away, she couldn't do it all. I had missed him and his presence and while the intensity of it scared me, the feeling of abject loneliness almost tempered the fear. He was my soulmate and I knew I would have to grow used to the intensity of the feelings I had for him.

"How are you?" His voice slid over me making me shudder. I curled up in the chair, pulling my knees up to my chest. I was thankful for the translator as I spoke to him. I wanted to close my eyes and just curl up with the sound of his voice rolling over me. It was so calming and peaceful.

"I've been better." I gave a small, almost raspy chuckle. I had only felt worse as he moved further and further away from me. I had stabilized somewhat yesterday, the symptoms hadn't gotten any worse, which I was thankful for. I assumed he made it to his training base.

"I know. Me too." He let out a heavy sigh and I could almost feel the weight of it pressing down on me. There was a faint moment of silence as I shifted, resting my chin on my knees and curling up a bit further in my chair. I wanted to urge him to keep talking but I didn't know how. Words felt strange in my mouth, how could I have pleasant conversation with him when I missed him to the point where I wanted to cry?

"I miss you." They were the only words that could roll off my tongue and I said it quietly and I felt almost a bit embarrassed at the admission. He was my mate but I wasn't fully aware of what that had meant for my emotions. Everything was different with him, stronger and more potent.

"I miss you too." He gave a small cough and I could hear people chattering in the background. There was a loud bark of laughter and I hoped that he had someone to help him out through the separation like I did. "What is your favourite colour?" The question caught me off guard and I couldn't help how I smiled at it.

"Light green." It had used to be ruby red but Rhex had changed that. He was changing a lot about me but I was finding I didn't particularly mind. I just hoped that I was changing him as well. It was selfish of me but I wanted him to think of something and be reminded of me.

"That does not have something to do with my eyes, does it?" There was a faint note of teasing to his voice and I felt my cheeks flush bright red. I glanced around and Ani was moving around the room as if not paying attention but I knew her. Her ears were wide open.

"Maybe." I said it quietly so she wouldn't hear but she whirled around.

"Look at you! Your face is all red!" Ani sidled closer to me and I waved her off, trying to hide my embarrassment. Ani would never let me live it down. She was a pest but she was for a reason. I appreciated her for doing what she did.

"Go away." I shoved at her playfully, wanting her to leave me alone for a moment. She was stuck to me like a barnacle, not that I minded. She was a very good friend. It felt nice to have a friend so close. I wanted Ami'la to be with me as well but she was busy with her work. I was happy that Ani was with me though, I wouldn't have switched her with anyone else out there in the universe.

"Who is that?" Rhex sounded curious and I gave a small chuckle as Ani pouted, her bottom lip sticking out. I stuck my tongue out at her in faint teasing.

"Ani. She's a new friend." I watched as Ani fluttered her eyelashes and pressed her hands to her chest as if I had said something touching. I smiled at her slightly, holding the phone tighter to my ear.

"Did you meet her at the Learning Centre?" Rhex sounded hesitant and I nodded despite the fact he couldn't see. I wondered if he knew what dangers were lurking for me while I learned about his culture.

"Yah. She helps me with my work." I was getting better, I knew a few more words of Orrian but it was slow going. Ani told me I was improving greatly and I knew all the thanks went to her for it. She was a patient teacher, a very patient one who dealt with me bursting into tears over my homework assignments because the feeling of missing Rhex became unbearable.

"That is good. You need allies." His voice was gruff but I could hear the notes of relief in his voice. He was relieved that I had someone else in my corner, that I would have someone here to protect me when he couldn't possibly reach me.

"Her face is red!" Ani said it loudly near the phone and I jumped. I hadn't seen her move closer. I gave a small groan as I shoved at her again, wanting her to move away before my face flushed even more with embarrassment.

"Go away!" I hissed it at her and I could hear Rhex chuckling. It was a rough and relaxed sound that had me relaxing as well.

"She is keeping you occupied?" There was a faint teasing note in his voice that had me scrunching my face up at Ani. She made a face at me in return before twirling around the room as if she were a ballet dancer.

"Yes." I watched her for a moment, she certainly kept me occupied with numerous things. There wasn't a day she didn't have me doing something to keep my mind occupied.

"She has my thanks." He said it with a note of serious respect and I knew Ani had made an ally with my mate. He respected her for what she was doing for me, for keeping me occupied when he was gone.

"You are welcome!" Ani stuck her head over my shoulder and I glared at her even as Rhex gave a bark of laughter.

"You're a pest." I shoved at her again and she slowly rolled down to the floor, moving in slow motion and making drawn out noises. She was making it seem as though my shove had a serious effect on her as she gave a long groan and pretended to die on the carpet.

"She seems happy." Rhex seemed amused and I grinned as I stuck my tongue out at her as her eyes cracked open.

"She's an obnoxiously happy individual." I made a face at her and she propped her head up on her hand with a rather shit eating grin on her face.

"Does that... does it help?" Rhex said it carefully and despite him not elaborating I knew what he was asking and I wondered if he had found someone to help him with how he was feeling. If I didn't have Ani I didn't know what I would do or how I would feel.

"It keeps it at bay for the most part." There were still moments when it got too much and I almost broke down but she helped keep most of it away from me. I was glad for it as well.

"For the most part?" He sounded uneasy and I let out a heavy sigh.

"I'm not going to lie, Rhex. This is hard. *Really* hard for me at times." There was no explanation for how it felt without him, as if half of my soul was gone. Like I was missing something important, like I had an important limb or organ taken from me but I wasn't sure what it was, I was just aware that it was gone.

"Fifteen weeks left, Liviya. That is all." There was a faint strain to his tone and I closed my eyes. Fifteen weeks might has well have been a lifetime away.

"That's a long time." It was too long to be away from the man who was my husband, the man who the Source had deemed was my one and true partner. The only one that would ever be for me. If I lost him I would lose the other half of who I was, it was how the soulmate system was.

"I know." He let out a heavy sigh and a small silence fell between us. Ani sat up and nudged at my knee with her foot, gesturing me to continue the conversation.

"How is training going?" It was all I could think of to say to keep the conversation going. I needed to know as much as I could about him.

"We have not done much. Just went through the itinerary and I will be busy." That was good. I felt relief that he would have something to take his attention off of things. I just hoped he would be busy enough that he wouldn't be able to dwell.

"That's good." It was because it pained me to think he would be feeling as I did when I could fix it. I didn't like the thought just as I knew he didn't.

"How are things in the Learning Centre? Are you learning much?" At that I gave a small grimace. People still hated me and Kher was probably still trying to plot my death.

I shook the thoughts away. "I'm learning a lot about the war with the Kengans and the general history. I know a few words of Orrian now." I was almost excited at the prospect of showing him how much I was learning about his culture.

"Really? Just give me a second." There was the sound of rustling as if the phone was set down before he came back. "Okay, I have my translator out. Show me?" I wanted him to be proud of me. I wanted to show him that I wasn't as different or as stupid as everyone thought I was.

"Star year is *seh'lan ahske*." I stumbled over the foreign words slightly and Rhex chuckled.

"Good! But it is *sEH'lan Ahske*. But it was good. You are doing very very well." His praise meant the world to me. There was a difference between Ani telling me I did good and having Rhex do it. There was more of a warmth, of a pride to it.

"Hello is *ahl'enhe*." That one I knew I had spot on and Rhex gave a noise of satisfaction that had me beaming.

"That was perfect." His voice was low and filled with pride and I wiggled in my seat happily. I was happy he thought I was doing well. I wanted to learn as much as I could about his language to actually talk to him without the translators.

"Kengan is *Slegranadeh*." At that my mood fell slightly. "It's really close to *slegrnd*." Ani winced at the use of the word and Rhex inhaled sharply.

"Do not use that term, Liviya." His words were harsh and I lowered my gaze to the floor. It was what I was called, a half-breed but they called me a name similar to the one they spat out about their longest standing enemy. It spoke of my place in their society. I wasn't wanted and because of my blood, because of my humanity, I never would be.

"Why? It just illustrates how your culture views me. I am similar to your most hated enemy." I glanced at Ani and she reached out and squeezed my leg, her eyes speaking an apology she had no business giving me. It wasn't her fault or her burden. She shouldn't have had to feel the need to apologize to me on behalf of her culture.

"I cannot understand you. Give me a moment." The rustling was back and Rhex said something guttural to someone in the background before he must have picked the phone back up. "You aren't to use that word, Liviya. Do not let that tarnish who you are." There was a serious reprimand to his tone and I shrugged. I was used to the word, nearly everyone spat it at me when I walked by.

"That is how everyone sees me. I am so close to an enemy-"

"No. You are not that name, Liviya. They call you it but you are Liviya Mary DharSon, you are my mate and my wife. You are more than they could imagine! Do not let that name destroy who you are as a person. You are more than your blood." There was a tense silence before he let out a breath. "Besides that name is inaccurate, you are more than a half-breed. More like two thirds-breed." At his words my mouth dropped open.

"Did you... did you just make a joke?" A wide smile crossed his face before he gave a small strained chuckle.

"Yes." At the rather sheepishly said word I burst out laughing. Ani tilted her head at me and I held my mouth over the phone receiver, trying to stifle my laughter.

"He just made a joke, a very funny inside one." I managed to get it out through chuckles and peals of laughter and Ani slowly nodded, giving me a look that had me laughing harder. I could hear Rhex laughing along with me and I felt a pang in my chest that had the laughter tapering off. "I miss you. *So much.*" Tears burned at my eyes as the words escaped and I pressed my hand to my forehead, fighting back the urge to cry. My dad had told me it would be painful but I didn't expect it would be this bad. I just wanted Rhex to be with me. I *ached* for it.

"The moon and the stars shined in your eyes the day I took you to the observatory. You looked like you should have been with them because you lit up like nothing I had ever seen before." There was a firm note of longing to his tone that made my breath hitch in my chest.

"Why are you telling me that?" I blinked back the tears but was forced to wipe my eyes to get them to disappear.

"Because I know that when I get back, it will not be the stars that make you light up. It will be me." His voice was rough and I felt my chin quiver from the need to cry. Tears once again flooded my eyes. "I hold onto that with everything that I am." His voice was rougher and he gave a small cough as if to clear a lump from his throat.

"Why does this have to be so messed up?" My words were a whisper and he made a sound in the back of his throat.

"Fifteen weeks. That is all I will ever ask of you, Liv." Fifteen weeks was too much but I had no other options. I had to go through it. I had to listen to his voice and know that he couldn't touch me, couldn't hold me and it *hurt*. It made everything ache even worse.

"You keep busy." I choked the words out. I couldn't keep it together for any longer and I didn't want him hear me cry.

"Liv..." He gave a heavy sigh. "There are no words to describe how much it aches without you by my side. I never knew how much a soul could ache before I left you." He said it low and I pinched my lips together to keep the sobs at bay as my vision blurred with tears that burned my cheeks. "I need to go but I will call again next week. Remember that I miss you with everything that I am." The line went dead and I sniffled as my chest tightened. I set the phone back in its cradle and closed my eyes. Ani shushed me gently as my shoulders shook from the sobs I stifled behind my hand.

"It will be okay. It will be fine. We will get you through this." She climbed onto the chair with me, wrapping her arms around me tightly, tucking me under her chin. The action reminded me of my mother and I let out a shuddering sob before I clung to her tightly.

Ani was all the comfort I had in this moment. I was alone in the world without her by my side. I was taken from my home and stuck in a sea of what I now knew was hate and I didn't know if I had the strength to keep swimming or if I would simply drown under it all.

"I am here for you and it will be okay." Her words were said with conviction and I held to her tightly. I knew she would be there for me but I also knew it wouldn't be okay until I was wrapped in Rhex's arms. Nothing would make it okay other than that.

27

Four weeks later

"What the *hell,* Liv?" Ani shoved my bedroom door open, throwing a full pill bottle onto my covers. I blinked at her slowly. I was too tired and feeling too crappy to listen to her rant at me. "We got those so you can *sleep!* You have not been taking them!" I pulled my covers over my head and closed my eyes. I just wanted to stay in bed and never leave, she had woken me up way too early.

I groaned as she ripped the blankets off my bed and jumped on me. "They upset my stomach." I tried to take them. I *really* did but when it made me feel like my stomach was turning inside out I couldn't justify taking them when they made me feel that horrible.

"That is why we got you the anti-nausea pills!" She shook me and I cracked an eye at her before rolling onto my back, shimmying underneath her to do so.

"Which give me migraines and cotton mouth which I take three other pills to combat and then with those I have to take pills for because of their side effects." So many pills it was hard to keep track of. However it was what Nadila and the medi-bot had forced me to take. Although Nadila and Ani had to physically restrain me from knocking the medi-bot's head off every time it said it diagnosed a separated bond and to find my soulmate to correct it.

"I'm on enough medication to choke a horse, Ani." I looked at her and she gave me a little shake again as she straddled my hips. I hated that this was now a daily occurrence. Ani was a morning person, I was not.

"What?" Her expression screwed up into confusion and I heaved out a sigh.

"It's an expression stating large volumes of something, sorry." I kept forgetting that while she spoke English very well, she did not have a full grasp of our sayings or expressions.

"Well you need to take them or you do not sleep well because of nightmares and you feel like shit." She poked my nose and I wrinkled it in distaste. That didn't matter.

"I feel like shit regardless. Except for when I-"

"For when you talk to your hot piece of ass, I know. I live with you remember?" She mimed crying and I tried to knee her in the back with a scowl but she twisted so I merely thumped against her spine. "Then you phone him and you are good for like a day and then you are back to being all weird." I grabbed my pillow from beneath my head and smacked her with it.

"Let's have your soulmate several thousand light years away and see how *you* feel." It was one thing to watch a person go through it and another entirely to experience it for one's self.

"*I* would turn on the shower." She stuck her tongue out and I gave an over exaggerated shudder at the mention.

"Ew. Keep your touchy feely mist to yourself." That was the last thing I wanted to do, once was enough for me. "Why are you really bothering me?" There was an actual reason for it, I just had to get it out of her.

"The pills." She picked up the pill bottle and shook them in my face, dodging my hand when I attempted to swat them away.

"I won't take them." I wouldn't. I had enough of taking ten pills in the morning and ten at night. I was done with that.

"I knew you would say that and that is why we are going to go see Ghilesh today. So get your butt out of bed! We are leaving in fifteen minutes." She hopped off of me and I let out a loud groan.

"It's too early!" It was far too early to wake up, especially since I had nightmares as I attempted to sleep. Ani would say it was my fault for not taking my pills and I had to reluctantly agree. I reached for my blankets and Ani grabbed them with a triumphant '*Ha!*' and ran from my room.

I sat up, pushing my hair back as I grumbled about her childish behaviour. I just wanted to sleep more, to just fall unconscious for a few more hours. It wasn't that much to ask for. I knew it was such a little thing to request but Early-Bird-Ani thought otherwise.

It had been four weeks since my first phone call with Rhex. I had another four calls to him, each one between only twenty minutes and half an hour. It didn't seem nearly long enough for me. I could have spent hours curled up with the phone listening to his voice. The calls were both happy and sad. They made me feel better but at the same time highlighted just how far away he was, which made me feel worse.

I was stuck on an emotional roller coaster and I couldn't get off. I wasn't used to that feeling, my hormones were all out of whack and I didn't know how to fix them. I rubbed at my face as I stood up, it was too early in the morning to think of my emotional state. When I was a sleep deprived zombie I didn't even want to think about getting dressed, let alone the state of my emotions. Which was somewhere between '*I am literally crying over spilled milk.*' and '*I laughed so hard I started crying because my brain can no longer tell the difference between happy and sad.*' It was ridiculous, completely and totally ridiculous.

"Hurry up, Liv!" Ani's voice held a warning that told me she would drag me out of the apartment half-naked if I didn't do as she said

"I hate you!" I grumbled as I got changed. She was so bossy at times.

"I love you too!" She sung it loudly and I practically stumbled out of my room as I rubbed my eyes.

"You better put my blanke-" I was cut off by the large bundle of blankets flying through the air and smacking me in the face. I stumbled backwards with a muffled cry and Ani laughed hysterically as I righted myself. "I'm going to murder you!" I tossed the blankets in the general direction of the bed before stalking into the living room to look for the pain in my ass.

"You love me too much to kill me." She made a kissy face at me and I flipped her off despite the upwards twitch my mouth was attempting to do. If there was one thing that Ani was good at, it was distraction.

"One of these days." I shook my head at her and she tossed my shoes in my direction before gesturing at them impatiently.

"Come on! We have to go!" She gestured to me again as she pulled on her own shoes and I scowled at her darkly.

"Why's there such a rush?" It was too early for her to be pushing me around and dragging me places. I would have thought that she would have understood by now just how much I was not a morning person. That issue was exasperated by being separated from Rhex. When all you wanted to do was lie in bed and sleep then having someone yank you out of it was not welcome.

"Because I told Ghilesh yesterday that we would be there early this morning. We are already running late." She came over as I was slipping on me shoes and I frowned in confusion, ignoring her as she started pushing me towards the door.

"When did you speak to Ghilesh?" I didn't particularly remember her talking to him yesterday and she made a sound in her throat.

"While you were trying to read your mushy love letter from Rhex." She stopped pushing me to open up the door and my face flared red.

"It wasn't a mushy love letter." I muttered the words out. It was simply a letter. He sent me one a week and they basically told me of little things about himself and what he was doing in training. I liked them.

"You are right. The man must be completely physical because his letters show me he has no imagination." She made a face at me and I punched her arm. She just stuck her tongue out at me, letting me know that the hit did nothing to her.

"I imagine it has something to do with the fact we have a snoopy person translating them." I pointed at her accusingly and she touched her chest as if offended.

"Me? Snoopy? *Please*, you have the wrong person." The smile tugging at her lips let me know just how much of a lie her words were. I rolled my eyes and stepped out of the apartment, Ani close behind me. I was ignored by the few Orrians that lingered. I was actually partial to the ignoring, at least I didn't feel as unsafe with that as I did with the blatant hatred.

Ani grabbed my hand and dragged me towards the stair well. I groaned but let her pull me along. The more she dictated my actions the less I had to think about things. It was easier when I didn't have to think, when I didn't have time to linger on the hollow ache where I felt my soul should be.

"Why are we going to Ghilesh?" I was a little concerned that she was making appointments for me without my knowledge. It didn't matter that I was scanning Rhex's letter looking for familiar words and simply staring at the lettering, wishing he was closer.

"Hush and you will see when we get there." She actually shushed me and I scowled at her back. It was really too early for me to be up and socializing.

"I don't like surprises." I *really* didn't. I wanted to know what was going on.

"I know." Her voice was far too cheery and I almost stumbled on the stairs as she pulled me.

"Ani, slow down." At my words she gave me a quick apology and slowed down before she pushed the door open to Ghilesh's floor level. As much as I hated getting up early, I really did like visiting with Ghilesh. I sought out his door, the number symbols were still confusing but I was getting better at recognizing familiar ones. The Learning Centre taught me the history and the culture but it didn't teach me the basics of their language. I was thankful for Ani in regards to her continued help in making sure I understood what was being taught and said.

"Oh look, pretenders." Ani's voice was tight with derision and I looked up, a stone faced couple stood outside of Ghilesh's door. I winced at the sight of them. That was what the Orrians had been reduced to, forcing bonds that were unnatural and expecting them to work properly. They said something rapidly in Orrian to each other and Ani gave a scoffing sound of disgust before she said a retort loudly, wrapping her arm around my shoulders.

"*Slegrnd.*" The word was spat at my feet by the man and I blinked at him. I had three choices when confronted by such people. I could turtle underneath the word, I could hurl the abuse back, or I could take the high road.

"*Ahl'enhe, heh'rsh.*" I bowed my head at him in the customary greeting and he looked slightly startled and off-balance at my words. I glanced at the woman and bowed my head at her as well. "*Reh'rsh.*" I smiled at them both, knowing I had nailed the customary greetings. "*Seh'lan ahske haf'hal'ma nel'met'sh.*" I knew my pronunciation was off slightly on the friendly but formal blessing but it conveyed what I wished to as the woman blinked at me, glancing up at the man in confusion.

He swallowed before giving me a quick bow of his head in return to the friendly greeting. "*She'lantha.*" The woman said the response quickly before she and the man moved off quickly. I smirked slightly and Ani was practically vibrating with excitement.

"Your pronunciation was off." Ghilesh's tone was slightly crusty and Ani waved him off.

"Oh hush. She is doing very well! I'm so proud of her!" She gave me a hard hug and I hid my slight wince behind a smile towards the old Soul Maker. Ani needed to remember that I wasn't as hardy as an Orrian.

"I can see why. He looked ready to swallow his tongue in surprise." He chuckled gleefully at the thought and waved us both in. His apartment was even more cluttered than the last time I had been in it and I noticed a set of metal chimes hanging from one of the empty spaces on his roof. "Got those this morning. Had to go pick them out of the trash. One man's trash is another man's soul medallion." He gave another rasping chuckle and I raised my eyebrow, glancing at Ani as she glanced at me. It must have been Soul Maker humour.

"So you are here to try it are you?" He gave me a pointed look with those amber eyes of his twinkled as if in excitement. I glanced at Ani in warning before looking at Ghilesh. Whatever those two had planned I honestly didn't want any part of it.

"Try what now?" I kept my tone even but kept it sharp with an edge of warning.

"You shall see." Ghilesh smiled at me brightly and within my mind I could almost imagine him as a wolf with that toothy grin. This did not bode well for me. I was going to be his guinea pig again.

It *really* was too early in the morning for this shit.

28

"Ghilesh, I'm not asking again. What am I supposedly trying?" I stared at him. I did not want to try anything he had cooked up, especially when I didn't remember agreeing to it.

"An obscure concoction I found that it supposed to help with soul separation." He smiled at me and I narrowed my eyes at him slightly, ignoring the faint pang of pain in my chest at the reminder. There was always a catch with him. The soulmate bond fascinated him intensely and I honestly didn't want to be a guinea pig again. "Why are you giving me that look, Liviya?" He moved around in his room and I narrowed my eyes further. Ani shoved at me with a look, I waved her off with a scowl.

"Because you have a catch, Ghilesh." I pointed at him and he scowled, muttering to himself as he gathered some pungent smelling herbs and dried plants.

"So trusting, Liviya." He looked at me and I made a face at him as he rolled eyes. "It is technically made for those that have lost their soul medallions and not for separated mate bonds." I knew it.

"Ghilesh." I drug his name out and he held up his hand.

"I have done some research and this *should* help with your separation." He gave me a stern look. "Yes, you will be a guinea pig but the best thing that could happen is that it helps and the worst is that it does nothing. There is honestly nothing you can really lose here, Liviya." He started to put the herbs and dried plants into his small cauldron. I watched him as I mulled it over. It might have been better than me taking my myriad of pills just so I could attempt to get a good night's sleep.

"Will it have any side effects?" That was the main thing I wanted to know. Those pills had far too many side effects for me take them in any way that made me feel safe.

"Do you have any allergies?" He started pouring things into the cauldron and I glanced at Ani as she cleared off a chair.

"Not that I'm aware of." I looked back at Ghilesh and he shook his head slightly.

"Then no. Sit. Sit." He waved absently at the empty chair across from Ani and I took it, sinking into the comfy chair with a wide yawn. I brought my knees up to my chest and wrapped my arms around them as I closed my eyes.

"No sleeping, Liv." Ani's voice was teasing and I cracked my eye open.

"Shush, Ani. Let me nap." A nap sounded so nice. I knew that if everyone was quiet for just a few seconds I would be able to fall asleep for just a little bit. There had been too many nightmares last night for me to sleep properly.

"Both of you need to be quiet. I need to concentrate." Ghilesh sounded slightly irritated and I smirked at Ani before closing my eyes again. She had to listen to Ghilesh and that meant I got some uninterrupted nap time. I sighed and sunk further into the chair. I needed the sleep, not being able to sleep was something I was not used to, nor did I like.

I was missing Rhex terribly. Ani had been some what right in her assertion that I was too distracted with Rhex's letter to pay attention to what was going on around me. Even though I couldn't read what he wrote, I simply liked looking at the lettering, looking at the strokes his pencil took on the paper. It made me feel closer to him to imagine him writing the letter to me.

Ani had translated it for me last night. It was his usual type of letter, basic statements about how his training was going and what he was doing. There was a few statements about how he missed me and how he was counting the weeks until he could get back. We were at ten weeks and six days left. It still felt like far too much for me to deal with but I had no choice.

I practically lived for the days when his letters arrived or when I could call him. I just needed that small piece of him that made him feel just a tiny fraction closer to me. Even if it was simply his voice or a faint scent on a piece of paper. It was almost pathetic if I thought about it long enough. I was never a person who felt like this for anyone that I had ever met before. I wasn't a person who felt like they would fall apart while not being in someone's presence. I wasn't this *needy*.

Ghilesh's muttering was a soothing background noise and I felt myself fall backwards into the cusp between sleep and consciousness. It was a familiar feeling just hanging between the two states. It happened often ever since Rhex had gone to training. Over a month of not being able to sleep or to sleep properly was draining for me.

"Have you two spoken to Nadila?" Ghilesh's question pulled me out of the state I had fallen into and I nodded.

"She said we could go down to visit my parents next week." That had been a brightening bit of news. Going to my parents and taking Ani to see the old ruins was a perfect way to spend the weekend. I hoped that it would be enough to take my mind off things. I just hoped that the trip there and back wouldn't be too stressful for me. I really did hate flying.

"Doing well at the Learning Centre then?" His tone was light and teasing as she glanced at me.

Ani chuckled happily, giving a clap of her hands. "She has good comprehension for the studies we are doing." Which was all thanks to her translating and walking me through it. I had learned much about their history even if I didn't comprehend much about their language. I could greet someone and use proper terms for them and I could almost hold a small talk conversation but I wasn't quite there.

"Good, good." He made a clucking sound with his tongue before it sounded like he shuffled some things around. I didn't feel like opening my eyes but Ghilesh grasping my hand and putting a cup into it had them opening regardless. "Drink." He watched me intently and I looked at the cup before slowly uncurling from my spot. I stared at the cup warily before looking into it. The liquid was a dark colour and when I sniffed it, it smelled minty.

I let out a heavy sigh, there was no getting out of it from my standpoint. I took a large gulp and the liquid was thicker than I thought it would be and it made me almost want to cough as I swallowed it down. It had a rather bland and stale taste with a hint of spice but it wasn't unpleasant, just strange. I finished the cup off and wrinkled my nose. I didn't feel any different.

"Alright. How do you feel?" Ghilesh had his notepad out and I rolled my eyes at it.

"The same." The moment the words escaped my mouth there was an uncomfortable heat that started in my belly and came up my chest and to my throat. Like it had followed the path the liquid had taken. "Okay. Something's happening." It felt slightly similar to when I had drank the bonding potion Ghilesh had made for Rhex and I but this felt heavier, more unnatural and slightly wrong. Like a shoe on the wrong foot.

"Explain." He scratched some notes onto his notepad and I made a face as it seemed to attempt to fill the place Rhex had vacated in his leaving. It was wrong. Nothing was fitting right.

"It's a heavier feeling, like my body feels too cramped. It's trying to fill the space where Rhex should be but it doesn't fit right." It felt weird and unnatural and it ached slightly, like the feeling one got when they ate just a bit too much but it was deeper within me.

"I bet that has to do with the fact that you are already bonded to another person. Rhex still occupies some space in your soul so it's not settling in the way it should." He frowned as he said it, his eyes on his note pad. "Are the effects of the separation gone?" I couldn't really focus on anything he was saying.

"No clue. I can't really think right now to be honest." That was the simple truth to it all. With my body feeling as strange as it did and my mind feeling a bit wonky, there was no time to think. I rubbed at my chest. It felt too cramped under my skin.

"Hmmmm... Hopefully it helps. We do not want you to feel so poorly. Not anymore, you are growing on us." He winked at me and I made a face, my cheeks flushing at the uncomfortable warmth that moved through my body.

"Her cheeks are really red." Ani tilted her head as she looked at me and I rubbed at my face.

"That's because I feel uncomfortably warm right now." It was like I had warm air blowing on my face and I couldn't escape it. I could almost feel the sweat starting to emerge. It was a gross feeling.

"Alright. Well you don't seem to be having any other issues with it." Ghilesh closed his notepad and set it off to the side. I looked at him through the corner of my eyes.

"*Yet.*" That was the clear distinction. I was not really liking the warmth that had taken residence underneath my skin and deep into my bones. It was just... weird and I didn't like the feeling it left in me. I had no clue what else could be waiting for me in regards to side effects.

"So trusting, Liv." Ghilesh smirked at me, his amber eyes twinkling.

"You're so lucky that I don't know how to cuss you out in Orrian." I glowered at him as I wiped my forehead. It was far too warm in my body at the moment and it wasn't a pleasant feeling. Like a fever without any other symptoms and it was almost growing slightly worse.

"Oh you are so dramatic." He smiled at me as he waved me away in an almost teasing way.

"You aren't the guinea pig so you can say that." I made a face at him and he shooed me slightly.

"Well this little guinea pig needs to go home." He moved closer, continuing his shooing motion.

I rolled my eyes and stood up with a groan at the same time Ani stood up. "I want a nap when I get home." I looked at Ani as I wrinkled my nose and she waved me off impatiently as she stretched.

"We have work to do, Liv." She smirked at me slightly and I narrowed my eyes at her slightly. I just wanted to have a nap. I deserved it after her waking me up so rudely.

"Like what, Ani?" I didn't truly want to know what she had planned for the day. I could imagine that it was something that kept me busy to the point where I would collapse into my bed at the end of the day.

"You two can argue on your way back to your apartment." Ghilesh put his hands on my shoulders as he pushed me towards the door. "You really *are* warm." He sounded almost surprised and I rolled my eyes again. They were starting to hurt I was rolling them that much.

"I wasn't lying." I threw a look at him over my shoulder and he winked at me, amusement clear on his face.

"You never do." He kissed my cheek and gently pushed me out of the door, Ani following me. "Tell me if you feel anything else." He gave me a small wave and I nodded with a small smile. The air on the balcony was slightly cooler than his apartments and it was a relief to me.

It brushed over my heated skin and I shivered in delight. Ani slipped her arm around my own, linking us together.

"So we are going to practice language today!" Her voice was incredibly chipper and I gave a heavy groan.

"Nooooo..." I drug the word out but she ignored me as she drug me towards the stairwell. I could see several Orrians staring at me but to my surprise there were very few glares.

Ani waved at them wildly. "*Ahl'enhe*!" She practically shouted the greeting and everyone looked away. I felt a smile tug at my lips at her exuberant nature. When I was tired it was more fun to have her energy directed at others rather than me.

"Hush, they might push us both over the railing if you are too loud." I felt a chuckle build in my throat as she gave a gasp and pressed her hand to her chest.

"Well, I never!" She said it loudly and threw a playful suspicious look around us, tugging me closer. "I do not know who to trust nowadays! Shame on them all!" She pointed her fingers at the others and they avoided looking at us. I chuckled low and leaned my head against her arm. As much Ani irritated me sometimes, she was a great friend.

"So anyway. Language is mandatory for the day. We are learning the alphabet!" She wiggled and I groaned heavily. Back to being irritated it was. I had seriously woken up too early for *that*.

29

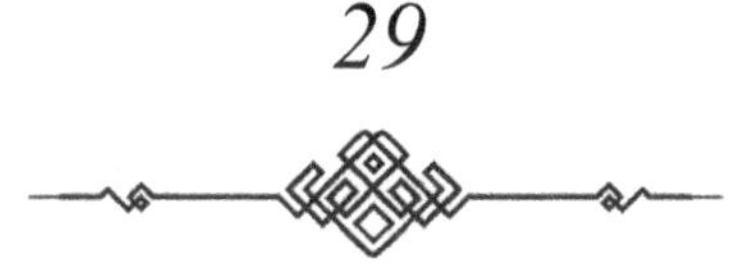

Three days later

I leaned over, taking in deep breaths and trying to get my shaking limbs under control as Ani rubbed my back. I *hated* flying. I could repeat it over and over again and it would never change. I crouched down, trying to keep my breakfast from coming back up.

"You *really* do not like flying." Ani said it slowly and I coughed, holding back a gag.

"No shit, Sherlock." I wheezed it out as I rubbed at my chest. It felt too tight and too heavy. I *really* hated flying.

"What?" She sounded so confused and I tried to focus on my breathing as I waved at her weakly.

"It's just a saying. I can't explain it right now. Need to breathe." I focused on my breathing. In and out. In and out. My limbs shook and I pressed a hand to the floor to help me stay upright so I wouldn't fall over into a trembling heap.

"Still have that issue, Liviya?" Ami'la's voice was teasing and I lifted my head to look at her. I gave her a weak smile. I was very happy to see her even though I knew I looked like a trembling, sweaty mess.

"Always, Ami'la." I doubted I would ever get over the fear I had of flying. I attempted to get to my feet and Ani helped me, keeping steady hands on me so I wouldn't fall over on my shaky legs.

"Come here and give me a hug." She moved over, I almost expected to hear her heels clicking on the floor but she was surprisingly dressed casually, with sneakers of all things. Her arms wrapped around me and she gave me a quick hug. Ani made a slightly disgruntled sound in her throat and I glanced at her as Ami'la let me go.

Ani looked rather wary of the new woman. "Who are *you* exactly?" She looked confused but her tone was hard and I gestured between them, even as Ami'la looked rather affronted by the tone.

"Ani'tah, this was my case worker and is my good friend Ami'la. Ami'la, this is my good friend Ani'tah from the ship, she's my roommate." I was starting to feel a bit better, my limbs not shaking as badly and the fear slowly seeping out of my body. I wiped at my forehead, hating the stickiness that I felt.

"Very pleased to meet you, Ani'tah." Ami'la held out her hand for Ani and she took it quickly, giving it a friendly and rather enthusiastic shake. All confusion and wariness gone from her form.

"Likewise. So are all Orrians down here friendly to humans or is it just you?" Her tone was earnest and I pinched my nose and closed my eyes with a sigh. Ani lacked tact sometimes.

"Umm, well..." Ami'la sounded a bit caught off guard at the question and I silently apologized to her. "A lot of us work closely with humans so we are generally friendly towards them. We wouldn't have a good working relationship otherwise." She started out slowly before she seemed to gain some confidence in what she was saying, losing the slight shock at the sudden question.

"Okay. I was just wondering because nearly everyone on the ship looks at Liv like they want to toss her over the railing into the shipping bay." At that Ami'la made a choked sound in the back of her throat.

I finally looked at her with a wry smile. "Ani doesn't know when to stop talking." I gave Ami'la a look, rolling my eyes slightly. I doubted Ani was listening to me or simply ignored me because she didn't react to my statement.

"I want to move to Earth after the Learning Centre. I will live right beside you if I can, Liv." She grabbed my arm, wrapping hers around it in excitement. I honestly didn't want to argue with her about it because living on Earth with Rhex was something that I hadn't actually thought about and it sounded wonderful. Not having to live among those that hated me and being in a community that would be more accepting of Rhex and I as a pairing was something I hoped to the Source we could have.

"Everything okay on the ship?" Ami'la looked at me and I shrugged slightly rubbing at my chest. The action more of a habit than me actually trying to rub the ache away. Surprisingly the concoction I had drunk had done its purpose. I was still prone to getting hot flashes randomly and that empty area that Rhex had occupied before still felt too full and unnatural but I wasn't in as much pain as before. I was still tired and still having some nightmares but it was better.

"People are getting used to me and no one has full on attempted to murder me yet, so that's good." I was still breathing, that was the main thing. I could deal with the aches and the separation as long as I was still surviving. Rhex would be back in almost ten weeks and I could survive that. I was nearly at the halfway point and it was enough for now.

"Still sarcastically morbid, I see." She raised an eyebrow at me and I smirked at her.

"Admit it, it's part of my charm." I needed the small conversation with her. I *needed* that normalcy, especially since everything was now in chaos for me. I lacked normalcy and so this was a treat for me. I was even happier that Ami'la was coming with us to my parent's home. I had sort of planned a get together with all of us and forgot to tell Ani that Ami'la was joining us. Although I had to admit I did it on purpose for her waking me up so goddamned early in the morning all week.

"Just like your hair. It's too long." She tugged on a strand of it, a soft smirk on her face. Her words were more to tease than to reprimand.

"Rhex likes it long." I patted it self-consciously, my face going slightly red.

"Oooooooooh." Ani nudged me repeatedly as she made the sound and wiggled her eyebrows. "Does he now? What else does he like? His hair being touched? Massages?" I rolled my eyes and looked at Ami'la as Ani continued to ramble.

"Ignore her. I try to." Try being the key word. Ani was hard to drown out sometimes.

The woman in question wiggled excitedly. "Does he like bubble baths? Oooooh does he like his toes being licked?" At that I shoved at her, making a disgusted face.

"*Ani*!" That was not something I wanted to imagine. She simply laughed loudly and poked my cheeks. I was glad she found humour. in her words because I was not. I glanced at Ami'la in slight embarrassment and my mouth dropped open when I saw she was covering her mouth, hiding her own giggles. "Oh you two are impossible!" I wiggled my arm out of Ani's grasp and walked away from them both quickly. Despite the slight embarrassment I felt, I was trying hard not to join in on their amusement.

"Oh come on, Liv." Ani gave a huff. "Lighten up. Just because Rhex likes his toes being licked-"

"Ani!" I covered my face and hurried away from them. They were both embarrassing. I had to admit that Ami'la probably deserved to embarrass me for all the times I made her squirm with my sense of humour but Ani was just being a brat.

I had an arm wrap around my shoulder and Ani chuckled as she gave me a friendly squeeze. "I am just teasing. I have never been down here so my excitement is off the charts!" She gave a happy little squeal as she practically vibrated with her excitement.

"You've never been down here before?" Ami'la sounded surprised as she looped her arm around mine on the opposite side from Ani.

"Never." Ani did a happy little wiggle as we walked down the hall and Ami'la made a noise in her throat.

"We have to take her for so many things, Liviya." She looked at me with wide eyes and I nodded. Ani was missing out on quite a few things and I was more than happy to show them to her.

"That we do but first we have to go to my parents." I was excited to see them again. I loved my parents dearly and not seeing them for a month was grating for me. I knew I still had a fair bit of time before I would see them again so I was going to savour the feeling of being at home.

"Are you sure I am alright to join in?" Ami'la sounded unsure about the situation and I didn't blame her. She felt like she was imposing and no matter how many times I told her it was okay.

I gave a quick nod. "Without a doubt. My parents are thrilled you're both coming." I had never brought friends home before so when Nadila had allowed me to talk to them to make plans they had been very excited to hear that I would be bringing some friends with me.

We finally made it out of the building and into the government supplied car. Ani stared at everything with wide eyes and both Ami'la and I chuckled at her innocence as she asked what the car was as we got in it. She pointed at numerous things and asked what they were as we drove by them. I hadn't realized how much she truly didn't know about my own culture. It was a fun change to teach her about my culture instead of her teaching me about hers.

Having her with me also highlighted just how separated our worlds were. There was nothing saying we couldn't mingle, share our cultures but prejudices kept us apart. Even when one *wanted* to mingle, the attitudes made it nearly impossible. Humans were accepting but Orrians simply weren't. It was a difficult time navigating the some time hostile waters between the two of them.

"So cars drive you from place to place. Like ships that do not leave the ground?" Ani looked at me and Ami'la and we both nodded. "And they use... *wheels*?" She sounded a bit off put by that and we nodded again. "That is so... *primitive*." She made a face and I laughed at it.

"It works." When something wasn't broken, you didn't fix it. I preferred them to the levitating models that one could get. Those ones reminded me too much of flying to use comfortably.

"It is just strange." Ani looked a bit off-kilter and I didn't blame her, experiencing a new culture was shocking at first.

"You will find many things strange. I know I did when I first started working on Earth. You get used to them and in most cases you start to prefer them. I can't really stomach ship food after years of human cuisine. They have so many different varieties and flavours." Ami'la let out a happy sigh and I nodded in agreement. Ship food was fairly bland and strange compared to the food I grew up on.

"I cannot wait!" She wiggled excitedly in her spot as the car slowed down to a stop in front of my family home. Once again my mother stood out on the lawn but this time my father stood out beside her. Apparently he had learned his lesson the last time. I came by my stubbornness honestly.

"We're here." I opened the door and waved at my parents.

My mother hurried over and yanked me into a hug. "I'm so glad to see you!" She peppered my face with kisses and I simply smiled, enjoying her embrace. "Look at you! I'm just so happy you're here!" She hugged me tightly and I glanced at my dad over her shoulder and he winked at me, smiling in amusement.

"Oh! You must be Ani!" She let me go abruptly to grab Ani's hand and yank her close to give her a hug as well. "Very pleased to meet you! We are so excited you're here!" I stepped back, allowing my mum to smother Ani in affection. She looked alarmed as my mother kissed her cheeks and looked her over, speaking about how excited she was to see her and how beautiful she thought she was.

My dad wrapped an arm around my shoulders, giving me a gentle squeeze in welcome. I leaned against him with a slight smile as my mother moved from Ani to Ami'la. It was a more subdued but no less enthusiastic greeting. My parents had already met Ami'la before but there was no less affection to the greeting.

Ani moved closer to me, eyeing my mum warily. I wanted to laugh at the look on her face. She kind of looked like Rhex did the first time my mother did that to him. I had forgotten about how jarring it was for an Orrian to be confronted by physical affection.

"You must be Ani." My dad stuck out his hand and she jumped slightly, staring at him with wide eyes. I reached out and nudged her and her face went red before she shook his hand quickly. "Don't worry about Eliza. She's friendly like that towards everyone." My dad smiled softly at my mum's back as she gestured wildly in her storytelling for Ami'la.

I felt a pang in my chest of longing. I was surprised it wasn't an actual sharp pain but the potion I took had pretty much nullified those feelings. It didn't remove them but it dampened them until I could barely feel them. It had its own drawbacks but I was trying my best to ignore those.

"My name is Louis." My dad gave her a wide smile and gave me another squeeze around the shoulders. It felt nice to be back on Earth with my family. It had a feeling of normalcy to it that I craved.

"Nice to meet you. I am Ani'tah." Ani tucked her hands in her pockets and rocked back and forth as she looked around. It was clear she felt a bit out of her element and a tad overwhelmed and I didn't blame her. I knew that feeling all too well.

"I know all about you. I pulled your file." My dad said it brightly and I smacked his chest with the back of my hand quickly.

"Dad!" There was no reason for him to be pulling files on anyone and getting in trouble because he was feeling overprotective. We didn't need Orrians poking their noses into our family business any further than they were.

"I'm kidding." He chuckled before letting me go and moving towards my mum to rescue Ami'la.

"This is..." Ani looked at a loss for words and I smiled at her.

"Weird? Confusing? Not at all what you were expecting?" There was a myriad of words and phrases she could possibly use to describe her feelings. I knew because I had experienced the culture shock she was currently feeling. Except some of my feelings included severe anxiety and fear as well.

"A bit of all three with a bit of simply nice mixed in." She said it slowly and gave me a hesitant smile. She was still unsure of herself and I nodded before looping my arm through hers.

"Come inside. My parents have a library you will want to live in." It wasn't a fancy library by any means but for an Orrian that loved human literature, Ani would *adore* the library regardless of how it looked. "Mum, dad. I'm taking Ani inside."

"Alright, Liv. We will be along shortly." My mum waved us off with a bright smile that I returned before I lead Ani up the stairs and into the house. Once we removed our shoes, she slowed down her steps as she slowly took everything in. Her hand reaching out to touch the paintings my mother had hung on the wall and even to touch the wooden frames on the door.

"Humans create such beautiful things." She sounded almost in awe as we moved down the hall and passed even more paintings and several glass blown vases. Ani seemed to take it all in with a child-like innocence. It was a heartwarming feeling to be the one responsible for the look on her face

"When we remained trapped on Earth. it was the one thing we could do. Create beauty from ordinary objects." It was the one thing humans truly had going for us. We were a highly creative people, be it words or carvings or paintings. We created beautiful, one of a kind masterpieces.

"I have never seen anything like these. What machines could create these images?" She touched a close painting of a starlit sky that was my mum's favourite.

I let her arm go to lift up her hand, spreading her fingers out. "These ones." I tapped on her palm and fingers and she looked stunned as she looked between the paintings and her hands. Sometimes beautiful things needed a touch of humanity to make them that more vivid.

"No." She said it softly. "Hands cannot create these... these... *marvels.*" She looked so confused and I chucked softly and nodded.

"Human hands are capable of great many things, Ani. Beauty or chaos, creation or death. We're creatures of habit and expressing ourselves through our hands and our words is just one of the more beautiful habits we have." We created and we destroyed. It was a cycle that had been repeated again and again and again throughout our history. I knew humans were flawed but what creatures weren't? We simply didn't hide our flaws and mistakes, we told the next generation of them in the hope that they wouldn't be repeated. Or at least we did now.

I pushed open the door to the library and her mouth dropped open, our conversation forgotten as she took in the shelves of books. She stood in shocked silence before she slowly closed her mouth and swallowed hard. I left her side to grab a familiar tome. I flipped it to the page I had memorized my entire life growing up before carrying it back to Ani.

"Here. Hero of Old. It's mine and my father's favourite poem. I think you will like it." I urged her to take the book and she did before sitting down in one of the overstuffed chairs, drawing her knees up to her chest as she scanned the page intently, her fingers following the words. I smiled at her.

Ani was one in a million. She was never satisfied in what she was told, she craved knowledge and stories and words. She devoured them quickly and with such joy. The library was a faint gift to her, to let her adjust to the culture shock in an environment she would be comfortable in.

I settled into a chair across from her, picking up a random book from the small table beside the chair. Ani's expression changed with the words she read before she seemed to wiggle further into her seat. I glanced down at the book I had picked up with an amused smile. There was no way I was getting her out of the library without a serious fight.

30

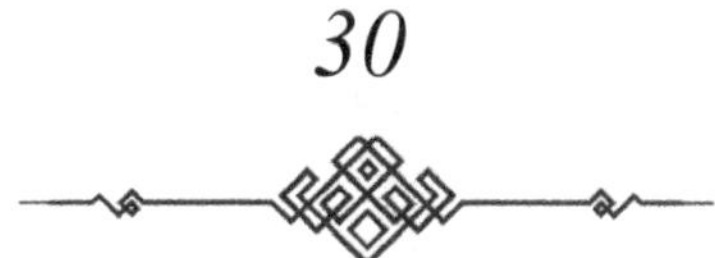

"Come on, Ani. You wanted to see the ruins up close." I was breathing heavy as I climbed up a pile of moss covered rubble. Ani had wanted to see the old ruins up close but now she was lagging behind. I thought it was amusing. Orrians were supposed to be stronger than humans but she was huffing and puffing as if we were climbing Mount Everest.

"I did not think there would be this much walking." She practically wheezed the words out and I smirked as I lifted myself up towards the slab of concrete above me.

"Out of shape are you?" I glanced back at her as I scrambled onto it.

"No one is as stubborn as you, Liviya." Ami'la glowered at me as she lagged behind Ani.

I stayed lying down on the flat piece of concrete that signalled the second last stop of the large pile. "You wanted to tag along, Ami'la." I glanced at her and she rolled her eyes as she gave Ani a boost to the edge before my spot. I sat up and looked around. I had apparently chosen one of the more difficult routes up the edge of rubble that signalled the beginning of the city.

"To keep *you* out of trouble." Her words were grumbled and I let out a chuckle.

"Trouble? Me? *Never.*" It felt good to tease one another again as I once again lifted myself up towards another slab of concrete. I knew the view was worth it though. It was one of my favourite places on Earth. I had grown up next to the ruins so seeing them was always something I enjoyed. It reminded me of simpler times. Happier times.

"Are we just about there?" Ani looked up at me and I nodded before I reached down and grabbed her hands. I helped to pull her up to the top of the pile. Once she scrambled up she lay down like I had, breathing heavy as I helped Ami'la onto the slab of concrete that signalled the top of the pile. I turned around and stared at the ruins.

Greenery had overtaken hollowed out, towering buildings that leaned haphazardly over top of craters that showed where the bombs had fallen centuries ago. Much of it was overtaken by nature but the scars in the Earth were something that would never go away. Humanity had made its mark within the Earth's surface and it wasn't something that could truly be healed. It showed the ugly side of humans and humanity but every time I saw it I was struck with awe.

Humans once had enough power in their hands to decimate cities and change the landscape of the planet we lived on. A select few had killed billions and thrown our world into utter chaos and darkness. Nuclear winters and the radioactive fallout. The shuddering of the tectonic plates that caused massive Earthquakes and volcanic explosions. We had once been powerful enough that the very Earth had shifted under our feet because of the actions of the few.

Some humans had taken brush to canvas or glass to fire and other had taken hands to keyboards and destroyed life as they had known it. I inhaled deeply as I stared at the magnitude of the scene in front of me. There was always a stillness in me, a sombreness that descended when I looked on the ruins. A deep acknowledgement that I was just as capable as those that had done such a terrible thing.

"*Wow...*" Ani's voice was practically breathless and I gave a small nod.

"I have never seen these up close before." Ami'la's voice was a soft whisper and I sat down.

"This is the other side of humans, Ani. With our hands we can create and with our hands we can destroy." I looked around the buildings, following a flock of birds with my eyes. There was a peacefulness in knowing that despite how much humans had destroyed the world, nature would always take it back. It would always find a way.

"Why did they do this?" Ani sounded slightly horrified at the thought and I didn't have an answer for her so I gave a small shrug.

"Greed, a strive for power, hate, revenge, religion. The list is endless. All I know is that we were left in the rubble and instead of taking all this down..." I gave a sweeping gesture to the ruins before us. "We left it up as a sombre reminder of what humanity is capable of." There were hundreds of thousands of cities just like the one we were staring at, that were all over the world and they all served as a reminder of what we had done. There would be no more tearing down our mistakes and rebuilding on top of them. We lived on the outskirts of grave yards filled with skeletons made of concrete and metal.

"I could see the tops of the buildings from my office but I've never actually seen them before." Ami'la sat beside me, her unique eyes scanned the area much like my own were doing.

"This was my backyard when I was growing up. I wasn't allowed into the ruins, no one is. It's too dangerous." Many of the crumbling, sky high towers had collapsed when I had been growing up. It wasn't safe to play in them or around them. They shifted and groaned and the ground was unstable.

"I have never seen so much green. Oria is more blue." Ani said it thoughtfully as she joined us.

"What is Oria like?" I had been learning of the history but no one had ever told me about it before, the planet itself. I wondered what it was like, if the air was as clean and clear as our own or if it had giant oceans like Earth.

"Our plants have a blueish tinge to them and the air is fresh, not as heavy as yours is. Your atmosphere has more oxygen than on Oria, not a lot more but enough to make a difference." Ami'la muttered it out faintly and I stared up at the sky. I could see the hovering ships high up in the sky, faint anomalies in the sky line.

"It is beautiful. The buildings are carved from stone. White stone that glistens in the sunlight." Ani let out a wistful sigh. "Everyone is softer there, not as harsh. We are not meant to live in the clouds." No one really was. The sky and clouds were for the birds and the ground was meant for the rest of us.

"It doesn't help that the ships contain a majority of war veterans and those who never wished to leave Oria. Resentment can breed very easily." Ami'la's voice was soft but her words carried a heavy truth. Resentment was so easily created and the effects of it took so long to disperse.

"Tell me more about Oria." I didn't want to think about the harsh resentment and anger that surrounded me on the ship, not while I was on Earth.

"It has two suns and is very similar to Earth. More land than water but our weather is much milder." Ani's voice was gentle with remembrance of her homeland and I felt a bit of a pang in my chest that she was so far from her homeland. "My parents had been born on Oria but myself was born on a fertility ship. I did not see Oria until I turned three." The words surprised me and I looked at her, her expression was sombre and she gave a slow shake of her head.

"All test tube children are required to stay on the ship because sometimes the genetic coding is wrong and they develop deformities that make them incompatible with life." She stared out over the ruins and I felt a pang in my chest. I didn't know. I could have never expected that. "One in five children die within the first three years." I had never heard that before and I reached over and grasped her hand. I hadn't realized that she hadn't actually grown within her mother, that she had all odds against her to survive but she succeeded in doing so anyway.

"Test tube babies." Ami'la's voice was tinged with sorrow as she said it. "It's hard to know that it is so easy for humans to create children when our own families can only grow children in glass vials after their genetic material has been forced together in an attempt to create life. My own children will never grow inside of me and it is a hard thing to know and accept." I hadn't ever thought of that perspective before and it made me feel especially saddened for my friends. I had the ability to grow life within me and they wouldn't be allowed to hold their children until they were three years old. It was a sombre and guilt ridden feeling that filled me at them.

"We do have hope though. If Liv and Rhex could possibly have babies maybe we could find our own mates and have children of our own." Ani sounded all manners of wistful and sad and I squeezed her hand again.

"Fair point, Ani." Ami'la let out a sigh and I reached over and grabbed her hand as well.

"So when did this city fall?" Ani's voice sounded forcefully chipper as she gestured to the ruined city.

"Over eight hundred years ago. It fell to the second round of bombings from ancient Russia." Such a large war for reasons that seemed to petty. Warring leaders turned to warring nations and young people had died for the whims of old men.

"Ancient Russia?" Ani made a humming sound in her throat and I nodded.

"It was called the Red Nation. Under a tyrannical dictator that flew under the flag of democracy. It was different from the Red Tide, which was ancient China. Very similar in ideologies but different cultures." So much history to learn on Earth and then I was being introduced to an entire history of the cultures within the universe. So much information to learn in such a small amount of time.

"The history humans have is so strange." Ani withdrew her hand from my own before lightly shoving me.

"I feel the same way about Orrian history." It was always strange when looking at it from the other side of the fence. The entire world was strange when one was stuck on the other side of the fence, forced to look through the wooden slats to see a glimpse of the other side.

"*You* two are strange." Ami'la chuckled as she patted my hand before she drew her legs to her chest and rested her chin on her knees.

"So says you." I made a face at her and she rolled her eyes.

"My life is perfectly ordinary, Liviya." And if there was one thing that Ami'la loved was when things were ordinary and precise and in order. I respected that. I needed a bit of order in my own life.

"Ordinary sounds great right about now. Nice house with a picket fence were Rhex and I can live happily." I gave a small sigh, staring off into the distance. I could almost see the image I had described. A little girl running around in the flower beds as Rhex laughed, his scar bunching, and his light green eyes sparkling.

"When you have so many people who look like they want to kill you, anyone would crave normal." Ani chuckled and I smiled at her with a small eye roll. She was certainly one who knew how to brighten a situation up, how to remove the veneer of seriousness.

"I can't argue with that." There was no lie in her words, in fact it was the honest truth. I had spent so long living in a borderline hostile environment that anything that was slightly better was something to crave. A comfortable silence fell as we looked over the ancient destruction humans had caused.

Ani shifted beside me and let out a heavy breath. "Your parents are... *something."*

"They're very affectionate." It was always something for an Orrian to get used to. Even Rhex had difficulties with my parents affection. I was learning it was normal for them to be unsure and wary of it. I didn't like the fact they had affection withheld from them but I knew I had to just accept it.

"My mother and father were never like that. They did not embrace me or kiss my cheeks." She sounded a bit lost at the thought. I didn't even want to think about how my childhood would have been without hugs that smelled of lemon and dirt and kisses that scratched my cheeks with stubble.

"I'm learning that Orrians are creatures that have a severe lack in affection. No child should lack in love as they grow up." It was a very sad thought. I would never allow my own children to lack in such a way.

"I think it would be nice to hug my children. To hug them and kiss their cheeks. It is a rather delightful feeling." Ani said it with conviction and Ami'la made a sound of agreement.

"When you live with humans you realize that while they are a species that are different from our own and considerably weaker, they have parts of their culture that are far greater than ours." She said it carefully before she reached over and squeezed my hand. "We have a great deal to learn from humans and their culture. We just need to open our eyes to see it." What a great deal different our worlds would be if we had simply opened our eyes just a bit wider to those that we lived closest to.

A thick silence fell as we slipped into our own thoughts. Despite the silence and the slightly sombre feeling that hovered over us, there was a comfortableness to our small bubble. I trusted both of the Orrian women I sat with. Trusted them enough that I would willingly place my life in their hands because I had never had more true friends.

I didn't know what I would have done if I had been isolated on the ship without Rhex or anyone else to lean on. I looked out over the ruins and gave a small half smile, trying my hardest to ignore the pressure of the false bond in my chest. Without those I could rely on, lean on. I doubted I would have lasted as long as I did. Hate was a hard thing to fight against when one was alone.

I was truly thankful that while I was a single human in a sea of Orrians, I was not, in fact, alone.

31

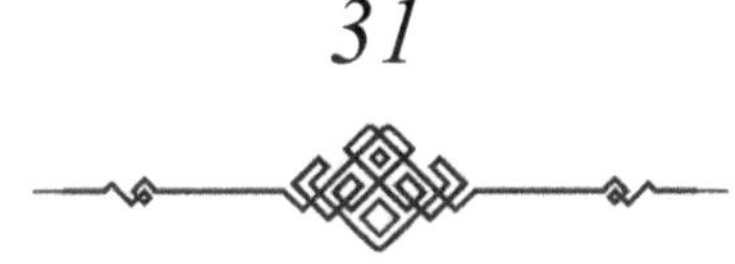

Three weeks later

I picked at my food, fighting the urge to yawn. I was starting to feel more and more drained. I had taken another dosage of the soul separation concoction a few days ago and it left me feeling rather poorly. Exactly like the other three times I had taken it.

"Do not pick at your food, Liviya." Nadila scolded me softly before she gestured at my plate, looking at me over her reading glasses. "Eat. You need it. Lost a bit too much weight." She turned back to her papers and shuffled them slightly.

I had asked her about why she used physical copies and she said it helped against tampering. She printed out time stamped copies of each piece of legislation and orders from Oria the moment she received them and it saved from someone hacking into her files and changing things. If they did, she had the official time stamped copies as originals to prove tampering occurred.

I took another small bite of the food and made a face. It was still hard to eat the ship food after the weekend we had on Earth. Ami'la and I had taken Ani to the store to pick up the best human delicacies and after we had her try all of it, we had taken her out for ice cream. I had never heard anyone squeal as loud as she did when she tried it. Ami'la laughed so hard she started snorting. It turned out that she had the exact same reaction to ice cream that Ani did.

I was happy that both Ani and Ami'la had bonded like they did. I had been a little wary because Ami'la was so serious and organized and Ani was pure unplanned chaos. I thought they would mix about as well as oil and water but they had hit it off very well. Ami'la had loosened up and Ani had reigned it in a bit, both things I hadn't thought were possible.

"Liviya." Nadila's voice filtered through my thoughts and I gave her a rather sheepish smile before taking a bite of the food. "You seem distracted." She took off her glasses and set them down on her papers.

"I'm not feeling well." I wasn't. I doubted I would be until Rhex got back. However that wasn't causing my issues. I wasn't sure if I was actually getting sick or just feeling the effects of the potion.

"I thought that gross tea Ghilesh was making for you was helping." She pushed her braid over her shoulder and I made a face.

"It causes its own problems." Hot flashes and the unknown effect of rather severe lethargy and appetite loss. Ghilesh was a bit worried about it, he was researching the side effects and the last time I had seen him he was gathering every dust covered tome he could find. All he could tell me was that it wasn't supposed to be used in the long term.

"I see." She drew the word out as she stared at me intently. "What other side effects are you experiencing?" The look she gave me told me not to lie and I let to a heavy sigh.

"The usual hot flashes but now there is the exhaustion and lethargy and then the loss of appetite. My body feels a bit too cramped to eat." I rubbed at my rib cage. It felt so very cramped inside of me. The pressure was starting to be felt on my organs and it was highly unpleasant.

"Alright. Well at least I can say that you are halfway through this whole ordeal." She was right with that. Only eight weeks left.

"That's the only bright side." When I talked to Rhex yesterday he had been more exuberant than usual, even the background had been loud and boisterous. I could hear him laughing as he tried to cheer me up over the phone.

To be honest just hearing him happy made me happy. When it had grown louder he had explained that his battalion mates had thrown him a rather loud party to celebrate making eight weeks without me. I thought it was sweet in a way, even though they were making lewd jokes in the background. Which I found was both embarrassing and hilarious. Especially because Rhex would sputter slightly at every single one he heard and apologize profusely for them.

"Do not be so down, Liv. Only eight short weeks left." She reached out and grasped my hand in hers gently. "They will fly-by before you know it." She patted my hand softly, her lilac eyes crinkling at the corners as she smiled before letting me go and putting on her glasses once more.

"Please eat some more." She flicked her hand at my plate and picked up her papers once more. I moved the rather unappealing food around the plate. I was not hungry enough to eat the sludge I was staring at. "How is the Learning Centre coming along?" I was waiting for that question since the moment I had stepped into her apartment.

"Which part? Her learning or her stalker?" Ani leaned her head over the edge of the sofa she had been quietly sitting on and Nadila's gaze snapped to me.

"Kher is *stalking* you?" I could see the flush crawling up her face that signalled that she was more than unimpressed with the news. In fact she was past unimpressed and that red flush meant she was down right pissed.

"Not *exactly* stalking." I was hesitant to call it anything because I knew Nadila would react poorly. Without any actual evidence of the behaviour, she would be spinning in circles and without concrete proof, that is exactly where Khos would want her.

"Not at all. Just excessively watching and showing up wherever we are without warning and all but trying to melt her face with his eyes." Ani grinned broadly from her spot, her head hanging upside down as she looked at us. I flipped her off before turning to Nadila.

"Why did not you tell me?" Her cheeks were flushed and her eyes were hard and I let out a heavy sigh.

"Because there's no proof that is substantial enough to bring anything against him. Telling you this does nothing but cause you to worry about the wrong things. Kher hasn't threatened me and I am positive this is all from Khos to distract you." I said it as calmly as I could. She needed to see *reason* and not jump on such an inconsequential thing.

"That makes sense. Khos has been trying to sneak some pretty nasty pieces of legislation through the council. I mean listen to this." She shuffled the papers and held one up, pointing to a small sentence outlined in red pen. "Rule six, subsection a-five. amendment seven. All non-Orrian personal aboard the ship must undergo rigorous vetting before being allowed in the general populous. To be effective retroactively." She threw the paper down in disgust.

"Then this one!" She dug through her papers and lifted another one. "Another amendment! All human subjects aboard ship two-nine-three are to undergo serious medical testing and if found faulty will be henceforth recycled! There are nearly forty in these papers alone!" She slammed her hand down on the papers before standing up.

"You are right, Liviya. Khos is playing a game with me. Distraction and diversion but I will not let him win this one. No no. Now that you have pointed this out, he is in for one hell of a fight." She glared at the papers and I heaved out a sigh of relief. "Eat your food." She gave me a look as she gathered all of the papers up into a tidy pile and I rolled my eyes.

"Yes, *mom.*" I poked at the sludge and took another half-hearted bite. I really wasn't feeling up to eating anything, let alone the questionable brown paste that was sticking to my plate.

"If I was your mum you would be in time out for your attitude." Nadila flashed me a smirk as she leaned over the table to gather the paper she threw.

"What attitude?" I gave her an innocent look, trying my hardest to look meek and sweet but it didn't work as she pointed at me.

"That one." She grabbed the paper and set it back on her pile, shuffling them so they all sat straight.

"Me? Never." I gave her a sweet smile as I took another bite of food, repressing the urge to spit it back out on the plate.

"You are getting far too smart, Liviya. Turn you into a politician yet." She gave me a rather wolfish grin and I shook my head, forcing myself to swallow the lump mouthful.

"*Ne'heta she'lantha.*" I shook my head as I said it. I was not getting into anything that put me closer to those that hated me. I was perfectly content sitting on the edges letting people like Nadila play the game.

"No thank you? My, my. You *are* getting better at the language. I will have to start paying attention to what I say around you." She gave me a rather teasing smile and I simply grinned. It felt nice to be in an environment that was welcoming and friendly.

"I wasn't lying." Ani sounded a bit petulant as she turned and looked over the arm of the couch.

"I *never* said you were, Ani'tah." Nadila winked at me before she tucked all of the papers into her file.

"Wait... are you mocking me?" Ani's face twisted into a frown and Nadila smirked at me before she quietly walked towards her office. Ani's eyes widened. "Nadila, where are you- Liv! Did she just mock me?" Her gaze turned towards me and I bit back a smile and gave a half-hearted shrug. I turned back to my plate and moved the food around on it. There was a muted thump before Ani stuck her face right close to mine.

"I know you are not eating it, Liv. No one wants to eat that crap." She had that right and I looked up at her innocently. "She was mocking me!" She gave an over exaggerated pout to try and hide the amusement twinkling in her eyes.

"She's a councilwoman. I'm fairly positive mocking people is below her." I was surprised the words didn't burn as they came out. All was fair when poking fun at friends.

"That is a lie. She mocks Khos all the time." Ani pointed at me and Nadila came out from her office empty handed.

"I merely point out his stupidity. There is no need to mock his hypocritical stupidity when he highlights it so well himself." She gave a toothy grin at that and Ani laughed loudly at that. I chuckled as I poked at the food with the fork. I really was unable to eat more. I rubbed at my rib cage again, it felt too cramped in there. "You do not have to finish it, Liviya." Nadila walked over, her heels clicking against the floor.

"No sense in forcing you to eat this mush if you cannot actually eat it." She grabbed the plate and raised an eyebrow at the food on it.

"Too cramped." I rubbed my rib cage with a small frown and Nadila nodded absently as she set the plate in the washing bubble.

"So you have said." She turned around and clapped her hands. "No worries, Liviya, halfway there. You can get through the rest." At her encouraging words I gave her a small smile and I watched her smooth down her suit jacket.

"She's right! Only eight short weeks left." Ani wrapped her arms around me, giving me a hug that lifted me off the ground. "Then you and your mate can make out all you want." She made a kissy face at me as she set me down and I shoved at her with a grin. It was rather uplifting to be surrounded by so much optimism, like being surrounded by a warm cloud that fuzzed all negativity out. Like being a cloud of happiness even when you felt half a moment's notice from letting tears pour out of you like rain.

32

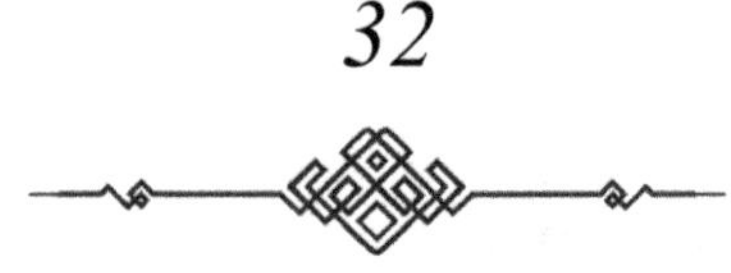

One week later

I stared at the board at the front of the class, trying my hardest to focus. I could only understand a few sporadic words, more than when I first started but most of it was still gibberish. The symbols across the board were the same, I could only recognize a few of them. It felt like class was dragging on. Mr. Dahgme's voice was practically a dial tone. One continuous monotone sound that droned on and on and *on*.

I wondered how close to the end of the day we were at. It had to be fairly close because I was positive that we had been there at least six hours. It was a long time to try and absorb something in a language you didn't understand. I looked away from the board and from my quick cursory glance over the class, I could see that many people shared that sentiment with me. I could see at least four Orrians almost falling asleep, their heads bobbing slightly towards their chests or their desks.

Ani was looking like she was ready to join them. Her eyes were glazed over slightly and she looked half dead from boredom. I glanced over and spotted Kher staring at me, his grey eyes narrowed intently. I swallowed and looked away just as quickly as I had spotted him. He was especially... weird today. He always stared and glowered and spat curses under his breath at me but now I saw him literally everywhere. If I was somewhere I could guarantee he would be there as well.

I wasn't sure if Ani had noticed or not but he was reaching levels where I was starting to get severely creeped out and borderline worried. I could still feel him staring so I focused on the board once more. However it was still just as confusing as the last time I looked so I buried my face in my arms. That was better than staring at the symbols that were now hurting my brain and fighting the urge to look at the crazy asshole who was, as Ani put it, trying to melt my face with his eyes.

“Do not die on me, Liv!" Ani grabbed my arm and gave me a frantic shake. I peeked at her over my arm and she winked at me before pressing the back of her hand to her forehead. "For if you die, I too shall perish! For I cannot survive with the painful shards of a broken heart that would linger in my chest!" She had discovered Shakespeare and so everything she did was even *more* dramatic but with the added flowery language that bordered on hysterical in use. I ducked my head back into my arms, my cheeks flushing slightly. If she was loud enough she was going to garner attention.

"Pray! Tis not true! My love has perished in this room of horrors, her mind broken by the four walls of injustice that surrounded her. Monotony! Boredom! Insanity! Thou art the cause of her death!" She touched my head with a fake gasping sob. "Sleep well, my sweet princess. For I shall join you in the morrow. When twilight seizes the air and when the injustice is fixed within the heavenly eye! Sleep well. Sleep well." She stroked my hair and I fought back giggles at her rather impromptu, and rather well done, monologue.

There was a gruff bark from Mr. Dahgme that let me know he did not appreciate Ani's theatrics. I peeked over my arm again as Ani crossed her arms over her chest and retorted something in a tone that looked to me as not entirely being polite. To be fair, Mr. Dahgme had been an incredible asshole to Ani since I joined the program and her disrespectful attitude was a consequence of his treatment of her.

There was an even more gruff response from him that Ani shot down with one of her own. "Can you believe this guy?" She gestured at him with a look of distaste as he raised his voice once more. "He just will not stop." I could see the utter dislike she had for him and it was an unusual experience for me because Ani was always super positive about everything, she never let her mood drop down into a low. I lifted my head higher as Mr. Dahgme stormed closer. I could see everyone staring at us with wide eyes as he approached and Ani crossed her arms over her chest and snapped something at him in Orrian.

He pointed to the door, his face red and a vein bulging in his forehead. I could almost see it moving with his heart beat. Ani shrugged before pointing at me and saying something rather calmly in Orrian. I tried to pick out words I knew but they were speaking too fast.

Mr. Dahgme started shouting, gesturing wildly at the door and Ani turned to look at me. "He is telling me to get out and I told him that you are supposed to accompany me wherever I go. He does not like that." She turned back to him and said something, my mind instantly grabbing onto the word councilwoman and Nadila. Mr. Dahgme's face turned even more red, which I hadn't thought was possible. He gestured wildly between the both of us and shouted the same line in Orrian again and again.

Ani stood up and patted my shoulder. "Well, we just got kicked out of class." She smiled at me brightly as she gripped my arm and practically lifted me from my chair. I let her pull me around the table. I looked at Mr. Dahgme and nodded my head.

"She'lantha." I was yanked forward by Ani as she moved towards the door of the classroom. Everyone's eyes followed after us as she pushed open the door and we stepped out. The moment the door closed behind us she started laughing.

"The look on that bloated balloon's face." She said something rapidly in Orrian, holding my shoulder as she laughed, leaning on me slightly. Once she managed to get herself somewhat under control she wiped her eyes, letting out sporadic chuckles as she did so. "Ohhhhh, that was funny. We need to go to the Dean's office. Protocol and all that." She linked her arm through mine and practically skipped beside me as we moved towards the Dean's office.

I doubted he would be happy, this was Ani's third time this month that she had gotten us kicked out of class. I didn't blame her, Mr. Dahgme was an asshole but the Dean didn't particularly care. He liked things to be orderly and to run smoothly. Which was surprising for me because he didn't mind my presence in the Learning Centre. In fact he encouraged me greatly to learn all I could.

"Dean Hilem will be upset with you." The Dean's office grew closer and Ani made a sound, waving her hand in the air as if shooing an irritating bug away. I reached into my pocket and pulled out my translator before tucking it into my ear.

"Oh posh. He knows how Mr. Dahgme is." She leaned her head on my shoulder with a chuckle. "I seriously thought he was going to burst a blood vessel in his brain. That vein just kept throbbing. Throb... throb... throb." She giggled. "I wanted to poke it. Next time I will. Just like this." She poked my forehead and I couldn't help but chuckle as I swatted her hand away.

"Leave Mr. Dahgme's pulsating forehead alone." I could only imagine how he would react to that. Despite how tempting the pulsating vein was.

"But Liiiiiv." She drug my name out as she stomped her feet like a child as we stopped in front of the Dean's office. She let my arm go and knocked on the door. There was an answer from inside that was too muffled by the door to make out but Ani pushed the door open anyway. "Hello, Dean Hilem." She pasted a sugary sweet smile on her face and the balding man glowered at her from over his reading glasses.

"Ani'tah SordaLam, do not tell me you were kicked out of class." He gave her a stern look and Ani sat down heavily into the chair in front of his desk. I took the one beside her.

"I was but he was being rude." She lifted her head up, setting her chin in defiance. She wouldn't ever back down from her position. I liked that about her. She was consistent and what was right was right and she would fight for that.

"He is an instructor, he needs to be treated with respect." The Dean's tone was low with warning and Ani scowled.

"He said humans are illogical and ridiculous creatures that are ruining our culture and customs." She glanced at me as she said it and I fought back a wince. Score a point on the asshole board for Mr. Dahgme.

"And *before* that?" He raised an eyebrow that told me that he was telling Ani not to lie.

She let out a huff of air. "I was reciting poetry." A very well thought out, Shakespearean inspired, dramatic monologue.

"Ani'tah, we must not disrupt the class." He shook his finger at her sternly and she leaned forward and slapped her hand on his desk.

"He is spreading malicious lies and *hate*." It bothered her a lot, I knew it did. She hated how everyone spoke about me and the rest of the humans. She loved and cared for me and my culture and heritage. She loved learning about it so hearing her own people deride it was hard for her.

"And I will have a discussion with him about that but you need to stop antagonizing him." Dean Hilem's voice was firm. He wasn't going to budge on his position. It was the same position he had taken numerous times before.

"He is mean to Liv." Ani's voice cracked slightly and Dean Hilem's eyes slid to me for a moment before he let out a heavy sigh.

"And I will continue to discuss that with him as well. It is not appropriate in a professional setting or in a classroom but he is a tenured instructor. He cannot simply be fired. You know this." He gave Ani a look that said he understood but he was stuck. He was always stuck. I knew what tenured meant, in the Orrian culture at least. It meant that Mr. Dahgme had been sent to the ship by the Oria council for a set term of service. It was nearly impossible to have them break that term.

"I also know he is an asshole." She muttered it underneath her breath and I winced because I knew the Dean had heard it.

He banged his fist on the table, causing me to jump at the bang. "Ani'tah SordaLam!" His voice was harshly reprimanding and Ani hunkered down in her chair.

"Sorry." She muttered it out and I glanced between the two of them as Dean Hilem pointed at her.

"I do not believe for a second that you are. You will not use such language in my office. The students and instructors can use it everywhere else but I will not abide by it here. *Especially* in the context of insulting an instructor." He turned his gaze to me and I gave him a small smile and his face relaxed. "How are your classes coming along?"

"Good. I'm learning more in Miss Geliensha's class than I am anywhere else." She was a sweetheart of an instructor. She was very patient and made sure everyone was understanding the topic of the day. I was just really upset that I only had her a few times a week

"Ancient laws and cultural teachings. I will have to commend Miss Geliensha on her incredible teaching habits. Perhaps implore some of the other instructors to pick up on them." He gave me a quick smile before looking down at his papers. "As it is, I am still writing you both up for this incident but you may both go home." He waved us off and I stood up before Ani. She seemed on the edge of sulking as she heaved herself out of the chair. I opened the door, saying a quick thank you in Orrian before I walked out.

"Ani'tah, I want no more incidents." His voice made my turn my head as Ani stopped to turn back to him. I went to grab the door when a large hand grabbed the chain of my medallion. I instantly looked forward but the person yanked hard, snapping the chain. I caught a glimpse of a face with hard edges and grey eyes before I felt like I was sucked from my body into nothingness.

33

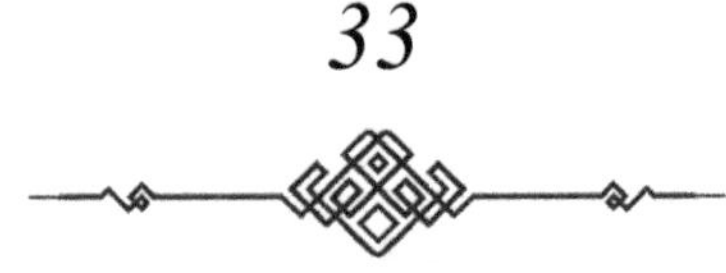

Unknown Passage of Time

I woke up slowly, like coming from a haze. It felt like fighting through molasses to reach a far shore. Difficult and exhausting but I still tried. When I did reach the far shore it was easier than I thought to push my body to move. I opened my eyes and expected to be standing in front of Dean Hilem's office but I was laying in a bed in a white room that reminded me of the medical clinic. Confusion swamped me and a beeping beside me picked up rapidly.

I looked around, attempting to sit up with trembling arms. Black dots swam in my vision and I slumped backwards, too weak to truly move from the spot. I swallowed convulsively my throat and mouth feeling like cotton, as if I hadn't drank anything for a very long time.

I couldn't grasp what was going on. I didn't remember what had happened after the chain of my medallion snapped. My hand snapped up to my neck and I felt the familiar links underneath my fingertips to my relief. It was a rather calming feeling and the beeping slowed down.

I turned my head slightly and noticed the machine was heart rate monitor. A wireless one that was probably hooked up to the bed rather than the person. They were much more efficient and required less wires. I blinked slowly before I stared up at the ceiling. My throat was really dry and I wanted to know what the fuck had happened.

"Hello, Liviya." Ghilesh's voice was soft and I turned my head to look at him. He looked worn out and tired as he stood in the doorway to the small medical like room. I opened my mouth to reply but the dryness made it impossible. He came forward with a soft smile and with a cup in his hand. I stared at it intently. "I bet you are thirsty." I nodded and he shuffled over before pressing a button on the side of the bed that helped me to sitting.

I wanted to thank him but he said nothing as he pressed the rim of the cup to my lips. I drank greedily and when I had drained half of the glass he pulled it away and then held a strange pan out in front of me. I looked at him and opened my mouth to ask him what it was for when I threw up.

My entire body seized as I heaved again and again. Tears filled my eyes as it felt like it wasn't going to stop. The vomit had a strange taste and came out black and thick almost like tar. It felt like something was pulling it from my body and my muscles clenched tightly as I continued heaving for what seemed like an eternity before it stopped entirely, leaving me feeling limp and exhausted.

"I am sorry, Liviya. That was not nice. I know." He pulled the pan away from me before patting my forehead with a cold damp cloth. I felt too tired to keep my eyes open and he smoothed the cloth down my cheeks. "It is okay. Sleep. I will be here when you wake up." His words faded and I fell backwards into nothingness once again.

Consciousness crept back onto me slowly but unlike the last time I awoke I was aware that time had passed. I slowly cracked my eyes open and winced at the light above my head. It seemed too bright even though I knew it was dimmed.

"Hello again, Liviya." Ghilesh appeared by my side with another cup in his hand, I eyed it warily. The last drink I had sent me into a heaving frenzy. "You have purged your system already. Besides, these are just ice chips." He shook the cup and I could hear the crushed ice moving around. I swallowed, that strange taste was still in my mouth and Ghilesh held me out an ice chip. I opened my mouth and he fed me several more before he moved a chair to right beside the bed.

"Do you remember what happened?" His amber eyes had heavy bags under them and he looked so worn out. I didn't like it.

"Dean Hilem's office. I stepped out." My voice was raspy and raw and my throat burned on every syllable. "Someone grabbed." I patted my medallion and swallowed with a wince. "Yanked it off." I frowned, trying to push through the pain in my head. I needed to remember what happened.

"Did you see who did it?" He asked it quietly and I shook my head. It hurt to think but I knew that much.

"Not well." I swallowed convulsively again and he fed me another ice chip. The coldness soothed my throat. "Grey eyes, sharp face. Just a glimpse." A tiny, tiny glimpse before I was sucked away, to where I didn't know. The heart rate increased as my heart started to beat faster at the thought of what happened.

Ghilesh grasped my arm and squeezed it softly, rubbing my skin in an attempt to get me to calm down. I breathed deeply, focusing on doing just that. "Was it Kher?" He asked it softly and I shrugged slightly. I was at a loss. I was nearly positive it was him deep down in my gut but I didn't see enough to make a formal decision.

"I don't know." I swallowed hard and turned to look at him. "What happened?" I wanted to know. I need to know what the hell had happened to me.

"Someone yanked off your medallion." His eyes darkened slightly in anger but his hand was gentle on my arm as he patted it. "It... it caused your soul to leave your body." I felt myself pale as my stomach rolled. I wanted to heave again. My soul had been disconnected from me, I hadn't gone unconscious like I thought. I had virtually *died.* "When the chain broke your medallion disintegrated into nothing, the magic it held simply returning to the Source." He moved his hand down and grabbed my own. "Your soul left with it." He looked saddened and I swallowed.

"Why?" Why would my soul simply leave my body. I didn't understand.

"It is what happens when a medallion is broken. Usually we can fix it quickly. The Source holding the souls until we can recreate the broken medallion and then place the soul back within it. You were... difficult." His eyes were almost watery as he said it. I didn't like that look.

"How?" My throat was so scratchy and sore it was nearly unbearable.

"When a mated pair is the subject of a medallion breaking, one soul will return to the other. We would know where it is and where to find it. Your soul got... confused." He swallowed and looked at his lap. "The potion you were taking confused your soul. It was meant to go back to Rhex, your soul would rest within his medallion until we could fix yours but the soul separation potion made your soul believe it had to go back to the Source." Tears burned my eyes. I had gotten *lost* out in the dark abyss of nothingness? I had been stuck out there alone?

"You were lost in the abyss of darkness, Liviya. And she was *mad."* Ghilesh shuddered under it as if he could still feel the fury from the person he spoke of. "She was so mad that her fury was felt through every medallion that came close to your body. We had to quarantine you to the lower bays because people were suffering third degree burns from their medallions." I blinked at that, reaching up to grab my medallion as Ghilesh squeezed my hand gently, as if afraid I was going to break.

"She screamed at all of the Soul Makers for days. Over and over again. She would not let us rest until we had your medallion ready and then she screamed at us to find you." He let out a heavy breath and I had a moment of realization that he was talking about the Source. The Source had been upset with my soul being lost. It was a rather disconcerting feeling to think about. "We almost couldn't find you. It took every bit of power we had to reach out towards where your soul had gotten stuck." He looked at me again and the tears finally fell down his face as he attempted to swipe them away.

"You were gone for a month, Liviya." His words made what ever calmness I felt, disappear entirely. My heart rate picked up and I felt my breathing come out in gasps. "Your body was dying and we could not find you. We tried so hard until we felt just a tiny pulse, a tiny call for help and then we realized we had been losing you too. The darkness wanted to consume you entirely." He wiped at his eyes again, as if the motion would stem the flow of tears and I had to look away from him, my mind racing with the information. I hadn't just died, my soul had nearly been extinguished entirely. I swallowed heavily against the bile that crawled into my throat. I hadn't thought I had enough in me to throw anything up again but apparently my body was showing me just how much was left.

"Rhex?" My voice was a hoarse croak as the tears trailed down my face. I just wanted to know if he was okay, that it didn't hurt him.

"He knew. He knew the moment it happened. He said he could not *feel* you anymore." He heaved out a breath. "They had to sedate him to keep him from going completely mad." My heart jumped into my throat and I squeezed Ghilesh's hand.

"Talk to him." I needed to talk to him. I needed to hear his voice just to assure myself that he was okay and safe. I just wanted to hear his voice because I was *scared.*

"You cannot right now." He said it gently, as if the tone of his voice could deliver the crushing words softly. I felt like my throat was constricting as it burned with sobs that wanted to escape. I *needed* to talk to Rhex.

"Talk to him." I watched him stand up and I held his hand as tightly as I could, my arm trembling from the whisper of a grip that I was using. "Ghilesh, *please*!" I wanted to beg him, to plead with him to *help* me.

His amber eyes were full of regret as he pull his wrinkled hand from my own. "You need to recover first, Liviya." He pressed a button on my bed and I felt a sudden, foggy warmth slowly start to spread through me.

"No." It came out as a faint, slurred whimper before that warm fog covered me completely, dragging me down, down, down.

34

"I stand amid the roar of a surf-tormented shore, and I hold in my hand grains of the golden sand--" The rasping, whispering words pulled me for my drugged slumber and I fought against the heaviness in my body to try and open my eyes. "How Few! Yet how they creep through my fingers to the deep. While I weep-- while I weep! Oh god! Can I not grasp them with a tighter clasp? Oh God! Can I not save *one* from the pitiless waves? Is that *all* that we see or seem but a dream within a dream?" The words were soothing being said in that rasping voice that tickled my memories. I knew it but I couldn't place it.

"I bet you are tired of hearing an old man speak of such desolate things. Let me try and find a poem that might brighten your dreams." The turning of pages could be heard and a faint humming of thought followed each one. My finger twitched and there was one more page turned. "Ahhhhhh, here we are. Forgive my voice once again. I am getting old." There was the faint sound of someone clearing their throat lightly.

"I carry your heart with me-- I carry it in my heart. I am never without it-- anywhere I go you go, my dear; and whatever is done by only me is your doing, my darling. I fear no fate-- for you are my fate, my sweet. I want no world-- for, beautiful, you are my world, my true." There was a slight pause as I heard skin against paper as if they had drawn their hand over the words. "And it's you are whatever a moon has always meant and whatever a sun will sing is always you. Here is the deepest secret nobody knows-- here is the root of the root and the bud of the bud and the sky of the sky of a tree called life; which grows higher than a soul can hope or mind can hide. And this is the wonder that's keeping the stars apart... I carry your heart-- I carry it in my heart." There was a faint sigh that I wanted to copy.

"That poem never fails to make me smile. What about you?" A hand touched my own. The skin like paper and my fingers twitched as I tried to force my body to work. I attempted to lift my eyelids and there was a rasping chuckle that reminded me of leaves on pavement. "There you are. Try just a bit harder, my dear." I managed to open them a crack and I looked towards the sound of the voice and blind eyes sat in a pale and heavily wrinkled face.

He patted my hand again. "There you are. I was starting to feel foolish reading poetry to a woman who could not appreciate it." He gave that rasping chuckle again and I forced my eyes open a touch more.

"Rhess?" I tried my hardest to struggle through the sludge that was my brain but I was fairly positive that was his name. It was Rhex's grandfather.

"Yes, my dear." He gave my hand a gentle squeeze. "You gave us quite the scare. It was strange seeing so many Soul Makers in one place. I cannot remember a time that it has happened before. And she was mad. So, so mad. I have not felt my medallion ever burn so hotly." He made a slight face.

"Kher will not be charged with what happened. Make no mistake we all know it was him but we have no proof. The camera for the area was conveniently broken the day it happened. Fools, all of them. The Source will punish those that do not heed her words and warnings." There was a fire and passion to his voice that made him sound years younger than his wrinkled face suggested.

"Rhex?" My throat still burned slightly but it wasn't nearly as bad as the second time I woke up.

"Oh yes. My boy is doing fine. Waiting rather impatiently for his lovely soulmate to wake up so he can talk to her." He had a rather curious look on his face as he said it and I frowned slightly. Ghilesh had told me no. Told me no and drugged me. I didn't want to have to go through that again.

"Allowed?" I was wary but I wasn't sure if my voice conveyed that well or not.

"Not even in the slightest." He gave that rasping chuckle as he leaned closer. "I might not look like much but in my younger years I was a rule breaker like no other and this is a very foolish rule." A wide grin crossed his wrinkled face. "No one suspects the blind old man of breaking the rules, so let us keep my double life secret and keep this phone call between us." He gave that rather endearing laugh again and I gave him the best smile that I could in my current condition. I was liking Rhess more and more.

He pulled out a cellphone and without actually looking at it, tapped the screen and placed it on the pillow next to my ear. "It has a built in translator. No worries, my dear." I nodded at him gratefully as it barely made half a ring before it was picked up.

"Grandfather, has there been any change? Is she awake? Is she doing okay?" Just hearing his rumbling voice was enough to make me want to curl up my exhausted and weak body and cry.

"Rhex." My voice croaked his name out and I could hear him inhale deeply.

There was a slight pause before he let out a shuddering breath. "Liviya, are you okay?" Worry and relief coated his tone thickly and I sniffled, the tears already starting to roll from my eyes.

I glanced towards Rhess but the old councilman had already disappeared. "Tired... scared. Miss you." I managed to roll onto my side and I painstakingly drew my legs up, so I was in the position I wanted to be in. My body didn't ache but it was so heavy and tired.

"Oh there are no words that I can say that can encompass how much I truly miss you. I have been so worried about you." His voice was filled with relief and I felt sobs building in my throat. I hadn't wanted him to feel as though he had lost me, that he had to worry about me.

"Sorry." I wanted to tell him everything that I felt but my throat was thick with tears and my rasping voice was making it impossible

"Do not apologize, Liv. *Please* do not. This is *not* your fault." His voice was low as he said it and I sniffled.

"Home?" I just wanted him back. I just wanted him to wrap me in his arms and tell me it would be okay. I needed him with me because what I went through was *terrifying* and I never wanted to experience that for us ever again.

"Two weeks." The words sent a sharp pain through my chest and I couldn't help the small sob that escaped. He made a sound before shushing me slightly. "I know. I am sorry. I am so sorry. I am trying to get a shuttle to pick me up sooner. I am. I am so sorry. I want to be there with you." He pulled the phone away and I could faintly hear him cursing as I tried to stop the sobs from escaping.

He let out another sigh. "I promise you, Liviya. I will come home and nothing like that will *ever* happen again." If he was with me I didn't doubt it. I would never doubt it. He was my shield to the world around me and I needed him to protect me from the world I found myself in.

"Talk till sleep?" The drugs were still heavy in my system and I just wanted to drift off to his voice. To trick myself and my body that he was actually here.

"I promise." He said it softly and I sniffled again, not even bothering to wipe away the tears. "It is too hot out here. We are finding dust from the old lake basin in every inch of our clothing and every crease of our skin. It is the dry season so it is to be expected but it is still bothersome." He continued on, telling me about his training, what I had missed in the month I had been away. He told me about everything and I felt my mind drifting further and further away, holding the phone in my hands but wishing with all my heart that it was Rhex instead.

35

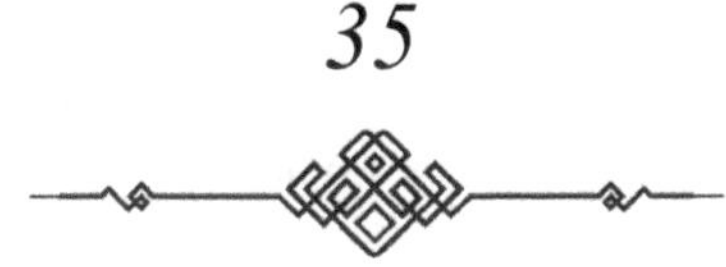

Over a week later

I walked back and forth from the kitchen to the living room. My legs still felt a bit unsteady but they were working better than they were yesterday. It had been slow progress. I had expected to simply be able to jump up and be ready for life but that turned out to be rather impossible.

I had to take everything slowly, my body was still weak from the stasis they had placed it in so it wouldn't die completely before my soul could be returned. That and the fit of my body sometimes didn't feel right. Like I was still settling under my skin.

I heaved out a heavy breath and moved across the room once more. I was doing a lot better than when I first woke up but I still had a bit to go to gain back all the muscle I had lost. I blew an errant strand of hair from my face as I heaved out another breath.

"Do not push yourself, Liv." Ani's voice came from her bedroom and I rolled my eyes slightly as I started the trek again after I touched the couch.

"I'm just a bit winded. I'm not done yet." Back and forth, back and forth until I was better. I didn't like feeling so vulnerable and weakened while still on the ship. Something was brewing. I wasn't sure what it was but I could feel it.

"I do not care. Take a rest." Her tone was stern and I rolled my eyes again as I touched the kitchen counter before turning around and heading back towards the living room.

"Fine, *mother.*" I emphasized the word and Ani made a sound of irritation.

"I have every right to mother you. Leave me to my incessant worry." She was right in that. Ghilesh and Nadila had told me she had been nearly inconsolable after the incident. She felt she had failed me, hadn't protected me like she should have. She refused to listen to anyone when they said there was nothing she could have done, the attack had been too quick to stop.

After I woken up, she hadn't left my side. She was with me everywhere I went, attached to my hip as she glowered at everyone who attempted to come close. She was worse than a dog with a bone. I couldn't say I disliked it, being so vulnerable and surrounded by people who hated me, I kind of liked her tenacity.

"Are you sitting down?" Her voice held a thread of warning and I touched the couch before sitting down on with a groan.

"Yes, mother." I sang it mockingly and I could hear her scoffing from my place on the couch. I didn't want to prove her right but sitting down did feel like heaven on my trembling legs. Perhaps I was pushing it a bit too far.

"Drink some water!" She turned on some music, the soft tones of the music were relaxing and I leaned my head against the back of the couch. My chest gave a faint ache but it had been not as bad as before.

I half wondered if it was because of the whole, nearly dying and having my soul ripped from my body thing. Like my soul was still settling into my body so I wasn't quite as aware of the separation as I should be. However the thought of Rhex pained me. I hadn't been allowed to call him for my usual weekly dose of hearing his voice.

I didn't like it. Not one single bit.

Those phone calls seemed to sometimes be my only grip on sanity. Without them I felt lost and alone. I hated that Rhex must have felt that a thousand times worse when I had been stripped from my body and lost in the darkness. I couldn't imagine that. I couldn't imagine feeling the loss of him *that* acutely and not perishing from a literal broken heart. The separation was bad enough, draining enough, *hard* enough.

I stared at the light blue ceiling, my eyes glazing over at the uniformity of it. No cracks, no bumps, just a flat clear surface that was enough to make someone tear their own hair out. I missed my old room that I had at my parents. The cracked paint and the unevenness that it had. I had it memorized but it was still *different*.

I had been stuck in the apartment for nearly a week, only leaving to see Ghilesh and the four other Soul Makers that had helped him find my soul. They had wanted to make sure I was situated properly, that my soul didn't have any long lasting issues and effects from being lost in the darkness. Other than seeing them, I would go to the medical bay and get checked out by the bots. My overall health seemed to be fine, it was just my soul that was settling, making me feel off.

"Ani." I was bored and feeling down and staring at the stupid ceiling was not going to help me.

"Drink some water." She seemed distracted and I wrinkled my nose as I talked myself into getting up. The couch was really comfortable and my legs were telling me not to get up rather nastily. I gave a heavy groan as I stood up on my shaking legs. They *really* weren't liking me at the moment.

I grabbed the arm of the couch, using it to prop myself up as I shuffled forward. Just one more trip to the kitchen and then back and I was good. I mentally pumped myself up as my legs dared me to take an actual step. I rubbed at my face. This was ridiculous.

I hesitated before I took a step and nearly cheered when my legs didn't buckle. I had succeeded in the first step, only thirty more to go. I made another step and my confidence was growing in my ability to actually make it to the kitchen and back. I smirked to myself, I could force myself to do it once more.

The door to our apartment was booted in rather violently. I jumped my eyes wide as I stumbled backwards several steps. My heart pounded hard in my chest as Ani gave an angry shout. My eyes landed on the intruder as he shouldered the door open. His form was large and foreboding and I whimpered slightly, unable to hide my fear. His face came up and my whimper turned into a cry as tears flooded my eyes.

"Rhex!" I held out my arms for him. His expression was severe as he stalked towards me, his chest heaving as he did so. I could hear Ani behind me but I took a trembling step towards him. He gave a low growling sound before his large hands wrapped around my waist and he threw me over his shoulder. He held me there tightly as he turned around and stalked out of the apartment.

I lifted my head and caught sight of Ani, her face red with anger and her eyes wide with fear. I smiled at her, trying to ease her fears. "I'm okay." My voice was a croak and I felt a lump form in my throat. Rhex was *here.* It didn't matter that he was early or that I still felt a bit weak, he was *here.*

My chest felt full and my chin trembled as I gripped the back of his dusty army jacket tightly in my hands. I wasn't going to let him go, never again. His hands were possessive on me, holding me tightly, as he kicked open the door to the stairwell, carrying me down the stairs.

I swallowed hard and tightened my grip on his jacket. He was taking the stairs two at a time, his long legs eating the distance between us and his apartment. I was going *home*. Tears leaked from my eyes as my fingers started to hurt from clutching his jacket so tightly but there was no way I was letting him go.

He pushed through another door and I glanced up. There were several soldiers who caught sight of me on Rhex's shoulder and cheered, smiles on their faces as they whistled and clapped loudly. I felt my face flush but was happy that Rhex had found such happy companions on his training detail.

I lifted myself up slightly, looking over my shoulder. Rhex's door came up quickly and without a word he shoved it open. The interior of the apartment was dark and it smelled almost stale, as if the air had been recycled too many times. The lights flickered on as he kicked the door shut.

I loosened my grip on him slightly, my hands needing a rest but before I could grasp him again he quickly set me on my feet. I felt suddenly dizzy at the head rush it gave me and swayed slightly. I glanced up at Rhex and his expression was severe, his mouth was set in a deep frown and his light green eyes had nearly darkened with anger. He looked almost... scary.

"Are you okay?" His words were rumbling as he quickly grabbed me looking me over as if searching for an injury I knew he wouldn't find. There were no outward signs that a soul had been torn from a person's body but I let him inspect me, lifting my arms and turning me around. I pressed my lips together and tried to blink the tears away as he turned me so I was once again facing him. "Are you *okay*?" He gave me a rather intense look and I shook my head.

"I was so scared!" It came out like a sob and I reached for him, needing him close as I sobbed out all of the terror I had felt in the past four months, especially the past two weeks. There had been much to fear since then. He pulled me close, pressing me to his chest tightly as he stroked my hair. There were no words to adequately express how much being in his arms meant to me. "I missed you *so* much." *So* much. Words could never describe the depths of how much I truly had missed him. The sobs tore at my throat and he made soft sounds in return, running his fingers through my hair, unravelling my braid as he did so.

"My Liviya. Shhhhhhh it will be alright. I will never let you go again." It was a soft promise that he whispered in my ear, his voice sounded more guttural than normal.

I sniffled and clung to him tightly. "Don't leave me." I couldn't bear it. I couldn't survive another separation, not after the last one. On Earth I would have a chance but on the ship, I wouldn't survive again. I had barely survived this one.

"Never again, Liviya. *Never* again." It was a harshly spoken promise that rasped against my ear, making me shudder in his arms. I felt safe, protected. "I could never abide it." He took in a deep shuddering breath that I found myself mimicking unconsciously.

"When I felt you disappear, there were no words I could use to explain it. Just unending sorrow and anger flooding my veins and filling up the space where you resided." His grip tightened on me, his fingers digging into my muscles but there was no pain or discomfort, just him and his touch. "I will *never* leave you to be harmed again. I wish to remove Kher's head for what he did but I cannot. I am bound by our laws." He trembled as hot rage curled around his words. I said nothing, there was nothing to say in response to it. I buried my face in his chest, inhaling the scent of dirt and ash into my lungs. He must have gone straight to the ship without changing his clothes. His need to be with me sooner, throwing everything else to the side.

His hands moved from my back to my face as he cupped it, his green eyes tracing my features as if committing them to memory. I let my eyes close slightly at the sheer pleasure I felt from his touch as his thumbs stroked my cheekbones, wiping away the tears. He brought his face down to mine, pressing his forehead to my own.

"Are you truly okay? Has this left any ill effects on your body?" His words were low as his eyes looked into mine. He was worried, it was painted clearly within them. I shook my head.

"It doesn't show up physically. How can it when your soul is not something one can touch?" When the attack was not physical, it wouldn't leave any visible marks. Rhex let my face go and grabbed my hand, his expression once again severe before he stepped around me and pulled me down the hall. "Rhex, what are you doing?" I wasn't sure what he wanted. I would follow him but I still wanted to know what he wanted to do.

"I need a shower." He glanced at me over his shoulder, his eyes narrowed slightly. "And to make sure my wife is all in one piece as she claims." His words made my mouth go dry and my eyes widen slightly.

"Oh." I couldn't help the small exclamation.

Oh indeed.

36

I felt a bit shy as he pulled me into the bathroom. He closed the door behind us before dropping my hand and stripping off his jacket. My legs trembled slightly, from the nerves or the weakness that had plagued me, I wasn't quite sure. I felt my cheek flush as he pulled his shirt over his head, even as my eyes greedily took in his form. He was a man that I felt was made perfectly. The large scar on the one side of his ribs didn't detract from his attractiveness, in fact it made him that much more appealing and rugged.

"You are shaking." His voice startled me slightly and I jerked my eyes up to meet his. He was frowning as he watched me trembling. I opened my mouth to respond before I closed it again. I simply nodded and he pulled off his bulky combat watch before he moved towards me, his muscles rippling. "Why?" His hand sank into my hair, tilting my head back as he did so, forcing me to look at him.

"Not sure." It was truly hard to concentrate with his half naked form being so close. The tanned skin and the sparse dark hair that dusted his sculpted chest. His light green eyes scanned my face and I felt myself tremble just a touch more. The hand in my hair tightened slightly as he brought his face closer, tilting my head back further.

"Nervous. Weak. I'm not sure which." The words came out almost breathless as he nuzzled my neck, inhaling before his lips brushed my skin. Heat flared through me and my lower belly clenched with a sudden need.

"You do not need to be nervous with me and if you are weak then I shall hold you." The words were said against my skin before he pulled back, his hand loosening in my hair. I swallowed thickly as his hand slid through the strands before both of his hands dipped to the hem of my shirt.

I kept my eyes locked on his as he pulled my shirt up, our gaze only breaking as he lifted it over my head. I lifted my arms to let him take my shirt off completely. He tossed it to the side as his gaze trailed down my body. I felt it almost like a touch that I wanted to arch into. I felt a bit of regret that I was wearing a plain bra and not one of my lace ones.

"I have waited four months too long to be allowed to look upon you like this." His voice was low and gravelly and I could almost feel it against my skin.

His hands did not hesitate before he grasped my waist. I sucked in a breath at the fire that licked at my skin at the touch. Goosebumps erupted over my skin as he trailed his hand over my skin, his fingers massaging slightly as he looked me over, his expression pensive as he slowly turned me around. His hands moved up my back, unhooking my bra. I hesitated, my first instinct was to catch it but I fought it back and let it drop to the floor.

I inhaled sharply as his hands slid down to my hips before he slid them around and undid my pants. I swallowed and couldn't help but lean back against him as his thumbs slipped into the waistband of my jeans and underwear. His lips pressed to my neck as he pushed the both down my hips, letting them fall to the floor. I trembled slightly as he turned me around, I kicked the clothes away and pulled my shoulders back.

I was nervous and I could feel the heat of a blush travelling down my chest as I looked up at him. His green eyes darkened slightly as he stared down at me, his eyes travelling from my breast to the thatch of hair between my legs. My heart pounded in my chest as his eyes trailed over my body. He brought his hand up to my face where he grasped my chin, lifting my face slightly before he gave me a soft kiss. My eyes fluttered closed against it and I swayed towards him.

He pulled back, kissing the corner of my mouth quickly, causing shivers to roll across my body. "Into the shower." He let his hand drop from my chin before he opened the shower door. I glanced up at him and he grasped my hip, gently pushing me towards the open shower. I tore my gaze away from him and stepped into the shower. The water turned on almost immediately and I tilted my head upwards, the warm water felt like heaven as I stepped further under it. My legs still felt a little weak and I closed my eyes as the water ran down my face.

The door opened behind me and I bit the inside of my cheek as I turned around. Rhex made the space seem small as he stepped inside. I felt my breath hitch in my throat as my eyes followed the line of hair his abdomen and down to his rather well crafted endowment. My eyes widened as I watched it twitch and swell under my gaze. I turned away quickly as he shut the door.

"Do not be shy with me now, Liviya." His voice rumbled in the space, creating a rather intimate atmosphere in the small shower. I looked up at him, a hard feat as my eyes caught the water droplets rolled over his form, wanting to follow them down their paths. "Come here." He reached out for me and without a thought I stepped towards him. His large hands rested on my shoulders and I shivered as they slid down my arms. His fingers spread out on my skin as he followed his touch with his eyes, fully looking me over.

His hands moved down to my hands before he grasped my waist and he started to trail his hands across my abdomen. My legs trembled under the feeling of his touch. They trembled at how fire licked at my body, heating me up, sending flashes of heat through my veins and a slow burn through my lower stomach. The water tickled already sensitive nerves and I had to stifle a moan as his hands moved upwards. I leaned into his touch and he gave a low sound of approval as his thumbs brushed the bottom of my breasts. They suddenly felt heavy and achy as my nipples tightened in response to the teasing swipes his thumbs were doing.

My breathing came out a touch more laboured and I couldn't help it as I reached out, grabbing his biceps, my entire body swaying towards him. He murmured something I couldn't quite catch before he buried his face into my neck and scraped my skin with his teeth as he finally covered one of my aching breasts with his large hand. I couldn't help the keening sound I made as I arched into his touch, my eyes fluttering closed.

He practically loomed over me, my body no longer being touched by the falling water as he nipped at my neck. I turned my head to the side, my breathing coming in pants as he gently caressed my skin before letting his hand drop and his other one take hold of me.

I sucked in a gasp, a breathy moan slipping from my mouth before I even knew it was there. He pulled his head from my neck but captured my lips with his own as his hand teased my breast and the other slid down my back to the slope of my ass. He yanked me closer to him. I could feel him pulsing against my stomach in time to his heartbeat.

His kiss felt claiming, *stealing,* as if he were reinforcing the belief that there was a part of me that no longer belonged to me, a part that he had taken. I opened up my mouth, allowing him to deepen the kiss. I shuddered under the possession I felt from it, heat roaring through me, making my mind fuzzy with desire.

Four *long* fucking months I had been waiting for him and in that moment it was incredibly worth it. I slid my hands up to his neck, his skin was slick with the water and I tangled my hands in the wet strands of his hair. I felt him groan as his hand dropped from my breast to my hip. I gave a slight whimper at the lose of contact but his hands slid down the curve of my ass and he gripped the backs of my thighs, lifting me up with an ease that surprised me. I wrapped around my arms around his neck, holding him tightly as he broke the kiss, letting me gasp in air that I hadn't even realized I had been missing.

He adjusted his grip on my thighs and I wrapped them around his waist. He captured my mouth once more as my back touched the cool tiles of the shower wall. Steam curled around us and my heartbeat in my chest rapidly as the need for Rhex grew nearly unbearable. I rolled my hips, needing something, *anything*, to help ease the ache I was experiencing. Rhex let out a groan as he broke the kiss. I leaned my head back against the tiles with hooded eyes, panting rapidly.

"You say there are no marks, Liviya, but I can see what this has done to you." His voice was deep and guttural, on the very edge of rasping as he looked me over his hands flexing on my ass. "What the Source had brought together, let no man, no being, tear asunder." He said the words darkly before one of his hands slid up my back and cupped the back of my neck. He pulled me to his neck and I nipped at the flesh I found, tasting it with my tongue. He gave another groan as he used his shoulder, shoving the shower door open. The cool air that brushed over my from the bathroom pulled me back out of the fuzzy daze just enough to think for a moment.

"What are you doing?" My heart clenched in my chest at the thought of him perhaps putting me down and not wishing to continue but the throbbing of his erection between us slowed the thoughts down.

"I have not seen my wife in four months and I will not claim her as mine against a shower wall." His words were a guttural sound as he drew his teeth over my jaw before kissing me again. My eyes fluttered closed at the pleasure it brought.

He was making my body heat up and burn for him in ways that I had never experienced before. I felt as though I would burn to ash without him, that if he were to leave me I would cease to be. I was barely aware of my surroundings until my back hit the softness of a mattress and his weight covered me. I gasped at the sudden change and he deepened the kiss, once again reinforcing his claim on me. I let my hands fall to his shoulders as I rolled my hips up against him. I needed *more.*

He pulled back before he bent down and nipped at my ear. He murmured something in my ear that might have sounded like the word greedy but I didn't care. I needed him, *ached* for him. I had been without him and his touch for too long and I needed to remind my body of who was our mate, of who belonged to us, who could sate us. I rolled my hips again again, gasping as he thrust against me at the same time. The touch was electric and I couldn't help how my head fell back and I moaned. I repeated the action and he gave a soft grunt as he thrust again.

He placed an open mouthed kiss on my throat before he shifted his weight on me, his hand trailing down my trembling skin. I arched into his touch. My nerves were alight with sensation and I was drawn to his touch, like a moth to a flame, except I was willing to touch the flames. My nails dug into his shoulders as he shifted on me, pressing against me. He felt too big for a moment before he gave a gentle push and my body gave way for him.

I gave a sharp cry, my nails digging into his shoulders more as he pressed another open mouthed kiss to my vibrating throat, the cry drawing itself out of me slowly. He murmured to me as he settled deeper within me, my slick flesh parting easily for him as if he had been inside me a thousand times before. It was an indescribable feeling. Like finally feeling completed for once in my life. There was no me without

Rhex and no him without me. He pulled out and thrust forward, my mouth dropped open, no sounds escaping but a harsh gasp.

"Liviya." He ground my name out before sliding a hand under my head and gripping a handful of hair, forcing me to look at him. His eyes were intense as he looked down at me, moving in me again and again. The sensations were an onslaught to my senses and I felt my body tense in anticipation. "Liviya." He gave a deep groan and bent his head, covering the tingle bud on my breast with his mouth.

"*Rhex*!" His name tore from my throat like a harsh plea, like a prayer for salvation. I felt tears fill my eyes as he increased his pace, moving faster and faster as he switched his head from one aching breast to the other. It was almost too much. Too much heat, too much friction, too much of *him*.

His arms went behind my back and he lifted me off the bed, moving me upright so I was chest to chest with him. I writhed on him, feeling like I wanted it to stop but *needing* it not to. My body was seeking that treasured height of pleasure it knew and it wanted me to jump over it to dash into a millions pieces as I hit the bottom.

His mouth bit at my throat lightly, sucking at my skin. I could almost feel him making a mark on my skin as he did so. I scratched his back, helpless not to claw into him and hold him tightly. I rocked on his lap, matching his thrusts that bounced me slightly. Curses tripped to the tip of my tongue but he latched back onto my mouth, stealing them from me like he was drawing the air from my lungs.

He gripped me tightly, his fingers digging into the flesh of my ass tightly as he pulled me down onto him again and again. It was too much. Too much. Slick heat and rough hands causing my nerves to ignite. There was too much fire burning through my veins and with one last thrust everything tightened to the point of pain before it shattered. I shattered around him, a keening cry escaping my lungs that he took into himself before he pulled his head back sucking in air as he did so.

Everything was hazy as I arched into him, throwing my head back as I let go of of everything and simply felt the slick and borderline painful pleasure he was causing within me. He bit my shoulder, stifling his own cry as he pulsed within me, thrusting as he did so. His arms wrapped around me tightly, so tight that I faintly wondered about bruises but never felt pain from his embrace. I *revelled* in it as the high came down.

I panted harshly, my heart beating hard and fast in my chest as he slowly lay me back down. He slowly slid from me, sending shivers through my entire body as the aftershocks still wracked my frame. He lay down beside me before he nuzzled my neck.

"*My* Liviya." His arm wrapped around me and he tugged me to his chest, not allowing a single inch of space between our bodies. A content limpness filled me and I could feel a small smile tug up my lips as he gave me a gentle kiss. "My miracle Liv." He ran his hand through my hair as he pressed another kiss to my forehead, holding his lips there as I caught my breath.

I could feel his heart pounding against me and I kissed one beautifully crafted pectoral. "I haven't felt this good in ages." I stretched slowly and he gave a deep groan, rubbing at his mouth as he stared at me.

"I will never get enough of you, Liviya." He kissed my throat before he moved down to my collarbone. My body shuddered, demanding more.

"I hope not." I tangled my fingers in his damp hair before pulling him up for a kiss. I shifted so I was beneath him and wanted to smirk as he got the message, once again settling himself between my legs. I would never get enough of him either.

37

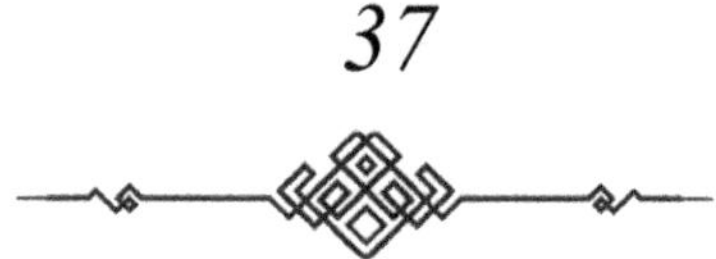

I lay on his chest, tracing patterns into skin as his hand rubbed up and down my back. He gave a rumble of pleasure at my touch and his hand moved lower. I scratched him in warning. I knew my limits and round four was more than pushing it. I was already feeling sore and in a more achy way rather than a delicious ‘I have been thoroughly tumbled through the sheets’ type of way. Not that I had much experience with that. I winced hard at the remembrance. I didn't need to remember that, not while tucked in Rhex's arms. It only hurt.

However the thoughts bombarded me, giving me no peace. "Are you okay with me not being pure?" The words tumbled out before I could stop them and Rhex's hand stilled on my back.

"I do not understand." There was a confused tone to his voice and I glanced up at him, my cheeks red with my shame before I had to look away. I bit my lip hard. I suddenly felt dirty and pulled away from him. "What is this that hurts you?" He grasped me tightly as he sat up. He refused my retreat and I felt sick.

"Do you mind that I had sex with another guy before you?" The words burned coming out and I wanted to bury my head in my hands. I wanted to hide in my shame.

"Why would I mind?" He tried to turn my face to look at him but I refused.

"Some men prefer their mates to be pure." So many of them did but I had allowed that gift to be sullied for Rhex. I had given it to some man I had a faint attraction to and nothing else. There was none of the connection, none of the fullness. I had been left empty and shamed at the end.

"I do not understand this. Pure means like snow or water. I do not understand." He sounded frustrated by his inability to understand what I said and I swallowed thickly.

"Untouched by others." Impure, tainted, and unwanted. The words hurt as if they had physically struck me. I went to pull away from him but he held me tight to his side, refusing to allow me to move an inch.

"I still do not understand. Do some men not wish their females to touch anyone in their lives? What foolishness is this?" He wasn't getting what I was saying and I rubbed at my eyes, trying to force the tears away.

"Intimacy Therapy." I ground the words out. How I *hated* it. I wanted to go to the shower and scrub my skin raw. It never felt like I would ever get clean when I had those moments.

Rhex made another sound of aggravation. "I do not understand."

"I had to have sex with men to try and spark a connection because I couldn't bond." I spat the words out. How it burned me now, knowing that such a connection could never been fucked into existence. It simply had to be and that thought burned me now.

"They forced you?" There was an angry heat to his words that had the emotion pushing at me slightly.

I gave a weak shrug. "Not exactly." It hadn't been forced but it had certainly felt like coercion. My potential life for a bit of sex. Who wouldn't trade their bodies for a chance to live?

"But you truly did not wish for it." His words were low and I shook my head.

"No." I hadn't wanted it at all. I had done it, enjoyed parts of it but, it had left me so unfulfilled and empty that it was never worth it and never would be.

"I do not care that you sought others. It is normal in Orrian culture to use sex as a tool to relieve stress or tension or to further one's self. Why would I condemn you for something I have done myself?" He gripped my chin and forced me to look at him. "My anger and upset comes from the fact that you were forced into a situation where you felt like you needed to trade your body for your life. The only thing that upsets me about this is the fact that it pains you deeply." His eyes searched my own as his jaw clenched over and over again.

"You could have been touched by thousands and it would not matter because I am the *last* of them. There will be no more after me, just like there would be no more women after you." He shook his head before kissing me, letting his lips linger on mine. "Do not think of this if it pains you to tears. Know that I want you no matter your past or who has touched you because they do not matter to me. *You* do." I frowned slightly as his tone turned more guttural and he paused in his speaking, his eyes darting back and forth as if searching for the right words to say. My eyes widened as it hit me that I wasn't wearing a translator.

"You're speaking English!" It was a quick exclamation and a slow smile crossed his face and seemed to light up his entire expression.

"I learned for you." He kissed my nose and let my chin go before he laid back down, dragging me down with him.

I didn't understand it. I couldn't believe he was actually speaking English. "But you... you were only gone for four months. I barely know any Orrian an-"

"You are doing very well with Orrian, Liviya. It is simply easier for an Orrian to learn English than for a human to learn Orrian." He resumed his stroking up and down my spine and I shivered under the touch. I was touched that he had learned English for me.

"How?" I didn't think any of his comrades would want him learning the half-breed language and he chuckled. It was a rich sound that made me shiver in delight to hear it.

"I transferred to an Orrian-Human combat unit. They taught me English." Pride coated his tone thickly and I felt a matching pride surge through me even as confusion warred with it heavily.

"You said that they don't do that anymore." He had. He had told me that humans and Orrians didn't mix anymore when it came to combat..

"Not on this ship and not with my original battalion. It was why I requested to be moved to a different one entirely." He smoothed his hand over my back and placed the other behind his head. "Those men we passed when I brought you home, they are part of my new battalion. They have all be stationed here under their own volition. We all wanted to be closer to the humans of our squad." He seemed much more relaxed and at ease. He didn't speak of his battalion with harsh sternness anymore and the way the men had cheered and smiled let me know that perhaps they were a lot closer than his previous one.

"Where are they?" I wondered where the humans were being held. I doubted Khos would allow them to stay on the ship.

"Still in training. They arrived two weeks late." He let out a small sigh and I rested my chin on his chest as I narrowed my eyes at him.

"About that. You came back early." He had come a whole week early. I wasn't complaining but I wondered how he had managed to do it.

"My battalion's bird was going to go up with an empty pod. I bribed my way onto it." He smirked down at me and I felt my cheeks flush under his rather intense look. "I could not stand spending one more day without you." I felt a lump appear in my throat and I nuzzled his chest, turning my face away from him so he couldn't see the tears that filled my eyes. He was so sweet sometimes and I was just an emotional mess.

There was a sudden banging on the front door that made me jump in fear. The banging was followed by the sound of raucous laughter on the other side. Rhex groaned heavily as someone shouted his name over the banging. He tightened his grip on me and buried his face in my hair. "If I ignore them. I think they will go away." The banging grew louder and I couldn't help the smile that spread out across my face.

"I think your friends want to see you." I stretched once more as Rhex got up. He looked down at me with a rather curious look on his face before he gave me a quick kiss.

"They want to see *you*." He moved off the bed and I felt my face flush brightly as I stared at him with wide eyes.

"Me?" Why on Earth would they wish to see me? I didn't entirely know how to feel about that.

"They want to see the beauty that I sang praises of every single day that I was in training." He pulled on a pair of pants and I felt my face flush even heavier as I sat up as well. He walked closer, my eyes were drawn to the rippling muscles of his torso, my eyes going half-lidded at the display. "And why would they not? You are even more perfect that the one I sang about." He grasped my face in his hands and gave me a rather hungry kiss that had me breathing heavy by the time he released me.

My thoughts were a jumbled mess due to the kiss when the realization sunk in. Source help me, I was going to be inspected by a group of large Orrian soldiers. My expression must have showed my shock and slight terror because Rhex gave me another kiss.

He pulled away as I grasped at him and I fought back a pout. He gave an amused chuckle at the look on my face. "Do not worry. They will love you." He gave me a rather rakish grin, his scar bunching rather adorably. "Just as I do." With that he left the bedroom, closing the door behind him. I stared at it, a heat blooming in my chest that had me burying my face in the blankets with a large grin.

Rhex *loved* me.

I quickly got out of the bed and moved towards the closet. None of my clothes were in there, I knew that but I needed something. I found a pair of boxer briefs and I snagged a t-shirt from one of the shelves. I pulled the clothes on, they were good enough and covered all that needed to be covered. I smoothed down my hair, swallowing nervously as the loud voice became louder as Rhex let them into the apartment.

I tried a bit harder to tame my sex tousled hair but finding it nearly impossible. My cheeks heated up and I hesitated at the bedroom door. I shifted my weight on me feet as I bit my lip. I let out a heavy sigh, trying to find some courage before I slowly opened the door and stepped out.

I searched quickly for Rhex, feeling a bit out of sorts without him near. There were several broad shouldered men standing in the living room and I swallowed thickly as I crept towards what felt like a lion's den. Loud baritone voices speaking Orrian seemed to rumble the air as they laughed loudly. I hesitated before peeking around the corner.

"They are not going to bite."Rhex's voice right beside my ear made me give a clipped cry as I jumped in surprise, my hand going to my chest as my heart pounded harshly.

I glowered at him, swatting at his bare chest. "That wasn't nice!" I scowled at him and he gave a shiver inducing chuckle before he pressed a quick kiss to my temple.

"Come." He placed his hand on my lower back and forced me to step out into the living room. The group of Orrians immediately stopped speaking to look at me. I felt a strong curling of fear begin in my stomach as they stared in silence.

"How the fuck is that fair?" A shorter man came through the front door, a wide smile on his face as his shaggy brown hair flopped into his eyes. The other men turned and cheered for him, pulling him into the group and pounding on his back. I looked up at Rhex but he simply let his hand drop from my back to go greet the newcomer. The shorter man walked over and thumped on his back. "Seriously, Rexy. How the fuck did you land such a gorgeous lady?" He moved closer to me, a wide smile on his face, his blue eyes twinkling.

"Hello, darlin'. The name is Bruce." He held out his hand and I took it with a tentative smile and he gave me a grin right before he yanked me close, giving me a tight hug. I was surprised by the action and he released me with a chuckle. "Well, lads? Let's give her a warm welcome." He threw a lazy arm around my shoulder and pulled me into the fray of exuberant Orrians who shook my hand or chucked my chin with wide smiles. Names flew from their mouths as they called out their introductions and I tried to hold onto them but it was a tad overwhelming.

As if sensing my slight distress, Rhex came in and wrapped an arm around my waist, pulling me to his side. "You recovered well." He nodded at Bruce who ruffled his shaggy hair with a grin.

"Damn right. There is nothing that can keep me down." He winked at me. "Training mishap. Rexy, here, took my spot on the shuttle. Deceptive bastard." There was an amusement to his tone that made him have almost a drawl, I stared at him for a moment before I realized he was human.

He grinned at me again. "That's right, darlin'. Just as human as you are. These lads have been my comrades for about... three years?" He turned to the group and they all called out five, shoving him lightly as if in play. "Sorry, sorry. I have been with them *five* years." He glanced between Rhex and I and gave a low whistle. "I haven't seen him that relaxed since I met him. You look good on him." He gave me a firm nod as if giving his approval and the large Orrians called out their agreement as they all fell into various seats in the living room.

Rhex kissed my temple again, his fingers tightening on my hip just a fraction. "They love you." He murmured it against my skin and I looked up at him with a smug grin.

"Just like I love you." I watched as his face softened before he bent down and brushed his nose along mine affectionately.

"And I you." He gave me a soft kiss that I melted into. I did not mind a touchy feely Rhex, in fact if he kept kissing me like he was, I would demand it.

"Get a room!" One of the Orrians, Lukesh if I remembered correctly, called it out and my face flared red. Rhex chuckled and said something in Orrian that had the whole room laughing and shoving at

Lukesh playfully. I pressed my face into Rhex's chest and inhaled deeply, taking in his scent of musk and cloves. He pulled me closer, wrapping me in his arms. As the laughter filled the apartment and Rhex's own rumbled his chest, I smiled.

It felt good to be surrounded by such happiness. It felt good to be wrapped in Rhex's arms.

It felt like... home.

38

A month later

I closed my eyes and curled up further in the bed. The lights were dimmed and I was attempting to have a nap. I hadn't slept well for the past few nights, nightmares plagued my sleep no matter how many times Rhex pulled me into his arms to quiet me.

One would have thought that falling into an exhausted and sated sleep would have kept the nightmares away but for the past week they had tormented me. I hadn't understood why but they had. I let out an exhausted sigh and buried my face further into the pillow. I had tried hard to make happy memories but I figured that everything surrounding the situation of my soul being torn from my body was catching up to me.

The past month had been wonderful for me. I had been surrounded by friends that swirled with happiness, laughter, and kindness. Ani had taken to the group of Orrian soldiers like a duck took to water. She was a favourite, rough housing and telling jokes with the best of them. It made me smile because I felt like for the first time in a very long time she felt like she *belonged* somewhere. With them she wasn't the odd one out, the one that was forced to the edges of the group. She was simply normal to them and I knew she loved that.

It took me a bit longer to get used to them. After so long of being scared of large Orrians, I had held back, trying to work through that fear. Rhex helped quite a bit, helping to pull me away when I would get too overwhelmed or just needed a break. None of the boys seemed to mind, always smiling at me even when I needed to retreat to gather my bearings. They never looked twice or poked fun at me needing my space. It seemed as they understood more than most why I would be timid and wary and I appreciated it.

I appreciated them all for making the past month a happy one for me. There were still those that glowered at me, muttering Orrian under their breath. I had learned even more of the language at the Learning Centre to know what they were saying more of the time. I had learned enough Orrian to carry on a small conversation and to understand a small portion of what was being talked about but I still had a ways to go.

The Learning Centre itself was even more difficult for me. I had thought that having Rhex back would ease some of the issues I had but it only seemed to highlight them. They *stared* at me like they hadn't before. Before it had simply been a string of words that told them I had been mated to an Orrian. Words were easy to shove away or ignore but my large Orrian husband coming to pick me up from my classes was not something they could ignore.

I had suddenly had a spotlight on me, they stared because I was different, an oddity, a *freak*. Kher's disgust had only grown since Rhex had returned and it had gotten to the point where even Dean Hilem had become concerned and had me permanently moved to Miss Geliensha's classes. It changed some of the core material I was taking and I had to supplement my lacking Orrian History education with books but it was safer.

To be honest I was simply happy to be away from Mr. Dahgme. He was nearly at the same level as Kher with his disgust. I hated having him pointing out humanity's flaws and calling down my relationship with Rhex as a simple mutation and something that should be reviled and squashed out. It was something I knew he was reprimanded severely for by Dean Hilem but prejudice sometimes ran deep and was hard to simply push away.

The dim lights turned up a fraction as the door creaked open. I turned my head on the pillow as Rhex moved over to the bed and crawled on it beside me. He lay down on his side before he brushed a lock of hair from my face. I closed my eyes in bliss at the contact. He had come back from training to be much more touchy and relaxed about our relationship. I appreciated it.

"Did you nap?" His accented voice made a small smile cross my face as it rolled over my skin. I wanted his fingers to follow the path his voice had. When I had said I would never get enough of him I hadn't been lying. There was nothing that I wanted more than Rhex touching me, being in my arms, or learning my body in such a way that had me uncontrollably shouting his name to the roof of our bedroom. "Liviya, as much as I like the trouble that expression on your face is painting, I need you to answer me." His words made me blush, despite the grin he had on his own face as one large hand covered my waist, his thumb brushing tantalizingly close to the bottom of my breast.

"No nap." I hadn't been able to and I couldn't place why. I should have been able to sleep, I was exhausted enough but I simply couldn't. Perhaps my brain was simply too busy at the moment.

"Are you feeling better?" His voice was low and I shrugged. I didn't think I did but lying in the dark had helped the ache in my head that I got from being overtired.

"Still tired but my head hurts less." As long as that faint throbbing pain was kept to a minimum I could deal with it.

"That is good. Do you want me to lay with you?" He asked the question rather hesitantly and I nodded wiggling closer to him. He chuckled before wrapping his arm around me and holding me close. I liked being close to him, relaxing with him. I was close enough I could feel the heat of his body and almost hear his heartbeat. Being in his arms made me feel that much more protected from the world I now lived in.

I relaxed even further as his fingers drew trailing patterns on my back, his touch burning through my shirt to sear my skin. I shivered under the feeling It gave me. He was an addiction I knew I would never be able to kick, even if I wanted to, which I absolutely did not. I was more than content to crave him and his proximity as if it were imperative to my very survival. I had known at the beginning that our bond did not mean love but I knew now that I loved Rhex more than anything.

I had fallen in love with him over phone calls and letters. I had fallen in love with him at every declaration of how much he missed me and every time he calmly told me that it was okay because he had only so many weeks to see me again. After he got back that love had grown.

It had grown with every touch, kiss, and embrace. It was in him stuttering over an unfamiliar English word as he practised the unfamiliar language he had learned for me. It had grown when he would awkwardly hug my mother back, when he would shake my father's hand. The growth was there when he would grin at me at the oddest times, when he would tuck some hair behind my ear and pull me close simply because he wanted to.

The Rhex that had left for training and the one I got back were so different it was nearly startling to me. The Rhex I had before had a tendency to lean away, to curl his hands into fists and pull them behind his back. That Rhex had expressed confusion about my want to touch, about his own want to touch. He was a man who told me that affection wasn't the Orrian way. The Rhex I had now was so vastly different. He reached out for me, gravitated to me like I did to him. He embraced me, revelled in affection and seemed *happy* about it.

"What did you do in training?" There had to have been something there that had taught him that contact was normal and acceptable. There was only so much that longing could do to change a person's perception of the world.

He made a faint noise in his throat as he slid his hand down my side. "Standard Army training. Gun handling, new tech training, explosiv-"

I tilted my head on the pillow to look at him. "Not that. You never did this before you left. You didn't like touching me before." He hadn't shied away from it. He had attempted before he had left but before that he had avoided touching me and when he did touch me he had seemed upset at it.

He met my gaze with his own and moved closer. "I loved touching you before, Liviya. Please do not take my retreating as me not liking the contact." His fingers had a bit more pressure, massaging my muscles instead of teasing my skin. "I grew up in a home where affection was absent. I was not used to contact because I had been conditioned into believing that such things were unnecessary and unnatural. My parents exhibited that behaviour, my classmate's parents, my instructors, and even the Council members I lived under. I was taught from a young age that the absence of affection and contact was *normal.*" He moved his head closer once more, kissing my forehead gently.

"The first memories of affection I ever had were from my grandfather and his soulmate. They patted heads, gave kisses to cheeks, and quick hugs but their behaviour was treated as if it was abnormal. They never truly mated, never exchanged medallions. They were content with each other and I believe love was there but they weren't like us or the others that bond." He let out a heavy sigh. "My grandparents decided to forgo tradition so the affection I was shown by them was labelled as unnatural. Hence my aversion to contact when I met you. I wanted to touch you, I ached for it but in my head I had hundreds of memories telling me that touching, that craving that contact was wrong." He had explained it to me before but not quite as in depth with his memories and his childhood social conditioning.

"Instinct against mind, like you told me before." I watched as he nodded before he rubbed my back in swirling motions, making my eyes go half-lidded.

"Exactly." He kissed my forehead again, letting his lips linger on my skin, causing me to shiver with faint pleasure. "When I transferred to my new battalion, I was surprised to see their camaraderie, their easiness with each other. With my old battalion it was all formation, structure and specific space. We never joked or laughed or even conversed about anything outside of our training or mission plans. It was a cold and sterile environment, just like how I had grown up." He pulled back slightly before rubbing his nose against my own.

"They were odd and strange and against everything I had been taught as I had grown up. I had not been given a chance to say no as they dragged me into everything they did. They told me that I was part of their family." His mouth had a softer edge to it and I could see he clearly cared about his new battalion. "The humans were just as much as family to them as an Orrian was. Species didn't matter, gender didn't matter to them. In my old battalion we were a unit, a formation, a number. With them I was Rexy, I was a part of something more. I was recognized, teased, and a member of a large family and when they found out about you... I was *celebrated*."

He swallowed before his light green eyes met my mine. "My pairing to you was a source of great joy for every single one of them. I have never seen more happiness in anyone when confronted about our pairing than with them." He chuckled, the sound rolling over me and I couldn't help but smile at it. "They demanded to know everything about you. They demanded I tell them what your laugh sounded like, what shade your eyes shined when you smiled. They spent *weeks* making me remember every facet of who you are. They forced me to think about you when there were moments when I felt like being without you made it so hard to breathe." They had my everlasting gratitude for helping him through our separation. I had known they had helped but to hear Rhex speak of it was just reinforcing it.

"It was Bruce who taught me that touching you was not something I had to shy away from. When I had explained it to him, explained to him that I felt such a barrier between us, he had asked me what I would do if I was on a road driving to a new post when my vehicle hit an odd bump in the road near a known Kengan junction." He let out a heavy sigh and I reached out, touching his chest, feeling his heart pounding beneath my fingertips. "I told him I would order a full retreat and bail on my rig because that bump was more than likely an IED. Bruce had stared at me before asking me how I knew that." Rhex grasped my hand in his own, linking our fingers together before he placed a kiss against the back of my hand.

"*Instinct.* It taught me that in order to save my battalion and my comrades I would need to order a retreat and bail before the device was triggered." He brushed his lips across my skin, creating a slow burn deep in my belly. "Bruce looked at me and told me that pushing myself to stop touching you was the same as me forcing my battalion to drive forward after my instinct told me that there was serious danger. It would be disastrous."

He kissed the back of my hand more fully as his eyes met mine. "He taught me that my instinct to touch should *never* be questioned or repressed because all I would be doing is damaging something much more important. *You.*" His words were sweeter than sugar and I felt a heated blush flood my cheeks.

"Bruce has my thanks." *All* of my thanks. He was the reason I was able to enjoy Rhex fully.

"Mine as well." He lifted himself over me and kissed me deeply. I melted under him, arching my back as his kiss built a rapidly growing fire within me. I would never get enough of his kisses. I tugged my hand from his and wrapped my arms around his neck, pulling him down. His lips moved from my mouth to trail down my jaw and to my neck. I inhaled quickly, shivering under the heat of his touch. I trailed my hand down his shirt to his pants when a hard, unusual shape in his pocket made me pause.

"What's this?" I tapped with with a raised eyebrow. He pulled himself away from me with a start as he went up to his knees quickly, digging it out of his pocket. It was a decently sized box and he smiled at it.

"I forgot." He opened it and showed me. I blinked as the lights turned up slightly. Two bracelets lay in the box, a smaller one inside of a larger one. He pulled out the smaller one before setting the box to the side. I grinned at the realization of what they were. "They were finally finished." The bracelet was a slightly thick weathered silver band with Orrian symbols carved into the surface. I took them in with a teary smile.

I brushed my fingers against the carvings. "*Mehba illeehd sirbaht onshe halh.*" The first of many loves will never be easy for its intensity is that of a thousand fiery suns. The Orrian and English translations of the poem wove around each other around the band.

Rhex nodded before gesturing for my hand. I lifted it quickly, sitting up as I wiped at my eyes. "Two beings caught in a raging inferno of the Source's creation. One cannot survive without the other and the other cannot survive without the one." He held the bracelet to my wrist and the side opened before it slid onto me gently, closing seamlessly. "Their love will be the spark that creates the beacons for those lost in the darkness. Their love will ignite the passions that have been faded for a millennia and it shall draw the lost ones from the darkness." I looked up at him before reaching out and grabbing his, my heart pounding in my chest. We would be truly bound in his culture. The gold rings were something Orrians barely looked at, the binding bracelets were their way of showing a bound couple.

"Without the first of many loves their souls are darkened, awaiting for the other half that will never come. Banished to the darkness as they had forsaken the light they wait without hope for the first of many to call them back home." I gestured for his own hand and he held it out. I held the bracelet to his wrist like he had done to mine and slid it onto him. "The first of many loves will never be easy for the winds of change blow harshly and the darkness will fight back against its fiery light." I looked up at him and locked my eyes to his. There was a softness to his face as some of his dark hair flopped into his face. He said nothing as he cupped my face and kissed me again. I grabbed the fabric of his shirt and pulled him closer, holding him tightly to me.

He deepened the kiss, gently moving me so I once again lay on my back, him hovering over me as he continued his mind scrambling kiss that made me feel like I was melting into the bed with the heat it caused. His hands moved under my shirt and I lifted my arms over my head, arching my back to help him pull my shirt off. I shivered as he slowly pushed my shirt up, his rough hands waking my nerves up, sending pleasurable things through my body.

He got it off halfway before someone banged on the door. We both gave a groan of disappointment at the interruption as he broke the kiss off. We both panted slightly and I couldn't help myself as I lifted my head and pressed a kiss to his lips. He returned it before the banging returned. He backed off, giving me several more pecks as he moved from off of me.

"I will be right back." His voice was husky and I liked the sound of his words. I stretched on the bed as he left the bedroom. I blinked at the ceiling but was distracted by the feminine voice that echoed through the apartment with apparent fury. I frowned and quickly got off the bed and left the bedroom. Nadila stood in the living room, her blond hair looking disarray as she threw her arms out. Rapid fire Orrian escaped her mouth. It was too fast for me to catch but Rhex barked back something in Orrian that sounded aggressive.

Nadila caught sight of me, her violet eyes filled with a rather dangerous fire. "You need to stick close to Rhex! There will be nothing but him to protect you." She spat the words out, her face red and I swallowed, looking between her and Rhex.

"What?" I didn't understand what was going on.

"The Oria Council had pulled Rhess, Lymirch, and I from our Council positions and has demanded we return to Oria. They have already sent our replacements. They will be here in two weeks." Her face expressed her anger but her tone expressed her panic and it mixed with the oppressive rage she was exuding.

I frowned, still not understanding what she was saying to us. "I don't-"

Her lilac eyes flashed with her anger as her chest heaved. "Khos has managed to convince the Oria council we needed to be transferred!" At that I swallowed, my throat dry with fear.

"You are *leaving*?" She couldn't leave. Nadila and Rhess and Lymirch were the only human friendly Orrians on the council. I never had much to do with Lymirch but his leanings were clear. Without them there was very little that was stopping Khos from doing as he wished

"Yes, and only the Source can help you now, Liviya." Her violet eyes spoke of her fear for me and as I tore my gaze to look at Rhex, his did as well.

39

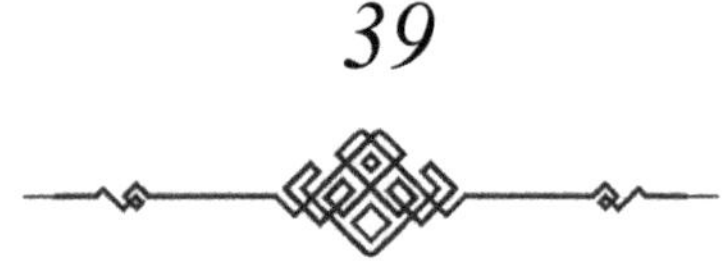

A week later

The week had been stressful. As Nadila had said, she and Rhess and Lymirch had been shipped off to Oria. Khos had personally shown up, his expression neutral except for the slight upwards tick of his mouth that had belayed his satisfaction for the goodbye.

Nadila had attempted to contact the Council numerous times before she was shipped out but her calls had fallen on deaf ears and were always countered simply with 'You are needed elsewhere'. I didn't understand it. I didn't understand why the Oria council was so unmoving towards her impassioned pleas.

I knew I was in danger, more now than I had ever been but for now I knew I was safe. With Rhex on the ship with me, I was protected from the worst of Khos' wrath. He couldn't harm me because with Rhex there, Khos was bound by the laws of his species. I was classified as an Orrian citizen and could not be separated from my mate. Not to mention they could not deny Rhex his mate, no matter who that person was. The law didn't care that I was human, the law only cared about the fact I was bound.

It was the only thing I clung to. It was my security blanket. I held onto it like I held onto Rhex. He had become so agitated and tense. I didn't blame him. I was just as tense as he was. I was also anxious enough that I was getting severe nausea and had a hard time eating anything because I worried myself to the point of throwing it all up again. Not to mention the nightmares. I would wake up crying some nights or screaming others. It was this entire fucked up situation that was wearing down on us both.

There was a loud knocking on the door and my heart jumped into my throat as Rhex gave me a look that told me to stay put as he moved towards the door. When he opened it two peace officers stared at him, one with a rather bored look on his face as he looked down at his clipboard.

"Rhex DharSon?" At his name Rhex nodded sharply, attempting to block view of me from the two officers. I quickly put my translator in, I needed to know what was being said. "Come with us." The one stepped out of the way and gestured for Rhex. I moved closer, my heart pounding hard in my chest.

"What grounds do you have for summoning me?" He snapped the words out and I swallowed, rubbing my arms as I watched his shoulder muscles tighten.

"You are late for your shuttle." The peace office gestured with with the clipboard and Rhex exhaled heavily.

It was clear he was agitated with the man and I didn't blame him. "What shuttle?" His tone was tense and clipped and held the heat of his anger.

"The one taking you to first section, Delta quadrant, soldier." At the words Rhex froze, his muscles locking up and I felt like my heart had stopped. Rhex wasn't supposed to be assigned anywhere. He was an inactive soldier, our bonding made it so he was free from service on the front.

"That is impossible. I am retired from the military. I am not to be reissued to war zones or training." His words were clipped with warning and the peace officer shrugged again. I remembered Nadila telling me they were in Khos' pocket. I felt fear thicken in my veins. This was *his* doing.

"It says here you are active." The officer tapped the clipboard and Rhex's grip on the door tightened. I could see his knuckles whitening.

"I filed the paperwork myself. I am no longer a soldier." Each word was said carefully and clearly but the officer made an exaggerated scan of the paper.

"It says here you *are*." His mouth nearly twitched upwards and I *knew* that this was Khos' doing, I could feel it in my very bones as the nausea swirled around me thickly at the implications. They were trying to take Rhex from me again.

"That is lying. I filed the paperwork correctly with the Army Resources Unit on level thirteen. It should have been processed." I had been with Rhex when he had done it. He had filed it a month ago. It was more than processed. The woman had assured us both that he would be taken off duty and listed as civilian.

"Are you resisting?" The other officer sounded amused and Rhex nodded.

"Yes, I am. This is *not* protocol." It wasn't, Khos was fucking with the system. I had the sudden urge to throw up as the anxiety and fear clashed inside of my stomach. This was bad. Very, very bad.

The other Peace Officer tapped his clipboard with a pen. "You are on the list. This *is* protocol."

"You cannot take me away from my mate to put me in a war zone. All mated soldiers are to no longer be reinstated for service." It was something Rhex had told me numerous times. It was all we had now that Nadila and the rest of the human friendly council members were gone.

"It says here you are not mated." The officer tapped the clipboard once more and Rhex pointed at him, his entire body shaking with rage.

"You *know* that is a lie!" There wasn't a person on the ship who couldn't tell that wasn't a lie. *Everyone* knew about Rhex and I. I swallowed back the vomit that wanted to climb into my throat.

"The Council no longer recognizes pairings between humans and Orrians. You have no mate." There was a smug look on the officer's face that I wanted to be wiped off. This wasn't some stupid game, this wasn't something that one could laugh about. They were messing with lives and taking away futures. They were *breaking* the law.

"The Council had no decree over what matings are to be had!" Rhex gestured at him harshly and I slowly backed away. Things were going to get violent and I knew I couldn't get in the way of an Orrian fist. It would break me.

"They do and they have done this. So, come quietly or not. It makes no difference to us. You are going to your shuttle and the human you are harbouring will be placed in the cell bays for trial." His eyes landed on me and my face drained of colour. The motion so quick that it actually made me dizzy. I knew it. I knew Khos hadn't been done with me.

"You cannot do this!" Rhex blocked his view of me and the peace officer gave a rather cold grin.

"It has already been done." He gave an amused shrug, his cold eyes landing on me once more.

"Not if I have a say." The words were ground out and my eyes went wide as Rhex wrapped his arm around one the peace officer's neck and kicked the other one in the side of the knee. I felt my stomach roll at the popping, crunch sound the joint made as it dislocated. The man screamed in pain as he fell to the floor clutching his knee.

With wide eyes I watched as Rhex spun the other man around before grabbing his arm. With what seemed like a lazy motion he twisted it and slammed the heel of his palm into the back of the man's elbow. I closed my eyes as it bent at an awkward angle. The man's harsh cry was jarring to my ears and as it added to the whimpering moans of the other man. I pressed my hands over my ears, not wanting to listen to their painful cries anymore.

I looked up at Rhex and his face was calm as it always was but there was a tinge of rage to the lines of his expression. This is what he was trained to do. True, he only did it on the battlefield but I wondered if it was as natural as breathing for him. He looked at me before he pitched forward and I saw another peace officer as he followed through with the tackle. I jumped back as Rhex hit the floor. With a small grunt he threw an elbow down and slammed it into the peace officer's neck before shoving him away.

I didn't know what to do, I wanted to help Rhex but I knew I couldn't endanger myself. They could seriously injure or kill me with a stray blow without meaning to. Another peace officer came into the apartment as Rhex managed to get to his feet. I called out a warning but it was too late as the newest officer slammed his fist into Rhex's side. I watched as pain flashed across his face and I took a step towards him. Almost instantly his eyes were on me, warning me off before he threw an elbow back and hit the officer in the face.

My eyes went wide and I dashed out of the way as Rhex threw the officer over his shoulder and over the sofa into the glass table. Glass shattered across the floor and I scurried away from it. Rhex was grappling with the officer who tackled him as I made a dash for the door. A hand grabbed my ankle and I fell. I put my hands out, allowing them to take most of the force and I gave a small cry as I kicked at the hand and was rewarded by being dragged back towards the officer with the dislocated elbow. I wasn't strong enough to fight off the grip but I tried my hardest to escape.

He gave a loud grunt as he popped the joint back into place. "I will break your ankle like a twig, half-breed" At his gritted words, time felt like it moved in slow motion as I looked over to Rhex and watched as he was slammed into again. I reached out for him, calling his name as they hit the wall with a crash. I could see the stunned confusion in Rhex's face right before the officer slammed his fist into his ribs again. I blinked as the peace officer grabbed me roughly by the arm and dragged me to my feet before pulling me towards the door.

The hand was so tight around my bicep, I felt needles in my fingertips as it cut off circulation. "Stop fighting, you little *bitch*." The curse was nasty and full of venom as I was pulled completely out of the house and into the housing square. I was jerked around as the officer grabbed my other wrist and brought his face close to mine. It felt like cotton was in my ears as he shouted at me, my eyes caught sight of a Rhex's comrades and my friends as they shoved against the line of peace officer's holding them back.

Kodlak, the eldest of the group, caught sight of me and pointed, his expression desperate. "Help her!" The words were louder than everything else and I watched as a Peace Keeper turned to look at me. "Help her!" It was a harsh order for the robot and I yanked against the crushing grip on my wrist.

"Stop fighting, half-breed! Now move!" The officer pushed me backwards with such force I hit the railing of the square and started to tip over it. My breath caught in my throat and I prepared to scream when a robotic hand grabbed my shirt and pulled me back to my feet.

"Please breath, citizen. You must not experience any unnecessary stress." The robotic voice brought tears to my eyes and I slid down the railing, my hand clutching my mouth. I felt vomit well up in my throat and I pressed a hand to my mouth to stop it from escaping. The peace officer strode towards me, his face twisted with anger. The peace keeper stepped in front of him, blocking his way. "Step back, officer, or I will be required to use lawful force to stop your approach." I watched with wide eyes as the officer pushed the peace keeper out to the way.

"Fucking piece of scrap, she is being arrested. Fucking little bitch has been enough trouble already." He reached for me and I gave a small chirp of fear as I tried to back away from his reach, unable to go very far as the railing resisted the movement.

"Lawful use of force engaged." The peace keeper grabbed the officer by the back of his jacket and slammed him into the ground, holding him down with one robotic arm. "Please, citizen, step back from the danger." The peace keeper's scanner moved over me, beeping as it did so.

"Where is Rhex?" I looked between the peace keeper and the door to Rhex's apartment. My heart pounded harshly in my chest as fear rolled through me. I glanced around and saw Rhex's form being dragged away from the apartment by two peace officers. My heart sank as he was pulled away. The group of our friends shoved against the line of peace officers hard. Their angry voices following Rhex while they looked back at me.

"Citizen, you have a warrant for your arrest. Please, come with me." Robotic hands grasped my arms and I gave a slight whimper as the peace keeper carefully lifted me to my feet. I felt tears burn my eyes and then my cheeks as they slid down my face. Three more peace keepers came to stand by me and when I looked between them, the peace officers were staring, like vultures at a corpse.

"She is our prisoner. Hand her over." The one that had been holding the clipboard stalked towards us and the peace keeper closest to him held out its arm.

"Please make way." Its robotic voice was comforting in a way. I felt far more safe with them, even if they were taking me to the cells.

"Hand her over." The officer's eyes burned into me and I stared at the floor, the lines of the tiles were blurry through my tears. I was fucked. So, so *fucked*.

"If you do not move, we shall have to use lawful force." At the words I glanced up and wiped at my eyes right as the officer shoved the keeper's arm away.

"Get the fuck out of the wa-"

"Lawful force engaged." With one smooth move the keeper took the officer's legs out from underneath him and shoved him to the floor. "Do not obstruct us in our task or more lawful force shall be used." The keeper grasped his arms before cuffing him. He struggled against them, glowering up at me.

One of the other officers stepped forward, pointing at the peace keeper. "She is-"

"To be taken to the cells. We have been alerted to her arrest warrant and have issued five more." The keeper's chest plate flashed and five pictures showed up, including the one of the officer on the ground, the one that nearly shoved me over the balcony, and the one currently questioning the keeper.

He looked just as surprised as I felt. "What the hell?! You cannot arrest us!" He pointed at the keepers surrounding me but only the one standing beside the already cuffed officer was paying any attention.

"Unlawful force against an Orrian citizen is a punishable offence. You will be detained. Please wait for the next available peace keeper or you shall be forced into compliance." The robot moved back to stand beside me and I felt a bit more comforted having them on all of my sides. I would take the peace keepers to the peace officers.

"That was lawful force!" He swung his arm wide and I moved closer to one of the keepers.

"Other citizen has sustained five broken ribs, a dislocated jaw, a severe concussion, and various skin abrasions. Lawful force contains, it does not harm. Anyone using unlawful force must be punished." The faces flashed once more before the keeper's chest plate went back to normal.

"Go fuck yourself, you tin can!" The officer stepped closer, right in front of the keeper.

"Obstruction of duty is a punishable offence." The robotic voice was quick as the keeper took a step and the officer bumped against it, barring it from moving forward.

"Hand her over!" He went to shove the keeper out of the way, his eyes on me when there was a faint clicking from the keeper.

"Lawful force engaged." Without warning he too was quickly taken down and cuffed. Two other keepers mechanically moved to the area and towards the bound men. Once the front keeper was back into place, they all started moving in tandem.

I rubbed my arms as I stared at the floor before looking at one of the robots. "What did I do?" I hadn't done anything. I hadn't broken the laws but I could only guess the ordinances that Khos had passed since Nadila and the others were gone.

"New ordinance of the council. Section five dash three point eighty-three. All humans on the ship must undergo medical testing within forty-eight hours. Amendment is retroactive. Citizen must be held for sentencing." At the words I felt my chin tremble as sobs built in my throat. I was going to die, they were going to learn of my DNA and I was going to be recycled.

"Okay... thank you." My voice warbled and the anxiety rushed through my stomach and into my chest. It made it hard to breathe, to think.

"Your stress levels are peaking, citizen. Lower them or lawful force will be engaged." I didn't know what it was saying but I tried to even my breathing out, not wanting to end up with my face pressed to the floor and cuffed. Everything was messed up and I knew I didn't have a chance in hell of escaping this situation alive. I sniffled and wiped at my eyes. I had no allies anymore.

I was as good as dead. Just like Khos wanted.

40

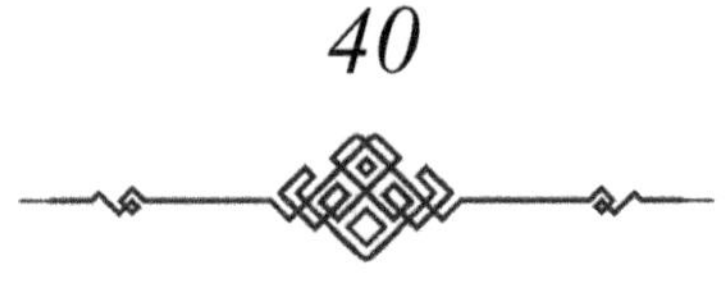

A week later

I stared at the white wall of my cell. I had been stuck in there for a week. A week of white walls, a hard cot and a scratchy blanket. I felt like I was losing my mind, there was nothing I could do except stare at the blank walls with eyes that weren't really seeing. The aching loneliness in my chest was nearly crushing and the first few days in the cell I had spent crying. Many times to the point where I would throw up.

The peace keepers had repeatedly told me to keep my stress levels down and when I became to inconsolable they had hooked me up to an IV with a mild sedative and started giving me pills and vitamins to help with the nausea so I could eat. Apparently that was their idea of lawful force. I was grateful for them, despite the fact they were my jailers. They made sure I had appropriate meals and vitamins as well as the fact they kept the peace officers away.

They had been trying to get to me since the moment I had been placed in the cell. Thankfully the peace keepers kept them out. They had also locked up numerous ones for obstructing their duty. Apparently the peace keepers locked the officers up much faster than Khos could get them out. It would have been amusing to witness had I not been locked in a cell with my soulmate going to one of the most dangerous places in the universe where he would probably die. No one came back from the section he was going into. The thought had a lump growing in my throat so I pushed it away.

I curled up on my bed, pressing my face to the pillow. I could hear Rhex's battalion speaking, their voices echoing down the hallway. They had tried to see me but the peace keepers kept everyone away. When I had attempted to count them I had managed to see twelve robotic bodies before I lost track of which ones I had already counted. The boys had still tried and when they couldn't get close they would speak to me, shouting down the hall, telling me that it would be okay, that they would help me out.

Several times I had heard Ani's voice but I hadn't been able to see her or the others. Without their voices I would have felt isolated and even more terrified than I currently was. Waiting in the cell had been nerve wracking and I knew Khos had done it on purpose, forcing me to wait, to agonize over what he was doing. Numerous rules would be written specifically so I would break them with my mere presence. Each one furthering his case for me to be recycled. I was an oddity, a mutation, a freak, something to be disposed of.

I pulled the covers over my head as I heard the mechanical clanking of a peace keeper coming to my cell. I didn't mind the robots, I truly didn't, but my head was hurting from the tears and the stress and I didn't want to have to deal with anyone.

"Citizen, you have been granted access to a visitor." At the robotic words I threw the covers off and jumped out of the bed. I grasped the cell bars tightly, looking for the visitor. Kodlak moved down the hall and I reached through the bars, my eyes blurring as I gave a small sob. He hurried over and grasped my hand in his before reaching through the bars and giving me a much needed hug.

"I am sorry we could not get to you sooner. It took us awhile to realize that we had to request visitation from the peace keepers themselves before we were allowed to see you." He held me gently, ever conscientious of his strength. I was just relieved to see a face, any face, that was friendly. I would have loved to see Ani but I knew I would have to take what I was given.

"Thank you, thank you so much for being here!" I had needed someone, anyone friendly to see and talk to.

Kodlak let me go slowly, still holding my hand. His face was lined with stress and I could only imagine how I looked. "It is okay,

Liviya. It is okay." He squeezed my hand gently, his shoulders slumping slightly.

"Rhex?" His name had to be forced out around a lump in my throat. I needed to know how he was doing.

"He is in hyper sleep still." Kodlak let my hand go and rubbed at his face. He looked so tired but I felt like that look right down to my bones.

"Will he be okay?" It had taken him a week to get to training, I wasn't aware of how long going to the front would take.

"He will be fine. The medical bay fixed him up before he got on the shuttle." As much as the news was relieving I still felt a new round of tears prick my eyes, warning me that they would fall if I spoke.

"What about after I'm-"

"*Do not,* Liviya. Do not think like that." He once again grabbed my hand, shaking his head. His aqua blue eyes were sad as he gently squeezed my hand before reaching through the bars and brushing away my tears.

"There are *no* other options, Kodlak." I was done. This was it, the last stop before Liviya Mary Burch had to get off. It was the end of my life and I knew it was. Khos would get what he wanted unless I was given a miracle and from my position it seemed like we were all out of miracles.

"Do not say that. Ani'tah, Lukesh, and Dhor are all searching the records for a way to get you down to Earth." As much as I wanted to hope I knew it wasn't really feasible or possible. Protocols needed to be followed and I knew those protocols would be blocked by Khos at every turn. He was going to do what he wished, regardless of who it affected.

"They need the Council's permission." And with Khos having a stranglehold on the Council I would never be free.

"I know but that is for Orrians. You are human, *maybe* there is a loophole for you." His voice was low and I felt a small spark of hope. If they could figure out how to wiggle around the permission from the council then I might have a chance of escaping.

"Do you really think there could be something?" I didn't want to hope because I didn't want it crushed but I couldn't help the small beam of it that bloomed in my chest.

"I am certain there is a way out. We just need to find it, we just need *time* to find it." He gave my hand one more squeeze before he let it go again.

"When do you think that they would have it figured out?" I needed a time frame. I needed *something* to keep my head above water. I tamped down the hope as best as I could.

"A day, maybe. They are trying very hard, Liviya." He gave me a tentative smile, it looked strained on his face and I didn't blame him. They had tried hard to keep Rhex off the shuttle and they were trying just as hard to keep me from the Council room.

"Okay." I gave a small nod and rubbed at my arms before wiping my eyes.

"Citizen, your visiting hour must be cut short. The prisoner has been called to the Council room." At the robotic voice that tiny bit of hope withered and my heart sank low into my belly.

"So much for that day, Kodlak." I stepped away from the bars, tears filling my eyes as the peace keeper led Kodlak away. I hated myself for allowing that small bit of hope into my grasp. I knew that there was no way that I was going to be okay.

"We will work this out, Liviya. I *promise* you." Words. They were just words and nothing else. I closed my eyes and sniffled slightly. Words couldn't save me. Nothing could now. I hated being so self-defeating but when your back is against the corner and wolves were closing in on the sides you had left, the outcome looked pretty bleak.

A peace keeper opened my cell door and stepped into the opening. "Please, prisoner, hold out your arms to the sides. I must scan you."The scanner beeped and I held out my arms, trying not to cry again. I needed to be done with tears. Just like the Hero of Old. I wanted to do this with my head held high but after being shown a life with my soulmate I couldn't imagine simply giving up. I knew I had to and I knew there was no hope but I ached and I was pained from knowing something so special and wonderful and then having it snuffed out.

The light flashed before the keeper scanned me for several moments, rolling up and down my body. I watched as data rapidly flashed on the screen in its chest before it went dark. There was a flashing red light for a few moments before the keeper once again moved.

"Scan complete. Mutation detected. Hand out." My heart jumped into my throat as I held out a shaky hand. The robot moved closer and took it carefully before it touched my wrist. There was a tiny sting before the screen flashed again, displaying a big sixty-three percent in big red letters. The keeper straightened before the screen died and it slumped, ceasing all noise. It looked like it was actually shut down.

"Apologies, prisoner, unit three-three-nine-eight-two has just experienced a remote deactivation." Another keeper came into the cell, moving the deactivated robot to the side. "Please come with me." It turned without another word and I quickly fell into step beside it, looking warily at the deactivated keeper.

"Why was it deactivated?" I glanced over my shoulder at my cell.

"It tried to process information that was denied by the main server. Unit three-three-eight-two would have been stuck in a processing loop without the deactivation." That made literally no sense. I frowned in confusion before numerous other keepers surrounded me. I counted eight of them.

"Do you always answer question?" They had never once denied me an answer when I asked them something.

"Yes. We are created to serve." All of them answered at the same time and I jumped slightly at the suddenness of it.

"Oh." I was lead past the small group of guys. I could see all the familiar faces but I couldn't look for long, it made my chest hurt and my head ache.

Kodlak lifted his hand in acknowledgement. "You will be okay, Liviya." His words were repeated through the small group and I turned my head forward without answering. There wasn't anything that pointed to me being okay. We walked through the halls, turning corners again and again. I was thankful that we didn't have to go up any stairs. They kept the cell bays on the same level as the Council room.

I shivered and rubbed at my arms. I was starting to tremble from the fear that was leaking into my limbs. I was walking into the lion's den and I knew that I probably wouldn't be walking out again. The large door to the Council room came into view and my legs shook as my heart pounded harshly in my chest. I reached up and checked my ear. The translator was firmly in place, the keepers had let me keep it.

"Calm yourself, prisoner." At the words I tried to breathe in and out to calm down but when death awaited a person behind the next door, it was hard to calm the erratic beating of my heart. The keepers moved to stand beside the door and I shook in my spot, my throat was dry and my heart continued to pound in my chest. "Please, prisoner, enter." The keeper closest to the door opened it and I moved forward, clutching my shirt hem in my hands as I entered the large room.

Half of the seats were empty and I felt a pang in my chest at the sight of them. I let my eyes drop to the floor as the door closed behind me. Two peace officers grabbed my arms and practically dragged me forward before shoving me down to the floor. My knees slammed against the metal and I stifled a cry at the pain it caused.

"Not surprised to see you here, half-breed." Khos's voice was smug and I stared at the floor, trying to hide my wince at the harsh grips that the peace officers had on me. "Look at all these infractions against you." I could hear paper shuffling and I bit my tongue against telling him that those infractions were of his own making and in no way actually my fault.

"I would list them but I doubt you can understand what I am saying besides, there is no need to review them verbally. You all have files on this half-breed. Now that the issues have been transferred we do not have to do every single thing by the book." There were chuckles from the two other council members and a door opened. I glanced over and a peace officer moved towards Khos.

"Councilman Khos, the Oria Council ship has docked." The words were said low but loud enough that I could hear. My heart jumped into my throat and I once again dropped my gaze to the floor.

"It has? Well then. Let us review this." Khos shuffled papers once more. "The half-breed claimed to be mated to an Orrian citizen. It has also broken many of our ordinances and has not complied with many of our laws and procedures." All of which were his doing. He had specifically made laws and ordinances so that I would unknowingly break them. He made them so just me being *human* would break them.

"The list is long. We cannot abide by having such a creature on the ship. We must have order." The speaker was Bilesh and I clenched my hands tightly, my nails digging into my palms.

"I agree. I suggest that we recycle this anomaly as we should have when it first appeared on the ship." Khos' words made my heart sink and I swallowed thickly.

It was over for me. There was no going back from this.

41

"Are you ready for sentencing?" Khos sounded amused and I bowed my head further.

"You would dare start without me?" A rather bulky man pushed open the far doors and I wiped at my eyes, trembling in my spot as I watched him. "Let her up. No need to shove her to the floor." At his rather gruff words I was let go rather abruptly as the Peace Officers backed away from me rapidly, heading for the door just as quickly. The man had three other bulky men following him as he moved closer.

"Ahhh, Councilman Rehnas. Very good of you to join us. Who are your colleagues?" Khos' voice was jovial and almost friendly and I shuddered on my spot. I *hated* that man with everything that I had.

"Councilmen Jonah, Kesparth, and Billimish." He gestured to each man as he said their name and their cold eyes made me shiver uncontrollably. My arms throbbed hotly with what I knew were bruises and I resisted the urge to curl into a ball and cry. I was dead. It was a fact I needed to get used to. "They were to accompany me to the ship on the behalf of the Oria council just as I was. Now please answer my question." He settled into Nadila's seat and I wanted to wince at the reminder that my friend was gone.

"I figured the quicker we got this... *nasty* business dealt with the sooner we could move on." He sneered the word nasty as he glanced at me and I shrunk under the gazes of the four men who turned to look at me. I swallowed hard and kept my gaze on the floor.

"Nasty business is quite an apt description for it but regardless, such an act needs to be done with a full council in place. You know this." Councilman Rehnas sounded bored and I glanced up as the other three moved to stand beside the table. The movement was odd because there were enough seats available for them to sit down.

"Apologies. Now would you like me to give you the details of this particular case?" Khos lifted a file and Rehnas shook his head.

"No. I am well versed in the case of Liviya Burch and Rhex DharSon. I had a long trip, lots of time to review it." He laced his fingers together and leaned against the table in a rather lazy manner. I let my gaze fall to the floor. My chest hurt and all I wanted was Rhex. My stomach flipped and flopped inside of me, making me nauseous and my entire body shake from nerves.

"Well then I suggest we move onto sentencing." Khos sounded almost delighted and I had to swallow back the vomit that climbed into my throat.

"If you do not mind, Councilman Khos. The Oria council has already passed a sentencing for this particular case." Rehnas picked up a file from the table and flipped it open.

"They have? How efficient. The floor is yours, Councilman Rehnas." Khos waved him on and I had a particular feeling that even if Khos had an issue with it, Rehnas wouldn't have paid him any attention.

"In the case of Liviya Burch and Rhex DharSon, the Oria council had deliberated and come to one very clear conclusion for this matter. As we are to preserve our race and our very people, the Oria council has decreed that action *must* be taken for this serious transgression." He said it calmly and evenly and my heart sank at each word. "In the preservation of our species and the future of our race, the Oria council had decreed that Councilman Khos and the rest of the council of ship two-nine-three are hereby stripped of their council positions and ranks and are to be banished to the outer realms for their treasonous actions against the people of Oria." My head snapped up and my eyes went wide as I stared at Rehnas. He stood up to his full height, his expression bored as he looked at Khos.

"*What?*" It was a collective cry as the three council members shot to their feet, their eyes wide with shock. I was fairly positive I looked the exact same as them.

"Detain them." At his words the three councilmen that had arrived with him moved over to them, grabbing them tightly as they cuffed the fighting council members.

"I demand you release me at once! This is an outrage! She is a human! A *half-breed!*" Khos's face was red and spit flew from his mouth in his rage and Rehnas moved around the table.

"Liviya Burch is a well known half-breed. One that the Oria council had decreed to be born." He moved closer and held out his hands for me to grasp and I shrank away from him slightly. Unsure of him. He crouched down and gently grasped my arms below the bruises, helping me to my feet as I tried to stand on wobbly legs. Everything was confusing. I didn't exactly know what he was saying. "Liviya Burch is one of eight thousand children who were born with more Orrian DNA than human. An experiment to see if a merging of our species would end our fall into extinction." I couldn't process his words but it sounded like the Oria council had ordered me to be born, *knowing* I was more Orrian than human.

"There is no extinction! Orrians will live as we always have!" Bilesh struggled against the cuffs on his arms and Rehnas shook his head.

"We had only three hundred Orrians born this star year. Next star year there will be less than twenty. Our extinction is rapidly growing closer and we found our cure." He rested a heavy but gentle hand on my shoulder as I tried to take in his words.

"I am trying to protect Orrians! I am trying to save them!" Khos fought hard against his cuffs and the other councilman shoved him against the table, holding him down. "You are going to ruin us by tainting our blood! Orrian life is precious!" He spat the words out as he fought hard to be released.

"Yes it is. That is why I am here." Rehnas said it carefully. "Orrian life *is* precious." He said the words slowly as his other hand covered my stomach. I wobbled slightly at the words. He wasn't saying what I thought he was saying, was he? I felt myself pale and my legs wobbled further, unable to hold my weight as my face drained of colour. "Easy, Liviya." He caught me surprisingly gently when my legs buckled before he set me on a nearby chair. I pressed my hands to my stomach. I was *pregnant*? The thought seemed so far fetched and unreal that it wasn't believable.

"That is a lie! There was no request for fertilization." Khos stared at me in horror and I lowered my gaze from him to where I was covering my stomach. It didn't seem real. *Nothing* seemed real.

"That is because fertilization was not needed." Rehnas stood beside me and I was almost comforted by his presence. "Human-Orrian pairs are naturally fertile. Liviya and Rhex's child, while celebrated on Oria as a rightful miracle, is just one of over a thousand that have been conceived naturally." I lifted my hand to my mouth and rubbed my stomach. I was going to have a baby, Rhex and I were going to have a baby.

Tears burned my eyes and I fought back a sob. The doors opened again and Rehnas moved quickly towards the newcomer. When I looked over it was a small, *human* woman that Rehnas kissed softly. The woman was holding a curly haired toddler who Rehnas gently picked out of her arms and smiled at as she hugged his neck.

"Just one of a thousand. Like my own daughter." Rehnas turned back to Khos. "You have been fighting against your own government and council for years. This is why you are being stripped of your rankings and being banished to the outer realms. Treason should result in death but *every* Orrian life is precious." He ruffled his daughter's curls before waving dismissively at the bound council members.

"Take them away." He pressed a kiss to his daughter's chubby cheeks and I wiped at my eyes with one hand, unwilling to let go of my stomach and the life that I had been told was growing within it. It seemed unbelievable.

"I'm sorry I took so long. I intercepted the wrong shuttle at first." Her voice was soft as she moved closer to him and Rehnas pulled her close, tucking her into his side. I felt my bottom lip tremble. I missed Rhex and I wanted him back but he was in hyper sleep somewhere in the galaxy on Khos's command. He was out of my reach.

"It is no matter, Margery. You are here now." He said the words softly and she smiled up at him before he turned his attention back towards me. I couldn't help but shrink under his gaze, both my hands going to cover my stomach as if that would protect the small life form growing within me.

"I am sorry about this unpleasantness, Liviya DharSon. I wished you could have been informed sooner but we needed to remain quiet if we were to gather enough evidence against this council and its treasonous affairs." He truly did seem apologetic and so I gave a rather shaky nod. I still wasn't entirely sure but the fact his soulmate was human and the fact he had banished Khos was enough to have me giving him some trust.

"It's okay." I wiped at my eyes and stood on unsteady legs.

Margery moved over and sat me back down, her hands flitting around me. "No. You must sit. You've had a *very* difficult week and stress is not good for the growing child." She patted my cheek with a friendly smile and I sniffled. My chest felt tight and all I wanted to do was cry. I wanted Rhex.

"Where is she?" The booming voice was familiar and my heart jumped into my throat as I shot to my feet, ignoring Margery as I sought out Rhex. "Liv!" His voice seemed to rattle the very air with his worried anger as he appeared in the doorway, his expression severe. I gave a cry and bolted for him. He dropped his pack and his rifle and caught me in his arms, holding me close. I started to sob, holding onto him tightly. I never wanted to let him go again. He held my tightly as I was holding him, his fingers digging into me so hard it nearly hurt but all it brought was unending comfort.

The sound of a throat clearing had Rhex loosening his grip on me just a fraction. "I hate to intrude upon your reunion but some things need to be discussed." Rehnas's voice was firm and Rhex slowly let me go, I clung to his side tightly, wiping my eyes as he held me close. "Because of Liviya's condition it is now apparent that until we fix the attitudes aboard this ship, we will need to place both you and her into a safer environment." The councilman gave me a soft smile but Rhex held me closer, gently moving me behind him and out of view.

"What do you mean her condition? What did they do to her?" His tone was severe and demanded retribution. I swallowed against the lump in my throat as I wiped my eyes, clutching his shirt with my free hand.

"It is what *you* did to her." Rehnas emphasized the word and I swallowed. Technically it was what we *both* did.

"*Excuse* me." Rhex's form stiffened as his hands curled into fists and I slowly stepped around him.

I grasped his fist in my hand, rubbing his arm as I silently urged him to relax. As soon as his muscles started to loosen and he looked at me, I swallowed hard. "Rhex... I'm pregnant." As much as I was having a hard time swallowing the news because of the suddenness of it all, both

Rehnas and his mate were positive I was. They obviously knew something I did not.

"What?" He looked stunned and confused and I didn't blame him. I still a bit shocked about it.

"She is roughly six weeks along. The peace keepers alerted us to her condition last week." Rehnas placed his hand on his soulmate's lower back as he gave us both a wide smile.

Rhex apprehended thunderstruck by the news and I knew I didn't fair much better with it. "We did not request fertilization." He turned to look at Rehnas, his face almost pale making his scar stand out and his stubble that much darker.

"Human-Orrian pairings do not need to." Margery gave him a soft smile as she took her squirming daughter from Rehnas.

"You are carrying my child?" Rhex slowly turned to look at me, his eyes searching for a lie, searching for something that told him it wasn't true.

"Apparently, yes." My voice came out as almost a squeak. I was terrified. I hadn't planned on having a baby, I hadn't even thought about it. Rhex pressed his face into my hair as his large hand went to cover my stomach, he rubbed it gently before he kissed my temple.

"I will kill him." His words were dark and deadly as he said them against my skin. I could feel the heat of them, could almost feel the promise they carried.

"He is being banished." Rehnas sounded unconcerned and Rhex whirled around to face him.

"He threatened my mate, my *wife,* and my unborn *child!* He had me sent away so he could do so!" Anger rolled off him in rather oppressive waves. He had been taken from me because I was to be recycled. Then he had learned that the threat hadn't just been against me but a child we had created and I could understand his anger fully. I could understand his need for vengeance. I knew that if I was in the right mind I would have as well.

"And he is being punished for such. You need to remain with Liviya and keep her happy and healthy while she creates the future generation." Rehnas kept calm and diplomatic in the face of Rhex's anger. He spoke as if it did not phase him and I was impressed. "And speaking of such. You two will be placed upon Earth. It is a safer and more relaxing environment. Many Human-Orrian pairings live on Earth. Much like your friend Ami'la Denmark." He gestured to me and I frowned in confusion.

"Denmark? Ami'la?" I hadn't heard anything about Ami'la pairing off. True it had been awhile since I had contact with anyone down on Earth but I was sure someone would have let me know.

"Yes, she was mated to a Bruce Denmark a few weeks ago when he entered her office, ironically, to find his soulmate." He seemed delighted at the irony of the situation and I blinked in confusion but it was Rhex who coughed to clear his throat.

"*Bruce,* Bruce?" He raised an eyebrow as he stared at the councilman and he gave a deep nod.

"The very same one that you spent your training with, Rhex." He gave a rather amused smile and Rhex blinked rapidly. I wanted to smile. Ami'la could truly use someone with Bruce's temperament.

"Oh." Oh indeed. I knew I would feel happy for Ami'la shortly but currently I was still confused as to what was happening and what was going on.

"Please, we extend our congratulations for your child to be but you are being asked to leave the ship on a permanent basis. Your belongings have already been transferred down to Earth." He gave us both an encouraging smile and I stared at him. I had pretty much hit my limit for taking in any new information.

"I don't understand." I didn't. I barely understood half of what he had said before.

"You and many human sympathizers are being moved to Earth on a permanent basis. It is time we unpacked the ships and started merging our cultures into one." He shifted his weight on his feet. "Your friend Ghilesh was far ahead of us in getting your things together and on Earth. Illegally at that but that is no matter." That explained why Ghilesh hadn't been seen or heard during my incarceration.

"I do not understand. Why are you doing this?" Rhex said it slowly as he reached out and pulled me close to his side. His rather tight grip let me know he wasn't going to let me go and I appreciated it.

"Because we have been building a chance for our species to survive for years. You and Liviya are just a small part of that chance." His words did little to clear the confusion I felt and I *knew* Rhex felt.

"Rehnas, he hasn't been told anything. We pulled him off of the ship in his pod." Margery said it quietly and Rehnas's face flushed slightly. It looked rather amusing on such a large man.

"Oh, my apologies." His eyes darted back and forth as if he were looking for the words to use to explain it. "Thirty years ago it was discovered that the reason we had become infertile as a species was because we were not copulating with our true soulmates. We had forsaken the Source and it had in turn forsaken us. It made us barren." My father had said as much as I was growing up. I was surprised no one had truly said it out loud as fact before Rehnas.

"We had then decided on an experiment. We contacted all the doctors and scientists that were looking into the fertility issues of our species and asked them to help us." He gestured as he spoke, his voice calm and even like a true neutral and impartial council member should be. "We requested that they pick out certain people, whom they trusted completely, to carry out this top secret experiment. Your father was among them, Liviya." He gave me a look and it all suddenly made sense. My father hadn't told me because he hadn't been allowed. He hadn't kept the secret of just my DNA but the project in its entirety. It was no wonder he hadn't said anything because he hadn't been allowed to.

"This experiment was to allow human children with more than fifty percent Orrian DNA to be born to see if we could jump start our soulmate process once more. Over eight thousand children were born but only about three thousand of those, all of which were above the sixty percent mark, were actually paired with Orrians. The rest were paired off with humans." He let out a breath before he gave me a rather small smile. "You might have thought you were alone in your inability to bond, Liviya, but you were far from the first. We simply kept everything about them under wraps. No one but the Oria council and the genetic scientists knew about you and the others." Everything was making sense to me. It was in how I had few friends growing up, in how I acted and how different I had felt. It was why I hadn't truly fit in because I was part of something much larger. Something the Source had shown them.

"From the moment you were conceived we controlled every move you made. We were the ones who kept your DNA from ever entering the system. The peace keeper in your room was deactivated by a source code we wrote and implemented in the main servers. A backup in case something slipped through." Rehnas paced slightly as his mate bounced their little girl with a happy smile. "When you turned twenty-five, we chose the ship you would be brought to, we chose the day it would happen, and we had every single Orrian we believed could be your soulmate within the recycling bay for when you arrived." The memories of that day entered my head and Rhex's fingers twitched on my side.

"The scheduling error." There was a note of realization to his words and Rehnas nodded.

"That was us. You were down there because we wanted you to be there, Rhex." They had controlled everything down to the most minor detail. This had been a plan thirty years in the making and I was in awe of how flawlessly they had executed it. “We also moved you from the military apartments to the student ones to prevent your DNA from being discovered. So many little things that brought us all to this moment. " He gestured to the council room with a smile.

"Why keep this a secret?" Rhex frowned slightly. "If it is the cure for our infertility, why continue to keep us in the dark?" That was also a very good question that I too wanted an answer for. Why the secrecy and the subterfuge?

"Because there are many like Khos. We are attempting to weed them out. By exposing Human-Orrian pairings one-by-one, ship-by-ship, we are flushing them out of the holes they have hidden themselves in. Our entire reasoning is to exterminate them. Our species can only survive by combining with humans." He gave a slow shake of his head before he pulled Margery close to his side, giving her a rather loving smile. "There is no other way and even if there was, there would be no other way I would be willing to take." I knew the feeling and from how Rhex shifted his grip so that he was holding me just a touch tighter, I knew he fully understood the feeling as well.

"So we needed to remove the source of the hate and the discrimination and the dissension. How does that human saying go? Remove the rotten apples before they spoil the entire barrel." He smiled at us once more and I nodded slowly. I was understanding more and more.

A few bad apples spoil the bunch.

They were getting rid of the bad apples and in order to do so they had to do it quietly. I was more than impressed.

"Now that we have that covered. You two need to head down to Earth and settle into your new house, Liviya." At that I gave a wide grin and leaned against Rhex. Rehnas returned my grin with one of his own. "It is time for you two to go home."

Home.

I laced my fingers through Rhex's before I brought his hand up to my mouth, kissing the back of it softly. A word had never sounded so wonderful.

42

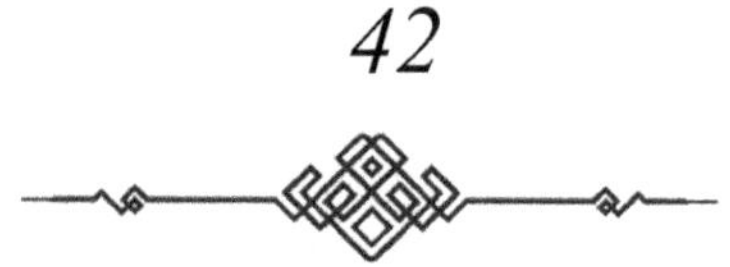

Five months later

I wiped at my forehead and pressed a hand to my back in an attempt to ease the slight twinge I had. I scowled at the crib. I had wanted it moved. It had sat in it's spot for the past four months but now the spot bothered me. I managed to move it a few feet but it seemed as though it has gotten heavier in those four months it had sat there.

I grabbed the side of the crib and pushed, grunting as I did so. It scraped across the floor as it moved several inches. This was far too difficult. Either it was getting heavier or I wasn't as strong as I had been. I rubbed my stomach as I pushed some hair from my face. I frowned. I was probably weaker. Carrying an Orrian baby was hard on human women and I was learning that first hand. I loved my little girl but she took a lot out of me. Not to mention she was a little... *rough.*

As if to punctuate my thought she gave me a rough kick that made me wince in pain and rub at the spot. She was strong and I happened to be a bit more delicate. She had a tendency to bruise me if she kicked too hard. I stared at the crib and gave a small huff and grabbed it again.

"Liviya..." Rhex's voice came from the doorway. It held a faint note of amusement and I scowled darkly.

"Don't use that tone with me. I just need to move this thing." I huffed the words out as I attempted to push the crib again. His footsteps came closer and he gently took my hands off the crib before moving the crib to the wall I was attempting to put it. I huffed and crossed my arms over my chest. "I could do it." I could have. Probably would have taken me over an hour but I would have done it.

"I know but you must limit yourself." He shuffled the crib until it was sitting where I wanted it and I almost stuck my bottom lip out.

"I don't like not being able to do things." The further I got into my pregnancy the less independent I was becoming and I felt like I was losing control and becoming a burden. I didn't like the feeling it gave me.

"You can still do things, just not the big things. You have limits now." How I hated that. I didn't like being limited or feeling trapped in my body but I *was*.

"I don't like that." Tears burned my eyes and I fought against them. I didn't want to go on another emotional tangent. The pregnancy were making my emotions go all over the place. I felt like I had no control over my own body and mind. I felt my chin tremble and Rhex's expression softened as he came over.

"I know. I know." He enclosed me into his arms and I clutched at him, sniffling. "Only a month and a half more." A month and a half and then I would be having a c-section to get our little girl out. If we let her go to term her strength would break my bones and she would be too big to have naturally. It was apparently common practice for human women with Orrian soulmates. Although they assured me that the more our DNA mixed down the generations the easier it would be on human women to naturally have children.

"A month and a half and then we get to meet her." He let me go and pressed a hand to my bulging belly. Our daughter thumped against the contact, her movements rather erratic and excited. I hid a wince as each kick thumped against his hand. My belly was starting to look slightly multi-coloured with the bruises that were just starting to show. "Are you done fighting with the nursery?" The amusement was back in his tone and I gave him a small frown.

I pushed the stray hairs away from my face as I looked around. Nothing was bothering me so I figured it looked okay. Well, for now at least. "I *think* so." I would probably start moving things around in a few days again anyway. I was highly indecisive and kept changing my mind about everything. I think that was just the anxiety about the pregnancy emerging in a different way. Growing a baby was a nerve wracking, anxiety filled process. My body was changing, hormones were surging and I had no control over myself anymore.

"Alright then." He scooped me up into my arms quickly and I gave a small cry of surprise.

"Put me down!" I still had my ability to walk and I would continue doing so until it became apparent that I couldn't.

"I am taking you downstairs. The guests will all be ready to leave by the time you finally make it down them yourself." At the teasing joke I tapped his cheek lightly in reprimand. He chuckled and carried me down the stairs regardless of my protests. He was a large protective pest. I huffed as he set me on the couch before crouching in front of me. "Are you going to pout?" He gave me a half grin that bunched up his scar and almost made me melt but I crossed my arms over my chest and looked away from him.

"Liviya, there is no need for this." He grasped my hand, amusement coating his tone as he kissed it softly. I humphed and pointedly looked away from him. "Just because you are mad it does not mean you do not love me." He kissed the back of my hand again and I fought to keep my expression from softening. He stood up and kissed my cheek, grasping my chin to pull my face towards his when the doorbell rang. He let out a small huff of irritation before giving me a quick peck on the side of my mouth.

He left to go answer the door and I couldn't help but gaze after him, a small smile tugging up the corners of my mouth. He was such a handsome man. I was happy in my life. I truly was. I could gripe and complain and feel anxious about what I was going through but with Rhex by my side it made it all worth it. Even when our daughter kicked me hard enough to make me lose my breath because each twinge of pain, each bruise, reminded me that I was carrying a bit of both of us within me, a miracle for the Orrian species.

"Rexy!" Bruce's jovial voice filled the entry way and he came around the corner, a wide grin splitting his face. "Lovely to see you, darlin'. Look at you!" He moved over, pressing his hands to my belly in welcome. "Oh she is getting big!" He smiled at me, his shaggy hair falling into his face as he gave my stomach and affectionate pat. "I can't wait for Ami'la to get this big." There was a twinkle in his eyes and I gasped.

"She's pregnant?" The happy excitement boiled over in my veins and I smiled broadly as he nodded.

"She is. We found out last week. Two months along." His grin was a proud one as both Ami'la and Rhex came into the living room.

"Congratulations to you both." Rhex slapped Bruce's shoulder and I opened my arms for Ami'la as I tried to make my way off the couch. She grasped my forearms and pressed her cheek to mine before she embraced me tightly. I held her back as tightly as I could. This was amazing news and when she pulled back there were tears in her eyes.

I touched her currently flat stomach with a large smile. "There is a baby in there." I looked up at her and she looked half a breath away from crying.

"This- I just-" She pressed her face into my shoulder, her own shaking with emotion.

Bruce made a slight face and grasped her gently. "Oh, love." He gathered her into his arms and I heaved myself off the couch to stand beside Rhex to give them some privacy. There was a heavy banging on the door and I moved towards the front door. Rhex hovered behind me and I waved him off as I pulled the door open.

"Surprise!" Nadila gave me a wide grin and threw up her arms. My mouth dropped open in shock as I stared at her.

"Nadila!" The last time I had seen her, she was being sent back to Oria and while I had been able to talk with her she never told me she was coming back.

She laughed and gave me a quick kiss to my cheek. "Close your mouth, you will swallow a fly." She kissed my cheek once more as she lifted my jaw, helping me close it.

"I can't believe you are here." I was stunned. She was supposed to still be in Oria. I couldn't believe she would trick me like that. I paused for a moment, I *totally* believed she would trick me like that.

"Well I would have come sooner but I was distracted by some... *political intrigue.*" She wiggled her eyebrows at me and sashayed into the house, her hips swaying in a rather exaggerated fashion. I blinked after her before there was a small cough, I turned and there was a rather unfamiliar bulky Orrian man holding a box with a purple bow.

"I hope you do not mind that I am here." He looked a little abashed, his eyes looking around me to land on Nadila. "I am-"

"Councilman Rhesthor." Rhex stepped beside me, holding out a hand for the councilman.

"I see my name precedes me." He gave Rhex's hand a shake and bowed at me. "I hope you do not mind the intrusion. I brought you a gift for your little one." His eyes landed on my belly and he gave me a warm, genuine smile.

"Not at all. Please, come in." I gestured to the interior of the house as Rhex moved to stand behind me once more. The large Orrian gave me another bow before passing into the house. I glanced at Rhex. "You don't think he and Nadila..." I let my voice trail off and Rhex's mouth twitched.

"He is Rehnas' father. Last I heard Rhesthor and Mah'dina chose to live separate lives and Nadila is a rather striking woman. Very ambitious and accomplished as well. Quite the catch for an unmated Orrian Councilman." Rhex rubbed at my lower backs. His fingers felt like heaven against my sore muscles.

"What about their soulmates?" With the way the tides were turning Orrians would start finding their soulmates more frequently.

"The Source sometimes surprises us and there is nothing wrong with enjoying each other's company until that time comes." rubbed my lower back and I just bit back a groan as he hit an unbearably achy spot.

He kissed the top of my head and I watched as a group of rowdy men came walking down the driveway. Rhex went out to greet his battalion and I crossed my arms, leaning against the doorway with a small smile on my face. There was a loud cheer from the group as he entered the group. I lifted a hand as they waved at me enthusiastically. They came up the sidewalk and each one kissed my cheek as they entered, several of them winking as they did so. I waved them off with an amused smile.

A car pulled up and Ani jumped out. I smiled and slowly made my way down the sidewalk towards her. She hurried towards me, a gift bag in her hand and gave me a big hug before she pulled back. "I am sorry. I took a later flight so I could give you your gift!" She held it out and I smiled, giving her another hug, holding onto her tightly. She was going halfway across the world and I was going to miss her greatly. I buried my face into her shoulder, feeling like I wanted to cry. "Hey now. I'm coming back. I should be back before the little one is born." She pushed me away and wiped at my face, cleaning away the tears I hadn't realized had fallen.

"It is just I need to go find me some dick." Her words made me burst out laughing and she cupped my face, a grin on her own. "I cannot sit here and see all the dick you and Ami'la get and not get me some of my own." She made a face at me and I gave a watery chuckle.

"You are terrible." I patted her cheek gently. I would miss her, even if she was gone for a day. She was one of my best friends and I didn't want to be without her.

"Nah, just bored of the shower." She wiggled her eyebrows and I gave another sad laugh before I looked at her. She brushed the tears away again. "Do not cry, Liv. I will always come back. After all, I might like guys but I *love* you." At that a little sob escaped and she shushed me, pulling me close. "Wherever you are, is my home because we are sisters and I would never be happy without you by my side." She let me go, kissing my cheek quickly before she made me take the gift back and slowly backed away, her own eyes shining with tears.

"I just need to go for a little bit. I will be home before the little pickle is born. I *promise* you." She lifted her hand before looking over my shoulder towards the house. "Congratulations, Ami'la. You are going to get *so* fat." Her chin trembled and she turned around, her shoulders hunching as she walked towards the car. I repressed the urge to call her back.

"You get your ass back here as soon as you can, Ani. Over turn every rock and when you find him, drag your man back with you." Ami'la's voice was stern and Ani lifted her hand, not looking back as she got into the car. I felt like I wanted to crumple in on myself. I was going to miss her so much that it hurt. I lifted my head and wiped at my eyes.

She was going to be fine. She was going to find her soulmate and the poor man wouldn't know what hit him. He would be stunned and amazed because Ani'tah was one beautiful, bold, intelligent woman. I watched the car pull away, holding onto the gift bag tightly.

"I feel like I am intruding." At the rather softly drawled voice my gaze snapped to a rather leggy dark haired woman with eyes that were such a light blue it was like they were made of ice. I stared at her in confusion and she ran her hand through her short bob and looked me up and down, her gaze lingering on my belly. "Well... *that* was not in the info Rhex gave us." She raised an eyebrow and I covered my belly with my hands as I looked at her. She moved closer and I narrowed my eyes slightly.

"What would mother and father think about being grandparents, Rhex?" She turned her gaze lazily towards the house, a slow smile crossing her face as she spotted Rhex. I looked between the two of them, spotting the slight similarities they had. Rhex took three steps and grasped her around the waist before lifting her up and spinning her around.

"Kati!" He hugged her tightly as he put her down. He ruffled her hair as she squirmed, a look of annoyance on her face as she tried to escape his grasp. "How are the parents?" He let her go and she attempted to straighten her hair and her clothes as a flush of embarrassment crossed her cheeks.

"Taking care of grandfather in his retirement." She tugged on her shirt to straighten it and Rhex reached out and ruffled her hair once more. She made a sound of disgust as she attempted to rearrange it. "Is he always like this?" She gave me a look and I nodded with a sly smile. “I swear. He was a huge pest growing up as well." She marched towards me and looped her arms through my own. "I need to get to know my sister-in-law. You can go bother someone else, Rhex." She lifted her nose in the air as she pulled me towards the house.

She glanced at me from the corner of her eyes and winked, a tiny smirk tugging at her mouth. I had a feeling I was going to like Kati. "So what are you going to name..." She glanced at me again, looking for an answer and I rubbed my stomach with my free hand.

"Her. It's a girl." At that she gave a smug smile.

"Another girl in the family? Mother is going to be pleased! So what is her name?" She looked at me in question as we entered the house and I frowned slightly. Rhex and I had yet to agree on a name

"Amy."

"Lynn." Rhex and I said the names at the same time and I made a face at him. He wasn't budging with Lynn and I wasn't budging with Amy. We had been butting heads since we learned it was a girl.

"Amy-Lynn? How cute. I approve" She let my arm go and moved further into noisy and full house.

I glanced at Rhex and he grinned as he met my gaze. "I like Amy-Lynn." He moved closer and gently pressed his hands to the bump and I smiled, giving a nod.

"I like it too." I watched as he got down to his knees, pushing my shirt up before kissing my belly.

"Hello, little Amy-Lynn. I cannot wait to meet you." He stared at my belly with a look of pure and unadulterated love that it made my heart flip in my chest. "I bet you are going to be just as beautiful as your mum." He looked up at me and I cupped his cheek in my hand, tears blurring my vision of him before the newly christened Amy-Lynn gave a rather strong kick that had me almost doubling over.

"And just as strong as her dad." I couldn't help but laugh as Rhex stood up, covering my belly up once more. He cupped my jaw with his hands, bending over me in a way that always made me feel protected. There was a soft look in his light green eyes that had my heart flipping once more in my chest.

"I thank the Source everyday that I saw you because I cannot imagine my life without you." He kissed me and I clung to him, melting towards him. He was my everything. He was my entire world and everything beyond it. He was the air I breathed and the heart that pounded in my chest. He was the father to our child and I thanked whichever deity that was listening that I had been allowed to grow up broken.

Epilogue

Part 1

Twenty seven years later

I had a duty to fulfill.

It was something that I had always been told. I was created to carry on the family name and to do my duty. As the years passed and I grew older the duty would change but the main thing that didn't was for me to carry on the family name. Now that I was twenty five my father was now adamant about it. He told me how he was going to find me a suitable, pureblood Orrian woman of good standing and high social ranking.

It was my duty as Kher LehnSon's only heir. I must continue on the traditional family practice. I had to carry on the name.

Except I had always had this niggling doubt in my head that my duty wasn't exactly to do as my father decreed. It had started with the Soul Maker and when she had given me my medallion.

I had expected something of distinguished importance that was befitting my family name but instead I had been given tarnished copper disk. It had blotches of blue green over old copper. It had been disappointing for me and my father. However when my father had left the Soul Maker's room and I had moved to follow, the wizened old woman grabbed my wrist, halting my process.

"You will be given a choice in this life, Keen LehnSon. Do what your father decrees is your duty. Follow in the dark footsteps of your family and lead your blood line in the darkness that will swallow you whole." She cackled loudly. "Or you can forge yourself a new path, create a new destiny and join your brothers and sisters in the light."

I had been confused because I had no siblings but when I went to ask her she had pushed me out the door and closed it quickly behind me.

That is when the doubt that surfaced but I shoved it all down and away. I did everything my father asked of me. I trained to be a soldier, gathered several medals on my two tours of duties against the Kengans. I had gone to the school of his choice and learned everything he dictated I should plus several that he could not control. Such as learning English and about humans.

My father *hated* them.

He had told me over and over again that they weren't to be trusted. That they had poisoned the Oria council against my grandfather and had him banished to the outer realms never to return. I had never seen anyone look so livid and cold before. When I had been a child it scared me. Now, I simply grew wary. Sometimes there seemed to be a glimmer of madness in my father's eyes that matched the cold glint in my mother's.

My childhood had been cold and I had always felt it was lacking. I had been well aware of those children whose parents would wrap them in their arms and press kisses to their cheeks. It made me wonder about more for me until my mother would yank me away, hissing about half-breeds and humans. So I would scowl at the children and their parents, hoping the hate would some how warm my mother and father up to me.

It never worked.

So I spent my life doing my duty, listening to my father, following in footsteps that had been set out before me. However that doubt always crawled back up, whispering about how uneven the steps were, how dark the path was. I would shove it away again and again but that little voice would always come back, whispering about how there was *more*. Such tantalizing whispers about how there was something greater for me out there. A faint chance at the warmth of love that I had craved as a child.

It was hard to ignore the voice as a child but I found it easier as I had grown, even though the doubt itself made me feel like I was wearing a mask my father had painted for me. It was a mask because underneath everything he taught me was a slight doubt and a disbelief that it wasn't true or right. As much as I tried to force it on, the mask never quite fit right. It rubbed me the wrong way no matter how many times I had tried to believe it didn't.

It was hard to believe in a man who tormented your nightmares as a child. My father was not a nice man. He wore a mask of false civilities to hide the twisted, dark creature that hid underneath. I had been at the brunt of his fury many times as I had grown up. I wasn't perfect and imperfection needed to be punished. It was the Orrian way he would say as he would pull his belt from his pants and point to a wall for me to press my hands against. If I wouldn't be perfect from creation, he would beat it into me.

My hand tightened into fists as a dark expression twisted my face at the memories. I didn't need to remember those. It only served to make the mask I wore itch and shift. I needed to be neutral and unaffected.

"Keen! Do not fiddle with that." My father's voice was sharp and my hand automatically dropped from my medallion to my side. My hand throbbed from the pressure of me squeezing it in my fist. Despite my strength the damned thing wouldn't break or bend. "Stand up straight and get that look off your face." I followed his instructions, forcing the thoughts away so that the dark look would smooth out into the classic LehnSon expression. Indifference with a hint of prideful smugness and derision. It was a reminder that everyone wanted to be a LehnSon but that they were all below our family name.

"I cannot believe they forced General Hamesk to have his headquarters on Earth. This is going too far. We are losing our culture while we breed with them like cattle." My father spit the words out and I nodded my agreement as he wished, my face twisting at the thought of how the humans created children.

Copulation.

True, I had my fair share of dalliances but that was with Orrian women and never for the purpose of reproducing. A true Orrian child was created on the fertility ships. It was what my father had always told me. We never rutted like animals for it. Sex was to be used for pleasure and for furthering your social standing. Nothing more.

I could understand why. Many, if not all, Orrian women were cold participants. Not truly into the experience and always with a bored look on their face. That little voice would always whisper in my ear that rutting like an animal in a manner that heated my skin and scored my back with nails would be more enjoyable than the cold indifference of the sex I was having. I wanted to wave the voice away but that doubt was always there. I stopped having sex because that voice was something I couldn't drown out anymore. It was starting to wet my curiosity as to how much better rutting like an animal could be.

I ground my teeth together and shoved the thoughts away. There would be no speculation as to what breeding like a human would be like. I was *fine* with the Orrian women. They satisfied me.

*Do they **really?***

The voice slithered into my mind and I clicked my teeth together against the possibilities it showed me. A touch that set fire to my blood and soft sounds that begged me to take what was mine. I clicked my teeth together in agitation once more and received a hard slap to the back of my head that jolted me forward.

"Pay attention and stop making that irritating sound! Hold it together, Keen, or you will ruin this family's chance at furthering ourselves!" His words were hissed and I gave a short nod, ignoring the faint throbbing from the back of my head.

"Yes, sir." I forced my teeth together tightly so I wouldn't click them before I pulled my hands behind my back and grabbed my left wrist tightly. I hoped the painful tightness of the grip would drown out that stupid little voice. I didn't need doubts. I needed General Hamesk to agree to my father's contract so I could bond to his daughter. It was all I needed in life. It was my duty.

*It is **really?***

The little voice was almost laughing at me. It reminded me of the Soul Maker's cackle, dry and brittle but full of amusement at my words and thoughts. It was *mocking* me.

My jaw hurt as I held it closed tighter and I resisted the urge to shake my head to get rid of it. Just a few more hours and then I hoped that the mocking little voice would disappear entirely.

"As you are acting like an imbecile, I will be the one speaking to the General. You are going to make yourself scarce and not fuck anything up." My father's hand gripped the back of my neck tightly as the shuttle came to a stop. His grip tightened sharply. "Am I understood?" His voice was low and deadly and I gave a short nod. He shoved my head down, squeezing the back of my neck tighter. "I did not quite hear you." He spat it out and I swallowed against the anger and the urge to retaliate.

"Yes, sir." I hid a wince as he let me go abruptly. I struggled to shove away the faint curlings of hate I had for the man whose DNA I shared. I repeated my mantra again and again until the bitter heat was buried deep down where I couldn't feel it anymore.

I must do my duty and carry on the family name.

That was all I was created for. Nothing more than that. Nothing less.

The door to the shuttle opened and I let my father exit first, as was proper, before I followed behind him. Always following in the footsteps of the generation before me. Uneven footsteps on a dark path. I clicked my teeth together in agitation and my father's shoulders tensed as he sent me a dark look back at me.

"Apologies, sir." I bowed my head slightly to appease him but he simply grabbed my arm and shoved me towards a nearby door.

"Get out to the air strip and do not speak to anyone until you can learn to control yourself. I will not allow you to make a mockery of our family name." The hissed words grated on my skin but I nodded anyway. Do my duty. I let the words bounce around in my head again and again.

"Yes, sir." The urge to spit them out was great but I fought it back. There would be no disrespect towards the family name and I would act like a LehnSon. I pushed the door open to the airfield tarmac.

A cool breeze blew against my neck as the warm sun beat down on me. Sunshine was always something I enjoyed. I had never lived outside of a ship before so sunshine and sweet breezes that carried the scent of life were something that was highly enjoyable for me. Even if they came from a planet overrun with humans and half-breeds.

I swallowed hard and chanted my mantra as that voice wiggled in the back of my mind. There was nothing for it to say. Nothing that it could do. I marched across the tarmac toward a tree that was close to the back fence. That was far enough away from everyone that I could compose myself.

*Compose yourself... Or **hide** yourself, Keen? Which is the truth?*

"Shut up." I spat the words out and the little voice cackled at me. The sound grating down my spine. I tensed against it, hurrying my steps towards the tree. A childhood habit of picking a spot and telling myself that if I reached it I would be safe. I always picked a spot furthest from my parents because even at that age I had known that there was no safety with them.

I brushed the thoughts away and clicked my teeth together in agitation. I needed to live by the mantra. Do my duty and carry on the family name. There was nothing more for me. My path had been set out.

Such a dark and lonely path. Do you ***really*** *want to go down it?*

I clicked my teeth together again. I *would* go down it because it was my *duty.* What did doubts and possibilities know about duty? *Nothing.* They knew nothing and it would be best if they simply stopped speaking.

It howled at me in amusement as if I had said something amusing. As if I had told it a joke that it could not help but laugh hysterically at.

I let a curse out and shook my head. It needed to go away. I reached out and touched the tree and my mind went blank. I let my shoulders droop with relief. I just needed quiet silence to simply think. To gather my composure and become ready to do my duty to the family. I took a step further into the shade, making note of the deep ditch that was behind me. It ran along the edge of the fence as if to deter trespassers.

I pulled myself away from looking at it to look out over the air strip. I watched shuttles land and leave and some military drop off ships make practice runs. When I looked up I could see fight ships running a practice formation above the military base. I almost missed the front lines. When I had been there the voice had been silent and I felt as if I were doing something *important,* something of *value* for this world.

Part 2

The cracking of a branch was all the warning I had before a slim form fell from the tree. I reflexively caught the unexpected person, the motion second nature since my time out on the front, but the movement sent both of us backwards into the steep ditch. We rolled down the incline together and I cursed harshly in Orrian as I tried and failed to stop, the person's arms tangling in mine to the point I could not use my own to stop us both.

We came to a stop at the bottom of the ditch and I landed heavily on my back, my head spinning from the rolling that I had unexpectedly done. My father would curse me for the rather improper behaviour, accident or not. LehnSons did not roll around in the grass and dirt. The person landed on top of me once more with a faint groan.

Anger rose up in my throat sharp and bitter but when I opened my mouth to reprimand the foolishness that the person had exhibited and the immature and despicable behaviour they had shown I had a small hand cover my mouth. A clear feminine voice muttered English close to my ear. I struggled to translate it but she had said it so quickly I could only catch a few words. I was more distracted by the soft hand that covered my mouth, how the touch seemed to sear me with a promise of something *more.*

I tried to focus on her words but all I got was: Quiet. Be. Caught. Corporal. The rest was gibberish.

My heart pounded in my rib cage as the small woman pressed her head into my chest, her form shaking slightly. I could feel my heart race unexpectedly in response to the contact and I frowned darkly. This was highly improper and my father would no doubt be punish me severely if I were to let him see me covered in grass stains and dirt. The woman pulled her hand away from my mouth and I faintly missed the contact. It was strange and I needed to get away from her. I sat up, pushing her away from me as I did so. She also sat up, faintly murmuring something I didn't care to listen to.

"Of all the stupid, illogical, and foolish things to do. No respectable lady climbs a tree! I can now tell why my father wants to keep me away from such brutish and uncultured *huma-*" My words died in my throat as she locked eyes with me. I felt like I had been sucker punched as her eyes, the multi-toned colour of my medallion, stared at me. She was something I had never experienced before. I had never viewed a woman more magnificent or stunning in my entire life. My mouth felt dry and I felt like something had connected us deep down, as if her gaze had stolen something from me and had left something of hers in return.

After a lifetime of craving it... Here is your something more. The voice whispered it softly before it faded off into the very back of my mind. It left me with stunned confusion.

There was no rational or logical explanation for what I was feeling as I looked at her. She was simply magnificent. Every inch of her face was unique and well formed. From her beautiful eyes to her thick lashes to her full lips that had a mischievous upwards tilt on the left side that made her mouth a tiny fraction uneven. The magnificence was in the delicateness of her face shape right down to the golden freckles across her nose and the tops of her cheeks.

I was pulled from my memorization of her face as she reached up and tucked some loose hairs behind her ears. I noticed her hair was in a long braid and it startled me slightly. Only important people wore their hair that long. Reality slapped me in the face and I ground my teeth together. I had been eyeing up a half-breed *human*. My father would be upset and I would tarnish the family name. I chanted my mantra in my head. I needed to focus on it and not *her.*

"*My name is Lacey.*" She was speaking English and I understood that clearly but I ignored it. I tried to ignore how the name suited her. A delicate name for a delicate fairy of a woman who had literally fallen from above. I tried to ignore how her voice rolled over my skin, bringing my nerves to life with a faint sound. "*Do you understand English?*" She gave me an imploring look but I avoided meeting her gaze. I didn't need to be sucked into that again. I *needed* to do my duty.

"I will not let such a brutish language sully my tongue." I spat the words out because anger was default. Anger was safe. It created distance and I needed distance from her. I stood up and attempted to brush off the dirt and grass that clung to my clothes. She let out such an explosive word that I nearly jumped as I immediately looked at her. I didn't need to catch the actual word to know it was a curse.

Her beautiful face was slowly turning red with anger and her unique and soulful eyes narrowed into a dark look. "An Orrian purist? I can't believe- Out of all the Source forsaken shit! I got paired with a fucking *purist!*" She spat the words out in rather flawless Orrian and I blinked at her rapidly. She was upset about this? I was the one supposed to be upset. This ruined every careful step that my father planned for me. It ruined the future plans he had for me and when his plans were ruined, mine were too because duty to my family was *everything* I had been taught. "I can't fucking believe this!" She ground the words out and I narrowed my eyes at her.

"*You* cannot believe this? What about me?" I thumped my chest. She had no right to be upset. Any woman, human or otherwise, should have been ecstatic to be paired with me. I was a coveted LehnSon. It would only elevate her status, it would simply drag mine down if anyone had even a tiny bit of knowledge about the pairing. I felt like my carefully planned footsteps were being scattered and blown away. I was lost.

"I should have listened to dad! I should have stayed away but no! I had to be a stubborn little brat because I wanted to see the birds come in!" She gestured wildly towards the air strip before she whirled around. "I cannot fucking believe this shit!" She stalked off and I stared after her in surprise, my eyes on the back of her old blue jumpsuit before my own anger rose up. She had no right to be angry. This wouldn't ruin *her* duty. This wouldn't bring punishment down on *her* head.

"Don't you dare walk away from me!" I glowered at her back but she simply moved further away as if she never heard me. I ground my teeth together. "Do *not* ignore me!" I stalked after her. There was no way I would be left looking like a fool by anyone. I was a LehnSon and I would be treated with the respect the name afforded. It was how it always was.

"I should have fucking listened. I could have led my life in blissful peace without the knowledge that I am fucking paired to an elitist Orrian *purist*!" She spat out the word with more hate and derision than my father ever used on the term half-breed. It was nearly disconcerting. "I'm such a stupid fucking idiot! Why the hell did the Source forsake me? Was it for all the times I lied and snuck out of the house? The Source needs to mind its own fucking business! God fucking damned bullshit!" The curses exploded out of her mouth and my long strides had caught me up to her rather quickly. I grabbed her shoulder to turn her around when she whirled around on her own, shoving my arm away rather violently and then shoving at my chest.

"Don't fucking touch me! You have no right to fucking touch me!" Her breathing was heaving in her chest and I narrowed my eyes. I pointed at her. I would *not* be disrespected by her, by *anyone*. I needed her to understand that I was just as upset as she was. I had a *duty* to fulfill and she was ruining that.

"Listen here you -"

"Shut the fuck up! I don't want to listen to you or even see your fucking face." She went to turn around but I grabbed her arm tightly, forcing her to stay and face me. I would not be left standing like a fool after being disrespected by her. I tried to ignore how touching her sent fire through my veins but it was hard.

"Excuse me! Do you know who I am?" I tightened my grip as she attempted to yank her arm out of it. I wasn't willing to let her go until she understood my positioning and stopped cursing at me like a foot soldier on grunt duty.

"The Mayor of *Prickville* from *Elitist* State in the great Republic of *Assholes*! I don't give two *shits* about who you are." The words were like pure venom and I would have flinched under them if I hadn't been taught from a young age to hide everything away. As much as I didn't want a soulmate, having her hurl such vile things at me was something that made my stomach feel slightly uneasy. I didn't want to hear that much hate being spit at me from her.

"You will *not* speak like that!" I would hear no more of her vile language. I wouldn't be derided that way any longer and I wouldn't be ignored.

"Get your hands off me!" She struggled to get out of my grip but I simply gave her a small shake. "Let me go!" Her hand swung and it connected against my cheek with a rather surprising amount of force. The sting came after the sound of it faded in the air. I felt a twisting rage in my gut that burned its way to my chest. I grabbed her other arm and gave her another firm shake.

"You will never strike me like that again! Do you understand me?" I had enough of such actions when I had been growing up. I would *not* take it from her.

"Then let me go!" She struggled against me and I gave her another shake.

"I will not because you have insulted me and derided me and I will not stand for it!" I would not let her go so she could assault me and then insult me as she did so. I would not stand by for it because I had heard enough of it as I grew up from my parents and I would *not* take it from her.

"Oh the shitty little half-breed hurt your feelings?" Hearing her referring to herself as such left a sour taste in my mouth that I wanted to spit out. "Cry me a river and then drown yourself in it!" She shoved at my chest as best as she could with me holding her arms before she attempted to pry my fingers off of her arms. I let one arm go and grabbed her jaw in a rather tight grip. It felt delicate in my hand and I held back, not willing to bruise her skin even though my cheek throbbed from her slap. I wanted to trail my hands across every inch of her soft skin. I shook my head slightly, trying to shake the thoughts away.

"You will not continue your tantrum! I have had enough of it!" I was growing weary of her continued tirades. She was speaking and shouting and cursing and refusing to listen. I *would* be listened to because I had a voice and I deserved to have my positioning heard. I clicked my teeth together in agitation.

"Just let me go! I don't want to look at you!" She tried to jerk her jaw out of my grasp but I forced her to face me. "I don't want to fucking look at you!" Her movements seemed almost frantic as her breathing heaved out of her chest and she shoved at me with a surprising strength.

Bitterness filled me at her struggles. "Cannot stand looking at me? Hmm? Can't stand to see the-"

"It fucking hurts to look at you!" That stunned me and my grip loosened on her. She shoved away from me, escaping my arms and moved away rather quickly.

My eyes narrowed in on her once the surprise of her admission wore off. "Don't you walk away-"

"Stop talking to me!" She threw a rather rude gesture at me over her shoulder and I narrowed my eyes further. I was done with that.

I pressed my lips into a thin line. "Don't you da-"

"Stop ordering me around! I'm not going to fucking listen!" Her stubbornness was grating on me. I deserved to be heard, to tell my side of the story. I wouldn't let that be taken from me.

"Stop cursing!" I was done with her belligerent attitude in refusing to let me speak.

"God! I need to find Ghilesh! Maybe he can do something about this stupid bond! Maybe he can fucking break it." Break it so both her and I could go our separate ways. I could bond to the perfect woman my father picked for me and she could bond to some human that would give her what I wouldn't. That thought was enough to have a dark and rather oppressive feeling fall over me. I grabbed her around the waist and lifted her up. "Put me down!" Her fists pounded on my arm and I slipped on my step backwards, sending us both to the ground. She scrambled to get away and I grabbed her quickly, pinning her to the ground, straddling her waist as I did so.

Part 3

There would be no human male in her future. I wouldn't abide by it. She struggled hard against me, shouting at me to get off her. I bent down close to her, the anger still coursing through me.

"I am *not* letting you go." I said it low and dark. I wouldn't be letting her go until she calmed down and let me speak. There was a faint whisper that urged me to *never* let her go at all. What was mine, was mine.

"*Please!* It hurts to look at you and know that I will never be good enough. That I will never be the perfect pureblood that you wanted." Tears made her eyes glisten before they rolled from the corners of them and across her temples to her hairline. The tears were enough to give me a pause, to lessen the anger a fraction until her face twisted into a scowl once more. "So fucking let me go so I can try and find someone else!" Her words were like an icy slap to the face and that dark oppressive feeling surged forward again.

I pinned her arms with one hand and reached up and yanked my medallion over my head. She thrashed under me, shouting angrily in a mixture of English and Orrian. I struggled slightly as I pulled my medallion over her head and grasped her own, tugging it out of her shirt. It was a jagged looking piece of obsidian that seemed to match my eyes.

"Don't fucking touch it!" Her voice had a panicked pitch to it and her thrashing grew stronger but I simply pulled it over her head and away from her. "Give it back!" She stared at it with wide eyes and I shook my head. She gave an angry shout tugging against my grip, attempting to bite my hands to get me to release her as I pulled her medallion over my own head.

The moment it landed on my chest the oppressive angry feeling left me and there was a warmth that rolled over my skin, like a comforting blanket had been wrapped around me. I liked it there and I liked mine on hers. What was mine, was *mine.* I wouldn't share her.

I felt her struggles lessen and she sniffled. "Please give it back. I will do *anything* you want but give it back to me." Her glassy, tear filled eyes were on the medallion I now wore and I swallowed hard. The old Soul Maker was right. I always had a choice.

I could follow in the steps that my father and grandfather and great grandfather had. I could give her medallion back in exchange for my own and bond to the woman my father picked for me or I could forge a new path. I could go against the centuries of LehnSon tradition and do as the Source decreed. I could throw my strong, vocal, spitfire of a mate over my shoulder and spend the rest of my life learning every inch of her body and her very soul.

If there was one good thing my father had taught me, it was to forever take what rightfully mine. Medals for military service, honours for my classes, and prestige for my rank. I had taken it all because it was rightfully mine and now I knew my father would demand I give up a dark haired fairy. The one with the foul mouth that spoke English and Orrian flawlessly and with elegance even when cursing me in both languages. He would demand I give up what was rightfully mine after instilling that drive deep within me.

"I will do anything. *Please.*" Her soft pleading entered my ears and I slowly loosened my grip from restraining to simply holding before I looked at her. The fairy with the eyes that matched my medallion. I had thought it had been useless and ugly but now all I could see was her. Even if I took it back all I would see would be her eyes. They would *haunt* me for the rest of my life if I let her go and I didn't wish to let her go. Not any more.

"Will you accept me?" I deliberately asked the question in English for her. I wanted to show her that I was willing to accept *all* of her.

What life would I have without her? What cold, harsh life would I have with a cold woman like my mother? Would I strike my child as well? Would I beat him because he didn't do things perfectly? Would I let him languish in cold and unfeeling darkness? My throat tightened at the thought of letting my own flesh and blood suffer as I did growing up.

"From this moment until our last?" I wanted what had been given to me. My stupid family duty be damned. I had been wearing the mask for so long that now that I could see how badly it fit. I wanted it off. She shook her head, more tears streaming from her eyes.

"No. You *hate* me. Prejudice doesn't just go away." She spoke in Orrian as she sniffled, tugging her hands from my own as she buried her face into them. Her shoulders shook with her sobs. They tore at me deeply. How could anyone throw away such a gift? Who would willingly choose a cold relationship over one that I knew would exude warmth and joy? Why would I give up the chance of experiencing the ever elusive love that I had seen as a child?

"I have been wearing a mask of my father's making for a very long time." I couldn't help myself and I trailed my lips across her skin to her ear. "Help me take it off and teach me how to *see*." Prejudices did run deep but I had never truly hated humans. I didn't have the intense dislike for them like my father had. I was indifferent but I pretended to make my father happy. I just needed her to understand I was willing to throw everything away for a slight chance to finally be in a warm beam of light. I knew it would take time but I was willing to try, to *change,* for her.

"Get off me please." At the soft plea I slowly moved off her, clenching my hands into fists so I wouldn't reach for her again. She rolled so her back was to me before she curled into a ball.

"Lacey." Her name felt right rolling off my tongue and I wanted to say it again and again as I trailed my lips across her skin, memorizing every curve and dip she had.

"No. You are just going to leave me." She sniffled and I frowned darkly before I stood up. I didn't want to hear any more of that. I reached down and lifted her up, throwing her over my shoulder.

"If there is one thing that you can be certain of, Lacey, it is the fact that I am *incredibly* selfish. I will always demand and take what is rightfully mine regardless of what or who is the in the way. The Source has given you to me and that makes you mine. You are going to demand I give you up?" I gave a sharp bark of cold amusement. "No, because I do not let go of things that are mine." I never had and I never would. I didn't care what my father would think and it felt freeing. I had been stuck following in footsteps that had always felt wrong to me and now I had a chance to *change* it. To go my own way.

"No. You are a purist, you hate humans." There was an edge of defiant stubbornness to her words and I started my climb up the hill. She wasn't struggling against me, which helped the ascent greatly.

"No I do not, not as you think I do, and you have until I find this Ghilesh to get onto my page, Lacey." It was the only warning she would get because, human or not, half-breed or not. Lacey was *my* soulmate and I wouldn't let her go. I didn't care what foolish worries she had because they didn't matter, *she* did. Even if I had to spend eternity showing her just how much she mattered to me.

"I won't say the words. I won't!" Her defiance had turned into slight petulance and I bit back a smirk at it. Ever the stubborn one. I didn't need to fully know her to understand that her stubbornness would be one issue I would encounter a lot. I looked forward to it. My mother had always agreed with my father. A cold indifferent acceptance but Lacey promised me a fiery chance at more and I wanted to feel that heat for myself.

"Then I will kiss you until you whimper them out." The idea sounded very, very appealing to me and her hand connected lightly with the back of my head right as we reached the top of the hill. Apparently the idea seemed more enraging than appealing to her. However the thought of kissing her made everything go out the window for me. I was now stuck on the thought of what it would feel like.

"Don't you fucking dare. I will bite your tongue off!" She spat the words out and I set her down on her feet, holding her waist before I pulled her close. I liked how she felt against me, her soft form moulding to my hard edges. A perfect fit as if we had been made for each other. I smirked slightly. We *had* been made for each other and I would turn into a sentimental fool to declare it to her as many times as I could.

"Lacey. Tell me why you will not." I wanted to know. I wanted to know if she found me lacking or wrong somehow. I knew she didn't like pureblood elitism, she had made that thoroughly clear but I made it clear I would change for her, that my prejudice was not my father's. I had doubts that perhaps she didn't want me. I hadn't entirely given her a reason to choose me.

"Because. What if some prettier pureblood comes along and you leave me?" Her bottom lip trembled and I winced at the sight of it. So many emotions. I wasn't used to them and I certainly didn't like them when they made her cry. "What if you wake up one morning and remember you hate me?" Hate her? The thought made my stomach churn unpleasantly. I could hate things, like her affinity to cursing and those tears but to hate *her*? It was nigh unthinkable. No, it *was* unthinkable.

"Hate you? You? A loud mouthed fairy who fell out of a tree on top of me and assaulted my person immediately after? Why would I hate you?" It seemed highly impossible for that to happen. "A spitfire woman that hurls insults faster than a soldier can fire bullets. A woman who disarmed me with only words and the touch of her skin against mine. The only chance I will ever have for a true future and the only woman whose eyes will haunt me for an eternity if I listen to her ridiculous excuses and walk away from her." I doubted she realized that the more she told me what to do, the less I was willing to do it. She was mine and I was hers and nothing she said would ever change that.

"Besides, I am the best you are possibly going to get." I smirked at the disgruntled look on her face.

"You're an ass." The words were muttered and she scowled darkly at my chest. It was almost as if she was refusing to look up at me.

"I have a rather inflated sense of self-importance." I wanted her to look at me, to *smile.* I knew her smile would have the potential to light up even the darkest parts of my soul and I wanted to see it.

"Also known as an ego." She glanced up at me before she looked away.

I frowned, pulling her closer. "I am a selfish and indifferent person who grew up without an ounce of love or affection. I was taught that hate, anger, and derision are a normal part of life. My father constantly told me that humans are responsible for my family's hardships and that they are a lower class, unworthy species that has ruined Orrian culture and lives." It was all that my father had said to me growing up. True it had never felt like me and I always felt like I was wearing a mask but it was still part of my upbringing. It was still a taught behaviour that shaped how I thought about certain things.

"Are you trying to sell yourself or scare me off?" She finally looked at me, raising one eyebrow as she wiped at her eyes. I wanted to push her hands away and do it myself, if only to touch her skin.

"I am letting you know that I was taught wrong and will require you to teach me how to live on a planet surround by the people I have been taught to hate my entire life but I am *willing* to learn for you." I would do *anything* to be with her. I wanted her to know that, to understand it. She was *my* soulmate and I wasn't about to let something of mine slip through my fingers for someone else to find.

"I don't know." She sounded so uncertain and I finally gave in and reached up, lifting her chin with a finger. She met my gaze and I could see her swallowing hard even as my mouth went dry. I slid my hand from her waist to the small of her back before yanking her close, leaving no space between us.

"Lacey... My father brought me down here to meet with a potential female to bond to." The thought of belonging to anyone but Lacey made my skin crawl and she trembled slightly, hurt clearly painted in her eyes. "I need you to get on the same page as me because I will not be going anywhere with that woman because I wish to be with *you.*" I *needed* her to understand that. "And I will kiss you a hundred times until you can say nothing but yes." Even if she did say yes I was quite firm on the idea of doing that anyway.

"I need to think." She pushed against my chest and I liked the feeling of her hands on me. My thoughts turned to her gripping my shoulders, pulling me closer. All those thoughts about rutting like animals became a very possible reality for me. I *liked* the thought of it.

"You have thirty seconds." Otherwise I was tempted to wave away her protests and kiss her anyway.

"Don't you dare kiss me." She scowled up at me and the moment my eyes drifted to her lips, they parted and her breathing deepened as if in response.

"I know you want me to." I wasn't sure how but I could *feel* it. As if my body was picking up the cues hers was sending out. A delicate push and pull, letting me know she was receptive to me.

"You can't kiss problems away." She scowled at me as a becoming pink flushed her cheeks.

"But we can try." I was always willing to try. I doubted I would ever turn away from the heat she promised. I had spent so long in the cold darkness that I would forever wish and crave to bask in that warmth.

She scowled at me despite the flush of embarrassment on her face. "No."

"Ten seconds." I was counting down and she had ten seconds to agree because after that I was going to do as I wanted.

"I won't kiss a man when I don't know his name." The words rushed out and I had to give her that.

"Keen." My last name was on the tip of my tongue but I held it back. My last name didn't matter anymore. I had spent too long protecting it, doing my duty for it that I simply wanted to let it go.

"What?" She looked confused and I slid my hand across her jaw and around to cup the back of her neck. Goosebumps followed my touch and she shivered against me.

"My name." I couldn't help how my voice lowered to a faint rumble.

"Oh." Her eyes went wide and her breathing quickened.

"Time is up." I lowered my head towards hers. All I wanted was to see what it would feel like to kiss her.

"Wait!" She pushed against my chest again. "What if you are a terrible kisser?" She looked genuine in her question and I narrowed my eyes.

"Now you are just asking for it." There was no reason for her to ever doubt me. *Especially* about that.

Part 4

"No, I'm no-" I cut her off, pressing my lips to hers. Heat and flames filled me from the contact and I burned with an oppressive need to consume her, body and soul. I leaned over her, a sound building in my throat as I leaned further, my hand reaching out and grabbing the bark of the tree, shifting her closer to it. Her hand went from pushing me to gripping my shirt and pulling me closer as she pressed against me.

Her lips were soft and warm and addicting. I could kiss her a hundred thousand times and never have my fill. The kiss was beyond describing and the need it brought was hot and burning. Her hands moved from my shirt to my neck, holding me close as she gave a soft whimper that made me clutch her tighter. I pulled back, needing air and she gave a small gasp.

"Please." It was a faint gasping plea as she pulled on my neck, attempting to bring me back into the kiss.

"What were you saying?" I smiled smugly at her and she gave a groan of frustration, her slightly swollen lips drawing my attention. "That yes you would accompany me to this Ghilesh to be bound?" She pouted, looking decidedly petulant and I chuckled softly before I kissed her again. It was just as wondrous as the first one and I ended it quickly as much as I didn't want to.

"I am still waiting on that answer." I wouldn't continue until I heard it. I was not above blackmail or manipulative tactics to get what I wanted.

"Kiss me again." She went up on her toes but I lifted my head higher so she couldn't kiss me.

"Not until you say it." I brought my face closer, letting my lips brush against hers, igniting a slow burn inside of my veins.

"Yes." She said it against my mouth and I pulled back.

"Yes what?" I wanted to hear her say it. I wanted to hear her acceptance of me and I wouldn't settle for less than that.

"Yes I will take you to Ghilesh." That was all I needed to hear. I captured her lips with my own once more. I felt as though I was starving and she was the only thing that could sate my hunger. I pressed her up against the tree as her hands tangled in my hair as she made soft noises in her throat. I moved my hand from her back to her hip before forcing my leg between hers and seeking to deepen the kiss. She gave a small gasp and I took advantage, meeting her tongue with my own as I slanted my mouth on hers. She was my paradise and my heaven wrapped up in a coarse grungy blue jumpsuit.

I pulled back from the kiss, looking at her flushed face, pink swollen lips and her fluttering eyes. She was pure perfection. "There we are." I couldn't help how raspy and low my voice was when I throbbed with the need to finish what I had started.

She pouted slightly as I let her go. "You're an asshole." She attempted to stand on slightly unsteady legs, her cheeks flushing prettily as she tucked the strands of hair behind her ears.

"We have been through this, Lacey, I also have a bit ego. Now, let us go." I pressed my hand to her lower back and put a bit of pressure on it. I wanted her close. As much as I wished to pin her up against the tree and take her as my nature and needs demanded of me, I wouldn't do that until I was bound to her completely. I wouldn't put her at risk like that. The longer we weren't bound the more risk she was in for my father's wrath.

"Are you always so pushy?" She crossed her arms over her chest but started walking anyway.

"Get used to it." I was pushy and I wouldn't deny it. There might be some times with her when I would perhaps let her win and perhaps not push too hard and concede but currently I was not in that mood.

The longer we went unbound the more danger she was in and I wouldn't abide by it.

"No." The petulance in her tone had only grown and I brought my mouth close to her ear.

"You have agreed, you cannot back out now." I wouldn't let her. My choice in keeping her put a target on her back that wouldn't disappear until we were bound. I didn't want there to be any chances for her to be harmed or taken from me. "Where is this man?" This ever elusive Ghilesh. It seemed she was partial to him so that is where we would go, besides I knew no other Soul Maker on this planet.

"He's probably with Aunty Ani in the Human-Orrian Resources department." Her voice trembled slightly, as if she were a bit scared of what was going to happen. I didn't wish for that and so I rubbed my thumb against her back, trying to soothe her fears and trepidation.

"Why would he be there?" It didn't make sense for him be hiding in the military base with her 'Aunty Ani'. Soul Makers never bonded so having a woman around him sounded more than strange.

"It's where they do the soul bonds. Aunty Ani is pestering him to let her help with the bonds despite her being pretty pregnant. She's tenacious." She glanced up at me and her face flushed again before she quickly looked away. I liked that I could cause that warm reaction from her. "He is probably trying to hide from her." I wondered what type of tenacious woman would cause such a man to hide from her. I could only imagine.

"Do we have to go through the building?" The tremble in her voice became more pronounced and I frowned as looked across the tarmac to the building that was growing ever closer.

"Yes." It was the easiest way to get to the civilian departments. "Why do you ask?" If she was wary then it was a cause for concern for me.

"Okay. I'm technically not supposed to be on the base at all. I snuck in." She cast me a guilty look and I kept my face even. My soulmate was a tried and true rule breaker, someone who knew a thing or two about forging her own path in life.

"So?" If we could avoid people then it was fine and if we were caught then I could explain I was simply escorting her off the premises. Potential problem solved before it could even happen.

"My dad is kind of a high ranking military official." She fiddled with her nails, her head down as she stared at the pavement and I shrugged before sliding my hand to her waist and tugging her closer.

Her dad was a high ranking military officer and mine was a cold and brutal asshole. We made quite the pair.

"Then we will stay away from where he is." If she knew his habits then we could avoid him easily. Another potential problem solved.

"You don't understand." She tried to stop walking as the door came closer but I pushed her forward. We needed to get bonded.

"I understand enough. My father is lurking around these premises as well and believe me we are better off running into yours." Her father could smack me around if he wanted but I wouldn't put her into a situation where she was anywhere near my father. He could deal serious damage if he wanted. I wouldn't allow that situation to even occur. "Simply tell me which part of the building he should be in and then we will avoid it." I pulled open the door and her shoulders slumped.

"He's supposed to be near the air tower watching the military flight formations." She gestured down the hall but didn't try to stop walking as we moved forward. She could tell me where we needed to go and we would follow that path, avoiding every unnecessary distraction along the way. "We need to stay away from any officers dressed in green. They will report me to my father." I nodded and kept my eyes out as she kept her head down as if attempting to not be seen.

"So why are you not allowed onto the base?" My curiosity wouldn't let me not ask the question. She had to have done something fairly serious to be barred from the base.

"I made some apparently 'unnecessary' adjustments to my sister's jet engine so it would conserve fuel and by-pass the max speed threshold." At the rather quietly said words, I raised my eyebrows.

"You tampered with a military jet?" To be honest, after dealing with her, it didn't seem that far fetched.

"I *fixed* a large military jet. There *is* a difference." She grumbled the words as she crossed her arms over her chest. I could almost imagine that tantalizing, pink bottom lip of hers sticking out in a pout. "The damned thing was getting a seventy-eight percent decrease in fuel consumption and an added thirty-seven percent increase in speed. Until they *ruined* it." She sounded highly disgusted at the thought and I had to admit I was impressed. I was never one who knew anything about the running schematics of the military birds. I flew them, I didn't fix them. So having a soulmate that knew how to not only fix but *improve* them was rather impressive to me.

"It wasn't even my fault. If they didn't want me fixing the birds dad should not have let me hang out in the repair bay with Uncle Bruce. That's where it all started." She hunched over herself and that imaginary image of her bottom lip sticking out was stuck in my head. As improper as it was, I wanted to kiss that pout off her face. "Stupid mechanical redundancies that minimized the maximum efficiency of the eighteen cylinder, false echoing, combustible engines." She muttered the words and I steered her down a corridor as I caught sight of a green uniform walking towards us.

"I do not understand what you are saying but any unauthorized changed to a pilot's bird is not allowed." Even I knew that. Having a simple sticker had to be authorized no less than twice.

"I know that but Amy said I could." That petulant tone was still strong and I frowned as I steered her down another corridor in avoidance of the green uniforms.

"Amy being?" I gestured for her to continue. I liked listening to her speak, it was calming for me, relaxing.

"My sister." At that she seemed to perk up rather quickly. "She's the best pilot in her flock. Ran six tours on the front lines, won eighteen medals for her service to our independence and people. Fastest flight times on Earth and in Oria *and* a highly coveted poker player. She can strip the shirt off your back without you even knowing it." Pride threaded every word she said and I could tell her and her sister were very close. My mind grasped what she had actually said. There was only one fucking pilot in the army that had that reputation.

"Wait... your sister is *Amy-Lynn DharSon*?" Amy-Lynn DharSon had absolutely *thrashed* everyone in my flock as well as everyone in *any* flock. She had proven time and time again that she was the *absolute* best damned pilot that Oria and Earth could offer. I knew because every single time that she beat my scores by a landslide my father saw fit to punish me because not only had a *half-breed* beat my scores but because she was a *DharSon*.

I wanted to roar with laughter. The Source hadn't paired me with any old half-breed human, it had paired me with a *DharSon*. My father's most *hated* nemesis. He hated the DharSons more than he hated humans and *that* was saying something.

"Yup. You heard of her?" She smiled up at me brightly and as soon as I saw it, everything faded away. It didn't matter that my father hated her family because I would do *anything* just to see that smile again.

"Who has not?" I doubted there was a person in the army that hadn't heard of Amy-Lynn DharSon. That and admitting it to her kept that smile glowing.

"True." She nodded, tucking those stray hairs behind her ears again. Her braid was coming undone, showing off the curls in her dark hair.

"It is you I have not heard much about." I hadn't even known of a second DharSon child. I would have thought my father would have mentioned something. If she was as good with mechanics as she said she was, then she should have made a name for herself by now. My little mate was turning into quite the little curiosity for me.

Part 5

"That's okay. I'm not a social person. I preferred the repair shop to actually flying. I love the birds, I do. But I am terrified of flying. Just like mum. So I didn't join the army. That and I'm a bit too short and I can't fire a gun to save my life. I am more of the creative fixing type." She looked so shy and timid as she said it that it made her all the more endearing. I had a soulmate who preferred to stay out of view, to tinker with things and leave the spotlight for others. I liked that, it was incredibly different from the power hungry women I had known before. "So yah, that's me. Just plain old-"

"*Lacey-Emmaline DharSon!*" At the booming voice she froze with a squeak, looking over her shoulder. I followed her gaze and it landed on a rather large man with a scar slashing down the side of his face, making him appear that much more severe and unapproachable. The infamous Rhex DharSon, the thought made my mouth twitch with amusement.

"Shit!" The curse was quickly spat out and she and I turned around. I could see the strained smile she put on her face.

"Where were you?" He moved towards us, pointing at Lacey, making her pull her shoulders back and set her jaw in what appeared to be defiance before she gave him one award winning smile.

"Showing him around." She pointed at me and I pulled my hands behind my back, holding my back straight and my shoulders back as his attention was immediately on me. His light green eyes were glinting hard as if he was searching for a lie.

"*You.*" He swung his finger so it pointed at me and I fought back a smile. My little mate was a *very* big trouble maker. "Did you see her near the bays at all? Near the birds?" I shook my head.

"No, sir. I fell into a ditch near the tarmac and she graciously offered to show me to the closest bathroom so I could get cleaned up." I was lying through my teeth at the General of the Human-Orrian Integrated Army so my troublesome little mate wouldn't get in shit and I was *enjoying* it.

"He was lost, daddy. I just wanted to help." She somehow made her voice seem innocent and almost childlike. I was impressed. She was *very* good at the game she was getting ready to play.

"Why are you in this portion of the building, Lacey? And you do not get to lie to me." His expression was the perfect image of fatherly sternness as he crossed his arms over his chest.

She inhaled deeply before starting to gesture with her hands. "Well I was helping Ghilesh in the bonding room but then Aunty Ani came in and you know how she gets and she started pestering Ghilesh about letting her help him but because she is so big with the twins he was like no. But you know how she can be. Doesn't listen and always pestering. You would have thought being pregnant would have changed that, right, daddy?" She inhaled again before starting her rambling story again.

I knew the tactic she was using. I had used it myself as a child. Distraction, confusion, and deflection. Give the person too much information and ask enough questions that they forgot what it was they had been upset about all together.

"So they started arguing and I just went outside to get some air when I saw Keen here, fall into the ditch and I went over right away to make sure he was okay. Which he is, as you can clearly see, right daddy? Just a bit dirty from the tumble. So I offered to escort him to the bathroom but because I would get into trouble for being in the building, we were trying to avoid your grunts so I could get him safely to bathroom without delays so he could clean himself up. And then you caught us and-"

"I know what you are doing, Lacey." He raised an eyebrow, clearly not buying anything Lacey was attempting to do. I felt almost disappointed he hadn't fallen for it. It would have been amusing to see a five star General confused by his daughter. Although I was tensing up at the entire situation, I wasn't one for confrontations between parents and their children. I knew how those went.

"I'm telling you what happened." She attempted to look meek and unassuming but he shook his head.

"In a very convoluted and confusing way so I will drop it. I am your father. I know all of the tricks that you use to keep yourself out of trouble." Surprisingly a smile tugged at his mouth. I had expected rage, that was the reaction my father would have had. Instead he looked amused.

"Fuck." Lacey's soft look twisted into agitation rather quickly at her trick being called out.

"Fuck is right. Now. The truth." He gave her a look, shifting on his feet.

"I was hiding in the tree watching the birds and I fell on him." She gestured to him and Rhex motioned his hand at her.

His arms crossed over his chest as he raised his eyebrow at her. "*And?*"

"We fell into the ditch. I wasn't lying about it." Defiance tainted the edges of her expression as she gritted the words out. Rhex's slightly soft look harden as he turned to me.

"Are you going to risk my temper by lying to me?" I was reminded of my father with his tone and that made my eyes narrow a fraction. I wasn't going to be treated like that anymore. Accepting Lacey had opened many doors I could step through in my life and I was going to take full advantage of them all.

"What she says is true. She fell out of the tree, landed on me, and we fell down a ditch." It was all he would be getting out of me. I would stick to whichever story Lacey came up with. I would forever protect her back, even from her father. *Especially* from her father.

"Keen! What have you been doing? You are *filthy.*" My father's voice instantly put me on edge as I looked around for him. He was in the corridor behind us. I turned to look at him and Lacey slowly slid slightly behind me at the rather hateful look on his face as he spotted her. "*Who* are you with, Keen?" The rather venomous question made me click my teeth together in agitation but I forced my face to remain even. I looked over the two people following behind him. One must have been the General Hamesk and the tall, willowy woman must have been his daughter.

"*Well?*" At his sharp question I lifted my chin.

"She was showing me around. I took a tumble down a ditch and could not find a bathroom to clean up." I moved away from Lacey, as much as I didn't want to. I needed to play this situation properly. I moved towards my father slowly, trying to keep his attention on me.

"*Kher.*" General Rhex's voice was clipped and Lacey was suddenly gone from behind me, no doubt now beside her father. There was no love lost between the two men and apparently Rhex was one who could see a threat from a mile away and my father was a serious threat.

"Rhex. How is your *little wife*?" My father's expression twisted slightly, his civil mask slipping slightly.

"Doing quite well. How is yours?" Rhex's voice was smooth and even, not a hitch or a hint that my father had gotten to him at all.

"Better than ever." My father lifted his head, his grey eyes hard like stone.

"That is great to hear. Why are you here?" All civility was gone and Rhex's voice was as hard and sharp as a forged blade.

My father's expression twisted into a heavy sneer. "I do not see why that is any of your busines-"

"It's *my* military base, Kher. I am supposed to know of any arriving guests and I was not informed of your arrival. I would have prepared for it." Even I could hear the slight threat his tone had and my father stiffened under it.

"It was a personal matter, rather than a business one." He turned his sharp glare towards me. "Speaking of which. Keen, this is Ti'ha." I inclined my head at the woman before moving towards my father.

"Father, did you bring the binding bracelets I picked out?" I smiled at Ti'ha and she lifted her head, a faint smile on her own face as her eyes looked me over as if she saw something she was pleased with. It made my skin crawl.

"Yes." His eyes narrowed at me and I nodded at him.

"May I see them?" I tried my hardest to not look back at Lacey and let her know it was alright, that there was no way I would choose the perfectly manufactured Ti'ha over her. There was no comparison.

Ti'ha had perfectly styled hair, her perfectly engineered facial features that were meant to be aesthetically pleasing, and her perfectly ratio-ed curves that were draped in expensive fabrics. I wouldn't deny she had been perfectly made but *Lacey*... Lacey was pure magnificence, even in her grungy, oil stained, torn, blue jump suit that I hadn't even cared she was wearing. The uneven tilt to her soft mouth, the freckles that dusted her cheeks and nose and wherever else I would find. The unruly hair that didn't like staying out of her face and those mesmerizing eyes. It all made her that much *more* than Ti'ha to me.

"Just to make sure they are intact." I held out my hand and my gaze flicked to the perfectly made Orrian woman. How could Ti'ha even *think* she could compare to Lacey?

"My son, Keen, is always one for preparation. Perhaps your... *daughter* should learn the same, Rhex." He threw a look of distaste towards Lacey that had me bristling. He had no right to say anything about Lacey. He had no right to look at her like that but I forced my expression to remain neutral as he pulled the box from his pocket. I took it with a small smile.

"Thank you, father." I grasped his shoulder with a wide smile. "If you ever look at my mate like that again, I will kill you." I released him as if he burned me before I turned around and headed straight for Lacey, her eyes were wide as they watched me. Rhex made a sound as I grabbed Lacey around the waist and threw her over my shoulder.

"Sir." I nodded at him in respect before I moved away from them all. I had made my choice and I was just doing as my father had taught me. Taking what was mine.

"Where do you think you are going?" My father's voice was livid as it followed me down the hall.

"I am going to get bonded." I threw the mocking words over my shoulder and Lacey giggled, a soft, tinkling sound that bolstered my rebellion.

She was my perfect match. Rebellious and headstrong, someone who was full of fire and courage, someone who could teach me how to walk my own path in life. She was someone who could teach me what love was and how to live in the warm light I had been denied for so long.

I grinned before I looked over my shoulder, my grin growing wider at the furious look on my father's face as Rhex barred him from following. "Who knows, father... maybe I will get a set of pretty gold rings for me and my *little wife*." His face turned red as I threw his mocking words back at him.

He sputtered, his face darkening with his rage. "I knew you were made wrong, Keen! I should have sent you back! I should have dealt with you when you were younger! This is how you repay me? This is how you treat the family name? You are a shame to this family. Your mind is twisted if you think I will ever accept this!" He cursed at me and I simply laughed, shifting Lacey on my shoulder as he continued his furious tirade. It felt good to be made wrong and it felt *great* to be my father's version of broken.

"He's mad." Her voice was filled with slightly strained giggles as I turned down a corridor, looking for signs that would lead me to the Soul Maker.

"He is." Furious and filled with rage. He was down right pissed off and it felt *great*.

"That's your father." She said it softly and I made an unconcerned sound in my throat.

"So? I have a new family now." *She* was my family now. I would be fine as long as I had her showing me how to break the rules, how to break with tradition.

"Really?" She sounded so unsure and my heart twisted slightly. The younger sister who must have felt always overlooked. She was scared, *terrified,* that I would leave her for something better but she didn't understand I was just as terrified as her.

"If you will have me, Lacey." I was terrified that she would see me as my family name and leave, that she would choose someone else, someone less fucked up or selfish. She had no idea that my entire world rested on her answer because I wanted no one else but her, in this life or the next.

"Always." She said it softly and I smiled before bumping her off my shoulder, swinging her slightly so I cradled her to my chest. I pressed my forehead to hers as I stepped around the corner that would take us to the Soul Maker.

"Then I have my family, from forever to always." And what a time that would be.

Duty be damned. The faint voice cackled in my head but this time I laughed with it.

Duty be damned indeed.

Author's Note

I decided to publish this story on a whim and it took me on a great adventure as I did so. I have learned many new things, changed some things within the story but there are so many others that remained the same.

This story is still a story that was born out of the prompt 'Love is never easy'. This is still a story I love and enjoy. I truly care about this small world I started just over two years ago. I left it for a time, editing it and then leaving it before I took the plunge and finished it off. It was perfect, with the help of some lovely friends of course, and ready for publishing.

This journey has showed me so much about my reading community. It's amazing to think I started out so small only to grow to have this wonderful and supportive community of people who encouraged me to follow my dreams. You guys have been with me every step of the way and it's incredible to see and be apart of. It truly is.

I have written many books so far but you guys are what I am proud of most. Your kindness and compassion and encouragement make me so so proud to claim you as my community. You are gracious and wonderful and imaginative, don't you let anyone tell you different.

There are so many of you I wish to thank but I know I don't have the space or the time to do so. So thank you all, you are wonderful and amazing.

Until next time,
Anna M. L. Koski

Love is Never Easy

(The prompt that started it all)

I looked at the clock and smoothed down my jeans and my favourite button up shirt. The invitation said to dress in what made you comfortable because what you were wearing didn't matter.

Today was my 18th birthday and the day I was to meet my soulmate. I felt nervous, so nervous the urge to throw up was nearly overpowering but I tried to force my body into submission. Everything would go smoothly, everything would be perfect. He would be perfect. I smiled at myself in the mirror, I fairly glowed with excitement and I hoped he would too.

"Liv, it's time to go." At my mum's voice the nervousness returned and I could see my face pale in the mirror. I forced myself to smile to hide it. After a moment of looking at myself, thinking how everything would be different when I came back, I turned away.

"Coming, mum." I rushed down the stairs and kissed my dad on his cheek before doing the same for my mum. They both looked so happy and I couldn't blame them. Their only daughter going out to meet the one she would love for eternity.

"We love you, sweety. Come back before the move and tell us everything." There were tears in my mum's eyes and she pressed her hand to her mouth.

"Bring your boy with you, we want to meet him. Deep breaths and don't forget to be respectful." My dad's eyes looked slightly watery and I flashed them one more smile before I rushed out the door. It was the beginning of forever.

The building wasn't as grand as I thought it would be. It was simple and grey. Its professional looking, I concluded as I stepped out of the government mandated vehicle. I would leave with a new car and a husband that would take me to our new house, government provided for all the new soulmates.

I took a deep breath in, my dad's words echoing in my head as I pulled the door open and stepped inside. The air was cool and I headed towards the front desk and the man sitting there pointed to a chair without looking at me.

Nervousness flooded my system once again as I sat down. It took all I had to not bounce my legs on my toes. My muscles jumped and twitched under my hands and I wondered if everyone felt like this before their meeting. If they felt this crushing mixture of nervousness, excitement, and pure happiness. This was the most important meeting in my life.

Since I was young everyone had told me what I was to expect on this day. That I would see him and the world would stop because in that moment all that mattered was him. That my heart would flutter in my chest and my mouth would feel dry because he was just so handsome. That I would want to laugh because I would know he felt the same way.

I clutched at my medallion where it hung between my breasts. Everyone was given one on their tenth birthday and it was to never be taken off until your eighteenth. On that day it would be removed and your soulmate's would take its place as yours would take theirs.

I worried that my medallion would be too plain. It was so simple, a flat metal oval, the edges worn slightly, with some strange symbols a gypsy at a fair I went to a few years ago said was Orrian. She told me she couldn't read it but my soulmate's medallion would look similar, his symbols completing mine.

The thought of the Orrians was a heart stopping one. Their species was divided. Half wished to help the humans and the other half wished to destroy us all. They had appeared over three hundred years ago and it was their intervention that started the soulmate program.

A tall woman walked towards me and I quickly got to my feet, nervousness twisting my insides once again. Her smile was calming and I felt myself take several deep breaths in, trying to relax. She motioned me to follow her and I do, mentally counting the steps it would take to lead me to my forever.

She pushed open a door and gestured at me to go inside and I hesitated for a moment, drawing in a breath before doing just that. I looked around the small room and my eyes finally land on a man sitting at the table in front of me. His eyes had gone wide and a large smile crossed his face. I blinked rapidly as he stood and I shook my head with a frown. It was all wrong, the man in front of me didn't make my heart flutter or my mouth go dry. I turned to look at the woman but the door was closed.

My heart thumped in my chest in panic, all of my worst fears had come true. I was broken because I did not want the stranger in front of me. So many times I had woken up as I had grown, screaming about just this nightmare. I closed my eyes and willed myself to wake up. I needed to wake up.

"My name is Mark." His voice was slightly wheezy as if he had asthma and I opened my eyes and looked at him. He looked at me like my dad looked at my mum and I felt sorry for him. I didn't love him like that. He was a stranger and would always be a stranger.

"I think there has been a mistake." My words sounded so foreign to my ears, they sounded so far away. My heart pounded hard in my chest and it drowned everything out. "There must be a mistake because you're not my soulmate." I watched as confusion crumbled the happiness that was on his face. He looked so confused but he wasn't experiencing what I was. He had love and I didn't. Not for him. He wasn't my soulmate and he would never be.

Tears filled my eyes as I thought of how disappointed my parents would be. About how disappointed his parents would be. All of that disappointment because I was broken, I was flawed because I didn't love my soulmate.

The door opened behind me and I turned around. Two large Orrians stepped inside, their neutral expressions couldn't hide their disdain and revulsion. My heart slammed into my rib cage. These weren't the nice Orrians. I could hear Mark shouting and I looked over my shoulder with wide eyes as two more Orrians grabbed him and dragged him from the room. I could see the fear in his eyes and my mouth went dry.

Rough hands grabbed my arms and spun me around before pulling them behind my back. The cold touch and click of handcuffs made fear surge through me. What was happening? I tried to think of other cases where soulmates were born broken but my brain froze.

I was pushed through the hallways, long twisting hallways to the point I felt dizzy, even if I escaped I could never find my way out. The two Orrians were speaking in their gruff language and I wanted to cry. What was going to happen to me? The answer came unbidden into my mind.

They will do to you what they do to all the other broken things. I started crying, tears running down my cheeks. I was going to be unmade. It is what they did to those with life altering defects, to those who didn't reach their proposed limits of perfection. I rejected my soulmate and so I was defective.

I didn't fight them, there was no point. Orrians were strong, far stronger than humans. I stood up straighter, my fate could not be changed. No one could escape the system, it was too perfect. I would be unmade and it is what I was destined for. My heart hurt for my parents. I wondered what story the Orrians would tell, I wondered if they would tell them the truth or if they would lie.

I felt the tears stop as I was pushed into a small room. One side was covered with buttons and screens and the others were glass. One of the Orrians closed the door before moving to the panel and pushing a few buttons. I felt the floor shift and then we were going up. I watched the windows but soon the rapidly passing floors made me dizzy and I closed my eyes. They would take me to one of their ships. Garbage disposal most likely. I felt a chuckle wanting to escape at my morbid attempt at humor but I bit it back.

Light soon filled the small ship and I risked opening my eyes. I wanted to close them again because we were going higher, far higher than I had ever been and the thought turned my stomach. It was a silly thing to want to vomit because of the height and not because I was going to be thrown into a garbage disposal.

I felt my legs grow weak and I closed my eyes. I didn't want to fall down, not without my hands to break the fall. I adjusted my hands behind my back, the cool metal had grown warmer from my skin but it still bit into it. I rolled my shoulders forward, trying to take off some of the strain but it didn't seem to help at all.

We went upwards for several more minutes before I felt the ship slow down. My heart did another lurch in my chest and the fear returned but I squared my shoulders as best I could. I was human and I wasn't going to let them tell all their other Orrian friends that I had fallen apart and fought them every step of the way. I would be brave and meet my fate like all the heroes of mythology. I would embrace death because it was inevitable. I was broken and this is what happened to the broken things.

The ship came to a stop and I stumbled slightly at the bump it made as it did. The two Orrians laughed and said something in their language before the door opened again. It was dark and one of the Orrians shoved me forward. I stumbled, nearly falling before I caught myself. Their laughter echoed in my ears as the door closed and I was left alone. I could hear movement around me and dull lights turned on. Several Orrians stared at me and I once again squared my shoulders and held my head high. I would not break at my fate. I would not weep for it. Their deep and guttural voices sounded around me but I kept my gaze straight.

"Rhex!" It sounded like a name and I glanced at the one who said it and he motioned for someone to come forward. My heart flipped in my chest as an Orrian stepped forward. He was large, his shoulders broad and it seemed like with every Orrian muscles came by him naturally. A scar went down his cheek and the corner of his mouth, giving him half a frown. His eyes were cold and he should have terrified me but he didn't.

The other Orrian said something else but it didn't matter, all that mattered was him. The Orrian called Rhex and his scarred face. He looked as though he had fought in many battles and had always emerged the victor. The thought made my mouth go dry, he would defeat all who opposed him and all who got between him and what he wanted.

The laughter that bubbled up was unexpected and I tried my best to force it back but I couldn't. I laughed and shook my head. I truly was broken because he was my soulmate. An Orrian and a human, never heard of but it was there, right in front of me. My mum used to say that the heart didn't lie and it seemed as though my heart wasn't, how I wished it was in that moment but it wasn't.

A large hand grabbed my arm and started dragging me down a long tunnel, he was muttering Orrian under his breath and I said nothing, just revelled in his presence. I wondered if this was what Mark had felt when he looked at me and the thought made me laugh again. I was fucked. I had an Orrian as a soulmate and I shook my head as the laughter died down.

Why did I have to be different? Why did I have to mess things up? Why was I so strange?

I let the questions bounce around my head as the person I was destined to love lead me to my death. His muttering became louder and he pulled me to a stop before pushing me up against the wall with one large hand. Fear bloomed in my chest at the angry look on his face and the fire in his eyes. He was dangerous, I knew that because all Orrians were dangerous. He pulled out a small device and pressed it to my neck. It pinched hard and I winced as he pulled it away. His gaze on the device.

He started shouting, I wondered if it was cursing. As he turned the device to my face, his tone sounded accusing and I tried to read the digital display but all I could make out was sixty-three percent. The numbers and the percentage sign flashed in my eyes and I didn't understand what it meant.

He abruptly dropped his hand and started pacing. I watched him warily, it was like watching the tigers pacing at the zoo. Only without the glass to protect you. He threw the device down the tunnel and I jumped as it shattered on the floor. He grabbed my arm and started pulling me down the tunnel once more. I was more and more certain that his mutterings were actually curses the further we moved along.

I wiggled my shoulders, hating how tight they were pulled back. He stopped again and I glanced over at him. His expression was blank and he turned me so I faced him. His hand reached down and pulled my medallion from my shirt. I almost gave a slight whimper of protest. My skin felt cold without it.

My dad told me that it was the physical representation of our souls and to be parted from it would mean aching loneliness forever. Without a medallion one could not claim their soulmate, they could not have children or ever be happy.

I watched as Rhex pulled out his own medallion, it looked similar to mine but the symbols were different. He muttered something, as if he had read the symbols. I looked up at his scarred face and it looked as though the harsh edges had softened. He held both the medallions in one hand and pointed to them. Repeating what he had just muttered.

"I don't understand. I can't speak Orrian." My voice was small, it almost didn't sound like my own and I watched frustration cross his face. He pointed at my medallion.

"Love is." His voice sounded so strange speaking English and I blinked in shock as his finger moved to his medallion. "Never easy." He looked at me and I blinked again.

"*Mehba illeehd sirbaht onshe halh.*" He said the words slowly and I realized he wanted me to say it.

"*Mehba illeehd sirbaht onshe halh.*" The repetition was slow and I stuttered over a few of the foreign words but he gave a quick nod before removing my medallion completely. I gave a noise of protest but the look he gave me silenced it in my throat. I watched as he removed his and replaced it with mine. He muttered something I couldn't understand before he gently pulled his medallion over my head, letting it fall into place. My skin warmed at the contact and I looked at him in confusion.

"Love is never easy." His gaze was as confused as mine but it appeared he had made a decision sometime during our trip down the tunnel.

Slowly, as if he was afraid I would run off, he reached behind me and released the cuffs. My shoulders ached with relief and I went to rub my wrists when he grabbed them instead. His rough fingers rubbed at the red marks, his voice was low as he spoke. He looked at me, his eyes were apologetic as he let my wrists go. I finally noticed in the dark lighting of the tunnel that his eyes were a pale green, a colour no one had on Earth. They were beautiful.

I reached up slowly, my fingers wanting to touch his scar, to touch the line that turned one corner of his mouth down into a perpetual frown. He jerked back slightly but I reached the rest of the distance anyway. The scar was smooth and the edges jagged as I trailed my fingertips from where it started to where it ended on his chin.

I did not know him or his past but in that moment all I wanted to do was take away that pain. To take away his scar and the memories that must have gone with it. I let out a sound of sympathy as I met his gaze, my fingertips still touching the scar.

"I am sorry this happened to you." I felt tears rush into my eyes as he reached up and took my hand in his. His palm was warm and large. He could hurt me without a thought but I knew he wouldn't. He couldn't hurt me anymore than I could hurt him.

"Never easy." The words were sighed and I realized we were going to have a hard time if we had a relationship. The language barrier alone would be hard to overcome but the intolerance of everyone else would be worse. Our relationship was unheard of for both humans and Orrians. We simply didn't mix but as his hand grasped the back of my neck and pulled me into a kiss, I didn't care.

Love is never easy. The words were branded into both of our souls, a mantra for a new beginning, our beginning. As he broke off the kiss and threw me over his shoulder in standard Orrian fashion when declaring a mate. I smiled, it felt good to be broken.

Acknowledgements

There are many people I wish to thank for helping me make this dream come true. These are the people to guided me when I felt lost and held my hand tightly when I was so overwhelmed by the process I was scared. The people who had my back through the thick and the thin and who I have forged long lasting, and hopefully life long bonds to.

I would firstly like to thank my sisters. They pushed me continually and believed in me every step of the way. They are the ones who continually demanded I publish and repeatedly told me that I had the talent to be a professional writer. Without their support I doubt I would have been as confident in this process as I was.

I would also like to thank Ericka, for whom the book is dedicated. She helped me with the strenuous editing process and made it so much easier for me to bear. She is always there when I need some quick advice and has been a wonderful friend.

I would also love to thank my readership and community for their unfailing support and appreciation in all that I do in my writing. They are always full of encouragement and happiness and never once let me fall.

And of course my last thank you. This is to my best friend and twinsie, Ashley. She was with me through late nights and early mornings. She was, and continues to be, right by my side through the thick and the thin of not just writing but life itself. She holds my hand tightly and guides me when I waver and is there to support me and lift me up when I am down. Although she is so very far away from me physically, she is never far from my heart.

I love you, Ashley. You are my other half, now and always.

About the Author

Anna M. L. Koski grew up on the family homestead in the rolling hills of Southern Saskatchewan. She has always been an avid writer and has a boundless love of literature.

Time has not lessened her desire to write but has only seemed to make her passion for it that much stronger as the years have gone by. You will likely find her staring at her laptop writing page after page of her stories even in the wee hours in the morning.

She has a great love of encouraging others to follow their dreams and to pursue their passions. She believes a life is only well lived if it is lived in happiness and contentment. She lives by her mother's motto and encourages others to do the same.

The tallest trees have the strongest roots.
Never forget where you came from.

Coming 2021

SHADOW of the BEAST

Twisted Dark

Anna M.L. Koski

Introducing book two of the sizzling and sexy Supernatural Romance Novella series Twisted Dark by Anna M. L. Koski

Read further for sneak peek of the newest instalment!

Violet has never belonged to herself.

She has been under the thumb of a cruel Elder Irma since she was born, stuck looking at the world and never being allowed to experience it. Her magick is bound tightly within her and with a chain around her ankle, she is trapped.

It all changes when a massive werewolf named, Jax, nearly destroys the shop and kidnaps her in his search of Irma. Yanked away from everything she knows, she's suddenly in the world she's never been able to touch with nothing but a dangerous werewolf to rely on.

Jax wants nothing but his brother but he soon sets his eyes on Violet, interest making them gleam. She's stuck between trusting him, her desire, and the world that threatens to destroy them both if she falls to the northern werewolf's charm.

However, without magick and no way to help Jax find Irma, she knows that the chain will forever remain around her ankle and she will continually be at the whims of those who hold the end of it. Be it a cruel witch or a rugged werewolf.

Clink Clack
Take your freedom back

Chapter One
Gold Coins

"One thousand eight hundred and thirty-three." I sighed out the number, setting my last gold coin on its stack. The brilliant yellow of the gold coins always made me feel better and if I needed to feel better it was now. I still hadn't quite recovered from Florence's... *visit*. A phantom pain ran over my nerves and I shivered at the memory of claws slowly moving through my flesh as the vicious witch had asked me the same questions again and again.

Where were the two werewolves? '*What werewolves*?' hadn't been acceptable.

Who were they with? '*I don't know*.' hadn't been acceptable.

Do you know where they went? '*I don't understand*.' hadn't been acceptable either.

It took me three long and drawn out deaths before I had finally cracked. I blinked back tears at that. I cursed the very day I was born and handed off to the brutality of Elder Irma. I shifted my left foot, the thin chain locked around my ankle forever reminding me of my position. I had no clue how Florence had learned of the time check spell on the chain and I had a sneaking suspicion it had been Irma who had told her.

I wasn't a fucking idiot, the very last witch I wanted to piss off was Miranda Lenkirion but I could only take being killed and regenerated so many times before my fear of it happening again overrode my fear of the powerful witch. The fucking time check *curse* on my chain meant that I could be killed but I wouldn't stay dead. I would be back in the land of the living when the time check spell lost my pulse. It reversed the damage and brought me back to the point of when the spell was last activated and it was activated daily.

It was like I was stuck in a form of hellish stasis. Dying was a *horrible* thing to endure and I had endured it a lot. It was why the gold was so comforting to me. I was trying to get enough gold to buy my freedom from Elder Irma. I had no clue what the debt I owed was but gold was hard to come by and I had gotten a significant amount of it. Nearly two thousand coins was a very generous amount and it was hard earned. I had to deal with illegal potions out of the back door of the shop to gather my gold. Elder Irma didn't pay me, slaves didn't get paid.

I shoved the thought away. I *would* pay for my freedom and I *would* be free of the chain on my ankle. I just needed to sell a few more potions and I would have over two thousand gold coins. I knew that Elder Irma would have a hard time refusing that size of payment. I just hoped it was tempting enough for her to accept it and let me go.

I took care of the shop for her but since I had grown up she hadn't used me for her experiments. I was thankful for that, very thankful for that, but I just wanted to be free.

I let out a small sigh as picked up my coin bag, slowly putting stacks of coins into it. I hadn't been allowed to practice my magick, hadn't been allowed to test for my levels. I had looked at the world around me through a cage my entire life. I just wanted to experience *something* without a chain rubbing my ankle raw.

I managed to clear the table of my coins and I closed the bag, trying it shut. It felt a bit heavier and I could hear the coins clinking around in the velvet. It had an ever space spell on it. I could put as much stuff as I wanted into and it wouldn't weigh too much or become full. I had managed to get it as a trade for a wellness potion I had created that created the illusion of youth and vitality. It was time and effort well spent in my opinion.

I stood up from my spot at the back table before I walked towards my corner I did my best to ignore the faint sound of the tiny chain moving along the floorboards behind me. It just reminded me of my place, as did my corner. A tiny, lumpy mattress on a rope bed frame ticked between several barrels was where I called home. I knelt down and shoved at one of the wooden boards of the barrel closest to my bed.

The piece shifted inwards and I wiggled the bag into place before pushing against the metal band of the barrel, popping the panel back into place.

I stood up, brushing my dusty hands off on my light dress. I knew I was being overly paranoid because Elder Irma never came around but I still didn't want to take any chances on anyone finding it. It paid to be paranoid, I knew that very well. I could hear the chime of the bell as the front door to the shop opened and I moved towards the warped mirror that stood over a rusty water basin and I smoothed down my hair, forcing a smile onto my face. There was no need for anyone to tell the Elder witch I wasn't being nice. She didn't come around but I also knew the witch never passed up on an opportunity to punish me.

I moved towards the front of the store, leaving the back quickly. The chain around my ankle became lighter and harder to see at the presence of another person around. Another little perk of the fucking chain, no one really knew it was there and I couldn't say anything about it or why I had it. Elder Irma didn't particularly like sharing and I knew that she knew that the spells on the chain made me a very special case if someone wanted to use me to get at her. That was probably also why I had no clue where Coven Thirteen was. The Elder witch was paranoid to a fault.

I tucked my hair behind my ears and once again pasted the smile on my face as I came around the front desk. "Welcome to the Broken Crow. How may I help you?" My voice trailed off as I blinked at the large form that nearly took up the entire doorway. I slowly looked up, my eyes following up the chest to a thick neck, that held several tattoos and a strong jaw and severely set mouth.

A glint of gold caught my attention as I spotted several small hoops rested along the male's ear lobe. My throat grew dry as I finally met the male's gaze. His eyes were a rather startling blue as they looked around the shop and his lips curled up into what looked like a snarl and his white teeth glinted against his tanned skin. The apparent and rather dangerous aura that hung off of him had my eyes widening and my heart racing with fear even before his eyes gleamed with a hint of ferality and a growl rumbled his chest.

A fucking *werewolf*.

I felt like my heart would escape my chest as I looked at the dangerous creature that had just decided to drop in. The last two times a werewolf had been in my shop something very bad had happened to me and I didn't think this time would be third time's the charm.

This book recognizes the upset this publishing has caused in certain individuals in a certain group but the author of this book does not care about the upset and those individuals can suck it.

Suck it.

www.ingramcontent.com/pod-product-compliance
Lightning Source LLC
Chambersburg PA
CBHW070547310726
48982CB00011B/1494/J